Samuel Warren

Passages From the Diary of a Late Physician

Volume 1

Samuel Warren

Passages From the Diary of a Late Physician
Volume 1

ISBN/EAN: 9783337126223

Printed in Europe, USA, Canada, Australia, Japan

Cover: Foto ©Andreas Hilbeck / pixelio.de

More available books at **www.hansebooks.com**

PASSAGES

FROM THE

DIARY OF A LATE PHYSICIAN

BY SAMUEL WARREN, F.R.S.,
AUTHOR OF "NOW AND THEN," "THE MERCHANT'S CLERK," ETC.

"...... nearest to us touches us most. The passions rise higher at domestic than at imperial tragedies."—Dr. JOHNSON.

IN THREE VOLUMES.

VOL. I.

𝔉rom the 𝔉ifth 𝔏ondon 𝔈dition.

NEW YORK:

HARPER & BROTHERS, PUBLISHERS,

FRANKLIN SQUARE.

1875.

THESE VOLUMES

ARE INSCRIBED TO

'R HENRY HALFORD, BARONET,

F.R.S., G.C.H.,

PRESIDENT OF THE ROYAL COLLEGE OF PHYSICIANS,

PHYSICIAN IN ORDINARY TO THE QUEEN,

&c., &c., &c.,

BY

THE AUTHOR.

PREFACE.

'THE first chapter of these " *Passages from the Diary of a late Physician*" appeared in Blackwood's Magazine in August, 1830, and the last in August, 1837. The first separate publication of them, in two volumes, took place in 1832, between which period and the present four very large impressions of them have been exhausted ; and it is a great satisfaction both to my publisher and myself to find that this has been effected without having in any way had recourse to the modern system of *puffing*, that miserable source of the deg radation of literature. A fifth edition having been called for, is accompanied by the third volume, which contains all the chapters that have since made their appearance in Blackwood's Magazine

As it lately became necessary, in the course of chancery proceedings instituted by Mr. Blackwood against parties who had pirated considerable portions of this work, that I should make oath of the fact of my being the sole author of it; and as it has been, both at home and abroad, long confidently attributed to other people, I now repeat the

statement that I am the sole author of every por
tion of the work, and, in deference to the wishes
of my family, place my name, as such author, upon
the title-page.* It is not necessary to trouble the
reader with the reasons that induced me so long
to abstain from doing so.

To account for any appearance of familiarity
with medical details in this work, I may add that
I was for six years actively engaged in the practical study of physic, a profession, however, which
I quitted in the month of September, 1827.

It may, perhaps, be not uninteresting to the
reader—merely, however, as a matter of petty literary detail—to be informed that the first chapter of
this " Diary"—the *Early Struggles*—was offered
by me successively to the conductors of three leading magazines in London, and rejected as " un-
suitable for their pages," and " not likely to interest the public." In despair I bethought myself of
the Great Northern Magazine. I remember taking
my packet to Mr. Cadell's, in the Strand, with a
sad suspicion that I should never see or hear any-
thing more of it; but at the close of the month I

---

* In three foreign editions of the " Diary" the name of ' Dr.
Harrison" is placed upon the title-page ; in England several
persons have actually stated themselves to be the writers of
this work ; others, that they have contributed towards it. I
need hardly say that all such statements are entirely untrue.

eceived a letter from Mr. Blackwood, informing me that he had inserted the chapter, and begging me to make arrangements for immediately proceeding regularly with the series. It expressed his cordial approval of the first chapter, and predicted that I was likely to produce a series of papers well suited for his magazine, and calculated to interest the public. It would be great affectation in me, and ingratitude towards the public, were I to conceal my belief that his expectations have been in some degree verified by the event. Here I wish to pay a brief and sincere tribute to the memory of my late friend, Mr. Blackwood. I shall ever cherish it with respect and affection. I have this morning been referring to nearly fifty letters which he wrote to me during the publication of the first fifteen chapters of the "Diary." The perusal of them has occasioned me lively emotion. All of them evidence the remarkable tact and energy with which he conducted his celebrated magazine Harassing as were his labours at the close of every month, he nevertheless invariably wrote to me a letter of considerable length, in style terse, igorous, and accurate, full of interesting comments on .iterary matters in general, and instructive suggestions concerning my own papers in particular. He was a man of strong intellect, of great practical sagacity, of unrivalled energy and industry, of high and inflexible honour in every transaction, great or small, that I ever heard of his being concerned in. But for him this work would certainly never have been in existence; and should it be so fortunate as *to live*, I wish it ever to be accompanied by the tribute I here sincerely and spontaneously pay to the memory of my departed friend William Blackwood.

I hope I may be permitted to add a word or two concerning the general nature of this work, and my design in writing it. I never desired to count myself among the myriad *novelists* of the present age. Even were I able, I have no ambition to attempt such a thing; all I wished was to present some of the results of my own personal observation of life and character in their most striking exemplification; to illustrate, as it were, the real practical working of virtues and vices. With this view I have ever, of set purpose, selected the most ordinary incidents, the simplest combinations of circumstances; never attempting to disturb or complicate the development of character and of feeling with intricacy of plot or novelty of incident. To this plan I have steadily adhered throughout the work, and I hope it has gained the approbation of sober and judicious readers. I trust I shall be pardoned, and not treated as vain or egotistical, if I venture to extract the following passages from the

" Preface by the 'Translator" prefixed to the German edition of this work, as they have greatly gratified *me*, and also given that particular *character* to my labours which I have always been so anxious to vindicate for them :

" This work is such an unusual literary production, that even on that account a translation of it into German can by no means appear an unworthy undertaking. A further and better acquaintance with the original has strengthened the translator in his purpose, and has also convinced him of the merits of these 'Passages.' Indeed, he is now of opinion that this work, though at first sight, perhaps, appearing to belong to the class of amusing literature, far distinguishes itself, by its intrinsic worth, from the usual run of fashionable literary productions. It contains a series of psychological sketches of human nature in various conditions, and especially in the last moments of life. * * * They bear on them the undoubted stamp of *genuineness*; and the reflecting reader must be convinced, by the many characteristic touches with which most of them abound, that these narratives are at least *founded* upon truth; he will further feel persuaded that facts—*facts* witnessed by the author—are related, though, undoubtedly, here and there the reality has been coloured and veiled by a fiction-like dress. * * * Although those narra-

I.—B

tives are, for the most part, of a peculiarly melancholy cast; and although, perhaps, we might have
wished that the author had more spared the feelings of his readers, and that many close dissec
tions of human misery had been omitted, yet it
must be owned that even the most gloomy and
heart-rending parts of these sketches are rich in
thrilling sensations and psychological perceptions;
that a bright fountain of advice and warning springs
from them all. The tendency of his work is
throughout pure and moral, which must secure for
him the most grateful acknowledgments from such
even of his readers (among whom the translator is
bound to place himself) as cannot perfectly agree
in the strict religious opinions of the author. * * *
The translation has been made with the greatest
accuracy; and, with the exception of a few polemical observations, nothing is altered."

I certainly feel much gratified by the approbation
of my labours here expressed, but am quite at a
loss to divine what can be the "*religious opinions*"
from which such a translator would dissent, or the
"*polemical observations*" he has found it necessary
to suppress. Being a firm believer in Christianity,
a conscientious member of the Church of England,
I hope and believe that nothing will be found in
this book inconsistent with such an avowal.

I do not intend to vindicate my selection of

characters, scenes, and incidents. Some of them
have been pretty freely remarked upon by the
press; all I can say, however, being that my aim
has been in every case for the best. One or two
exceedingly severe, perhaps I might add, wanton
and malignant attacks, have been made upon some
of them; but I heartily forgive those who have
done so, whoever they may be. In conclusion, I
know, alas! that this work has many imperfections;
but it has been too long in too many forms before
the world for me to attempt, even were I so disposed, extensive alterations. Such as it is, I now
finally commit it, in this its complete and authentic
form, to the judgment of the public, very thankful
for their approbation and deferential to their censure. The duties of a laborious profession *may*
not admit of my making any further contributions
to literature, or I might, perhaps, attempt to prove
myself worthier of the favour I have experienced,
and cheerfully exclaim,

    "To-morrow to fresh woods and pastures new!"

Samuel Warren

Inner Temple, London, 31st Oct., 1837.

CONTENTS.

AFFECTING SCENES:

BEING

PASSAGES FROM THE DIARY

OF

A PHYSICIAN.

PASSAGES

FROM THE

DIARY OF A LATE PHYSICIAN.

CHAPTER I.

EARLY STRUGGLES.

* * * CAN any thing be conceived more dreary
and disheartening than the prospect before a young
London physician, who, without friends or fortune,
yet with high aspirations after professional eminence, is striving to weave around him what is tech-
nically called "a connexion?" Such was my case.
After having exhausted the slender finances allotted
me from the funds of a poor but somewhat ambitious family in passing through the usual routine of
a college and medical education, I found myself,
about my twenty-sixth year, in London,—possessed
of about 100*l.* in cash, a few books, a tolerable ward-
robe, an inexhaustible fund of animal spirits, and a
wife—a lovely young creature whom I had been
absurd enough, some few weeks before, to marry,
merely because we loved each other. She was the
only daughter of a very worthy fellow-townsman of
mine, a widower; whose fortunes, alas! had decayed
long before their possessor. Emily was the glory
of his age, and, need I add, the pride of my youth,
and after having assiduously attended her fathe

through his last illness, the sole and rich return was his daughter's heart.

I must own that when we found ourselves fairly housed in the mighty metropolis of England, with so poor an exchequer, and the means of replenishing it so remote and contingent, we were somewhat startled at the boldness of the step we had taken. "Nothing venture, nothing have," however, was my maxim; and I felt supported by that unaccountable conviction which clings to all in such circumstances as mine, up to the very pinching moment, but no longer—that there *must* be thousands of ways of getting a livelihood to which we can turn at a moment's warning. And then the swelling thought of being the architect of one's own fortunes! As, however, daily drafts began to diminish my 100*l*., my spirits faltered a little. I discovered that I might indeed as well

"————lie pack'd in mine own grave,"

as continue in London without money or the means of getting it; and, after resolving endless schemes, the only conceivable mode of doing so seemed by calling in the *generous* assistance of the Jews. My father had fortunately effected a policy on my life for 2000*l*. at an early period, on which some fourteen premiums had been paid; and this available security, added to the powerful influence of a young nobleman to whom I had rendered some service at college, enabled me to succeed in wringing a loan from old Amos L—— of 3000*l*., at the trifling interest of fifteen per cent., payable by way of redeemable annuity. It was with fear and trembling that I called myself master of this large sum, and with the utmost diffidence that I could bring myself to exercise what the lawyers would call *acts of owner-ship* on it. As, however, there was no time to lose, I took a respectable house in C—— street, west—

furnished it neatly and respectably—fortunately enough let the first floor to a rich old East India bachelor—beheld "Dr.——" glisten conspicuously on my door—and then dropped my little line into the great waters of London, resolved to abide the issue with patience.

Blessed with buoyant and sanguine spirits, I did not lay it much to heart that my only occupation during the first six months was—abroad, to practise the pardonable solecism of hurrying *haud passibus æquis* through the streets, as if in attendance on numerous patients; and at home to ponder pleasantly over my books, and enjoy the company of my cheerful and affectionate wife. But when I had numbered twelve months, almost without feeling a pulse or receiving a fee, and was reminded by old L—— that the second half-yearly instalment of 225*l.* was due, I began to look forward with some apprehension to the overcast future. Of the 3000*l.*, for the use of which I was paying so cruel and exorbitant a premium, little more than half remained; and this notwithstanding we had practised the most rigid economy in our household expenditure, and devoted as little to dress as was compatible with maintaining a respectable exterior. To my sorrow, I found myself unavoidably contracting debts, which, with the interest due to old L——, I found it would be impossible to discharge. If matters went on as they seemed to threaten, what was to become of me in a year or two? Putting every thing else out of the question, where was I to find funds to meet old L——'s annual demand of 450*l.*? Relying on my prospects of professional success, I had bound myself to return the 3000*l.* within five years of the time of borrowing it; and now I thought I must have been mad to do so. If my profession failed me, I had nothing else to look to. I had no family resources; for my father had died since I came to London, very much embarrassed in his circumstances; and my mother, who was aged and infirm, had gone to reside with some relatives, who were few and poor. My wife, as I have stated, was in like plight. I do not think she had a relative in England (for her father and all his family were Germans) except

> "—— him whose brightest joy
> Was that he called her ' wife.' "

Lord ——, the nobleman before mentioned, who I am sure would have rejoiced in assisting me, either by pecuniary advances or professional introductions, had been on the continent ever since I commenced practice. Being of studious habits and a very bashful and reserved disposition while at Cambridge, I could number but few college friends—none of whom I knew where to find in London. Neither my wife nor I knew more than five people besides our India lodger; for to tell the truth we were, like many a fond and foolish couple before us, all the world to one another, and cared little for scraping together promiscuous acquaintances. If we had even been inclined to visiting, our straitened circumstances would have forbid our incurring the expenses attached to it. What then was to be done? My wife would say, "Pho, love, we shall contrive to get on as well as our neighbours;" but the simple fact was, we were *not* getting on like our neighbours —nor did I see any prospect of our ever doing so. I began, therefore, to pass sleepless nights and days of despondency—casting about in every direction for any employment consistent with my profession and redoubling my fruitless efforts to obtain practice.

It is almost laughable to say, that our only receipts were a few paltry guineas sent at long intervals from old Asperne, the proprietor of the European Magazine, as remuneration for a sort of monthly medical summary; and a trifle or two from

Mr. Nicholls, of the Gentleman's Magazine, as an acknowledgment for several sweet sonnets sent by my wife. Knowing the success which often attended professional authorship, as tending to acquire for the writer a reputation for skill in the subject of which he treated, and introduce him to the notice of the higher members of his own profession, I determined to turn my attention that way. For several months I was up early and late at a work on Diseases of the Lungs. I bestowed incredible pains on it; and my toil was sweetened by my wife, who would sit by me in the long summer evenings like an angel, consoling and encouraging me with predictions of success. She lightened my labour by undertaking the transcription of the manuscript; and I thought that two or three hundred sheets of fair and regular handwriting were heavily purchased by the impaired eyesight of the beloved amanuensis. When at length it was completed, having been read and revised twenty times, so that there was not a comma wanted, I hurried, full of fluttering hopes and fears, to a well-known medical bookseller, expecting he would at once purchase the copyright. Fifty pounds I had fixed in my own mind as the minimum of what I would accept; and I had already appropriated part of it towards buying a handsome silk dress for my wife. Alas! even in this branch of my profession my hopes were doomed to meet with disappointment. The bookseller received me with great civility; listened to every word I had to say; seemed to take some interest in the new views of the disease treated of, which I explained to him, and repeated, and ventured to assure him that they would certainly attract public attention. My heart leaped for joy as I saw his business-like eye settled upon me with an expression of attentive interest. After having almost talked myself hoarse, and flushed myself all over with excitement, he removed his spectacles, and politely assured me of his approbation of the work; but that he had determined never to publish any more medical works on his own account. I have the most vivid recollection of my almost turning sick with chagrin. With a faltering voice I asked him if that was his unalterable determination. He replied, it was; for he had "lost too much by speculations of that sort." I tied up the manuscript, and withdrew. As soon as I left his shop, I let fall a scorching tear of mingled sorrow and mortification. I could almost have wept aloud. At that moment whom should I meet but my dear wife; for we had both been talking all night long, and at breakfast-time, about the probable result of my interview with the bookseller; and her anxious affection would not permit her to wait my return. She had been pacing to and fro on the other side of the street, and flew to me on my leaving the shop. I could not speak to her; I felt almost choked. At last her continued expressions of tenderness and sympathy soothed me into a more equable frame of mind, and we returned to dinner. In the afternoon I offered it to another bookseller, who, John Trot like, told me at once he never did that sort of thing. I offered it subsequently to every medical bookseller I could find—with like success. One fat fellow actually whiffled out, "if he might make so bold," he would advise me to leave off book-making, and stick to my practice. Another assured me he had got two similar works then in the press; and the last I consulted told me I was too young, he thought, to have seen enough of practice for writing "a book of that nature," as his words were. "Publish it on your own account, love," said my wife. That, however, was out of the question, whatever might be the merits of the work—for I had no friends; and a kind-hearted bookseller, to whom I mentioned the project, assured me that if I went to press my work would fall from it stillborn. When I returned home from making this last attempt I flung myself into a chair by the fireside, opposite my wife, without speaking. There was an anxious smile of sweet solicitude in her face. My agitated and mortified air convinced her that I was finally disappointed, an1 that six months' hard labour was thrown away. In a fit of uncontrollable pique and passion I flung the manuscript on the fire; but Emily suddenly snatched it from the flames—gazed at me with a look such as none but a fond and devoted wife could give —threw her arms round my neck, and kissed me back to calmness, if not happiness. I laid the manuscript in question on a shelf in my study; and it was my first and last attempt at medical bookmaking.

From what cause or combination of causes I know not, but I seemed marked out for failure in my profession. Though my name shone on my door, and the respectable neighbourhood could not out have noticed the regularity and decorum of my habits and manners, yet none ever thought of calling me in! Had I been able to exhibit a line of carriages at my door—or to open my house for the re ception of company—or to dash about town in an elegant equipage—or be seen at the opera and theatres,—had I been able to do this the case might have been different. In candour I must acknowledge, that another probable cause of my ill-success was a somewhat insignificant person, and unprepossessing countenance. I could not wear such an eternal smirk of conceited complacency, or keep my head perpetually bowing mandarin-like, as many of my professional brothers; still there were thousands to whom these deficiencies proved no serious obstacles. The great misfortune in my case was undoubtedly the want of introductions. There was a man of considerable rank and great wealth, who was a sort of fiftieth cousin of mine, resided in one of the fashionable squares not far from me, and on whom I had called to claim kindred and solicit his patronage; but after having sent up my name and address, I was suffered to wait so long in an anteroom, that, what with the noise of servants bustling past with insolent familiarity, I quite forgot the relationship, and left the house, wondering what had brought me there. I never felt inclined to go near it again; so there was an end of all prospects of introduction from that quarter. I was left, therefore, to rely exclusively on my own efforts, and trust to chance for patients. It is true, that in the time I have mentioned I was twice called in at an instant's warning; but in both cases the objects of my visits had expired before my arrival, probably before a messenger could be despatched for me; and the manner in which my fees were proffered convinced me that I should be cursed for a mercenary wretch if I accepted them. I was therefore induced in each case to decline the guinea, though it would have purchased me a week's happiness! I was also on several occasions called in to visit the inferior members of families in the neighbourhood—servants, housekeepers, porters, &c.; and of all the trying, the mortifying occurrences in the life of a young physician, such occasions as these are the most irritating. You go to the house—a large one, probably —and are instructed not to knock at the front door, but to go down by the area to your patient! I think it was about this time that I was summoned in haste to young Sir Charles F——, who resided near May fair. Delighted at the prospect of securing so distinguished a patient, I hurried to his house, resolved to do my utmost to give satisfaction. When I entered the room, I found the sprig of fashion enveloped in a crimson silk dressing-gown, sitting conceitedly on the sofa, and sipping a cup of coffee from which he desisted a moment to examine me through his eye-glass, and then direct me to inspect the swelled foot of a favourite pointer! Darting a look of anger at the insulting coxcomb, I instantly withdrew, without uttering a word. *Five years* afterward did that young man make use of the most strenuous efforts to oust me from the confidence of a family of distinction to which he was distantly related.*

A more mortifying incident occurred shortly after-ward. I had the misfortune to be called on a sudden emergency into consultation with the late cele-brated Dr. ——. It was the first consultational visit that I had ever paid; and I was of course very anxious to acquit myself creditably. Shall I ever forget or forgive the air of insolent condescension with which he received me, or the remark he made in the presence of several individuals, professional as well as unprofessional—" I assure you, Dr. ——, there is *really* some difference between apoplexy and epilepsy; at least there was when I was a young man!" He accompanied these words with a look of supercilious commiseration, directed to the lady, whose husband was our patient; and I need not add that my future services were dispensed with. My heart ached to think that such a fellow as this should have it in his power, as it were, to take the bread out of the mouth of an unpretending and almost spirit-broken professional brother; but I had no remedy. I am happy to have it in my power to say how much the tone of consulting physicians is now (1824) lowered towards their brethren who may happen to be of a few years' less standing, and consequently less firmly fixed in the confidence of their patients. It was by a few similar incidents to those above related that my spirit began to be soured; and had it not been for the unvarying

* This anecdote calls to my mind one told me by the late Dr. Hamil ton. He was sent for once in great haste by Lady P——, to see—abs.> lutely a little favourite *monkey*, which was almost suffocated with its morning feed. When the doctor entered the room, he saw only her ladyship, her young son (a lad of ten years old, who was most absurdly dressed), and his patient. Looking at each of the two latter, he said ~oolly to Lady P—— " My lady, which is the monkey?"

I.—C

sweetness and cheerfulness of my incomparable wife, existence would not have been tolerable. My professional efforts were paralyzed; failure attended every attempt; my ruin seemed sealed. My re-sources were rapidly melting away; my expendi-ture, moderate as it was, was counterbalanced by no incomings. A prison and starvation scowled before me.

Despairing of finding any better source of emolu-. ment, I was induced to send an advertisement to one of the daily papers, stating that "a graduate of Cambridge University, having a little spare time at his disposal, was willing to give private instructions in the classics, in the evenings, to gentlemen pre-paring for college—or to others!" After about a week's interval, I received one solitary communica-tion. It was from a young man holding some sub-ordinate situation under government, and residing at Pimlico. This person offered me two guineas a-month, if I would attend him *at his own house,* for two hours on the evenings of Monday, Wednesday and Friday. With these hard terms was I obliged to comply—yes, a gentleman, and a member of an English university, was driven so low as to attend. for these terms, an ignorant underling, and endea-vour to instil a few drops of classic lore into the turbid and shallow waters of his understanding. I had hardly given him a month's attendance, before this fellow assured me, with a flippant air, that as he had now acquired "a practical knowledge of the classics," he would dispense with my further ser vices. Dull dunce! he could not, in Latin. be brought to comprehend the difference between a neuter and an active verb; while, as for Greek, he was an absolute choke-pear,—so he nibbled on to ῥώ, and then gave it up. Bitter but unavailing were my regrets as I returned from paying my last visit to this promising scholar, that I had not en-tered the army and gone to America, or even ne-

taken myself to some subordinate commercial situation.   A thousand and a thousand times did I curse
the ambition which brought me up to London, and
the egregious vanity which led me to rely so implicitly on my talents for success.   Had I but been
content with the humbler sphere of a general practitioner, I might have laid out my dearly-bought
1000*l.* with a reasonable prospect of soon repaying
t, and acquiring a respectable livelihood.   But all
hese soberer thoughts, as is usual, came only time
*nough to enhance the mortification of failure.

*   *   *   *   *   *   *   *

About 300*l.* was now the miserable remnant of tne
money borrowed from the Jew; and half a year's
interest (225*l.*), together with my rent, was due in
about a fortnight's time.   I was, besides, indebted to
many tradesmen—who were becoming every day
more querulous—for articles of food, clothing, and
furniture.   My poor Emily was in daily expectation
of her accouchement; and my own health was sensibly sinking under the combined pressure of anxiety
and excessive parsimony.   What was to be done?
Despair was clinging to me, and shedding blight and
mildew over all my faculties.   Every avenue was
closed against me.   I never knew what it was to
have more than one or two hours' sleep at night, and
that so heavy, so troubled, and interrupted, that I
woke each morning more dead than alive.   I lay tossing in bed, revolving all conceivable schemes and
fancies in my tortured brain, till at length, from mere
iteration, they began to assume a feasible aspect;
but, alas! they would none of them bear the blush
of daylight—but faded away as extravagant and
absurd.   I would endeavour to set afloat a popular
Medical Journal—to give lectures on diseases of the
lungs (a department with which I was familiar)—I
would advertise for a small medical partnership as a
general practitioner—I would do a thousand things of
the sort: but where was my capital to set out with?

I had 300*l.* in the world, and 450*l.* yearly to pay to an extortionating old miser; that was the simple fact and it almost drove me to despair to advert to it for one instant. Wretched, however, as I was, and almost every instant loathing my existence, the idea of suicide was never entertained for a moment. If the fiend would occasionally flit across the dreary chamber of my heart—a strong, an unceasing confidence in the goodness and power of my Maker always repelled the fearful visitant. Even yet, rapidly as I seemed approaching the precipice of ruin, I could not avoid cherishing a feeble hope that some unexpected avenue would open to better fortune; and the thought of it would for a time soothe my troubled breast, and nerve it to bear up against the inroads of my present misfortunes.

I recollect sitting down one day in St. James's Park on one of the benches, weary with wandering the whole morning I knew not whither. I felt faint and ill, and more than usually depressed in mind. I had that morning paid one of my tradesmen's bills, amounting to 10*l.*; and the fellow told my servant, that as he had so much trouble in getting his money, he did not want the honour of my custom any longer The thought that my credit was failing in the neighbourhood was insupportable. Ruin and disgrace would then be accelerated; and being unable to meet my creditors, I should be proclaimed little less than a swindler, and shaken like a viper from the lap of society Fearful as were such thoughts, I had not enough of energy of feeling left to suffer much agitation from them. I folded my arms on my breast in sullen apathy, and wished only that, whatever might be my fate, certainty might be substituted for suspense.

While indulging in thoughts like these, a glittering troop of soldiers passed by me, preceded by their band, playing a merry air. How the sounds jarred on the broken strings of my heart! And many a bright face, dressed in smiles of gayety and happiness, thronged past, attracted by the music—little thinking of the wretchedness of him who was sitting by. I could not prevent the tears of anguish from gushing forth. I thought of Emily—of her delicate and interesting, but to me melancholy, situation. I could not bear the thought of returning home to encounter her affectionate looks,—her meek and gentle resignation to her bitter fortunes. Why had I married her, without first having considered whether I could support her? Passionately fond of me as I well knew she was, could she avoid frequently recurring to the days of our courtship, when I reiteratedly assured her of my certainty of professional success as soon as I could get settled in London? Where now were all the fair and flourishing scenes to which my childish enthusiasm had taught me to look forward? Would not the bitter contrast she was now experiencing, and seemed doomed long yet to experience, alienate from me a portion of her affections, and induce feelings of anger and contempt? Could I blame her for all this? If the goodly superstructure of my fortunes fell, was it not I that had loosened and destroyed the foundation?—Reflections like these were harassing and scourging me, when an elderly gentleman, evidently an invalid, tottered slowly to the bench where I was sitting, and sat down beside me. He seemed a man of wealth and consideration; for his servant, on whose arm he had been leaning, stood behind the bench on which he was sitting. He was almost shaken to pieces by an asthmatic cough, and was besides suffering from another severe disorder, which need not be more particularly named. He looked at me once or twice, in a manner which seemed to say that he would not take it rudely if I addressed him. I did so. I said, "I am afraid you are in great pain from that cough, sir?"—"Yes," he gasped faintly, "and I don't know how to get rid of it. I am an old man, you see, sir

and methinks my summons to the grave might have
been less loud and painful." After a little pause, I
ventured to ask him how long he had been subject to
the cough which now harassed him? He said, more
or less, for the last ten years; but that latterly it had
increased so much upon him, that he could not derive
any benefit from medical advice. "I should think,
sir, the more violent symptoms of your disorder
might be mitigated," said I; and proceeded to question him minutely as to the origin and progress of
the complaints which now afflicted him. He answered all my questions with civility; and as I went
on, seemed to be roused into something like curiosity
and interest. I need not say more than that I discovered he had not been in the hands of a skilful
practitioner; and that I assured him very few and
simple means would give him great relief from at
least the more violent symptoms. He, of course
perceived I was in the medical profession; and after
some apparent hesitation, evidently as to whether or
not I should feel hurt, tendered me a guinea. I
refused it promptly and decidedly, and assured him
that he was quite welcome to the very trifling advice
I had rendered him. At that moment, a young
man of fashionable appearance walked up, and told
him their carriage was waiting at the corner of the
Stable-yard. This last gentleman, who seemed to
be either the son or nephew of the old gentleman,
eyed me, I thought, with a certain superciliousness,
which was not lessened when the invalid told him I
had given him some excellent advice, for which he
could not prevail on me to receive a fee. "We are
vastly obliged to you, sir; but are going home to the
family physician," said the young man, haughtily;
and placing the invalid's arm in his, led him slowly
away. He was addressed several times by the servant as "*Sir*" something, *Wilton* or *William*, I think
but I could not distinctly catch it, so that it was evi
dently a person of some rank that I had been addres

ing. How many there are, thought I, that, with a more plausible and insinuating address than mine is, would have contrived to have got into the confidence of this gentleman, and become his medical attendant! How foolish was I not to give him my card when he proffered me a fee, and thus, in all probability, be sent for the next morning to pay a regular professional visit! and to what lucrative introductions might not that have led! A thousand times I cursed my absurd diffidence—my sensitiveness as to professional etiquette—and my inability to seize the advantages occasionally offered by a fortunate conjuncture of circumstances. I was fitter, I thought, for La Trappe than the bustling world of business. I deserved my ill fortune; and professional failure was the natural consequence of the *mauvaise honte* .which has injured so many. As the day, however, was far advancing, I left the seat, and turned my steps towards my cheerless home.

As was generally the case, I found Emily busily engaged in painting little firescreens and other ornamental toys, which, when completed, I was in the habit of carrying to a kind of private bazaar in Oxford-street, where I was not known, and where, with an aching heart, I disposed of the delicate and beautiful productions of my poor wife, for a trifle hardly worth taking home. Could any man, pretending to the slightest feeling, contemplate his young wife— far advanced in pregnancy, in a critical state of health, and requiring air, exercise, and cheerful company—toiling, in the manner I have related, from morning to night, and for a miserably inadequate remuneration? She submitted, however, to our misfortunes with infinitely more firmness and equanimity than I could pretend to; and her uniform cheerfulness of demeanour, together with the passionate fervour of her fondness for me, contributed to fling a few rays of trembling and evanescent lustre over the gloomy prospects of the future. Still, however

the dreadful question incessantly presented itself—
What, in God's name, is to become of us? I cannot
say that we were at this time in absolute literal want·
though our parsimonious fare hardly deserved the
name of food, especially such as my wife's delicate
situation required. It was the hopelessness of all
prospective resources that kept us in perpetual thral-
dom. With infinite effort we might contrive to hold
on to a given period—say till the next half-yearly
demand of old I——; and then we must sink altogether, unless a miracle intervened to save us. Had
I been alone in the world, I might have braved the
worst—have turned my hands to a thousand things
—have accommodated myself to almost any circumstances, and borne the extremest privations with fortitude. But my darling—my meek, smiling, gentle
Emily!—my heart bled for her.

Not to leave any stone unturned, seeing an advertisement addressed " To Medical Men," I applied for
the situation of assistant to a general practitioner,
though I had but little skill in the practical part of
compounding medicines. I applied personally to the
advertiser, a fat, red-faced, vulgar fellow, who had
contrived to gain a very large practice, by what
means God only knows. His terms were—and these
named in the most offensive contemptuousness of
manner—80*l.* a year, board and lodge out, and give
all my time in the day to my employer! Absurd as
was the idea of acceding to terms like these, I
thought I might still consider them. I pressed hard
for 100*l.* a-year, and told him I was married—

" Married!" said he, with a loud laugh, " No, no,
sir; you're not the man for my money—so I wish
you good morning."*

Thus was I baffled in every attempt to obtain a
permanent source of support from my profession.

* This worthy (a Mr. C—— by name) lived at this time in the region
of St George's in the east.

it brought me about 40*l.* per annum; I gained by occasional contributions to magazines an average sum annually of about 25*l.*; my wife earned about that sum by her pencil: and these were all the funds I had to meet the enormous interest due half-yearly to old L——, to discharge my rent, and the various other expenses of housekeeping, &c. Might I not well despair! I did—and God's goodness only preserved me from the frightful calamity which has suddenly terminated the earthly miseries of thousands in similar circumstances.

And is it possible, I often thought, with all the tormenting incredulousness of a man half-stupified with his misfortunes—is it possible that, in the very heart of this metropolis of splendour, wealth, and extravagance, a gentleman and a scholar, who has laboured long in the honourable toil of acquiring professional knowledge, cannot contrive to scrape together even a competent subsistence?—and that, too, while ignorance and infamy are wallowing in wealth—while charlatanry and quackery of all kinds are bloated with success! Full of such thoughts as these, how often have I slunk stealthily along the streets of London, on cold and dreary winter evenings, almost fainting with long abstinence, yet reluctant to return home and incur the expense of an ordinary family dinner, while my wife's situation required the most rigorous economy to enable us to meet, even in a poor and small way, the exigencies of her approaching accouchement! How often—ay, hundreds of times—have I envied the coarse and filthy fare of the minor eatinghouses, and been content to interrupt a twelve hours' fast with a bun or biscuit, and a draught of water or turbid table-beer, under the wretched pretence of being in too great a hurry to go home to dinner! I have often gazed with envy—once, I recollect, in particular—on dogs eating their huge daily slice of boiled horse's flesh, and envied their contented and satiated looks! With what anguish of heart have I seen carriages setting down company at the door of a house, illuminated by the glare of a hundred tapers, where were ladies dressed in the extreme of fashion, whose cast-off clothes would have enabled me to acquire a tolerably respectable livelihood!—O! ye sons and daughters of luxury and extravagance, how many thousands of needy and deserving families would rejoice to eat of the crumbs which fa'l from your tables—and they may not!

I have stood many a time at my parlour window, and envied the kitchen fare of the servants of my wealthy opposite neighbour; while I protest I have been ashamed to look our own servant in the face, as she, day after day, served up for two what was little more than sufficient for one: and yet, bitter mockery! I was to support abroad the farce of a cheerful and respectable professional exterior!

    *   *   *   *   *   *   *   *

Two days after the occurrence in St. James's Park above related, I was as usual reading the columns of advertisements in one of the daily papers, when my eyes lit on the following:—

" The professional gentleman who a day or two ago had some conversation on the subject of asthma with an *invalid* on one of the benches in St. James's Park, is particularly requested to forward his name and address to W. J., care of Messrs. ———."

I almost let the paper fall from my hands with delighted surprise. That I was the " professional gentleman" alluded to was clear; and on the slender foundation of this advertisement, I had in a few moments built a large and splendid superstructure of good fortune. I had hardly calmness enough to call my wife, who was engaged with some small household matters, for the purpose of communicating the good news to her. I need hardly say with what eagerness I complied with the requisitions of the advertisement. Half an hour beheld my name and

address in an envelope, with the superscription " W.
T." lying at Messrs. ——'s, who were stationers.
After passing a most anxious and sleepless night,
agitated by all kinds of hopes and fears, my wife and
I were sitting at breakfast, when a livery-servant
knocked at the door; and after inquiring whether
" Dr. ——" was at home, left a letter.   It was an en-
velope containing the card of address of Sir William
——, No. 26, —— street, accompanied with the fol-
owing note :—

" Sir William ——'s compliments to Dr. ——, and
will feel obliged by his looking in in the course of the
morning."

" Now be calm, my dear ——," said Emily, as she
saw my fluttering excitement of manner.   But alas!
that was impossible.   I was impatient for the hour
of twelve, and precisely as the clock struck I sallied
forth to visit my titled patient.   All the way I went
I was taxing my ingenuity for palliatives, remedies
for asthma; I would new-regulate his diet and plan
of life—in short, I would do wonders!

Sir William, who was sitting gasping by the fireside, received me with great courtesy; and after
motioning his niece, a charming young woman, to
retire, told me he had been so much interested by my
remarks the other day in the Park, that he felt inclined to follow my advice, and put himself under my
care altogether.   He then entered on a history of his
complaints.   I found his constitution was entirely
broken up, and that in a very little it would fall to pieces.
I told him, however, that if he would adhere strictly
to the regimen I proposed, I could promise him great,
if not permanent relief.   He listened to what I said
with the utmost interest.   " Do you think you could
prolong my life, doctor, for two years ?" said he, with
emotion.   I told him I certainly could not pretend to
promise him so much.   " My only reason for asking
the question," he replied, " is my beloved niece, that
young lady who has just left us.   If I cannot live

for two years or eighteen months longer, it will be a
bitter thing for her!" He sighed deeply, and added
abruptly—"but of that more hereafter. I hope to
see you to-morrow, doctor." He insisted on my
accepting five guineas in return for the *two* visits
he said he had received, and I took my departure.
I felt altogether a new man as I walked home. My
spirits were more light and buoyant than they had
been for many a long month; for I could not help
thinking that I had now a fair chance of introduction
into respectable practice. My wife shared my joy,
and we were as happy for the rest of that day as if
we had already surmounted the heavy difficulties
which oppressed us.

I attended Sir William every day that week, and
received a fee of two guineas for each visit. On
Sunday I met the family physician, Dr. ——, who
had just been released from attendance on one of the
royal family. He was a polite but haughty man, and
seemed inclined to be much displeased with Sir William for calling me in. When I entered, Sir William
introduced me to him as "Dr. ——." " Dr. —— of
—— Square?" inquired the other physician, care-
lessly. I told him where I lived. He affected to be
reflecting where the street was; it was the one next
to that in which he himself resided. There is nothing in the world so easy as for the eminent members of our profession to take the bread out of the
mouths of their younger brethren with the best grace
in the world. So Sir —— contrived in the present
case. He assured Sir William that nothing was calculated to do him so much good as change of air—of
course I could not but assent. The sooner, he said,
Sir William left town the better. Sir William asked
me if I concurred in that opinion? Certainly. He
set off for Worthing two days after; and I lost the
best and almost the only patient I had then ever had
for Sir William died after three weeks' residence at
Worthing.

This circumstance occasioned me great depression
of spirits. Nothing that I touched seemed to pros-
per; and the transient glimpses I occasionally obtained of good fortune seemed given only to tantalize me and enhance the bitterness of the contract.
My store of money was reduced at last from 3000*l.*
to 25*l.* in cash; my debts amounted to upwards of
100*l.*, and in six months another 225*l.* would be due
to old L——! My wife, too, had been confined, and
there was another source of expense, for both she
and my little daughter were in a very feeble state of
health. Still, secretly wishful to accommodate herself to one lowered in circumstances, she almost
broke my heart with the proposal of dismissing our
servant, the whole of whose labour my sweet Emily
herself undertook to perform! No, no, this was too
much; the tears of agony gushed from my eyes as I
folded her delicate frame in my arms, and assured
her that Providence would never permit so much
virtue and gentleness to be degraded into such humiliating servitude. I *said* this : but my heart heavily
misgave me that a more wretched prospect was before her!

I have often sat by my small, solitary parlour fire.
and pondered over my misery and misfortunes till I
have been almost phrensied with the violence of my
emotions. Where was I to look for relief? What
earthly remedy was there? Oh, my God! thou alone
knowest what this poor heart of mine suffered in
such times as these, not on my own account, but for
those beloved beings whose ruin was implicated in
mine! What, however, was to be done at the present crisis, seeing at Christmas old L—— would
come upon me for his interest, and my other creditors would insist on payment? A dewy mist came
over my mind's eye whenever I attempted to look
steadily forward into futurity. I had written several
times to my kind and condescending friend Lord
——, who still continued abroad; but as I knew not

to what part of the continent to direct, and the servants of his family pretended they knew not, I left my letters at his town-house to be forwarded with his quarterly packages. I suppose my letters must have been opened and burnt as little other than pestering, begging letters; for I never heard from him.

I had often heard from my father that we had a sort of fiftieth cousin in London, a baronet of great wealth, who had married a distant relation of our family on account solely of her beauty; but that he was one of the most haughty and arrogant men breathing, had in the most insolent manner disavowed the relationship, and treated my father on one occasion very contumeliously. Since I had been in London, and suffered from the pressure of accumulated misfortunes, the idea of applying to this man, and stating my circumstances, had presented itself a thousand times. As one is easily induced to believe what one *wishes* to be true, I could not help thinking that surely he must in some degree relent if informed of our utter misery; but my heart always failed when I took my pen in hand to write to him. I was at a loss for terms in which to state our distress most feelingly, and in a manner best calculated to arrest his attention. I had, however, after infinite reluctance, addressed a letter of this sort to his lady, who, I am sorry to say, shared all Sir ——'s *hauteur*, and received an answer from a fashionable watering-place, where her ladyship was spending the summer months. This is it :—

" Lady ——'s compliments to Dr. ——, and having received his letter, and given it her best consideration, is happy in being able to request Dr. ——'s acceptance of the enclosed ; which, however, owing to Sir ——'s temporary embarrassment in pecuniary matters, she has had some difficulty in sending. She is, therefore, under the painful necessity of requesting Dr. —— to abstain from future applications of this sort. As to Dr. ——'s offer of his medical services to Lady ——'s family when in town, Lady —— must beg to decline them, as the present physician has attended the family for years, and neither Lady —— nor Sir —— see any reason for changing.

"W—— to Dr. H——."

The enclosure was 10*l.*, which I was on the point of returning in a blank envelope, indignant at the cold and unfeeling letter which accompanied it; but I thought of my wife, and retained it. To return. Recollecting the reception of this application, my heart was frozen at the very idea of a similar one to Sir ——. To what, however, will not misfortune compel a man! I determined at length to call upon Sir ——, to insist upon being shown to him. I set out for this purpose without telling my errand to my wife, who, as I have before stated, was confined to her bed, and in a very feeble state of health. It was a fine sunny morning, or rather noon; all that I passed seemed happy and contented; their spirits exhilarated by the genial weather, and sustained by the successful prosecution of business. *My* heart, however, was fluttering feebly beneath the pressure of anticipated disappointment. I was going in the spirit of a forlorn hope, with a dogged determination to make the *attempt*, to *know* that even this door was shut against me. My knees trembled beneath me as I entered —— Place, and saw elegant equipages standing at the doors of most of the gloomy but magnificent houses, which seemed to frown off such insignificant and wretched individuals as myself. How could I ever muster resolution enough, I thought, to ascend the steps, and knock and ring in a sufficiently authoritative manner to be attended to? It is laughable to relate, but I could not refrain from stepping back into a by street, and getting a small glass of some cordial spirit to give me a little firmness. Although I ventured again into —— Place, and found Sir ——'s house on the opposite side, there was no one to be seen but some men-servants

in undress lolling indolently at the dining-room window, and making their remarks on passers-by.   I
dreaded these fellows as much as their master!   It
was no use, however, indulging in thoughts of that
kind; so I crossed over, and lifting the huge knocker,
made a tolerably decided application of it, and pulled
the bell with what I fancied was a sudden and im-
perative jerk.   The summons was instantly answered
by the corpulent porter, who, seeing nothing but a
plain pedestrian, kept hold of the door, and leaning
against the door-post, asked me familiarly what were
my commands.

"Is Sir —— at home?"

"He is," said the fellow, in a supercilious tone;
"and what then, sir?"

"Can he be spoken to?"

"I think he can't, for he wasn't home till six
o'clock this morning from the Dutchess of ——'s."

"Can I wait for him? and will you show him this
card," said I, tendering it to him, "and say I have
particular business?"

"You couldn't look in again at four, could you?"
inquired he, in the same tone of vulgar assurance.

"No, sir," I replied, kindling with indignation;
"my business is urgent—I shall wait now."

He opened the door for me, and called to a servant
to show me into the antechamber, saying, I must
make up my mind to wait an hour or two, as Sir
—— was then only just getting up, and would be an
hour at least at his breakfast.   He then left me, saying he would send my card up to his master.   My
spirits were somewhat ruffled and agitated with having forced my way so far through the frozen island
of English aristocracy, and I sat down determined
to wait patiently till I was summoned up to Sir ——.
I could hear several equipages dashing up to the
door, and the visiters they brought were always
shown up immediately.   I rung the bell, and asked a

servant why I was suffered to wait so long, as Sir
—— was clearly visible now.

"'Pon honour, I don't know, indeed," said the fel-
ow, coolly, shutting the door.

Boiling with indignation, I resumed my seat, then
walked to and fro, and then sat down again. Presently I heard the French valet ordering the carriage
to be in readiness in half an hour. I rung again;
the same servant answered. He walked into the
room, and standing near me, asked in a familiar tone
what I wanted. "Show me up to Sir ——, for I
shall wait no longer," said I, sternly.

" Can't, sir, indeed," he replied, with a smirk in his
face.

" Has my card been shown to Sir ——?" I inquired, struggling to preserve my temper.

" I'll ask the porter if he gave it to Sir ——'s
valet," he replied, and shut the door.

About ten minutes afterward a carriage drove up;
there was a bustle on the stairs and in the hall. I
heard a voice, saying, " If Lord —— calls, tell him
I am gone to his house." In a few moments the
steps of the carriage were let down—the carriage
drove off—and all was quiet. Once more I rung.

" Is Sir —— *now* at liberty ?"

" Oh, he's gone out, sir," said the same servant,
who had twice before answered my summons. The
valet then entered. I asked him, with lips quivering
with indignation, why I had not seen Sir ——? I
was given to understand that my card had been shown
the baronet—that he said, " I've no time to attend to
this person," or words to that effect, and had left his
house without deigning to notice me ! Without uttering more than "Show me the door, sir," to the
servant, I took my departure, determining to perish
rather than make a second application. To antici
pate my narrative a little, I may state, that ten years
afterward, Sir ——, who had become dreadfully addicted to gambling, lost all his property, and died

I.—D

suddenly of an apoplectic seizure brought on by a paroxysm of fury! Thus did Providence reward this selfish and unfeeling man.

I walked about the town for several hours, endeavouring to wear off that air of chagrin and sorrow which had been occasioned by my reception at Sir ——'s. Something *must* be done, and that immediately ; for absolute starvation was now before us. I could think of but two other quarters where I could apply for a little temporary relief. I resolved to write a note to a very celebrated and successful brother practitioner, stating my necessities, acquainting him candidly with my whole circumstances, and soliciting the favour of a temporary accommodation of a few pounds—twenty was the sum I ventured to name. I wrote the letter at a coffee-house, and returned home. I spent all that evening in attempting to picture to myself the reception it would met with. I tried to put myself in the place of him I had written to, and fancy the feelings with which I should receive a similar application. I need not, however, tantalize the reader. After nearly a fortnight's suspense, I received the following reply to my letter. I shall give it *verbatim*, after premising that the writer of it was at that time making about 10,000*l.* or 12,000*l.* a-year.

"—— encloses a trifle (*one guinea*) to Dr. ——, wishes it may be serviceable; but must say, that when young men attempt a station in life without competent funds to meet it, they cannot wonder if they fail.

"—— Square."

The other quarter was old Mr. G——, our Indian lodger. Though an eccentric and reserved man, shunning all company except that of a favourite black servant, I thought he might yet be liberal. As he was something of a character, I must be allowed a word or two about him in passing. Though he occupied the whole of the first floor of

my house, I seldom saw him. In truth he was little
else than a bronze fireside fixture all day long, summer and winter,—protected from the intrusion of
draughts and visiters, which equally annoyed him,
by a huge folding screen. Swathed, mummy-like,
in flannel and furs; squalling incessant execrations
against the chilly English climate; and solacing
himself alternately with sleep, caudle, and curry.
He would sit for hours listening to a strange,
cluttering (I know no word but this can give any
thing like an idea of it), and most melancholy noise,
uttered by his black grizzle-headed servant—which
I was given to understand was a species of Indian
song—evincing his satisfaction by a face curiously
puckered together, and small beady black eyes,
glittering with the light of vertical suns: thus, I
say, he would sit till both dropped asleep. He
was very fond of this servant (whose name was
Clinquabor, or something of that sort), and yet
would kick and strike him with great violence on
the slightest occasions.

Without being self-interested, I candidly acknowledge, that on receiving him into our house, and
submitting to divers inconveniences from his strange
foreign fancies, I had calculated on his proving a
lucrative lodger. I was, however, very much mistaken. He uniformly discouraged my visits, by
evincing the utmost restlessness and even trepidation whenever I approached. He was more tolerant
to my wife's visits; but even to her could not help
intimating, in pretty plain terms, on more occasions
than one, that he had no idea of being " drugged to
death by his landlord." On one occasion, however,
his servant came stuttering with agitation into my
room, that "hib massa wis to see—a—a doctor." I
found him suffering from the heart-burn; submitted
to his asthmatic querulousness for nearly half an
hour; prescribed the usual remedies; and received
in return—a guinea? No; a curious, ugly, and per

fectly useless cane, with which (to enhance its va lue) he assured me he had once kept a large snake at bay! On another occasion, in return for similar professional assistance, he dismissed me ·without tendering me a fee, or any thing instead of it; but sent for my wife, in the course of the afternoon, and presented her with a hideous little cracked china teapot, the lid fastened with a dingy silver chain, and the lip of the spout bearing evident marks of an ancient compound fracture. He was singularly exact in every thing he did: he paid his rent, for instance, at ten o'clock in the morning every quar-ter-day, as long as he lived with me.

Such was the man whose assistance I had at last determined to ask. With infinite hesitation and embarrassment I stated my circumstances. He fidgeted sadly, till I concluded, almost inarticulate with agitation, by soliciting the loan of 300*l.*—offer-ing, at the same time, to deposite with him the lease of my house, as a collateral security for what he might advance me.

"My God!" he exclaimed, falling back in his chair, and elevating his hands.

"Would you favour me with this sum, Mr. G——?" I inquired, in a respectful tone.

"Do you take me, doctor, for a money-lender?"

"No, indeed, sir; but for an obliging friend, as well as lodger—if you will allow me the liberty."

"Ha! you think me a rich old hunks come from India to fling his gold at every one he sees."

"May I beg an answer, sir?" said I, after a pause.

"I cannot lend it you, doctor," he replied, calmly, and bowed me to the door. I rushed down stairs, almost gnashing my teeth with fury. The Deity seemed to have marked me with a curse. No one would listen to me!

The next day my rent was due; which, with Mr. G——'s rent and the savings of excruciating parsi

mony, I contrived to meet.   Then came old L——'
Good God! what were my feelings when I saw him
hobble up to my door.   I civilly assured him, with
a quaking heart and ashy cheeks, but with the calmness of despair, that, though it was not convenient
to-day, he should have it on the morning of the next
day.   His greedy, black, Jewish eye seemed to dart
into my very soul.   He retired, apparently satisfied,
and I almost fell down and blessed him on my knees
for his forbearance.

It was on Wednesday, two days after Christmas,
that my dear Emily came down-stairs after her confinement.   Though pale and languid, she looked
very lovely, and her fondness for me seemed re-
doubled.   By way of honouring the season, and
welcoming my dear wife down-stairs, in spite of my
fearful embarrassments, I expended my last guinea
in providing a tolerably comfortable dinner, such as
I had not sat down to for many a long week.   I was
determined to cast care aside for one day at least.
The little table was set; the small but savoury
roast-beef was on; and I was just drawing the cork
of a solitary bottle of port, when a heavy knock was
heard at the street-door.   I almost fainted at the
sound, I knew not why.   The servant answered the
door, and two men entered the very parlour, holding
a thin slip of parchment in their hands.

"In God's name, who are you?   What brings
you here?" while my wife sat silent, trembling, and
ooking very faint.

"Are you the gentleman that is named here?"
inquired one of the men, in a civil and even com-
passionate tone, showing me a *writ* issued against
me by old L——, for the money I owed him!   My
poor wife saw my agitation; and the servant arrived
just in time to preserve her from falling, for she had
fainted.   I had her carried to bed, and was permitted to wait by her bedside for a few moments
when, more dead than alive, I surrendered myself

into the hands of the officers. I shall never forget that half-hour, if I were to live a thousand years. I felt as if I were stepping into my grave. My heart was utterly withered within me.

A few hours beheld me the sullen and despairing occupant of the back attic of a sponging-house near Leicester-square. The weather was bitterly inclement, yet no fire was allowed one who had not a farthing in his pocket. Had it not been for my poor Emily and my child, I think I should have put an end to my miserable existence; for *to prison I must go;* there was no miracle to save me; and what was to become of Emily and her little one? Jewels she had none to pawn; my books had nearly all disappeared; the scanty remnants of our furniture were not worth selling. Great God! I was nearly frantic when I thought of all this. I sat up the whole night without fire or candle (for the brutal wretch in whose custody I was, suspected I had money with me and would not part with it), till nearly seven o'clock in the morning, when I sunk in a state of stupor on the bed, and fell asleep. How long I continued so I know not, for I was roused from a dreary dream by some one embracing me, and reiteratedly kissing my lips and forehead. It was my poor Emily, who, at the imminent risk of her life, having found out where I was, had hurried to bring me the news of release; for she had succeeded in obtaining the sum of 300*l.* from our lodger, which I had in vain solicited. We returned home immediately. I hastened up-stairs to our lodger to express the most enthusiastic thanks. He listened without interruption, and then coldly replied, " I would rather have your note of hand, sir!" Almost choked with mortification at receiving such an unfeeling rebuff, I gave him what he asked, expecting nothing more than that he would presently act the part of old L——. He did not, however, trouble me.

The few pounds above what was due to our re-

lentless creditor L—— sufficed to meet some of our
more pressing exigencies; but as they gradually
disappeared, my prospects became darker than ever.
The agitation and distress which recent occurrences
had occasioned threw my wife into a low, nervous,
hysterical state, which added to my misfortunes;
and her little infant was sensibly pining away, as if
in unconscious sympathy with its wretched parents.
Where *now* were we to look for help? We had a
new creditor, to a serious amount, in Mr. G——, our
lodger; whatever, therefore, might be the extremity
of our distress, applying to *him* was out of the question; nay, it would be well if he proved a lenient
creditor. The hateful annuity was again becoming
due. It pressed like an incubus upon us. The
form of old L—— flitted incessantly around us, as
though it were a fiend goading us on to destruction.
I am sure I must often have raved frightfully in my
sleep; for more than once I was waked by my wife
clinging to me, and exclaiming, in terrified accents,
" Oh, hush, hush, ——, don't for heaven's sake say
so !"

To add to my misery, she and the infant began to
keep their bed; and our lodger, whose constitution
had been long ago broken up, began to fail rapidly.
I was in daily attendance, but of course could not
expect a fee, as I was already his debtor to a large
amount. I had three patients who paid me regularly, but only one was a daily patient; and I was
obliged to lay by, out of these small incomings, a
cruel portion to meet my rent and L——'s annuity.
Surely my situation was now like that of the fabled
scorpion, surrounded with fiery destruction! Every
one in the house, and my few acquaintances without, expressed surprise and commiseration at my
wretched appearance. I was worn almost to a skeleton; and when I looked suddenly in the glass, my
wan and hollow looks startled me. My fears magnified the illness of my wife: the whole world

seemed melting away from me into gloom and darkness.

My thoughts, I well recollect, seemed to be perpetually occupied with the dreary image of a desolate churchyard, wet and cold with the sleets and storms of winter. Oh that I and my wife and child, I have sometimes madly thought, were sleeping peacefully in our long home! Why were we brought into the world? why did my nature prompt me to seek my present station in society? merely for the purpose of reducing me to the dreadful condition of him of old, whose only consolation from his friends was, " Curse God and die!" What had I done—what had our forefathers done—that Providence should thus come upon us, and thwart us in every thing we attempted?

Fortune, however, at last seemed tired of persecuting me ; and my affairs took a favourable turn when most they needed it, and when least I expected it. On what small and insignificant things do our fates depend. Truly,

> " There is a tide in the affairs of men,
>   Which, taken at the flood, leads on to fortune."

About eight o'clock one evening, in the month of March, I was walking down the Haymarket, as usual in a very disconsolate mood, in search of some shop where I might execute a small commission for my wife. The whole neighbourhood in front of the Opera-house door exhibited the usual scene of uproar arising from clashing carriages and quarrelsome coachmen. I was standing at the box-door, and watching the company descend from their carriages, when a cry was heard from the very centre of the crowd of coaches, " Run for a doctor!" I rushed instantly to the spot, at the peril of my life, announcing my profession. I soon made my way up to the open door of a carriage, from which issued the moanings of a female, evidently in great agony.

The accident was this: a young lady had suddenly stretched out her arm through the open window of the carriage conveying her to the opera, for the purpose of pointing out to one of her companions a brilliant illumination of one of the opposite houses. At that instant their coachman, dashing forward to gain the open space opposite the box-door, shot with great velocity, and within a hair's breadth distance, past a retiring carriage. The consequence was inevitable: a sudden shriek announced the dislocation of the young lady's shoulder, and the shocking laceration of the forearm and hand. When I arrived at the carriage-door the unfortunate sufferer was lying motionless in the arms of an elderly gentleman and a young lady, both of them, as might be expected dreadfully agitated. It was the Earl of —— and his two daughters. Having entered the carriage, I placed my fair patient in such a position as would prevent her suffering more than was necessary from the motion of the carriage; despatched one of the servants for Mr. Cline, to meet us on our arrival home; and then the coachman was ordered to drive home as fast as possible. I need not say more, than that by Mr. Cline's skill the dislocation was quickly reduced, and the wounded hand and arm duly dressed. I then prescribed what medicines were necessary; received a check for ten guineas from the earl, accompanied with fervent thanks for my prompt attentions; and was requested to call as early as possible the next morning.

As soon as I had left his lordship's door, I shot home like an arrow. My good fortune (truly it is an ill wind that blows *nobody* any good) was almost too much for me. I could scarce repress the violence of my emotions, but felt a continual inclination to relieve myself by singing, shouting, or committing some other such extravagance. I arrived at home in a very few minutes, and rushed breathless up stairs, joy glittering in my eyes, to commu

I.—E

nicate my good fortune to my wife, and congratulate ourselves that the door of professional success was at last opened to us. How tenderly she tried to calm my excitement, and moderate my expectations, without at the same time depressing my spirits! I did certainly feel somewhat damped, when I recol·lected the little incident of my introduction to Sir William ——, and its abrupt and unexpected termination. This, however, differed from that; and the event proved that my expectations were not ill founded.

I continued in constant attendance on my fair patient, who was really a very lovely girl; and by my unremitting and anxious attentions so conciliated the favour of the earl and the rest of his family, that the countess, who had long been an invalid, was committed to my care, jointly with that of the family physician. I need hardly say that my poor services were most nobly remunerated; and more than this, having succeeded in securing the confidence of the family, it was not many weeks before I had the honour of visiting one or two other families of high rank; and I felt conscious that I was laying the foundation of a fashionable and lucrative practice. With joy unutterable I contrived to be ready for our half-yearly tormentor, old L——; and somewhat surprised him by asking, with an easy air, when he wished for a return of his principal. Of course he was not desirous of losing such interest as I was paying!

I had seen too much of the bitterness of adversity to suffer the dawn of good fortune to elate me into too great confidence. I now husbanded my resources with rigorous economy, and had in return the inexpressible satisfaction of being able to pay my way and stand fair with *all* my creditors. My beloved Emily appeared in that society which she was born to ornament; and we numbered several families of high respectability among our visiting friends. As is usual, whenever accident threw me in the way of those who formerly scowled upon me contemptuously, I was received with an excess of civility. The very physician who sent me the munificent donation of a guinea I met in consultation, and made his cheeks tingle by returning him the *loan* he had advanced me!

In four years' time from the occurrence at the Haymarket I contrived to repay old L—— his 3000*l.* (though he did not live a month after signing the receipt), and thus escaped for ever from the fangs of the money-lenders. A word or two, also, about our Indian lodger. He died about eighteen months after the accident I have been relating. His sole heir was a young lieutenant in the navy; and very much to my surprise and gratification, in a codicil to old Mr. G——'s will I was left a legacy of 2000*l.*, including the 300*l.* he had lent me, saying it was some return for the many attentions he had received from us since he had been our lodger, and as a mark of his approbation of the honourable and virtuous principles by which, he said, he had always perceived our conduct to be actuated.

Twelve years from this period my income amounted to between 3000*l.* and 4000*l.* a-year; and as my family was increasing, I thought my means warranted a more extensive establishment. I therefore removed into a large and elegant house, and set up my carriage. The recollection of past times has taught me at least one useful lesson, whether my life be long or short, to bear success with moderation, and never to turn a deaf ear to applications from the younger and less successful members of my profession.

> " Sweet are the uses of adversity ;
> Which, like a toad, ugly and venomous,
> Wears yet a precious jewel in his head.'

CHAPTER II.

CANCER—THE DENTIST AND THE COMEDIAN—A SCHOLAR'S
DEATH-BED—PREPARING FOR THE HOUSE—DUELLING.

Cancer.

ONE often hears of the great firmness of the female
sex, and their powers of enduring a degree of physical pain which would utterly break down the stubborn strength of man.   An interesting exemplification of this remark will be found in the short narrative immediately following.   The event made a
strong impression on my mind at the time, and I
thought it well worthy of an entry in my Diary.

I had for several months been in constant attendance on a Mrs. St——, a young married lady, of considerable family and fortune, who was the victim of
that terrible scourge of the female sex—a cancer.
To great personal attractions she added uncommon
sweetness of disposition: and the fortitude with
which she submitted to the agonizing inroads of her
malady, together with her ardent expressions of
gratitude for such temporary alleviations as her
anxious medical attendants could supply, contributed
to inspire me with a very lively interest in her fate.
I can conscientiously say, that during the whole
period of my attendance I never heard a word of complaint fall from her, nor witnessed any indications
of impatience or irritability.   I found her, one morning, stretched on the crimson sofa in the drawing-
room; and though her pallid features and gently
corrugated eyebrows evidenced the intense agony
she was suffering—on my inquiring what sort of a
night she had passed, she replied in a calm but tremulous tone, "Oh, doctor ! I have had a dreadful

night; but I am glad Captain St—— was not with me, for it would have made him very wretched!" At that moment a fine flaxen-haired little boy, her first and only child, came running into the room, his blue laughing eyes glittering with innocent merriment. I took him on my knee, and amused him with my watch, in order that he might not disturb his mother. The poor sufferer, after gazing on him with an air of intense fondness for some moments, suddenly covered her eyes with her hand (oh, how slender —how snowy—how almost transparent was it!)— and I presently saw the tears trickling through her fingers—but she uttered not a word. There was the *mother!*—The aggravated malignity of her disorder rendered an operation at length inevitable. The eminent surgeon who, jointly with myself, was in regular attendance on her feelingly communicated the intelligence, and asked whether she thought she had fortitude enough to submit to an operation. She assured him, with a sweet smile of resignation, that she had for some time been suspecting as much, and had made up her mind to submit to it—but on two conditions—that her husband (who was then at sea) should not be informed of it till it was over ; and that during the operation she should not be in anywise bound or blindfolded. Her calm and decisive manner convinced me that remonstrance would be useless. Sir —— looked at me with a doubtful air. She observed it ; and said, "I see what you are thinking, Sir ——; but I hope to show you that a woman has more courage than you seem willing to give her credit for." In short, after the surgeon had acquiesced in the latter condition—to which he had especially demurred—a day was fixed for the operation —subject, of course, to Mrs. St——'s state of health. When the Wednesday arrived, it was with some agitation that I entered Sir ——'s carriage, in company with himself and his senior pupil, Mr. ——. I could scarce avoid a certain nervous tremor—unprofessional as it may seem—when I saw the servant place the operating case on the seat of the carriage. "Are you sure you have every thing ready, Mr. ——?" inquired Sir ——, with a calm and businesslike air, which somewhat irritated me. On being assured of the affirmative, and after cautiously casting his eye over the case of instruments,* to make assurance doubly sure, we drove off. We arrived at Mrs. St——'s, —who resided a few miles from town,—about two o'clock in the afternoon, and were immediately ushered into the room in which the operation was to be performed—a back parlour, the window of which looked into a beautiful garden. I shall be pardoned, I hope, for acknowledging that the glimpse I caught of the pale and disordered countenance of the servant, as he retired after showing us into the room, somewhat disconcerted me; for in addition to the deep interest I felt in the fate of the lovely sufferer, I had always an abhorrence for the operative part of the profession, which many years of practice did not suffice to remove. The necessary arrangements being at length completed,—consisting of a hateful array of instruments,—cloths,—sponge,—warm water, &c. &c.,—a message was sent to Mrs. St——, to inform her all was ready.

Sir —— was just making a jocular and not very well-timed allusion to my agitated air. when the door was opened, and Mrs. St—— entered, followed by her two attendants. Her step was firm, her air composed, and her pale features irradiated with a smile—sad, however, as the cold twilight of October. She was then about twenty-six or seven years of age, and under all the disadvantageous circumstances in which she was placed, looked at that moment a beautiful woman. Her hair was light auburn,

---

* I once saw the life of a patient lost, merely through the want of such laudable precaution as that of Sir —— in the present instance. An indispensable instrument was suddenly required, in the middle of the operation ; and, to the dismay of the operator and those around him there was r one at hand'

and hung back neglectedly over a forehead and neck white as marble. Her full blue eyes, which usually beamed with a delicious pensive expression from beneath

———" the soft languor of the drooping lid,"

were now lighted with the glitter of a restlessness and agitation which the noblest degree of self-command could not entirely conceal or repress. Her features were regular, her nose and mouth were exquisitely chiselled, and her complexion fair, almost to transparency. Indeed, an eminent medical writer has remarked that the most beautiful women are generally the subjects of this terrible disease. A large Indian shawl was thrown over her shoulders, and she wore a white muslin dressing-gown. And was it this innocent and beautiful being who was doomed to writhe beneath the torture and disfigurement of the operating knife? My heart ached. A decanter of port wine and some glasses were placed on a small table near the window; she beckoned me towards it, and was going to speak.

"Allow me, my dear madam, to pour you a glass of wine," said I.

"If it would do me good, doctor," she whispered. She barely touched the glass with her lips, and then handed it to me, saying, with assumed cheerfulness, "Come, doctor, I see you need it as much as I do, after all. Yes, doctor," she continued with emphasis, "you are very, *very* kind and feeling to me." When I had set down the glass, she continued, "Dear doctor, do forgive a woman's weakness; and try if you can hold this letter, which I received yesterday from Captain St——, and in which he speaks very fondly, so that my eyes may rest on his dear handwriting all the while I am sitting here, without being noticed by any one else; will you?"

"Madam, you must really excuse me—it will agitate you—I must beg—"

" You are mistaken," she replied, with firmness; " it will rather compose me.   And if 1 *should*—" expire, she was going to have said, but her tongue refused utterance.   She then put the letter into my hand ; hers was cold, icy cold, and clammy, but I did not perceive it tremble.

" In return, madam, you must give me leave to hold your hand during the operation."

" What ! you fear me, doctor ?" she replied, with a faint smile, but did not refuse my request.   At this moment, Sir —— approached us with a cheerful air, saying, " Well, madam, is your tête-à-tête finished ? I want to get this little matter over, and give you permanent ease."   I do not think there ever lived a professional man who could speak with such an assuring air as Sir ——.

" I am ready, Sir ——.   Are the servants sent out ?" she inquired of one of the women present.

" Yes, madam," she replied, in tears.

" And my little Harry ?"   Mrs. St—— asked, in a fainter tone.   She was answered in the affirmative.

" Then I am prepared," said she, and sat down in the chair that was placed for her.   One of the attendants then removed the shawl from her shoulders, and Mrs. St—— herself, with perfect composure, assisted in displacing as much of her dress as was necessary.   She then suffered Sir —— to place her on the corner side of the chair, with her left arm thrown over the back of it, and her face looking over her right shoulder.   She gave me her right hand; and with my left I endeavoured to hold Captain St——'s letter, as she had desired.   She smiled sweetly, as if to assure me of her fortitude; and there was something so indescribably affecting in the expression of her full blue eyes, that it almost broke my heart.   I shall never forget that smile as long as I live !   Half-closing her eyes, she fixed them on the letter I held, and did not once remove them till all was over.   Nothing could console me

at this trying moment, but the conviction of the consummate skill of Sir ——, who now, with a calm
eye and a steady hand, commenced the operation.
At the instant of the first incision her whole frame
quivered with a convulsive shudder, and her cheeks
became ashy pale.   I prayed inwardly that she might
faint, so that the earlier stage of the operation might
be got over while she was in a state of insensibility.
It was not the case, however; her eyes continued
riveted in one long burning gaze of fondness on the
beloved handwriting of her husband; and she moved
not a limb, nor uttered more than an occasional
sigh, during the whole of the protracted and painful
operation.   When the last bandage had been applied,
she whispered, almost inarticulately, "Is it all over,
doctor?"

"Yes, madam," I replied; "and we are going to
carry you up to bed."

"No, no—I think I can walk; I will try," said
she, and endeavoured to rise; but on Sir —— assuring her that the motion might perhaps induce fatal
consequences, she desisted, and we carried her,
sitting in the chair, up to bed.   The instant we had
laid her down she swooned, and continued so long
insensible that Sir —— held a looking-glass over her
mouth and nostrils, apprehensive that the vital energies had at last sunk under the terrible struggle.
She recovered, however; and under the influence of
an opiate draught, slept for several hours.

*   *   *   *   *   *   *   *

Mrs. St—— recovered, though very slowly; and I
attended her assiduously, sometimes two or three
times a-day, till she could be removed to the seaside.   I shall not easily forget an observation she
made at the last visit I paid her.   She was alluding,
one morning, distantly and delicately to the personal
disfigurement she had suffered.   I, of course, said
all that was soothing.

"But, doctor, my *husband*—" said she, suddenly

while a faint crimson mantled on her cheek ; adding
falteringly, after a pause, " I think St—— will love
me yet !"

The Dentist and the Comedian.

FRIDAY, — 18—. A ludicrous contretems happened
to-day, which I wish I could describe as forcibly as
it struck me. Mr. ——, the well-known comedian,
with whom I was on terms of intimacy, after having
suffered so severely from the toothache as to be prevented for two evenings from taking his part in the
play, sent, under my direction, for Mons. ——, a
fashionable dentist, then but recently imported from
France. While I was sitting with my friend, endeavouring to " screw his courage up to the stick-
ing-place," monsieur arrived, duly furnished with
the " tools of his craft." The comedian sat down
with a rueful visage, and eyed the dentist's formidable preparations with a piteous and disconcerted
air. As soon as I had taken my station behind, for
the purpose of holding the patient's head, the gum
was lanced without much ado ; but as the doomed
tooth was a very formidable broad-rooted molar,
monsieur prepared for a vigorous effort. He was
just commencing the dreadful wrench, when he
suddenly relaxed his hold, retired a step or two from
his patient, and burst into a loud fit of laughter ! Up
started the astounded comedian, and with clenched
fists demanded furiously, " What the d—l he meant by
such conduct ?" The little bewhiskered foreigner,
nowever, continued standing at a little distance, still
so convulsed with laughter as to disregard the menacing movements of his patient ; and exclaiming,
" Ah, mon Dieu !—ver good—ver good—bien ! ha,
na !—Be Gar, monsieur, you pull one such d——d
queer, extraordinaire comique face ; be Gar, like one
big fiddle !" or words to that effect. The dentist was
right : Mr. ——'s features were odd enough at all
times ; but on the present occasion they suffered

such excruciating contortions—such a strange puckering together of the mouth and cheeks, and upturn-
ing of the eyes, that it was ten thousand times more
laughable than any artificially distorted features with
which he used to set Drury-Lane in a roar.—Oh that
a painter had been present!—There was, on one
side, my friend, standing in menacing attitude, with
both fists clenched, his left cheek swelled, and looking
as if the mastication of a large apple had been suddenly suspended, and his whole features creating a
grotesque expression of mingled pain, indecision, and
fury. Then there was the operator beginning to
look a little startled at the probable consequences
of his sally; and, lastly, I stood a little aside, almost
suffocated with suppressed laughter! At length,
however, ——'s perception of the ridiculous prevailed; and after a very hearty laugh, and exclaiming, " I *must* have looked d——d odd, I suppose !" he
once more resigned himself into the hands of
monsieur, and the tooth was out in a twinkling.

A Scholar's Death-bed.

[The following short but melancholy narrative will, it is hoped, be
perused with additional interest, when the reader is assured that it is
FACT. Much more might have been committed to press; but as it would
have related chiefly to a mad devotion to *alchymy*, which some of
Mr. ——'s few posthumous papers abundantly evidence, it is omitted,
lest the reader should consider the details as romantic or improbable.
All that is worth recording is told; and it is hoped that some young
men of powerful, undisciplined, and ambitious minds will find their ac
count in an attentive consideration of the fate of a kindred spirit.—*Bene
facit, qui ex aliorum erroribus sibi exemplum sumat.*]

THINKING, one morning, that I had gone through
the whole of my usual levee of home-patients, I
was preparing to go out, when the servant informed
me there was one yet to be spoken with, who, he
thought, must have been asleep in a corner of the
room, or he should not have failed to summon him
in his turn. Directing him to be shown in immediately, I retook my place at my desk. The servant

in a few moments ushered in a young man, who seemed to have scarce strength enough, even with the assistance of a walking-stick, to totter to a chair opposite me. I was much struck with his appear-ance, which was that of one in reduced circum-stances. His clothes, though perfectly clean and neat, were faded and threadbare; and his coat was buttoned up to his chin, where it was joined by a black silk neck-kerchief, in such a manner as to lead me to suspect the absence of a shirt. He was rather below than above the average height, and seemed wasted almost to a shadow. There was an air of superior ease and politeness in his demeanour; and an expression about his countenance, sickly and sallow though it was, so melancholy, mild, and intel-ligent that I could not help viewing him with pecu-liar interest.

"I was afraid, my friend, I should have missed you," said I, in a kind tone, "as I was on the point of going out."—"I heard your carriage drive up to the door, doctor, and shall not detain you more than a few moments; nay, I will call to-morrow, if that would be more convenient," he replied, faintly, sud-denly pressing his hand to his side, as though the effort of speaking occasioned him pain. I assured him I had a quarter of an hour at his service, and begged he would proceed at once to state the nature of his complaint. He detailed—what I had antici-pated from his appearance—all the symptoms of a very advanced stage of pulmonary consumption. He expressed himself in very select and forcible language; and once or twice, when at a loss for what he conceived an adequate expression in Eng-lish, chose such an appropriate Latin phrase, that the thought perpetually suggested itself to me, while he was speaking—"*a starved scholar!*"—He made not the most distant allusion to poverty, but confined himself to the leading symptoms of his indisposition I determined, however, (*haud præteritorum imme-*

mor!) to ascertain his circumstances, with a view, if possible, of relieving them. I asked if he ate animal food with relish,—enjoyed his dinner,—whether his meals were regular. He coloured, and hesitated a little, for I put the question searchingly; and replied, with some embarrassment, that he did not certainly *then* eat regularly, nor enjoy his food when he did. I soon found that he was in very straitened circumstances; that, in short, he was sinking rapidly under the pressure of want and harassing anxiety, which alone had accelerated, if not wholly induced, his present illness; and that all he had to expect from medical aid was a little alleviation. I prescribed a few simple medicines, and then asked him in what part of the town he resided.

"I am afraid, doctor," said he, modestly, "I shall be unable to afford your visiting me at my own lodgings. I will occasionally call on you here, as a morning patient," and he proffered me half-a-guinea. The conviction that it was probably the very last he had in the world, and a keen recollection of similar scenes in my own history, almost brought the tears into my eyes. I refused the fee, of course; and prevailed on him to let me set him down, as I was driving close past his residence. He seemed overwhelmed with gratitude; and with a blush hinted that he was "not quite in carriage costume." He lived in one of the small streets leading from Mayfair; and after having made a note in my tablets of his name and number, I set him down, promising him an early call.

The clammy pressure of his wasted fingers, as I shook his hand at parting, remained with me all that day. I could not dismiss from my mind the wild and sorrowful countenance of this young man, go where I would; and I was on the point of mentioning the incident to a most excellent and generous nobleman, whom I was then attending, and soliciting his assistance, but the thought that it was pre-

nature checked me. There *might* be something unworthy in the young man; he might *possibly* be an—impostor. These were hard thoughts—chilling and unworthy suspicions, but I could not resist them, alas! an eighteen years' intercourse with a deceitful world has alone taught me how to entertain them!

As my wife dined a little out of town that evening I hastily swallowed a solitary meal, and set out in quest of my morning patient. With some difficulty I found the house; it was the meanest and in the meanest street I had visited for months. I knocked at the door, which was open, and surrounded by a babbling throng of dirty children. A slatternly woman, with a child in her arms, answered my summons. Mr. ——, she said, lived there, in the top floor; but he was just gone out for a few moments, she supposed, " to get a mouthful of victuals, but I was welcome to go up and wait for him, since there was not much to make away with, howsoever," said the rude and vulgar creature. One of her children led me up the narrow dirty staircase, and having ushered me into the room, left me to my meditations. A wretched hole it was in which I was sitting! The evening sun streamed in discoloured rays through the unwashed panes, here and there mended with brown paper, and sufficed to show me that the only furniture consisted of a miserable, curtainless bed (the disordered clothes showing that the weary limbs of the wretched occupant had but recently left it)— three old rush-bottomed chairs—and a rickety deal table, on which were scattered several pages of manuscript—a letter or two—pens, ink, and a few books. There was no chest of drawers—nor did I see any thing likely to serve as a substitute. Poor Mr. —— probably carried about with him all he had in the world! There was a small sheet of writing paper pinned over the mantelpiece (if such it deserved to be called), which I gazed at with a sigh; it bore simply the outline of a coffin, with Mr. ——'s initials, and "*obiit* ——, 18—," evidently in his own handwriting. Curious to see the kind of books he preferred, I took them up and examined them. There were—if I recollect right—a small Amsterdam edition of Plautus—a Horace—a much befingered copy of Aristophanes—a neat pocket edition of Æschylus— a small copy of the works of Lactantius—and two odd volumes of English **books.** I had no intention of being impertinently inquisitive, but my eye accidentally lit on the uppermost manuscript, and seeing it to be in the Greek character, I took it up, and found a few verses of Greek sapphics, entitled— Εἰς τὴν νύκτα τελευταίαν—evidently the recent composition of Mr. ——. He entered the room as I was laying down the paper, and started at seeing a stranger, for it seems the people of the house had not taken the trouble to inform him I was waiting. On discovering who it was, he bowed politely, and gave me his hand; but the sudden agitation my presence had occasioned deprived him of utterance. I thought I could almost *hear* the palpitation of his heart. I brought him to a chair, and begged him to be calm.

"You are not worse, Mr. ——, I hope, since I saw you this morning?" I inquired. He whispered almost inarticulately, holding his hand to his left side, that he was always worse in the evenings. I felt his pulse; it beat 130! I discovered that he had gone out for the purpose of trying to get employment in a neighbouring printing-office, but having failed, was returned in a state of deeper depression than usual. The perspiration rolled from his brow almost faster than he could wipe it away. I sat by him for nearly two minutes, holding his hand, without uttering a word, for I was deeply affected. At length I begged he would forgive my inquiring how it was that a young man of talent and education like himself could be reduced to a state of such utter destitution? While I was waiting for an answer, he suddenly fell from his chair in a swoon. The exertion

·f walking, the pressure of disappointment, and, 1 fear, the almost unbroken fast of the day, had completely prostrated the small remains of his strength. When he had a little revived, I succeeded in laying him on the bed, and instantly summoned the woman of the house. After some time, she sauntered lazily to the door, and asked me what I wanted. "Are you the person that attends on this gentleman, my good woman?" I inquired.

"Marry come up, sir!" she replied in a loud tone. "I've no manner of cause for attending on him, not I; he ought to attend on himself; and as for his being a *gentleman*," she continued, with an insolent sneer, for which I felt inclined to throw her down stairs, "not a stiver of his money have I seen for this three weeks for his rent, and"—— Seeing the fluent virago was warming, and approaching close to my unfortunate patient's bedside, I stopped her short by putting half-a-guinea into her hand, and directing her to purchase a bottle of port wine; at the same time hinting, that if she conducted herself properly I would see her rent paid myself. I then shut the door, and resumed my seat by Mr. ——, who was trembling violently all over with agitation, and endeavoured to soothe him. The more I said, however, and the kinder were my tones, the more was he affected. At length he burst into a flood of tears, and continued weeping for some time like a child. I saw it was hysterical, and that it was best to let his feelings have their full course. His nervous excitement at last gradually subsided, and he began to converse with tolerable coolness.

"Doctor," he faltered, "your conduct is very— very noble—it *must* be disinterested," pointing, with a bitter air, to the wretched room in which we were sitting.

"I feel sure, Mr. - —, that you have done nothing to *merit* your present misfortunes," I replied, with a serious and inquiring air.

" Yes—yes, I have!—I have indulged in wild am·
bitious hopes,—lived in absurd dreams of future great.
ness,—been educated beyond my fortunes,—and
formed tastes, and cherished feelings, incompatible
with the station it seems I was born to—beggary or
daily labour!" was his answer, with as much vehemence as his weakness would allow.

" But, Mr. ——, your friends—your relatives—they
cannot be apprized of your situation."

" Alas, doctor, friends I have none—unless you
will permit me to name the last and noblest, yourself; relatives, several."

" And they, of course, do not know of your illness
and straitened circumstances?"

" They do, doctor, and kindly assure me I brought
it on myself. To do them justice, however,
they could not, I believe, efficiently help me, if they
would."

" Why, have you offended them, Mr. ——? Have
they cast you off?"

" Not avowedly—not in so many words. They
have simply refused to receive or answer any more
of my letters. Possibly I may have offended them.
but am content to meet them hereafter, and try the
justice of the case—*there*," said Mr. ——, solemnly
pointing upwards. " Well I know, and so do you,
doctor, that my days on earth are very few, and
likely to be very bitter also." It was in vain I
pressed him to tell me who his relatives were, and
suffer me to solicit their personal attendance on his
last moments. " It is altogether useless, doctor, to
ask me further," said he, raising himself a little in
bed; " my father and mother are both dead, and no
power on earth shall extract from me a syllable
further. It *is* hard," he continued, bursting again
into tears, " if I must *die* amid their taunts and
reproaches." I felt quite at a loss what to say to
all this. There was something very singular, if not
reprehensible, in this manner of alluding to his rela-

I —F

tives, which led me to fear that he was by no means free from blame. Had I not felt myself very delicately situated, and dreaded even the possibility of hurting his morbidly irritable feelings, I felt inclined to have asked him how he thought of *existing* without their aid, especially in his forlorn and helpless state; having neither friends nor the means of obtaining them. I thought, also, that short as had been my intimacy with him, I had discerned symptoms of a certain obstinacy and haughty imperiousness of temper which would sufficiently account, if not for occasioning, at least for widening, any unhappy breach which might have occurred in his family. But what was to be done? I could not let him starve; as I had voluntarily stepped in to his assistance, I determined to make his last moments easy—at least as far as lay in my power.

A little to anticipate the course of my narrative, I may here state what little information concerning him was elicited in the course of our various interviews. His father and mother had left Ireland, their native place, early, and gone to Jamaica, where they lived as slave-superintendents. They left their only son to the care of the wife's brother-in-law, who put him to school, where he much distinguished himself. On the faith of it he contrived to get to the college in Dublin, where he stayed two years: and then, in a confident reliance on his own talents, and the sum of 50*l.* which was sent him from Jamaica, with the intelligence of the death of both his parents in impoverished circumstances, he had come up to London, it seems, with no definite end in view. Here he had continued for about two years; but in addition to the failure of his health, all his efforts to establish himself proved abortive. He contrived to glean a scanty sum, God knows how, which was gradually lessening at a time when his impaired health rather required that his resources should be augmented. He had no friends in respectable life, whose influence or wealth might have been serviceable; and at the time he called on me, he had not more in the world than the solitary half-guinea he proffered to me as a fee. I never learned the names of any of his relatives; but from several things occasionally dropped in the heat of conversation, it was clear there must have been unhappy differences.

To return, however. As the evening was far advancing, and I had one or two patients yet to visit, I began to think of taking my departure. I enjoined him strictly to keep his bed till I saw him again, to preserve as calm and equable a frame of mind as possible, and to dismiss all anxiety for the future, as I would gladly supply his present necessities, and send him a civil and attentive nurse. He tried to thank me, but his emotions choked his utterance. He grasped my hand with convulsive energy. His eye spoke eloquently—but, alas! it shone with the fierce and unnatural lustre of consumption, as though, I have often thought in such cases, the conscious soul was glowing with the reflected light of its kindred element—eternity. I knew it was impossible for him to survive many days, from several unequivocal symptoms of what is called, in common language, a galloping consumption. I was as good as my word, and sent him a nurse (the mother of one of my servants), who was charged to pay him the utmost attention in her power. My wife also sent him a little bed-furniture, linen, preserves, jellies, and other small matters of that sort. I visited him every evening, and found him on each occasion verifying my apprehensions, for he was sinking rapidly. His mental energies, however, seemed to increase in an inverse ratio with the decline of his physical powers. His conversation was animated, various, and, at times, enchainingly interesting. I have sometimes sat at his bedside for several hours together, wondering how one so young (he was not more than two or three-and-twenty) could have acquired so much information. He spoke with spirit and justness on the leading political topics of the day; and I particularly recollect his making some very noble reflections on the character and exploits of Buonaparte, who was then blazing in the zenith of his glory. Still, however, the current of his thoughts and language was frequently tinged with the enthusiasm and extravagance of delirium. Of this he seemed himself conscious; for he would sometimes suddenly stop, and pressing his hand to his forehead, exclaim, "Doctor, doctor, I am failing here—*here!*" He acknowledged that he had from his childhood given himself up to the dominion of ambition; and that his whole life had been spent in the most extravagant and visionary expectations. He would smile bitterly when he recounted some of what he justly stigma- tized as his insane projects. "The objects of my ambition," he said, "have been vague and general; I never knew exactly where or what I would be. Had my powers, such as they are, been concentrated on one point—had I formed a more just and modest estimate of my abilities, I might possibly have be- come something.* * * Besides, doctor, I had no *money* —no solid substratum to build upon—there was the rotten point!—Oh, doctor," he continued, with a deep sigh, "if I could but have seen these things three years ago as I see them *now*, I might at this moment have been a sober and respectable member of society; but now I am dying a hanger-on—a fool —a beggar!" and he burst into tears. "You, doctor," he presently continued, "are accustomed, I suppose, to listen to these death-bed repinings—these soul- scourgings—these wailings over a badly-spent life! —Oh, yes—as I am nearing eternity, I seem to look at things—at my own mind and heart especially— through the medium of a strange, searching, un- couthly light. Oh, how many, many things it makes distinct, which I would fain have forgotten for ever! Do you recollect the terrible language of Scripture, doctor, which compares the human breast to *a cage of unclean birds!*"—I left him that evening deeply convinced of the compulsory truths he had uttered; I never thought so seriously before. It is some Scotch divine who has said, that one death-bed preaches a more startling sermon than a bench of bishops.

* * * * * * * *

Mr. —— was an excellent and thorough Greek scholar, perfectly well versed in the Greek dramatists, and passionately fond, in particular, of Sophocles. I recollect his reciting, one evening, with great force and feeling, the touching exclamation of the chorus in the Œdipus Tyrannus—

> Ω πόποι—ἀναρίθμα γὰρ
> φέρω πήματα,
> νοσεῖ δέ μοί πρόπας στόλος,
> οὐδ' ἔνι φροντίδος ἔγχος
> ᾧ τις ἀλεξέται,*
>   &c. &c., 167-171.

—which, he said, was never absent from his mind, sleeping or waking. I once asked him if he did not regret having devoted his life almost exclusively to the study of the classics. He replied, with enthusiasm, " No, doctor—no, no! I should be an ingrate if I did. How can I regret having lived in constant converse, through their works, with the greatest and noblest men that ever breathed! I have lived in Elysium—have breathed the celestial air of those hallowed plains, while engaged in the study of the philosophy and poetry of Greece and Rome. Yes, it is a consolation even for my bitter and premature death-bed, to think that my mind will quit this wretched, diseased, unworthy body, imbued with the refinement—redolent of the eternal freshness and beauty of the most exquisite poetry and philosophy

---

* Ah me! I groan beneath the pressure of innumerable sorrows truly my substance is languishing away, nor can I devise any means of bettering my condition, or discover any source of consolation.

the world ever saw! With my faculties quickened and strengthened, I shall go confidently, and claim kindred with the great ones of Eternity. They know I love their works—have consumed all the oil of my life in their study, and they will welcome their son —their disciple!" Ill as he was, Mr. —— uttered these sentiments (as nearly as I can recollect, in the very words I have given) with an energy, an enthusiasm, and an eloquence which I never saw surpassed. He faltered suddenly, however, from this lofty pitch of excitement, and complained bitterly that his devotion to ancient literature had engendered a morbid sensibility, which had rendered him totally unfit for the ordinary business of life or intermixture with society.   *   *   *

Often I found him sitting up in bed, and reading his favourite play, the *Prometheus Vinctus* of Æschylus, while his pale and wasted features glowed with delighted enthusiasm. He told me that in his estimation there was an air of grandeur and romance about that play, such as was not equalled by any of the productions of the other Greek dramatists; and that the opening dialogue was peculiarly impressive and affecting. He had committed to memory nearly three-fourths of the whole play! I on one occasion asked him, how it came to pass that a person of his superior classical attainments had not obtained some tolerably lucrative engagements as an usher or tutor? He answered, with rather a haughty air, that he would rather have broken stones on the highway.

"To hear," said he, "the magnificent language of Greece—the harmonious cadences of the Romans, mangled and disfigured by stupid lads and duller ushers—oh, it would have been such a profanation as the sacred groves of old suffered, when their solemn silence was disturbed by a rude unhallowed throng of Bacchanalians. I should have expired doctor!" I told him, I could not help lamenting such an absurd and morbid sensitiveness—at which he seemed exceedingly piqued.   He possibly thought I should rather have admired than reprobated the lofty tone he assumed!   I asked him if the stations of which he spoke with such supercilious contempt had not been joyfully occupied by some of the greatest scholars that had ever lived?   He replied simply, with a cold air, that it was his misfortune—not his fault.   He told me, however, that his classical ac- quirements had certainly been capable of something like a profitable employment; for that about two months before he had called on me, he had nearly come to terms with a bookseller for publishing a poetical version of the comedies of Aristophanes: that he had nearly completed one—the ΝΕΦΕΛΑΙ, if I recollect right—when the great difficulty of the task, and the wretched remuneration offered, so dispirited him, that he threw it aside in disgust.*   His only means of subsistence had been the sorry pay of an occasional reader for the press, as well as a contri- butor to the columns of a daily paper.   He had parted with almost the whole of his slender stock of books, his watch, and all his clothes, except what he wore when he called on me.   "And you never try any of

---

* Among his papers I found the following spirited and close version of one of the choral odes in the *Nubes*, commencing,

'Αμφί μοι αὖτε Φοῖβ' ἄναξ
Δήλει, &c.

"Thee, too, great Phœbus, I invoke,
  Thou Delian King,
Who dwell'st on Cynthia's lofty rock!
  Thy passage hither wing,
Blest Goddess! whom Ephesian splendours hold
  In temple bright with gold,
Mid Lydian maidens nobly worshipping!
And thee, our native deity,
  Pallas, our city's guardian, thou!
  Who wield'st the dreadful Ægis.   Thee,
Thee, too, gay Bacchus, from Parnassian height,
  Ruddy with festive torches' glow—
To crown the sacred choir, I thee invite!"

Those who are conversant with the original will perceive that many of the difficult Greek expressions are rendered into literal English.

the magazines?" I inquired; "for they afford to
many young men of talent a fair livelihood." He
said he had indeed struggled hard to gain a footing
in one of the popular periodicals, but that his com-
munications were invariably returned, "with polite
acknowledgments." One of these notes I saw, and
have now in my possession. It was thus:—

"Mr. M'—— begs to return the enclosed, '*Remarks on English Versions of Euripides*,' with many
thanks for the writer's polite offer of it to the E——
M——; but fears that, though an able performance, it is not exactly suited for the readers of the
E—— M——."

To Δ. Δ.

A series of similar disappointments, and the consequent poverty and embarrassment into which he
sunk, had gradually undermined a constitution naturally feeble; and he told me, with much agitation,
that had it not been for the trifling but timely assistance of myself and family, he saw no means of
escaping literal starvation! Could I help sympa-
thizing deeply with him? Alas! his misfortunes
were very nearly paralleled by my own. While
listening to his melancholy details, I seemed living
over again the first four wretched years of my professional career.

* * * * * * * *

I must hasten, however, to the closing scene. I
had left word with the nurse that when Mr. ——
appeared dying, I should be instantly summoned.
About five o'clock in the evening of the 6th of July,
18—, I received a message from Mr. —— himself,
saying that he wished to breathe his last in my presence, as the only friend he had on earth. Unavoid-
able and pressing professional engagements detained
me until half-past six; and it was seven o'clock
before I reached his bedside.

"Lord, Lord, doctor, poor Mr. —— is dying, sure!"
exclaimed the woman of the house, as she opened

the door. "Mrs. Jones says he has been picking and clearing the bedclothes awfully, so he must be dying!"* On entering the room, I found he had dropped asleep. The nurse told me he had been wandering a good deal in his mind. I asked what he had talked about? "*Larning*, doctor," she replied, "and a proud young lady." I sat down by his bedside. I saw the dews of death were stealing rapidly over him. His eyes, which were naturally very dark and piercing, were now far sunk into their sockets; his cheeks were hollow, and his hair matted with perspiration over his damp and pallid forehead. While I was gazing silently on the melancholy spectacle, and reflecting what great but undisciplined powers of mind were about soon to be disunited from the body, Mr. —— opened his eyes, and seeing me, said, in a low, but clear and steady tone of voice, "Doctor—the last act of the tragedy!" He gave me his hand. It was all he could do to lift it into mine. I could not speak—the tears were nearly gushing forth. I felt as if I were gazing on my dying *son*.

"I have been dreaming, doctor, since you went," said he; "and what do you think about? I thought I had squared the circle, and was to perish for ever for my discovery."

* This very prevalent but absurd notion is not confined to the vulgar; and as I have in the course of my practice met with hundreds of respectable and intelligent people, who have held that a patient's "*picking and clearing the bedclothes*" is a symptom of death, and who consequently view it with a kind of superstitious horror, I cannot refrain from explaining the philosophy of it to the unprofessional readers of this volume in the simple and satisfactory words of Mr. C. Bell:—

· It is very common," he says, "to see the patient picking the bedclothes, or catching at the empty air. This proceeds from an appearance of *motes* or *flies* passing before the eyes, and is occasioned by an affection of the retina, producing in it a sensation similar to that produced by the impression of images; and what is deficient in sensation *the imagination supplies*: for although the resemblance between those diseased affections of the retina and the idea conveyed to the brain may be very remote, yet by that slight resemblance the idea usually associated with the sensation will be excited in the mind."—*Bell's Anatomy*, vol. iii. p. 57, 58.

The secret lies in a disordered circulation of the blood forcing the red globules into the minute vessels of the retina.

" I hope, Mr. ——," I replied, in a serious tone, and with something of displeasure in my manner—" I hope that at this awful moment, you have more suitable and consolatory thoughts to occupy your mind with than those ?"

He sighed. " The clergyman you were so good as to send me," he said, after a pause, " was here this afternoon. He is a good man, I dare say, but weak, and has his head stuffed with the quibbles of the schools. He wanted to discuss the question of *free will* with a dying man, doctor!"

" I hope he did not leave without administering the ordinances of religion ?" I inquired.

" He read me some of the church prayers, which were exquisitely touching and beautiful, and the fifteenth chapter of Corinthians, which is very sublime. He could not help giving me a rehearsal of what he was shortly to repeat over my grave!" exclaimed the dying man, with a melancholy smile. I felt some irritation at the light tone of his remarks, but concealed it.

" You received the sacrament, I hope, Mr. ——?"

He paused a few moments, and his brow was clouded. " No, doctor, to tell the truth, I declined it"—

" *Declined* the sacrament!" I exclaimed with surprise.

" Yes—but, dear doctor, I beg—I entreat you not to ask me about it any further," replied Mr. ——, gloomily, and lapsed into a fit of abstraction for some moments. Unnoticed by him, I despatched the nurse for another clergyman, an excellent and learned man, who was my intimate friend. I was gazing earnestly on Mr. ——, as he lay with closed eyes; and was surprised to see the tears trickling from them.

" Mr. ——, you have nothing, I hope, on your mind, to render your last moments unhappy?" I asked, in a gentle tone.

" No—nothing material," he replied, with a deep sigh; continuing, with his eyes closed, " I was only thinking what a bitter thing it is to be struck down so soon from among the bright throng of the living —to leave this fair, this beautiful world, after so short and sorrowful a sojourn. Oh, it *is* hard !" He shortly opened his eyes. His agitation had apparently passed away, and delirium was hovering over and disarranging his thoughts.

" Doctor, doctor, what a strange passage that is," said he suddenly, startling me with his altered voice, and the dreamy, thoughtful expression of his eyes, " in the chorus of the Medea—

$$\text{Ἄνω ποταμῶν ἱερῶν χωροῦσι παγαὶ}$$
$$\text{καὶ δίκα καὶ πάντα πάλιν στρέφεται} *$$

Is there not something very mysterious and romantic about these lines? I could never exactly understand what was meant by them." Finding I continued silent,—for I did not wish to encourage his indulging in a train of thought so foreign to his situation,—he kept murmuring at intervals, metrically,

$$\text{ἄνω ποταμῶν ἱερῶν,}$$

in a most melancholy, monotonous tone. He then wandered on from one topic of classical literature to another, till he suddenly stopped short, and turning to me, said, " Doctor, I am raving very absurdly. I feel I am ; but I cannot dismiss from my thoughts. even though I know I am dying, the subjects about which my mind has been occupied nearly all my life through —Oh !" changing the subject abruptly, " tell me, doctor, do those who die of my disorder generally continue in the possession of their intellects to the last ?" I told him I thought they generally did.

" Then I shall burn brightly to the last ! Thank God !—And yet," with a shudder, " it is shocking

* Eurip. Med. 411-13.

too, to find one's self gradually ceasing to exist.—
Doctor, I should recover, I am sure I should, if you
were to bleed me," said he—his intellects were
wandering.

The nurse now returned, and, to my vexation, unaccompanied by Dr. ——, who had gone that morning
into the country. I did not send for any one else.
His frame of mind was peculiar, and very unsatis-
factory; but I thought it, on the whole, better not to
disturb or irritate him by alluding to a subject he
evidently disliked. I ordered candles to be brought,
as it was now nearly nine o'clock. "Doctor," said
the dying young man, in a feeble tone, "I think you
will find a copy of Lactantius lying on my table.
He has been a great favourite with me. May I
trouble you to read me a passage—the eighth chapter
of the seventh book—on the immortality of the soul?
I should like to die thoroughly convinced of that
noble truth—if truth it is—and I have often read that
chapter with much satisfaction." I went to the
table, and found the book—a pocket copy—the leaves
of which were ready turned down to the very page I
wanted. I therefore read to him, slowly and empha-
tically, the whole of the eighth and ninth chapters,
beginning, "*Num est igitur summum bonum immor-
talitas, ad quam capiendam, et formati a principio, et
nati sumus.*" When I had got as far as the allusion
to Cicero's vacillating views, Mr. —— repeated with
me, sighing, the words, "*harum inquit sententiarum,
quæ vera sit, Deus aliquis viderit.*"—As an instance
of the

" Ruling passion, strong in death,"

I may mention, though somewhat to my own dis-
credit, that he briskly corrected a false quantity
which slipped from me, "Allow me, doctor—'*ex-
pĕtit,*' not '*expetit.*'" He made no other observation
when I had concluded reading the chapters from
Lactantius, than, " I certainly wish I had early

formed fixed principles on religious subjects—but it is now too late." He then dropped asleep, but presently began murmuring very sorrowfully—"Emma, Emma! haughty one! Not *one* look?—I am dying—and you don't know it—nor care for me! * * * How beautiful she looked stepping from the carriage! How magnificently dressed! I *think* she saw—*why* can't she love me? She cannot love somebody else—No—madness—no!"—In this strain he continued soliloquizing for some minutes longer. It was the first time I had ever heard any thing of the kind fall from him. At length he asked, "I wonder if they ever came to her hands?" as if striving to recollect something. The nurse whispered that she had often heard him talk in the night-time about this lady, and that he would go on till he stopped in tears. I discovered, from a scrap or two found among his papers, after his decease, that the person he addressed as Emma was a young lady in the higher circles of society, of considerable beauty, whom he first saw by accident, and fancied she had a regard for him. He had, in turn, indulged in the most extravagant and hopeless passion for her. He suspected himself, that she was wholly unconscious of being the object of his almost phrensied admiration. When he was asking "if something came to her hands," I have no doubt he alluded to some copy of verses he had sent to her—of which the following fragments, written in pencil on a blank leaf of his Aristophanes, probably formed a part. There is some merit in them, but more extravagance.

> " I could go through the world with thee,
> To spend with thee eternity!
>   *   *   *   *   *
> " To see thy blue and passionate eye,
> Light on another scornfully,
> But fix its melting glance on me,
> And blend"——

> " Read the poor heart that throbs for thee,
> Imprint all o'er with thy dear name—

> Yet withering 'neath a lonely flame,
> That warms *thee* not, yet me consumes!"
>
>   *   *   *   *   *
>
> " Ay, I would have thee all my own,
> Thy love, thy life, mine, *mine* alone;
> See nothing in the world but me,
> Since nought *I* know, or love, but thee!
>
> " The eyes that on a thousand fall,
> I would collect their glances all,
> And fling their lustre on my soul,
> Till it imbibed, absorb'd the whole."

These are followed by several lines more; but these will suffice. This insane attachment was exactly what I might have expected from one of his ardent and enthusiastic temperament. To return, however, once more. Towards eleven o'clock, he began to fail rapidly. I had my fingers on his pulse, which beat very feebly, almost imperceptibly. He opened his eyes slowly, and gazed upwards with a vacant air.

" Why are you taking the candles away, nurse?" he inquired, feebly. They had not been touched. His cold fingers gently compressed my hand—they were stiffening with death. " Don't, *don't* put the candles out, doctor," he commenced again, looking at me with an eye on which the thick mists and shadows of the grave were settling fast—they were filmy and glazed.

" Don't blow them out—don't—don't!" he again exclaimed, almost inaudibly.

" No, we will not!—My dear Mr. ——, both candles are burning brightly beside you, on the table," I replied tremulously,—for I saw the senses were forgetting their functions—that life and consciousness were fast retiring!

" Well," he murmured, almost inarticulately, " I am now quite in darkness!—Oh, there is something at my heart—cold, cold!—*Doctor, keep them off!**—

---

* I once before heard these strange words fall from the lips of a dying patient—a lady. To me they suggest very unpleasant, I may say fearful thoughts. *What* is to be kept off?

Why—oh, death—" He ceased. He had spoken his last on earth. The intervals of respiration became gradually longer and longer; and the precise moment when he ceased to breathe at all cou'd not be ascertained. Yes; it was all over. Poor Mr.—— was dead. I shall never forget him.

Preparing for the House.

" Do, dear doctor, be so good as to drop in at ——-Place, in the course of the morning, *by accident;* for I want you to see Mr.——. He has, I verily believe, bid adieu to his senses; for he is conducting himself very strangely. To tell you the truth, he is resolved on going down to the House this evening, for the purpose of speaking on the ——. bill, and will, I fear, act so absurdly as to make himself the laughing-stock of the whole country; at least I suspect as much, from what I have heard of his preparations. Ask to be shown up at once to Mr.——, when you arrive, and gradually direct the conversation to politics—when you will soon see what is the matter. But mind, doctor, not a word of this note! Your visit will be quite *accidental,* you know. Believe me, my dear doctor, yours, &c. &c."—Such was the note put into my hands by a servant, as my carriage was driving off on my first morning round. I knew Mrs.——, the fair writer of it, very intimately—as, indeed, the familiar and confidential strain of her note will suffice to show. She was a very amiable and clever woman—and would not have complained, I was sure, without reason. Wishing, therefore, to oblige her by a prompt attention to her request, and in the full expectation, from what I knew of the worthy member's eccentricities, of encountering some singular scene, I directed the horses' heads to be turned towards —— Place. I reached the house about twelve o'clock, and went up stairs at once to the drawing-room, where I understood Mr.—— had

taken up quarters for the day.   The servant opened
the door and announced me.

"Oh—show Dr. —— in." I entered.   The object
of my visit, I may just say, was the very *beau ideal*
of a county member; somewhat inclined to corpu-
lency, with a fine, fresh, rubicund, good-natured face
—and that bluff old English frankness of manner
which flings you back into the age of Sir Roger De
Coverley.   He was dressed in a long gray woollen
morning-gown; and, with his hands crammed into
the hind pockets, was pacing rapidly to and fro from
one end of the spacious room to the other.   At one
extremity was a table, on which lay a sheet of fools-
cap, closely written, and crumpled as if with constant handling—his gold repeater, and a half-emptied
decanter of sherry, with a wineglass.   A glance at
all these paraphernalia convinced me of the nature
of Mr. ——'s occupation; he was committing his
speech to memory!

"How d'ye do—how d'ye do, doctor?" he exclaimed, in a hearty but hurried tone; "you must
not keep me long: busy—very busy indeed, doctor."
I had looked in by accident, I assured him, and did
not intend to detain him an instant.   I remarked that
I supposed he was busy preparing for the House.

"Ah, right, doctor—right! Ay, a d——d good
hit, too!   I shall peg it into them to-night, doctor!
—I'll let them know what an English county member is!   I'll make the House too hot to hold them!"
said Mr. ——, walking to and fro, at an accelerated
pace.   He was evidently boiling over with excitement.

"You are going to speak to-night, then, on the
great —— question, I suppose?" said I, hardly able
to repress a smile.

"Speak, doctor?   I'll burst on them with such a
view-halloo as shall startle the whole pack!   *I'll* show
my Lord —— what kind of stuff I'm made of—I will,
oy ——.   He was pleased to tell the House, the

other evening—curse his impudence!—that the two
members for ——shire were a mere couple of dumb-
bells—he did, by ——! But *I'll* show him whether
or not *I*, for one of them, am to be jeered and flammed
with impunity! Ha, doctor—what d'ye think of
this?" said he, hurrying to the table, and taking up
the manuscript I have mentioned. He was going to
read it to me, but suddenly stopped short and laid it
down again on the table, exclaiming, " Nay, d——e,
I know it off by this time—so listen! Have at ye,
doctor!"

After a pompous hem! hem! he commenced, and
with infinite energy and boisterousness of manner,
recited the whole oration. It was certainly a wonderful—a matchless performance—parcelled out with
a rigid adherence to the rules of ancient rhetoric.
As he proceeded, he recited such astounding absurdities—such preposterous, high-flown Bombastes-fu-
rioso declamations; as, had it but been uttered in
the House, would assuredly have procured the triumphant speaker six or seven distinct rounds of convulsive laughter! Had I not known well the simplicity and sincerity—the perfect *bonhomie*—of
Mr. ——, I should have supposed he was hoaxing me
—but I assuredly suspected he was *himself* the
hoaxed party—the joking-post of some witty wag
who had determined to afford the House a night's
sport at poor Mr. ——'s expense! Indeed, I never
in my life listened to such pitifully puerile, such
almost idiotic, *gallimatia.* I felt certain it could never
have been the composition of fox-hunting Mr. ——!
There was a hackneyed quotation from Horace—from
the Septuagint (!), and from Locke; and then a
scampering through the whole flowery realms of
rhetorical ornament—and a glancing at every topic
of foreign or domestic policy that could conceivably
attract the attention of the most erratic fancy. In
short, there never before was such a speech composed
since the world began! And this was the sort of
    I.—G

thing that poor Mr. —— actually intended to delive
that memorable evening in the House of Commons
As for myself, I could not control my risible faculties ; but accompanied the peroration with a perfect
shout of laughter! Mr. —— laid down the paper
(which he had twisted into a sort of scroll) in an
ecstasy, and joined me in full chorus, slapping me
on the shoulder, and exclaiming—"Ah! d——e,
doctor, I *knew* you would like it! It's just the thing
—isn't it? There will be no standing me at the next
election for ——shire, if I can only deliver all this in
the House to-night! Old Turnpenny, that's going
to start against me, backed by the manufacturing
interest—won't come up—and you see if he does!—
Curse it! I thought it was *in* me ; and would come
out, some of these days.—They shall have it all to-
night—they shall, by ——! Only be on the look-
out for the morning papers, doctor—that's all!" and
he set off, walking rapidly, with long strides, from
one end of the room to the other. I began to be
apprehensive that there was too much ground for
Mrs. ——'s suspicions, that he had literally "taken
leave of his senses." Recollecting, at length the
object of my visit, which the amusing exhibition I
have been attempting to describe had almost driven
from my memory, I endeavoured to think, on the
spur of the moment, of some scheme for diverting
him from his purpose, and preventing the lamentable
exposure he was preparing for himself. I could think
of nothing else than attacking him on a sore point
—one on which he had been hipped for years, and
not without reason — an hereditary tendency to
apoplexy.

"But, my dear sir," said I, "this excitement will
destroy you—you will bring on a fit of apoplexy. if
you go on for an hour longer. in this way—you will
indeed!" He stood still, changed colour a little,
and stammered, "What! eh, d——e, apoplexy! You
don't say so. doctor? Hem! how is my pulse?" ex

... ling his wrist. I felt it—looked at my watch,
... I shook my head.

" Eh—what, doctor! *Newmarket*, eh?" said he,
with an alarmed air; meaning to ask me whether his
pulse was beating rapidly.

" It is, indeed, Mr. ——.   It beats upwards of one
hundred and fifteen a minute," I replied, still keeping
my fingers at his wrist, and my eyes riveted on my
watch—for I dared not trust myself with looking in
his countenance. He started from me without uttering a syllable; hurried to the table, poured out a
glass of wine, and gulped it down instantly. I suppose he caught an unfortunate smile or a smirk on
my face—for he came up to me, and in a coaxing
but disturbed manner, said—" Now, come, come,
doctor—doctor, no humbug! I feel well enough all
over! D——e, I *will* speak in the House to-night,
come what may, that's flat! Why, there'll be a
general election in a few months, and it's of consequence for me to do something—to make a figure
in the House. Besides—it is a great constitutional"——

" Well, well, Mr. ——, undoubtedly you must
please yourself," said I, seriously; " but if a fit
should—you'll remember I did my duty, and warned
you how to avert it!"—" Hem, ahem!" he ejaculated,
with a somewhat puzzled air. I thought I had succeeded in shaking his purpose. I was, however, too
sanguine in my expectations. " I must bid you good
morning, doctor. I *must* speak! I *will* try it, to-
night, at all events; but I'll be calm—I will! And if
I *should* die—but d— it, that's *impossible*, you know!
But if I should—why, it will be a martyr's death; I
shall die a patriot—ha, ha, ha! Good morning,
doctor."   He led me to the door, laughing as he
went, but not so heartily or boisterously as formerly.
' was hurrying down stairs, when Mr. —— reopened
the drawing-room door, and called out, " Doctor,
doctor, just be so good as to look in on my good lady

before you go. She's somewhere about the house —in her *boudoir*, I dare say. She's not quite well this morning—a fit of the vapours—hem! You understand me, doctor?" putting his finger to the side of his nose, with a wise air. I could not help smiling at the reciprocal anxiety for each other's health simultaneously manifested by this worthy couple.

"Well, doctor, am not I right?" exclaimed Mrs. ——, in a low tone, opening the dining-room door, and beckoning me in.

"Yes, indeed, madam. My interview was little else than a running commentary on your note to me."

"How did you find him engaged, doctor?—Learning his *speech*, as he calls it—eh?" inquired the lady with a chagrined air, which was heightened when I recounted what had passed up-stairs.

"Oh, absurd! monstrous! doctor, I am ready to expire with vexation to see Mr. —— acting so foolishly. But it is all owing to that odious Dr. ——, the village rector, who is up in town now, and an immense crony of Mr. ——'s. I suspected there was something brewing between them; for they have been laying their wise heads together for a week past. Did not he repeat *the speech* to you, doctor?—the whole of it?"

"Yes, indeed, madam, he did," I replied, smiling at the recollection.

"Ah—hideous rant it was, I dare say!—I'll tell you a secret, doctor. I know it was every word composed by that abominable old addle-head, Dr. ——, a noodle that he is!—(I wonder what brought him up from his parish!)—And it is he that has inflamed Mr. ——'s fancy with making *a great hit* in the House, as they call it. That precious piece of stuff which they call a speech, poor Mr. —— has been learning for this week past; and has several times woke me in the night with ranting snatches of it." I begged Mrs. —— not to take it so seriously.

"Now, tell me candidly, Dr. ——, did you ever hear such nonsense in your life? It is all that country parson's small-beer trash! I'm sure our name will run the gauntlet of all the papers in England, for a fortnight to come!" I said, I was sorry to be compelled to acquiesce in the truth of what she was saying.

"Really," she continued, pressing her hand to her forehead, "I feel quite poorly myself, with agitation at the thought of to-night's farce. Did you attempt to dissuade him? You might have frightened him with a hint or two about his tendency to apoplexy, you know."

"I did my utmost, madam, I assure you; and certainly startled him not a little. But, alas! he rallied, and good-humouredly sent me from the room, telling me, that if the effort of speaking killed him he should share the fate of Lord Chatham, or something of that sort."

"Preposterous!" exclaimed Mrs. ——, almost shedding tears with vexation. "But, *entre nous,* doctor, could you not think of any thing—hem!— something in the medical way—to prevent his going to the House to-night?—A—a sleeping draught—eh, doctor?"

"Really, my dear madam," said I, seriously, "I should not feel justified in going so far as that."

"Oh, dear, dear doctor, what possible harm can there be in it? Do consent to my wishes for once, and I shall be eternally obliged to you. *Do* order a simple sleeping draught—strong enough to keep him in bed till five or six o'clock in the morning—and I will myself slip it into his wine·at dinner."—In short, there was no resisting the importunities and distress of so fine a woman as Mrs. ——; so I ordered about five-and-thirty drops of laudanum, in a little sirup and water. But, alas! this scheme was frustrated by Mr. ——'s, two hours afterward, unexpectedly ordering the carriage (while Mrs. —— was her-

self gone to procure his *quietus*,, and leaving word
he should dine with some members that evening at
Brookes's.　After all, however, a lucky accident accomplished Mrs. ——'s wishes, though it deprived
her husband of that opportunity of wearing the
laurels of parliamentary eloquence; for the ministry,
finding the measure against which Mr. —— had intended to level his oration to be extremely unpopu-
lar, and anticipating that they should be dead beat,
wisely postponed it *sine die.*

Duelling. *

I had been invited by young Lord ——, the noble
man mentioned in my former chapter, to spend the
latter part of my last college vacation with his lordship at his shooting-box in ——shire.　As his destined profession was the army, he had already a
tolerably numerous retinue of military friends, several
of whom were engaged to join us on our arrival at
——; so that we anticipated a very gay and jovial
season.　Our expectations were not disappointed.
What with fishing, shooting, and riding abroad—
billiards, songs, and high *feeding* at home—our days
and nights glided as merrily away as fun and frolic
would make them.　One of the many schemes of
amusement devised by our party was giving a sort
of military subscription ball at the small town of
——, from which we were distant not more than four
or five miles.　All my Lord ——'s party, of course,
were to be there, as well as several others of his
friends scattered at a little distance from him in the
country.　On the appointed day all went off admira-
bly.　The little town of —— absolutely reeled beneath the unusual excitement of music, dancing, and
universal fêting.　It was, in short, a sort of minia-

* The melancholy facts on which the ensuing narrative is founded, I
find entered in the Diary as far back as nearly twenty-five years ago
and I am convinced, after some little inquiry, that there is no one now
living whose feelings could be shocked at reading it.

ture carnival, which the inhabitants, for several reasons, but more especially the melancholy one I am
going to mention, have not yet forgotten. It is not
very wonderful that all the rustic beauty of the place
was there. Many a village belle was there, in truth,
panting and fluttering with delighted agitation at the
unusual attentions of their handsome and agreeable
partners ; for there was not a young military member of our party but merited the epithets. As for myself,
being cursed, as I once before hinted, with a very insignificant person, and not the most attractive or communicative manners, being utterly incapable of pouring
that soft, delicious nonsense, that fascinating, searching small-talk, which has stolen so often right through
a lady's ear into the very centre of her heart,—being
no hand, I say, at this, I contented myself with dancing a set or two with a young woman whom nobody
else seemed inclined to lead out ; and continued for
the rest of the evening more a *spectator* than a par-
taker of the gayeties of the scene. There was one
girl there—the daughter of a reputable, retired tradesman—of singular beauty, and known in the neighbourhood by the name of " *The Blue Bell of——*."
Of course she was the object of universal admiration, and literally besieged the whole evening with
applications for the " honour of her hand." I do not
exaggerate, when I say that, in my opinion, this
young woman was perfectly beautiful. Her complexion was of dazzling purity and transparence ;
her symmetrical features of a placid bustlike character, which, however, would perhaps have been
considered insipid had it not been for a brilliant pair
of large, languishing, soft blue eyes, resembling

> ——" blue water-lilies, when the breeze
> Maketh the crystal waters round them tremble,"

which it was almost madness to look upon. And
then her light auburn hair, which hung in loose and
easy curls, and settled on each cheek like a soft

golden cloud flitting past the moon!   Her figure was
in keeping with her countenance—slender, graceful
and delicate—with a most exquisitely turned foot and
ankle. I have spent so many words about her descrip
tion, because I have never since seen any woman that
I thought equalled her, and because her beauty was
the cause of what I am about to relate.   She riveted
the attention of all our party except my young host
Lord ——, who adhered all the evening to a sweet
creature he had selected on first entering the room
I observed, however, one of our party, a dashing
young captain in the Guards, highly connected, and
of handsome and prepossessing person and manners,
and a gentleman of nearly equal personal pretensions,
who had been invited from —— Hall, his father's
seat, to exceed every one present in their attentions
to sweet Mary ——; and as she occasionally smiled
on one or the other of the rivals, I saw the countenance of either alternately clouded with displeasure
Captain —— was soliciting her hand for the last set
—a country dance—when his rival (whom for distinction's sake I shall call *Trevor*, though that, of
course, is very far from his real name), stepping up
to her, seized her hand, and said, in rather a sharp
and quick tone, "Captain ——, she has promised me
the last set; I beg, therefore, you will resign her.   I
am right, Miss ——?" he inquired of the girl, who
blushingly replied, "I think I did promise Mr. Trevor
but I would dance with both if I could.   Captain,
you are not angry with me, are you?" she smiled,
appealingly.
   "Certainly not, madam," he replied, with a peculiar
emphasis; and after directing an eye which kindled
like a star to his more successful rival, retired haughtily a few paces, and soon afterward left the room.
A strong conviction seized me that even this small
and trifling incident would be attended with mischief
between those two haughty and undisciplined spirits
for I occasionally saw Mr Trevor turn a moment

from his beautiful partner, and cast a stern, inquiring glance round the room, as if in search of Captain ——. I saw he had noticed the haughty frown with which the captain had retired.

Most of the gentlemen who had accompanied Lord —— to this ball were engaged to dine with him on the next Sunday evening. Mr. Trevor and the captain (who, I think, I mentioned was staying a few days with his lordship) would meet at this party, and I determined to watch their demeanour. Captain —— was at the window, when Mr. Trevor, on horseback, attended by his groom, alighted at the door, and on seeing who it was, walked away to another part of the room with an air of assumed indifference; but I caught his quick and restless glance invariably directed at the door through which Mr. Trevor would enter. They saluted each other with civility—rather coldly I thought—but there was nothing particularly marked in the manner of either. About twenty sat down to dinner. All promised to go off well; for the cooking was admirable, the wines first rate, and conversation brisk and various. Captain —— and Mr. Trevor were seated at some distance from each other; the former was my next neighbour. The cloth was not removed till a few minutes after eight, when a dessert and a fresh and large supply of wine were introduced. The late ball, of course, was a prominent topic of conversation; and after a few of the usual bachelor toasts had been drunk with noisy enthusiasm, and we all felt the elevating influence of the wine we had been drinking, Lord —— stood up, and said, " Now, my dear fellows, I have a toast in my eye that will delight you all; so bumpers, gentlemen—bumpers!—up to the very brim. So make sure your glasses are full, while I propose to you the health of a beautiful—nay, by ——! the most beautiful girl we have any of us seen for this year! Ha! I see all anticipate me, so to be short—here is the health of Mary ——, the Blue Bell of ——!" It was

I.—H

drunk with acclamation. I thought I perceived Captain ——'s hand, however, shake a little as he lifted his glass to his mouth.

"Who is to return thanks for her?"—"Her favourite beau, to be sure."—"Who is he?"—"Legs—rise—legs—whoever he is!" was shouted, asked, and answered in a breath. "Oh, Trevor is the happy man, there's no doubt of that; he monopolized her all the evening—*I* could not get her hand once," exclaimed one near Mr. Trevor. "Nor I"—"Nor I," echoed several. Mr. Trevor looked with a delighted and triumphant air round the room, and seemed about to rise, but there was a cry—'No—Trevor is not the man—*I* say captain —— is the favourite!"—"Ay, ten to one on the captain!" roared a young hero of Ascot. "Stuff—stuff!" muttered the captain, cutting an apple to fritters, and now and then casting a fierce glance towards Mr. Trevor. There were many noisy maintainers of both Trevor and the captain.

"Come, come, gentlemen," said a young Cornish baronet, good-humouredly, seeing the two young men appeared to view the affair very seriously, "the best way, since I dare be sworn the girl herself does not know which she likes best, will be to *toss up* who shall be given the credit of her beau!" A loud laugh followed this droll proposal, in which all joined except Trevor and the captain. The latter had poured out some claret while Sir —— was speaking, and sipped it with an air of assumed carelessness. I observed, however, that he never removed his eye from his glass, and that his face was pale, as if from some strong internal emotion. Mr. Trevor's demeanour, however, also indicated considerable embarrassment, but he was older than the captain, and had much more command of manner. I was amazed, for my own part, to see them take up such an insignificant affair so seriously; but these things generally involve so much of the strong passions of our youthful nature, especially our vanity and jealousy, that on second thoughts my surprise abated.

"I certainly fancied you were the favourite, captain; for I saw her blush with satisfaction when you squeezed her hand," I whispered.

"You are right, ——," he answered, with a forced smile; "I don't think Trevor can have any pretensions to her favour." The noisiness of the party was now subsiding, and, nobody knew why, an air of blank embarrassment seemed to pervade all present.

"Upon my honour, gentlemen, this is a vastly silly affair altogether, and quite unworthy such a stir as it has excited," said Mr. Trevor; "but as so much notice has been taken of it, I cannot help saying, though it is monstrously absurd, perhaps, that I think the beautiful ' Blue Bell of ——' is mine—mine alone. I believe I have good ground for saying I am the sole winner of the prize, and have distanced my military competitor," continued Mr. Trevor, turning to Captain —— with a grim air, which was very foreign to his real feelings, "though his bright eyes, his debonair demeanour, that fascinating *je ne sais quoi* of his"——

"Trevor, don't be insolent!" exclaimed the captain sternly, reddening with passion.

"*Insolent!* captain? What the deuse do you mean? I'm sure you don't want to quarrel with me—oh, it's impossible! If I have said what was offensive, by —— I did not mean it; and, as we said at Rugby, *indictum puta*, and there's an end of it. But as for my smart little Blue Bell, I know—am perfectly certain—ay, spite of the captain's dark looks—that I am the happy man. So, gentlemen, *de jure* and *de facto*—for her I return you thanks." He sat down. There was so much kindness in his manner, and he had so handsomely disavowed any intentions of hurting Captain ——'s feelings, that I hoped the young Hotspur beside me was quieted. Not so, however

"Trevor," said he, in a hurried tone, "you are mis-taken—you are, by ——! You don't know what passed between Mary —— and myself that evening On my word and honour, she told me she wished she could be off her engagement with you."

"Nonsense! nonsense! She must have said it to amuse you, captain—she *could* have had no other intention. The very next morning she told me"—

"The very next morning!" shouted Captain ——; "why, what the —— could you have wanted with Mary —— the next morning?"

"That is my affair, captain, not yours. And since you will have it out, I tell you for your consolation, that Mary and I have met every day since!" said Mr. Trevor, loudly, even vehemently. He was getting a little *flustered*, as the phrase is, with wine, which he was pouring down glass after glass, or of course he could never have made such an absurd. such an unusual disclosure.

"Trevor, I must say you act very meanly in telling us, if it really is so," said the captain, with an intensely chagrined and mortified air; "and if you intend to ruin that sweet and innocent creature, I shall take leave to say that you are a—a—a—curse on it, it WILL out—a villain!" continued the captain, slowly and deliberately. My heart flew up to my throat, where it fluttered as though it would have choked me. There was an instant and dead silence.

"A *villain!* did you say, captain? and accuse me of meanness?" inquired Mr. Trevor, coolly, while the colour suddenly faded from his darkening features; and rising from his chair, he stepped forward and stood nearly opposite to the captain, with his half-emptied glass in his hand, which, however, was not observed by him he addressed. "Yes, sir, I *did* say so," replied the captain, firmly, "and what then?"

"Then of course you will see the necessity of apolo-gizing for it instantly," rejoined Mr. Trevor.

" As I am not in the habit, Mr. Trevor, of saying what requires an apology, I have none to offer," said Captain ——, drawing himself up in his chair, and eying Mr. Trevor with a steady look of composed intrepidity.

" Then, captain, don't expect me to apologize for *this!*" thundered Mr. Trevor, at the same time hurling his glass, wine and all, at the captain's head. Part of the wine fell on me, but the glass glanced at the ear of Captain ——, and cut it slightly; for he had started aside on seeing Mr. Trevor's intention. A mist seemed to cover my eyes as I saw every one present rising from his chair. The room was, of course, in an uproar. The two who had quarrelled were the only calm persons present. Mr. Trevor re mained standing on the same spot, with his arms folded on his breast, while Captain —— calmly wiped off the stains of wine from his shirt-ruffles and white waistcoat, walked up to Lord ——, who was at but a yard or two's distance, and inquired, in a low tone of voice, " Your lordship has pistols here, of course We had better settle this little matter now and here. Captain V——, you will kindly do what is necessary for me ?"

" My dear fellow, be calm! This is really a very absurd quarrel,—likely to be a dreadful business though!" replied his lordship, with great agitation; " come, shake hands and be friends!—come, don't let a trumpery dinner brawl lead to bloodshed—and in my house, too!—make it up like men of sense"—

" That your lordship, of course, knows as well as I do is impossible. Will you, Captain V——, be good enough to bring the pistols? You will find them in his lordship's shooting gallery—we had better adjourn there, by the way, eh?" inquired the captain, coolly. He had seen many of these *affairs!*

" Then bring them—bring them, by all means,"— " In God's name, let this quarrel be settled on the spot!" exclaimed ——, and ——, and ——.

"We all know they *must* fight—that's as clear as the sun—so the sooner the better!" exclaimed the honourable Mr. ——, a hot-headed cousin of Lord ——'s.

"Eternal curses on the silly slut!" groaned his lordship; "here will be bloodshed for her! My dear Trevor!" said he, hurrying to that gentleman, who, with seven or eight people round him, was conversing on the affair with perfect composure; "do, I implore—I beg—I supplicate that you would leave my house! Oh, don't let it be said I ask people here to kill one another! Why may not this wretched business be made up? By —— it *shall* be," said he, vehemently; and putting his arm into that of Mr. Trevor, he endeavoured to draw him towards the spot where Captain —— was standing.

"Your lordship is very good, but it's useless," replied Mr. Trevor, struggling to disengage his arm from that of Lord ——. "Your lordship knows the business *must* be settled, and the sooner the better. My friend Sir —— has undertaken to do what is correct on the occasion. Come," addressing the young baronet, "away! and join Captain V——." All this was uttered with *real* nonchalance. Somebody present told him that the captain was one of the best shots in England—could hit a sixpence at ten yards' distance. "Can he, by ——?" said he, with a smile, without evincing the slightest symptoms of trepidation; "why, then, I may as well make my will, for I'm as blind as a mole!—Ha! I have it." He walked out from among those who were standing round him, and strode up to Captain ——, who was conversing earnestly with one or two of his brother officers.

"Captain ——," said Mr. Trevor, firmly, extending his right hand with his glove half drawn on. The captain turned suddenly towards him with a furious scowl.—"I am told you are a dead shot, eh?"

"Well, sir, and what of that?" inquired the cap-

ain, haughtily, and with some curiosity in his countenance.

" You know I am short-sighted, blind as a beetle.
and not very well used in shooting matters." Every
one present started, and looked with surprise and displeasure at the speaker; and one muttered in my
ear—" Eh! d——! Trevor showing the white fea-
ther! I *am* astonished!"

" Why, what do you mean by all this, sir?" inquired
the captain, with a contemptuous sneer.

" Oh, merely that we ought not to fight on unequal
terms. Do you think, my good sir, I will stand to
be shot at without having a chance of returning the
favour? I have to say, therefore, merely, that since
this quarrel is of your own seeking, and your own
d——d folly only has brought it about, I shall insist
on our fighting breast to breast—muzzle to muzzle—
and across a table. Yes," he continued, elevating
his voice to nearly a shout; " we will go down to hell
together, if we go at all—that is some consolation."

" Infamous!"—" Monstrous!" was echoed from all
present. They would not, they said, hear of such a
thing—they would not stand to see such butchery!
Eight or ten left the room abruptly, and did not return.
Captain —— made no reply to Trevor's proposal,
but was conversing anxiously with his friends.

" *Now*, sir, who is the coward?" inquired Mr. Tre
vor, sarcastically.

" A few moments will show," replied the captain,
stepping forward, with no sign of agitation except a
countenance of an ashy hue; " for I accede to your
terms, ruffianly—murderous as they are; and may
the curse of a ruined house overwhelm you and your
family for ever!" faltered Captain ——, who saw, of
course, that certain death was before both. " Are
the pistols preparing?" inquired Mr. Trevor, without
regarding the exclamation of Captain ——. He was
answered in the affirmative, that Captain V—— and
Sir — were both absent on that errand. It was

agreed that the distressing affair should take place in
the shooting gallery, where their noise would be less
likely to alarm the servants.   It is hardly necessary
to repeat the exclamations of "Murder!—downright,
savage, deliberate murder!" which burst from all
around.   Two gentlemen left abruptly, saddled their
horses, and galloped after peace-officers; while Lord
——, who was almost distracted, hurried, accompanied by several gentlemen and myself, to the shooting gallery, leaving the captain and a friend in the
dining-room, while Mr. Trevor with another betook
themselves to the shrubbery walk.   His lordship informed Captain V—— and the baronet of the dreadful nature of the combat that had been determined
on since they had left the room.   They both threw
down the pistols they were in the act of loading, and,
horror-struck, swore they would have no concern
whatever in such a barbarous and bloody transaction.
A sudden suggestion of Lord ——'s, however, was
adopted.   They agreed, after much hesitation and
doubt as to the success of the project, to charge the
pistols with powder only, and put them into the hands
of the captain and Mr. Trevor as though they were
loaded with ball.   Lord —— was sanguine enough
to suppose, that when they had both stood fire, and
indisputably proved their courage, the affair might be
settled amicably.   As soon as the necessary preparations were completed, and two dreary lights were
placed in the shooting gallery, both the hostile parties
were summoned.   As it was well known that I was
preparing for the medical profession, my services
were put into requisition for both.

"But have you any instruments or bandages?"
inquired some one.

"It is of little consequence; we are not likely to
want them, I think, if our pistols do their duty," said
Mr. Trevor.

But a servant was mounted on the fleetest horse in
Lord ——'s stable, and despatched for the surgeon,

who resided at not more than half a mile's distance, with a note requesting him to come furnished with the necessary instruments for a gun-shot wound. As the principals were impatient, and the seconds as well as the others present were in the secret of the blank charge in the pistols, and anticipated nothing like bloodshed, the pistols were placed in the hands of each in dead silence, and the two parties, with their respective friends, retired to a little distance from each other.

"Are you prepared, Mr. Trevor?" inquired one of Captain ——'s party; and being answered in the affirmative, in a moment after the two principals, pistol in hand, approached one another. Though I was almost blinded with agitation, and was, in common with those around, quaking for the success of our scheme, my eyes were riveted on their every movement. There was something solemn and impressive in their demeanour. Though stepping to certain death, as they supposed, there was not the slightest symptom of terror or agitation visible—no swaggering—no affectation of a calmness they did not feel. The countenance of each was deadly pale and damp; but not a muscle trembled.

"Who is to give us the word?" asked the captain in a whisper, which, though low, was heard all over the room; "for in this sort of affair, if one fires a second before the other he is a murderer." At that moment there was a noise heard; it was the surgeon who had arrived, and now entered breathless. "Step out, and give the word at once," said Mr. Trevor, impatiently. Both the captain and Mr. Trevor returned and shook hands, with a melancholy smile, with their friends, and then retook their places. The gentleman who was to give the signal then stepped towards them, and closing his eyes with his hands, said, in a tremulous tone, "Raise your pistols!"— the muzzles were instantly touching one another's breasts—"and when I have counted three, fire. One

—two—three!" They fired—both recoiled with the shock several paces, and their friends rushed forward.

"Why, what is the meaning of this!" exclaimed both in a breath. "Who has dared to mock us in this way?—there were no balls in the pistols!" exclaimed Trevor, fiercely. Lord —— and the seconds explained the well-meant artifice, and received an indignant curse for their pains. It was in vain we all implored them to be reconciled, as each had done amply sufficient to vindicate his honour. Trevor almost gnashed his teeth with fury. There was something fiendish, I thought, in the expression of his countenance. "It is easily remedied," said Captain ——, as his eye caught several small-swords hanging up. He took down two, measured them, and proffered one to his antagonist, who clutched it eagerly. "There *can* be no deception here, however," said he; "and now"—each put himself into posture—"stand off there!"

We fell back horror-struck at the relentless and revengeful spirit with which they seemed animated. I do not know which was the better swordsman; I recollect only seeing a rapid glancing of their weapons flashing about like sparks of fire, and a hurrying about in all directions, which lasted for several moments, when one of them fell. It was the captain; for the strong and skilful arm of Mr. Trevor had thrust his sword nearly up to the hilt in the side of his antagonist. His very heart was cloven! The unfortunate young man fell without uttering a groan—his sword dropped from his grasp—he pressed his right hand to his heart—and with a quivering motion of the lips, as if struggling to speak, expired! "Oh, my great God!" exclaimed Trevor, in a broken and hollow tone, with a face so blanched and horror-stricken that it froze my very blood to look upon; "what have I done? *Can all this be* REAL?" He continued on his knees by the side of his fallen an-

.agonist, with his hands clasped convulsively, and his
eyes glaring upwards for several moments.

*   *   *   *   *   *   *   *

A haze of horror is spread over that black transaction; and if it is dissipated for an instant when my
mind's eye suddenly looks back through the vista of
years, the scene seems rather the gloomy representa-
tion or picture of some occurrence which I cannot
persuade myself that I *actually witnessed*. To this
hour, when I advert to it I am not free from fits of
incredulousness. The affair created a great ferment
at the time. The unhappy survivor (who in this narrative has passed under the name of Trevor) instantly
left England, and died in the south of France about
five years afterward, in truth, broken-hearted. In a
word, since that day I have never seen men entering
into discussion, when warming with wine, and approaching never so slowly towards the confines of
formality, without reverting with a shudder to the
trifling, the utterly insignificant circumstances which
wine and the hot passions of youth kindled into the
fatal brawl which cost poor Captain —— his life, and
drove Mr. —— abroad to die a broken-hearted exile.

———

CHAPTER III.

THE BROKEN HEART.

Intriguing and Madness.

When I have seen a beautiful and popular actress,
I have often thought how many young play-goers
these women must intoxicate—how many even sensible and otherwise sober heads they must turn
upside down! Some years ago, a case came under

my care which showed fully the justness of this reflection; and I now relate it, as I consider it pregnant
both with interest and instruction.   It will show how
the energies of even a powerful and well-informed
mind may be prostrated by the indulgence of un-
bridled passions.   Late one evening in November, I
was summoned in haste to visit a gentleman who was
staying at one of the hotels in Covent Garden, and
informed in a note that he had manifested symptoms
of insanity.   As there is no time to be lost in such
cases, I hurried to the —— hotel, which I reached
about nine o'clock.   The proprietor gave me some
preliminary information about the patient to whom I
was summoned, which, with what I subsequently
gleaned from the party himself, and other quarters, I
shall present connectedly to the reader, before introducing him to the sick man's chamber.

Mr. Warningham—for that name may serve to
indicate him through this narrative—was a young
man of considerable fortune, some family, and a
member of —— College, Cambridge.   His person and
manners were gentlemanly; and his countenan:,
without possessing any claims to the charact:: of
handsome, faithfully indicated a powerful and cuiti-
vated mind.   He had mingled largely in college
gayeties and dissipations, but knew little or nothing
of what is called "town-life;" which may, in a great
measure, account for much of the simplicity and extravagance of the conduct I am about to relate.
Having from his youth upwards been accustomed
to the instant gratification of almost every wish he
could form, the slightest obstacle in his way was suf
ficient to irritate him almost to phrensy.   His temperament was very ardent, his imagination lively and
active.   In short, he passed every where for what he
really was—a very clever man—extensively read in
elegant literature, and particularly intimate with the
dramatic writers.   About a fortnight before the day
on which I was summoned to him, he had come up

from college to visit a young lady whom he was addressing; but finding her unexpectedly gone to Paris, he resolved to continue in London the whole time he had proposed to himself, and enjoy all the amusements about town—particularly the theatres. The evening of the day on which he arrived at the —— hotel, beheld him at Drury-lane, witnessing a new and, as the event proved, a very powerful tragedy. In the afterpiece, Miss —— was a prominent performer; and her beauty of person—her "maddening eyes," as Mr. Warningham often called them—added to her fascinating *naïveté* of manner, and the interesting character she sustained that evening—at once laid prostrate poor Mr. Warningham among the throng of worshippers at the feet of this "Diana of the Ephesians."

As he found she played again the next evening, he took care to engage the stage-box; and fancied he had succeeded in attracting her attention. He thought her lustrous eyes fell on him several times during the evening, and that they were instantly withdrawn, with an air of conscious confusion and embarrassment, from the intense and passionate gaze which they encountered. This was sufficient to fire the train of Mr. Warningham's susceptible feelings; and his whole heart was in a blaze instantly. Miss —— sung that evening one of her favourite songs—an exquisitely pensive and beautiful air; and Mr. Warningham, almost frantic with excitement, applauded with such obstreperous vehemence, and continued shouting "*encore—encore*"—so long after the general calls of the house had ceased, as to attract all eyes for an instant to his box. Miss —— could not, of course, fail to observe his conduct; and presently herself looked up with what he considered a gratified air. Quivering with excitement and nervous irritability, Mr. Warningham could scarcely sit out the rest of the play; and the moment the curtain fell, he hurried round to the stage door. determined to wait and see ner leave, for the purpose, if possible, of speaking to her. He presently saw her approach the door, closely muffled, veiled, and bonneted, leaning on the arm of a man of military appearance, who handed her into a very gay chariot. He perceived at once that it was the well-known Captain ——. Will it be believed that this enthusiastic young man actually jumped up behind the carriage which contained the object of his idolatrous homage, and did not alight till it drew up opposite a large house in the western suburbs; and that this absurd feat, moreover, was performed amid an incessant shower of small searching rain? He was informed by the footman, whom he had bribed with five shillings, that Miss ——'s own house was in another part of the town, and that her stay at Captain ——'s was only for a day or two. He returned to his hotel in a state of tumultuous excitement, which can be better con ceived than described. As may be supposed, he slept little that night; and the first thing he did in the morning was to despatch his groom, with orders to establish himself in some public-house which could command a view of Miss ——'s residence, and return to Covent Garden as soon as he had seen her or her maid enter. It was not till seven o'clock that he brought word to his master, that no one had entered but Miss ——'s maid. The papers informed him that Miss —— played again that evening; and though he could not but be aware of the sort of intimacy which subsisted between Miss —— and the captain, his enthusiastic passion only increased with increasing obstacles. Though seriously unwell with a determination of blood to the head, induced by the perpetual excitement of his feelings, and a severe cold caught through exposure to the rain on the preceding evening—he was dressing for the play, when, to his infinite mortification, his friendly medical attendant happening to step in positively forbade his leaving his room, and consigned him to bed and physic instead of the maddening scenes of the theatre. The next morning he felt relieved from the more urgent symptoms; and his servant having brought him word that he had at last watched Miss —— enter her house, unaccompanied, except by her maid, Mr. Warningham despatched him with a copy of passionate verses, enclosed in a blank envelope. . He trusted that some adroit allusions in them, might possibly give her a clew to the discovery of the writer—especially if he could contrive to be seen by her that evening in the same box he had occupied formerly; for to the play he was resolved to go, in defiance of the threats of his medical attendant. To his vexation he found the box in question pre-engaged for a family party: and—will it be credited?—he actually entertained the idea of discovering who they were, for the purpose of prevailing on them to vacate in his favour! Finding that, however, of course out of the question, he was compelled to content himself with the corresponding box opposite, where he was duly ensconced the moment the doors were opened.

Miss —— appeared that evening in only one piece, but in the course of it she had to sing some of her most admired songs. The character she played, also, was a favourite both with herself and the public. Her dress was exquisitely tasteful and picturesque, and calculated to set off her figure to the utmost advantage. When, at a particular crisis of the play, Mr. Warningham, by the softened lustre of the lowered foot-lights, beheld Miss —— emerging from a romantic glen with a cloak thrown over her shoulders, her head covered with a velvet cap, over which drooped, in snowy pendency, an ostrich-feather, while her hair strayed from beneath the cincture of her cap in loose negligent curls, down her face and beautiful cheeks; when he saw the timid and alarmed air which her part required her to assume, and the sweet and sad expression of her eyes, while she stole about as if avoiding a pursuer

—when, at length, as the raised foot-lights were restored to their former glare, she let fall the cloak
which had enveloped her, and, like a metamorphosed
chrysalis, burst in beauty on the applauding house,
habited in a costume, which, without being positively
indelicate, was calculated to excite the most volup-
tuous thoughts;—when, I say, poor Mr. Warningham
saw all this he was almost overpowered, and leaned
back in his box, breathless with agitation.

A little before Miss —— quitted the stage for the
last time that evening, the order of the play required
that she should stand for some minutes on that part
of the stage next to Mr. Warningham's box.   While
she was standing in a pensive attitude, with her face
turned full towards Mr. Warningham, he whispered,
in a quivering and under-tone,—" Oh, beautiful, beautiful creature!"   Miss —— heard him, looked at him
with a little surprise; her features relaxed into a
smile, and, with a gentle shake of the head, as if
hinting that he should not endeavour to distract her
attention, she moved away to proceed with her part.
Mr. Warningham trembled violently; he fancied she
encouraged his attentions—and, God knows how—
had recognised in him the writer of the verses she
had received.   When the play was over, he hurried
as on a former occasion to the stage-door, where he
mingled with the inquisitive little throng usually to
be found there, and waited till she made her appearance, enveloped as before in a large shawl, but followed only by a maid-servant, carrying a bandbox.
They stepped into a hackney-coach, and, though Mr.
Warningham had gone there for the express purpose
of speaking to her, his knees knocked together, and
he felt so sick with agitation that he did not even
attempt to hand her into the coach.   He jumped into
the one which drew up next, and ordered the coachman to follow the preceding one wherever it went.
When it approached the street where he knew she
resided, he ordered it to stop, got out, and hurried on

foot towards the house, which he reached just as she was alighting. He offered her his arm. She looked at him with astonishment, and something like apprehension. At length, she appeared to recognise in him the person who had attracted her attention by whispering when at the theatre, and seemed, he thought, a little discomposed. She declined his proffered assistance, said her maid was with her; and was going to knock at the door, when Mr. Warningham stammered, faintly, "Dear madam, do allow me the honour of calling in the morning, and inquiring how you are after the great exertions at the theatre this evening!" She replied, in a cold and discouraging manner; could not conceive to what she was indebted for the honour of his particular attentions, and interest in her welfare, so suddenly felt by an utter stranger—unusual—singular—improper—unpleasant—&c. She said that as for his calling in the morning, if he felt so inclined, she, of course, could not prevent him; but if he expected to see her when he called, he would find himself "perfectly mistaken." The door that moment was opened, and closed upon her, as she made him a cold bow, leaving Mr. Warningham, what with chagrin and excessive passion for her, almost distracted. He seriously assured me that he walked to and fro before her door till nearly six o'clock in the morning; that he repeatedly ascended the steps, and endeavoured, as nearly as he could recollect, to stand on *the very spot* she had occupied while speaking to him, and would remain gazing at what he fancied was the window of her bedroom for ten minutes together; and all this extravagance, to boot, was perpetrated amid an incessant fall of snow, and at a time—Heaven save the mark—when he was an accepted suitor of Miss ——, the young lady whom he had come to town for the express purpose of visiting! I several times asked him how it was that he could bring himself to consider such conduct consistent with honour or deli-

I.—I

cacy. or feel a spark of real attachment for the lady to whom he was engaged, if it was not sufficient to steel his heart and close his eyes against the charms of any other woman in the world? His only reply was, that he "really could not help it;"—he felt "rather the patient, than agent." Miss —— took his heart, he said, by storm, and forcibly ejected, for a while, his love for any other woman breathing!

To return, however: About half past six, he jumped into a hackney-coach which happened to be passing through the street, drove home to the hotel in Covent Garden, and threw himself on the bed, in a state of utter exhaustion both of mind and body. He slept on heavily till twelve o'clock at noon, when he awoke seriously indisposed. In the first few mo·ments, he could not dispossess himself of the idea that Miss —— was standing by his bedside, in the dress she wore the preceding evening, and smiled encouragingly on him. So strong was the delusion, that he actually addressed several sentences to her! About three o'clock he drove out, and called on one of his gay friends, who was perfectly *au fait* at mat·ters of this sort, and resolved to make him his con·fidant in the affair. Under the advice of this mentor, Mr. Warningham purchased a very beautiful emerald ring, which he sent off instantly to Miss ——, with a polite note, saying it was some slight acknowledg·ment of the delight with which he witnessed her ex·quisite acting, &c. &c. &c. This, his friend assured him, *must* call forth an answer of some sort or other, which would lead to another—and another—and another—and so on. He was right. A twopenny-post letter was put into Mr. Warningham's hands the next morning before he rose, which was from Miss ——, elegantly written, and thanked him for the "tasteful present" he had sent her, which she should, with great pleasure, take an early opportunity of gratifying him by wearing in public. There never yet lived an actress, I verily believe, who had forti-bile enough to refuse a present of jewelry! What was to be done next? He did not exactly know. But having succeeded at last in opening an avenue of communication with her, and induced her so easily to lie under an obligation to him, he felt con vinced that his way was now clear.   He determined, therefore, to call and see her that very afternoon; but his medical friend, seeing the state of feverish excitement in which he continued, absolutely inter-dicted him from leaving the house.   The next day ne felt considerably better, but was not allowed to leave the house.   He could, therefore, find no other means of consoling himself, than writing a note to Miss ——, saying he had " something important" to communicate to her, and begging to know when she would permit him to wait upon her for that purpose. What does the reader imagine this pretext of " some-thing important" was?   To ask her to sit for her portrait to a young artist!   His stratagem succeeded; for he received, in the course of the next day, a polite invitation to breakfast with Miss —— on the next Sunday morning; with a hint that he might expect no other company, and that Miss —— was " curious" to know what his particular business with her was.   Poor Mr. Warningham!   How was he to exist in the interval between this day and Sunday? He would fain have annihilated it!

Sunday morning at last arrived; and about nine o'clock he sallied from his hotel, the first time he had left it for several days, and drove to the house. With a fluttering heart he knocked at the door, and a maid-servant ushered him into an elegant apart-ment, in which breakfast was laid.   An elderly lady, some female relative of the actress, was reading a newspaper at the breakfast-table; and Miss —— herself was seated at the piano, practising one of those exquisite songs which had been listened to with breathless rapture by thousands.   She wore an

elegant morning dress; and though her infatuated
visiter had come prepared to see her to great disadvantage—divested of the dazzling complexion she
exhibited on the stage—her pale, and somewhat
sallow features, which wore a pensive and fatigued
expression, served to rivet the chains of his admiration still stronger, with the feelings of sympathy.
Her beautiful eyes beamed on him with sweetness
and affability; and there was an ease, a gentleness
in her manners, and a soft animating tone in her
voice, which filled Mr. Warningham with emotions
of indescribable tenderness. A few moments beheld
them seated at the breakfast-table; and when Mr.
Warningham gazed at his fair hostess, and reflected
on his envied contiguity to one whose beauty and
talents were the theme of universal admiration—
listened to her lively and varied conversation, and
perceived a faint crimson steal for an instant over
her countenance, when he reminded her of his exclamation at the theatre—he felt a swelling excitement
which would barely suffer him to preserve an exterior
calmness of demeanour. He felt, as he expressed it—
(for he has often recounted these scenes to me)—that
she was *maddening* him! Of course, he exerted himself in conversation to the utmost; and his observations on almost every topic of polite literature were
met with equal spirit and sprightliness by Miss ——.
He found her fully capable of appreciating the noblest
passages from Shakspeare and some of the older
English dramatists, and that was sufficient to lay
enthusiastic Mr. Warningham at the feet of any
woman. He was reciting a passionate passage from
Romeo and Juliet, to which Miss —— was listening
with an apparent air of kindling enthusiasm, when a
phaeton dashed up to the door, and an impetuous
thundering of the knocker announced the arrival of
some aristocratical visiter. The elderly lady, who
was sitting with them, started, coloured, and ex

claimed—"Good God, will you receive *the man* this morning!"

"Oh, it's only Lord ——," exclaimed Miss —— with an air of indifference, after having examined the equipage through the window-blinds, "and I won't see the man—that's flat.   He pesters me to death," she continued, turning to Mr. Warningham, with a pretty peevish air.   It had its effect on him.—"What an enviable fellow I am to be received, when *lords* are refused!" thought Mr. Warningham.

"Not at home!" drawled Miss ——, coldly, as the servant brought in Lord ——'s card.   "You know one can't see *every* body, Mr. Warningham," she said, with a smile.   "Oh, Mr. Warningham,—lud, lud!— don't go to the window till the man's gone!" she exclaimed; and her small white hand, with his emerald ring glistening on her second finger, was hurriedly laid on his shoulder, to prevent his going to the window.   Mr. Warningham declared to me he could that moment have settled his whole fortune on her!

After the breakfast things were removed, she sat down, at his request, to the piano—a very magnificent present from the Duke of ——, Mrs. —— assured him,—and sung and played whatever he asked. She played a certain well-known arch air, with the most bewitching simplicity; Mr. Warningham could only *look* his feelings.   As she concluded it, and was dashing off the symphony in a careless, but rapid and brilliant style, Mrs. ——, the lady once or twice before mentioned, left the room; and Mr. Warningham, scarce knowing what he did, suddenly sunk on one knee, from the chair on which he was sitting by Miss ——, grasped her hand, and uttered some exclamation of passionate fondness.   Miss —— turned to him a moment with a surprised air, her large, liquid blue eyes almost entirely hid beneath her half-closed lids, her features relaxed into a coquettish smile: she disengaged her hand, and went on playing and singing.

> " He sighs—' Beauty! I adore thee,
> See me fainting thus before thee :'
> But I say—
>   Fal, lal, lal, la!   Fal, lal, lal, la!
>   Fal lal, &c."

"Fascinating, angelic woman! glorious creature of intellect and beauty, I cannot live but in your presence!" gasped Mr. Warningham.

"Oh, Lord, what an actor you would have made Mr. Warningham—indeed you would! Only think how it would sound—' *Romeo, Mr. Warningham!*'—Lud, lud—the man would almost persuade me that he was in earnest!" replied Miss ——, with the most enchanting air, and ceased playing. Mr. Warningham continued addressing her in the most extravagant manner; indeed, he afterward told me, he felt 'as though his wits were slipping from him every instant."

"Why don't you *go* on the stage, Mr. Warningnam?" inquired Miss ——, with a more earnest and serious air than she had hitherto manifested, and gazing at him with an eye which expressed real admiration,—for she was touched by the winning, persuasive, and passionate eloquence with which Mr. Warningham expressed himself. She had hardly uttered the words, when a loud and long knock was heard at the street door. Miss —— suddenly started from the piano; turned pale, and exclaimed in a hurried and agitated tone,—" Lord, Lord, what's to be done!—Captain —— !—whatever can have brought him up to town—oh, my——"

"Good God, madam, what can possibly alarm you in this manner?" exclaimed Mr. Warningham, with a surprised air. " What in the earth can there be in this Captain —— to startle you in this manner? What can the man want here if his presence is disagreeable to you? Pray, madam, give him the same answer you gave Lord ——!" "Oh, Mr. Warn—dear, dear' the door is opened—what *will* become of me if Cap tain —— sees you here?   Ah! I have it—you must —country manager—provincial enga—" hurriedly muttered Miss ——, as the room-door opened, and a gentleman of a lofty and military bearing, dressed in a blue surtout and white trousers, with a slight walking cane in his hand, entered, and without observing Mr. Warningham, who at the moment happened to be standing rather behind the door, hurried towards Miss ——, exclaiming, with a gay and fond air, "Ha, my charming De Medici, how d'ye?—Why, who the —— have we *here?*" he inquired, suddenly breaking off, and turning with an astonished air towards Mr. Warningham.

"What possible business can *this person* have here, Miss ——?" inquired the captain, with a cold and angry air, letting fall her hand, which he had grasped on entering, and eying Mr. Warningham with a furious scowl.   Miss —— muttered something indistinctly about business—a provincial engagement —and looked appealingly towards Mr. Warningham, as if beseeching him to take the cue, and assume the character of a country manager.   Mr. Warningham, however, was not experienced enough in matters of this kind to take the hint.

"My good sir—I beg pardon, *captain*"—said he, buttoning his coat, and speaking in a voice almost choked with fury—" what is the meaning of all this? What do you mean, sir, by this insolent bearing towards me?"

"Good God! Do you know, sir, whom you are speaking to?" inquired the captain, with an air of wonder.

"I care as little as I know, sir; but *this* I know— I shall give you to understand that, whoever you are, I won't be *bullied* by you.'

"The devil!" exclaimed the captain, slowly, as if he hardly comprehended what was passing. Miss ——, pale as a statue, and trembling from head to foot, leaned speechless against the corner of the piano, apparently stupified by the scene that was passing.

"Oh, by ——! this will never do," at length exclaimed the captain, as he rushed up to Mr. Warningham, and struck him furiously over the shoulders with his cane. He was going to seize Mr. Warningham's collar with his left hand, as if for the purpose of inflicting further chastisement, when Mr. Warn ingham, who was a very muscular man, shook him off, and dashed his right hand full into the face of the captain. Miss —— shrieked for assistance—while the captain put himself instantly into attitude, and being a first-rate "miller," as the phrase is, before Mr. Warningham could prepare himself for the encounter, planted a sudden shower of blows about Mr. Warningham's head and breast, that fell on him like the strokes of a sledge-hammer. He was of course instantly laid prostrate on the floor in a state of insensibility, and recollected nothing further till he found himself lying on his bed at the —— hotel, about the middle of the night, faint and weak with the loss of blood, his head bandaged, and amid all the paraphernalia and attendance of a sick man's chamber. How or when he had been conveyed to the hotel he knew not, till he was informed some weeks afterward that Captain ——, having learned his residence from Miss ——, had brought him in his carriage, in a state of stupor.   All the circumstances above related combined to throw Mr. Warningham into a fever, which incieased upon him ; the state of nervous excitement in which he had lived for the last few days aggravated the other symptoms—and delirium at last deepened into downright madness.   The medical man, who has been several times before mentioned as a friendly attendant of Mr. Warningham, finding that matters grew so serious, and being unwilling any longer to bear the sole responsibility of the case, advised Mr. Warningham's friends, who had been summoned from a distant county to his bedside, to call me in; and this was the *statu quo* of affairs when I paid him my first visit.

On entering the room, I found a keeper sitting on each side of the bed on which lay Mr. Warningham, who was raving frightfully, gnashing his teeth, and imprecating the most fearful curses upon Captain ——. It was with the utmost difficulty that the keepers could hold him down, even though my unfortunate patient was suffering under the restraint of a strait waistcoat. His countenance, which I think I mentioned was naturally very expressive, if not handsome, exhibited the most ghastly contortions. His eyes glared into every corner of the room, and seemed about to start from their sockets. After standing for some moments a silent spectator of this painful scene, endeavouring to watch the current of his malady, and at the same time soothe the affliction of his uncle, who was standing by my side dreadfully agitated, I ventured to approach nearer, observing him nearly exhausted, and relapsing into silence—undisturbed but by heavy and stertorous breathing He lay with his face buried in the pillow; and on my putting my fingers to his temples, he suddenly turned his face towards me. " God bless me—M*. K_an !" said he, in an altered tone, "this is really a very unexpected honour!" He seemed embarrassed at seeing me. I determined to humour his fancy,—the only rational method of dealing with such patients. I may as well say, in passing, that some persons have not unfrequently found a resemblance—faint and slight, if any at all—between my features and those of the celebrated tragedian for whom I was on the present occasion mistaken.

" Oh, yours are terrible eyes, Mr. Kean—very, very terrible! Where did you get them? What fiend touched them with such unnatural lustre? These are not human—no, no! What do you think I have often fancied they resembled ?"

"Really, I can't pretend to say. sir," I replied with some curiosity.

"Why, one of the damned inmates of hell—glaring through the fiery bars of their prison," replied Mr. Warningham, with a shudder. "Isn't that a ghastly fancy?" he inquired.

"'Tis horrible enough, indeed," said I, determined to humour him.

"Ha, ha, ha!—Ha, ha, ha!" roared the wretched maniac, with a laugh which made us all quake round his bedside. "I can say better things than that,—though it *is* d——d good; it's nothing like the way in which I shall talk to-morrow morning—ha, ha, ha!—for I am going down to hell, to learn some of the fiends' talk; and when I come back, I'll give you a lesson, Mr. Kean, shall be worth two thousand a-year to you—ha, ha, ha!   What d'ye say to that, Othello?"

He paused, and continued mumbling something to himself in a strangely different tone of voice from that in which he had just addressed me.

"Mr. Kean, Mr. Kean," said he, suddenly, "you're the very man I want; I suppose they had told you I had been asking for you, eh?"

"Yes, certainly, I heard"—

"Very good—'twas civil of them; but, now you are here, just shade those basilisk eyes of yours, for they blight my soul within me."   I did as he directed—"Now, I'll tell you what I've been thinking —I've got a tragedy ready, very nearly at least, and there's a magnificent character for you in it,—expressly written for you—a compound of Richard, Shylock, and Sir Giles—your masterpieces—a sort of *quartum quiddam*—eh—you hear me, Mr. Kean?"

"Ay, and mark thee, too, Hal." thinking a quotation from his favourite Shakspeare would soothe and flatter his inflamed fancy.

"Ah—aptly quoted—happy, happy!   By-the-way, talking of that, I don't at all admire your personation of Macbeth—by ——, Mr. Kean, I don't. 'Tis ut-

terly misconceived—wrong from beginning to end;
it is, really.   You see what an independent, straight-
forward critic I am—ha, ha, ha!" accompanying the
words with a laugh, if not as loud, as fearful as his
former ones.   I told him I bowed to his judgment.

"Good," he answered; "genius should always
be candid.   Macready has a single whisper, when he
inquires, '*Is it the King?*' which is worth all *your*
fiendish mutterings and gaspings—ha, ha!   'Does the
galled jade wince?   Her withers are unwrung.'   Mr.
Kean, how absurd you are, ill-mannered, pardon me
for saying it, for interrupting me," he said, after a
pause; adding, with a puzzled air, "What was it I
was talking about when you interrupted me?"   "Do
you mean the tragedy?"—(I had not opened my lips
to interrupt him.)   "Ha! the tragedy!

'The play, the play's the thing,
Wherein I'll catch the conscience of the king.'

—Ah—*the tragedy* was it I was mentioning?   *Rem
acu—acu tetigisti*—that's Latin, Mr. Kean!   Did you
ever learn Latin and Greek, eh?"   I told him I had
studied it a little.

"What *can* you mean by interrupting me thus un
mannerly?   Mr. Kean, I won't stand it—once more,
what was it I was talking about a few minutes ago?"
He had again let slip the thread of his thoughts.   "A
digression this, Mr. Kean; I must be mad—*indeed* I
must!" he continued, with a shudder, and a look of
sudden sanity; "I must be mad, and I can't help
thinking what a profound knowledge of human nature Shakspeare shows when he makes memory the
test of sanity—a d—d depth of philosophy in it, eh?
d'ye recollect the passage—eh, Kean?"   I said I certainly could not call it to mind.

"Then it's infamous—a shame and a disgrace for
you.   It's quite true what people say of you—you
are a mere tragedy hack!   Why won't you try to
get out of that mill-horse round of your hackneyed
characters!   Excuse me: you know I'm a vast ad-

mirer of yours, but an *honest* one. Curse me," after
a sudden pause, adding with a bewildered and angry
air, "*what* was it I was going to say? I've lost it
again!—oh, a passage from Shakspeare—memory—
test of—Ah, *now* we have him! 'Tis this:—mark
and remember it—'tis in King Lear—

> ————' Bring me to the test,
> And I *the matter will re-word*, which *madness*
> Would gambol from.'

Profoundly true; isn't it, Kean?" Of course I acquiesced.

"Ah," he resumed, with a pleased smile, " nobody
now can write like that except myself—go it, Harry,
ha, ha, ha!—Who—oo—o!" uttering the strangest
kind of revolting cry I ever heard. " Oh dear, dear
me, *what* was it I was saying? The thought keeps
slipping from me like a lithe eel; I can't hold it.
Eels, by-the-way, are nothing but a sort of water-
snake; 'tis brutal to eat them! What made me name
eels, Mr. Kean?" I reminded him. " Ah, there *must*
be a screw loose—something wrong *here*," shaking
his head; " it's all upside down—ha! *what* the d—l
was it now?" I once more recalled it to his mind,
for I saw he was fretting himself with vexation at
being unable to take up the chain of his thoughts.

" Ah! well now, once more—I said I'd a character
for you—good; do it justice, or d—me, I'll hiss you
like a huge boa coiled in the middle of the pit!—
There's a thought—stay—he's losing the thought
again—hold it—hold it."

" The tragedy, sir."

" Ah, to be sure! I've another character for Miss
—— (naming the actress before mentioned)—magni
ficent queen of beauty—nightingale of song—radiant,
peerless—Ah, lady, look on me! look on me!" and
he suddenly burst into one of the most tigerlike
howls I could conceive capable of being uttered by
a human being. It must have been heard in the street
and market without. We who were round him sto

listening, chilled with horror.   When he had ceased, I said, in a soothing whisper, " Compose yourself, Mr. Warningham, you'll see her by-and-by. "   He looked me full in the face, and uttered as shocking a yell as before.

" Avaunt!—out on ye !—scoundrels !—fiends !" he shouted, struggling with the men who were endeavouring to hold him down; " are you come to murder me ?   Ha—a—a !" and he fell back as though he was in the act of being choked or throttled.

" Where—where is the fiend who struck me ?" he groaned, in a fierce under-tone ; " and in HER presence, too; and she stood by looking on !—cruel, beautiful, deceitful woman !   Did she turn pale and tremble ?   Oh, will not I have his blood—blood— blood !" and he clutched his fists with a savage and murderous force.   " Ah! you around me, say, does not blood cleanse the deepest, foulest stain, or hide it ?   Pour it on warm and reeking—a crimson flood —and never trust me if it does not wash out insult for ever !   Ha—ha—ha !   Oh, let me loose !   Let me loose !   Let me but cast my eyes on the insolent ruffian—the brutal bully—let me but lay hands on him !" and he drew in his breath with a long, fierce, and deep respiration.   " Will I not shake him out of his military trappings and fooleries ?   Ha, devils !. unhand me, I say ; unhand me, and let me loose on this Captain ———."

In this strain the unhappy young man continued raving for about ten minutes longer, till he utterly exhausted himself.   The paroxysm was over for the present.   The keepers, aware of this (for of course they were accustomed to such fearful scenes as these, and preserved the most cool and matter-of-fact demeanour conceivable), relaxed their hold.   Mr. Warningham lay perfectly motionless, with his eyes closed, breathing slow and heavily, while the perspiration burst from every pore.   His pulse and other symptoms showed me that a few more similar paoxysms would destroy him; and that, consequently, the most active remedies must be had recourse to immediately. I therefore directed what was to be done: his head to be shaved; that he should be bled copiously; kept perfectly cool and tranquil; and prescribed such medicines as I conceived most calculated to effect this object. On my way down stairs I encountered Mr. ——, the proprietor or landlord of the hotel, who, with a very agitated air, told me he must insist on having Mr. Warningham removed immediately from the hotel; for that his ravings disturbed and agitated everybody in the place, and had been loudly complained of. Seeing the reasonableness of this, my patient was, with my sanction, conveyed that evening to airy and genteel lodgings in one of the adjoining streets. The three or four following visits I paid him presented scenes little varying from the one I have above been attempting to describe. They gradually, however, abated in violence. I shall not be guilty of extravagance or exaggeration if I protest that there was sometimes a vein of sublimity in his ravings. He really said some of the very finest things I ever heard. This need not occasion wonder, if it be recollected that "out of the fulness of the heart the mouth speaketh;" and Mr. Warningham's naturally powerful mind was filled with accumulated stores, acquired from almost every region of literature. His fancy was deeply tinged with Germanism, with *diablerie;* and some of his ghostly images used to haunt and creep after me like spirits, gibbering and chattering the expressions with which the maniac had conjured them into being.

To me nothing is so affecting, so terrible, so humiliating, as to see a powerful intellect, like that of Mr. Warningham, the prey of insanity, exhibiting glimpses of greatness and beauty amid all the chaotic gloom and havoc of madness; reminding one of the mighty fragments of some dilapidated structure of Greece or Rome mouldering apart from the another, still displaying the exquisite moulding and chiselling of the artist, and enhancing the beholder's regret that so glorious a fabric should have been destroyed by the ruthless hand of time. Insanity, indeed, makes the most fearful inroads on an intellect distinguished by its *activity*; and the flame is fed rapidly by the fuel afforded from an excitable and vigorous fancy. A tremendous responsibility is incurred, in such cases, by the medical attendants. Long experience has convinced me, that the only sensible way of dealing with such patients as Mr. Warningham is, chiming in readily with their various fancies, without seeming in the slightest degree shocked or alarmed by the most monstrous extravagances. The patient must never be startled by any appearance of surprise or apprehension from those around him; never irritated by contradiction or indications of impatience. Should this be done by some inexperienced attendant, the mischief may prove irremediable by any subsequent treatment; the flame will blaze out with a fury which will consume instantly every vestige of the intellectual structure, leaving the body—the shell—bare, blackened walls alone,

> " A scoff, a jest, a by-word through the world "

Let the patient have sea-room; allow him to dash about for a while in the tempest and whirlwind of his disordered faculties; while all that is necessary from those around is, to watch the critical moment, and pour the oil of soothing acquiescence on the foaming waters. Depend upon it, the uproar will subside when the winds of opposition cease.

To return, however, to Mr. Warningham. The incubus which had brooded over his intellects for more than a week at length disappeared, leaving its victim trembling on the very verge of the grave. In truth, I do not recollect ever seeing a patient whose energies, both physical and mental, were so dread-

fully shattered. He had lost almost all muscular
power. He could not raise his hand to his head,
alter his position in the bed, or even masticate his
food. For several days it could barely be said that
he existed. He could utter nothing more than an
almost inaudible whisper, and seemed utterly unconscious of what was passing around him. His sister,
a young and very interesting woman, had flown to
his bedside immediately the family were acquainted
with his illness, and had continued ever since in daily
and nightly attendance on him, till she herself seemed
almost worn out. How I loved her for her pallid,
exhausted, anxious, yet affectionate looks! Had not
this illness intervened, she would have been before
this time married to a rising young man at the bar;
yet her devoted sisterly sympathies attached her to
her brother's bedside without repining, and she would
never think of leaving him. Her feelings may be
conceived, when it is known that she was in a great
measure acquainted with the cause of her brother's
sudden illness; and it was her painful duty to sit and
listen to many unconscious disclosures of the most
afflicting nature. This latter circumstance furnished
the first source of uneasiness to Mr. Warningham on
recovering the exercise of his rational faculties; he
was excessively agitated at the idea of his having
alluded to and described the dissipated and profligate
scenes of his college life; and when he had once
compelled me to acknowledge that his sister and
other relations were apprized of the events which led
to his illness, he sunk into moody silence for some
time, evidently scourging himself with the heaviest
self-reproaches, and presently exclaimed—" Well,
doctor, thus you see has

' Even-handed justice
Compell'd the poison'd chalice to my lips,'

and I have drunk the foul draught to the dregs! Yet
though I would at this moment lay down half my
fortune to blot from their memories what they must

have heard me utter, I shall submit in silence—I have richly earned it. I now, however, bid farewell for ever to debauchery, profligacy, dissipation, for ever!" I interrupted him by saying, I was not aware, nor were his relatives, that he had been publicly distinguished as a debauchee. "Why, doctor," he replied, "possibly not; there may be others who have exposed themselves more absurdly than I have—who have drunk and raked more—but mine has been the vile profligacy of the *heart*—the dissipation of the *feelings*. But it shall cease! God knows I never thoroughly enjoyed it, though it has occasioned me a delicious sort of excitement which has at length nearly destroyed me. I have clambered out of the scorching crater of Etna, scathed, but not consumed. I will now descend into the tranquil vales of virtue, and never, never leave them!" He wept, for he had not yet recovered the tone or mastery of his feelings. These salutary thoughts led to a permanent reformation; his illness had produced its effect. One other thing there was which yet occasioned him disquietude and uncertainty: he said he felt bound to seek the usual "satisfaction" from Captain ——! I and all around him, to whom he hinted it, scouted the idea; and he himself relinquished it on hearing that Captain —— had called often during his illness, and left many cards, with the most anxious inquiries after his health; and in a day or two had a private interview with Mr. Warningham, when he apologized in the most prompt and handsome manner for his violent conduct, and expressed the liveliest regrets at the serious consequences with which it had been attended.

Mr. Warningham, to conclude, recovered but slowly; and as soon as his weakness would admit of the journey, removed to the family house in ——shire; from thence he went to the seaside, and staid there till the close of the autumn, reading philosophy and some of the leading writers on morals He was married

.I.—K

in October, and set off for the continent in the spring.
His constitution, however, had received a shock from
which it never recovered; and two years after Mr
Warningham died of a decline at Genoa.

The Broken Heart.

There was a large and gay party assembled one
evening, in the memorable month of June, 1815, at a
house in the remote western suburbs of London.
Throngs of handsome and well-dressed women—a
large retinue of the leading men about town—the
dazzling light of chandeliers, blazing like three suns
overhead—the charms of music and dancing—toge
ther with that tone of excitement then pervading society at large, owing to our successful continental
campaigns which maddened England into almost
daily annunciations of victory;—all these circumstances, I say, combined to supply spirit to every
party.   In fact, England was almost turned upside
down with universal fêting!   Mrs. ——, the lady
whose party I have just been mentioning, was in
ecstasy at the eclât with which the whole was going
off, and charmed with the buoyant animation with
which all seemed inclined to contribute their quota
to the evening's amusement.   A young lady of some
personal attractions, most amiable manners, and great
accomplishments, particularly musical, had been repeatedly solicited to sit down to the piano, for the
purpose of favouring the company with the favourite
Scottish air " *The Banks of Allan Water.*"   For a long
time, however, she steadfastly resisted their importunities on the plea of low spirits.   There was evidently an air of deep pensiveness, if not melancholy,
about her, which ought to have corroborated the
truth of the plea she urged.   She did not seem to
gather excitement with the rest, and rather endured
than shared the gayeties of the evening.   Of course,
the young folks around her of her own sex whispered

.heir suspicions that she was in love ; and in point of
fact, it was well known by several present that Miss
—— was engaged to a young officer who had earned
considerable distinction in the peninsular campaign,
and to whom she was to be united on his return from
the continent. It need not, therefore, be wondered
at that a thought of the various casualties to which
a soldier's life is exposed,—especially a bold and
brave young soldier, such as her intended had proved
himself—and the possibility, if not probability, that
he might, alas ! never

> " Return to claim his blushing bride,"

—but be left behind among the glorious throng of the
fallen, sufficed to overcast her mind with gloomy anxieties and apprehensions. It was, indeed, owing
solely to the affectionate importunities of her relatives that she was prevailed on to be seen in society
at all. Had her own inclinations been consulted, she
would have sought solitude, where she might, with
weeping and trembling, commend her hopes to the
hands of Him "who seeth in secret," and " whose
are the issues" of battle. As, however, Miss ——'s
rich contralto voice and skilful powers of accompaniment were much talked of, the company would listen
to no excuses or apologies ; so the poor girl was absolutely *baited* into sitting down to the piano, when
she ran over a few melancholy chords with an air of
reluctance and displacency. Her sympathies were
soon excited by the fine tones—the tumultuous me-
lody of the keys she touched; and she struck into
the soft and soothing symphony of " The Banks of
Allan Water." The breathless silence of the by-
standers (for nearly all the company was thronged
around) was at length broken by her voice, stealing,
" like faint blue gushing streams," on the delighted
ears of her auditors, as she commenced singing that
exquisite little ballad with the most touching pathos
and simplicity. She had just commenced the verse,

> " For his bride a soldier sought her,
> And a winning tongue had he !"

when, to the surprise of everybody around her, s!
suddenly ceased playing and singing, without remov
ing her hands from the instrument, and gazed stead
fastly forward with a vacant air, while the colou
faded from her cheeks, and left them pale as the lily
She continued thus for some moments, to the alaru
and astonishment of the company—motionless, and
apparently unconscious of any one's presence.   He
elder sister, much agitated, stepped towards her
placed her hand on her shoulder, endeavoured gently
to rouse her, and said hurriedly, " Anne, Anne! what
now is the matter ?" Miss —— made no answer; but
a few moments after, without moving her eyes, suddenly burst into a piercing shriek!   Consternation
seized all present.

" Sister—sister!—dear Anne, are you ill ?" again
inquired her trembling sister, endeavouring to rouse
her, but in vain.   Miss —— did not seem either to
see or hear her.   Her eyes still gazed fixedly forward, till they seemed gradually to expand, as it
were, with an expression of glassy horror.   All present seemed utterly confounded and afraid to interfere with her.   Whispers were heard, " She's ill—in
a fit—run for some water.—Good God, how strange!
—what a piercing shriek!" &c. &c.   At length Miss
——'s lips moved.   She began to mutter inaudibly;
but by-and-by those immediately near her could dis.
tinguish the words, " There!—there they are witl
their lanterns!—Oh! they are looking out for the
d——a——d!—They turn over the heaps.—Ah!—now
—no!—that little hill of slain—see, see!—they are
turning them over one by one.—There!—THERE HE
IS!—Oh, horror! horror! horror!—RIGHT THROUGH THE
HEART!" and with a long shuddering groan she fell
senseless into the arms of her horror-struck sister
Of course all were in confusion and dismay; not
face present but was blanched with agitation and
fright on hearing the extraordinary words she ut

\ered. With true delicacy and propriety of feeling all those whose carriages had happened to have al ready arrived instantly took their departure, to pre-vent their presence embarrassing or interfering with the family, who were already sufficiently bewildered. The room was soon thinned of all except those whr were immediately engaged in rendering their serv.ces to the young lady, and the servant was instantly despatched with a horse for me. On my arrival, ! found her in bed, still at the house where the party was given, which was that of the young lady's sister-in-law. She had fallen into a succession of swoons ever since she had been carried up from the drawing-room, and was perfectly senseless when I entered the bedchamber where she lay. She had not spoker a syllable since uttering the singular words just re-lated, and her whole frame was cold and rigid; in fact, she scemed to have received some strange shock which had altogether paralyzed her. By the use, however, of strong stimulants, we succeeded in at length restoring her to something like consciousness, but I think it would have been better for her, judging from the event, never to have woke again from for-getfulness. She opened her eyes under the influence of the searching stimulants we applied, and stared vacantly for an instant on those standing round her bedside. Her countenance, of an ashy hue, was damp with clammy perspiration, and she lay perfectly motionless, except when her frame undulated with long, deep-drawn sighs.

"Oh, wretched, wretched, wretched girl!" she mur-mured at length, "why have I lived till now? Why did you not suffer me to expire? He called me to join him—I was going—and you will not let me—but I must go—yes, yes!"

"Ar.ie, dearest! why do you talk so? Charles is not gr.ie. He will return soon; he will, indeed," sor., ' her sister.

"...., never, never! You could not see what I

saw, Jane," she shuddered; "Oh, it was frightful How they tumbled about the heaps of the dead!— How they stripped!—oh, horror! horror!"

"My dear Miss ——, you are dreaming—raving— indeed you are," said I, holding her hand in mine "come, come, you must not give way to such gloomy, such nervous fancies; you must not, indeed. You are frightening your friends to no purpose."

"What do you mean?" she replied, looking me suddenly full in the face; "I tell you it is true! Ah, me! Charles is dead—I know it—I saw him!—*Sho right through the heart!* They were stripping him, when—" and heaving three or four short, convulsive sobs, she again swooned. Mrs. ——, the lady of the house (the sister-in-law of Miss ——, as I think I have mentioned) could endure the distressing scene no longer, and was carried out of the room fainting in the arms of her husband. With great difficulty we succeeded in restoring Miss —— once more to con- sciousness; but the frequency and duration of her relapses began seriously to alarm me. The spirit being brought so often to the brink, might at last suddenly flit off into eternity without any one's being aware of it. I of course did all that my professional knowledge and experience suggested; and after ex- pressing my readiness to remain all night in the house, in the event of any sudden alteration in Miss —— for the worse, I took my departure, promising to call very early in the morning. Before leaving, Mr. —— had acquainted me with all the particulars above related; and as I rode home, I could not help feeling the liveliest curiosity, mingled with the most intense sympathy for the unfortunate sufferer, to see whether the corroborating event would stamp the present as one of those extraordinary occurrences which occasionally "come o'er us like a summer cloud," astonishing and perplexing every one.

The next morning, about nine o'clock, I was again at Miss ——'s bedside. She was nearly in the same

state as that in which I had left her the preceding
evening, only feebler, and almost continually stupified. She seemed, as it were, stunned with some
severe but invisible stroke. She said scarcely any
thing, but often uttered a low, moaning, indistinct
sound, and whispered at intervals, " Yes—shortly,
Charles, shortly—to-morrow." There was no rous-
ing her by conversation; she noticed no one, and
would answer no questions. I suggested the propriety of calling in additional medical assistance;
and in the evening met two eminent brother physicians in consultation at her bedside. We came to
the conclusion that she was sinking rapidly, and that,
unless some miracle intervened to restore her energies, she would continue with us but a very little
'onger. After my brother physicians had left, I re-
urned to the sick chamber, and sat by Miss——'s
bedside for more than an hour. My feelings were
much agitated at witnessing her singular and affecting situation. There was such a sweet and sorrowful expression about her pallid features, deepening
occasionally into such hopelessness of heart-broken
anguish, as no one could contemplate without deep
emotion. There was besides something mysterious
and awing—something of what in Scotland is called
second sight—in the circumstances which had occasioned her illness.

" Gone—gone !" she murmured, with closed eyes,
while I was sitting and gazing in silence on her;
" gone—and in glory! Ah! I shall see the young
conqueror—I shall! How he will love me! Ah! I
recollect," she continued, after a long interval, " it
was the ' Banks of Allan Water' those cruel people
made me sing—and my heart breaking the while
What was the verse I was singing when I saw"
she shuddered—" oh! this—

  ' For his bride a soldier sought her
   And a winning tongue had he -
  On the banks of Allan water
   None so gay as she '

> But the summer grief had brought her.
> And the soldier—false was he—'

Oh, no, no, never, Charles! my poor, murdered Charles —-never!" she groaned, and spoke no more that night. She continued utterly deaf to all that was said in the way of sympathy or remonstrance; and if her lips moved at all, it was only to utter faintly some such words as " Oh, let me—let me leave in peace!" During the next two days she continued drooping rapidly The only circumstance about her demeanour particu larly noticed was, that she once moved her hands for a moment over the counterpane, as though she were playing the piano; a sudden flush overspread her features; her eyes stared, as though she were startled by the appearance of some phantom or other, and she gasped, "There—there!" after which she relapsed into her former state of stupor.

How will it be credited, that on the fourth morning of Miss ——'s illness, a letter was received from Paris by her family, with a black seal, and franked by the noble colonel of the regiment in which Charles —— had served, communicating the melancholy intelligence that the young captain had fallen towards the close of the battle of Waterloo; for while in the act of charging at the head of his corps, a French cavalry officer shot him with his pistol *right through the art!* The whole family, with all their acquaintance, were unutterably shocked at the news—almost petrified with amazement at the strange corroboration of Miss ——'s prediction. How to communicate it to the poor sufferer was now a serious question, or whether to communicate it at all at present. The family, at last, considering that it would be unjustifiable in them any longer to withhold the intelligence, intrusted the painful duty to me. I therefore repaired to her bedside alone, in the evening of the day on which the letter had been received : that evening was the last of her life! I sat down in my usual place beside her, and her pulse, countenance, breathing, old extremities, together with the fact that she had taken no nourishment whatever since she had been laid on her bed, convinced me that the poor girl's sufferings were soon to terminate. I was at a loss for a length of time how to break the oppressive silence. Observing, however, her fading eyes fixed on me, I determined, as it were, accidentally, to attract them to the fatal letter which I then held in my hand. After a while she observed it; her eye suddenly settled on the ample coroneted seal, and the sight operated something like an electric shock. She seemed struggling to speak, but in vain. I now wished to heaven I had never agreed to undertake the duty which had been imposed upon me. I opened the letter, and looking steadfastly at her, said, in as soothing tones as my agitation could command, "My dear girl, now don't be alarmed, or I shall not tell you what I am going to tell you." She trembled, and her sensibilities seemed suddenly restored; for her eye assumed an expression of alarmed intelligence, and her lips moved about like those of a person who feels them parched with agitation, and endeavours to moisten them. "This letter has been received to-day from Paris," I continued; "it is from Colonel Lord ——, and brings word that—that—that—" I felt suddenly choked, and could not bring out the words.

"That my Charles is DEAD! I know it. Did I not tell you so?" said Miss ——, interrupting me, with as clear and distinct a tone of voice as she ever had in her life. I felt confounded. Had the unexpected operation of the news I brought been able to dissolve the spell which had withered her mental energies, and afford promise of her restoration to health?

Has the reader ever watched a candle which is flickering and expiring in its socket, suddenly shoot up into an instantaneous brilliance, and then be utterly extinguished? I soon saw it was thus with poor Miss —— All the expiring energies of her soul were

suddenly collected to receive this corroboration of he
vision (if such it may be called), and then she would

> " Like a lily drooping,
> Bow her head, and die."

To return. She begged me, in a faltering voice, to
read her all the letter. She listened with closed eyes,
and made no remark when I had concluded. After
a long pause, I exclaimed, " God be praised, my dear
Miss ——, that you have been able to receive this
dreadful news so firmly!"

" Doctor, tell me, have you no medicine that could
make me weep ? Oh, give it me, give it me; it would
relieve me, for I feel a mountain on my breast—it is
pressing me," replied she, feebly, uttering the words
at long intervals. Pressing her hand in mine, I begged
her to be calm, and the oppression would soon dis-
appear.

" Oh—oh—oh, that I could weep, doctor !" She
whispered something else, but inaudibly. I put my
ear close to her mouth, and distinguished something
like the words, " I am—I am—call her—hush," accompanied with a faint, fluttering, gurgling sound.
Alas! I too well understood it ! With much trepidation I ordered the nurse to summon the family into
the room instantly. Her sister Jane was the first
that entered, her eyes swollen with weeping, and
seemingly half-suffocated with the effort to conceal
her emotions.

" Oh, my darling, precious, precious sister Anne !"
she sobbed, and knelt down at the bedside, flinging
her arms round her sister's neck, kissing the gentle
sufferer's cheeks and mouth.

" Anne !—love !—darling !—Don't you know me ?"
she groaned, kissing her forehead repeatedly. Could
I help weeping? All who had entered were standing around the bed, sobbing, and in tears. I kept my
fingers at the wrist of the dying sufferer, but could
not feel whether or not the pulse beat ; which, how
ever, I attributed to my own agitation.

"Speak—speak—my darling Anne! Speak to me —I am your poor sister Jane!" sobbed the agonized girl, continuing fondly kissing her sister's cold lips and forehead. She suddenly started, exclaimed "Oh God, *she's dead!*" and sunk instantly senseless on the floor. Alas! alas! it was too true; my sweet and broken-hearted patient was no more!

CHAPTER IV.

CONSUMPTION—THE SPECTRAL DOG—THE FORGER.

Consumption.

CONSUMPTION!—Terrible, insatiable tyrant! who can arrest thy progress, or number thy victims? why dost thou attack almost exclusively the fairest and loveliest of our species? why select blooming and beautiful youth instead of haggard and exhausted age? why strike down those who are bounding blithely from the starting-post of life, rather than the decrepit beings tottering towards its goal? By what infernal subtlety hast thou contrived hitherto to baffle the profoundest skill of science, to frustrate utterly the uses of experience, and disclose thyself only when thou hast irretrievably secured thy victim, and thy fangs are crimsoned with its blood? Destroying angel!—why art thou commissioned thus to smite down the first-born of agonized humanity? What are the strange purposes of Providence, that thus letteth thee loose upon the objects of its infinite goodness?

Alas! how many aching hearts have been agitated with these unanswerable questions, and how many myriads are yet to be wrung and tortured by them!

—Let me proceed to lay before the reader a shor. and simple statement of one of the many cases of consumption, and all its attendant broken-heartedness, with which a tolerably extensive practice has, alas! *crowded* my memory. The one immediately following has been selected, because it seemed to me, though destitute of varied and stirring incident, calculated on various accounts to excite peculiar interest and sympathy. Possibly there are a few who may consider the ensuing pages pervaded by a tone of exaggeration. It is not so. My heart has really ached under the task of recording the bitter premature fate of one of the most lovely and accomplished young women I ever knew; and the vivid recollection of her sufferings, as well as those of her anguished relations, may have led me to adopt strong language; but not strong enough adequately to express my feelings.

Miss Herbert lost both her father and mother before she had attained her tenth year, and was solemnly committed by each to the care of her uncle, a baronet, who was unmarried, and, through disappointment in a first attachment, seemed likely to continue so to the end of his life. Two years after his brother's death, he was appointed to an eminent official situation in India, as the fortune attached to his baronetcy had suffered severely from the extravagance of his predecessors. He was for some time at a loss how to dispose of his little niece. Should he take her with him to India, accompanied by a first rate governess, and have her carefully educated under his own eye? or leave her behind in England, at one of the fashionable boarding-schools, and trust to the general *surveillance* of a distant female relation? He decided on the former course; and accordingly, very shortly after completing her twelfth year, this little blooming exotic was transplanted to the scorched soil, and destined to "waste its sweetness" on the sultry air of India. A more delicate

and lovely little creature than was Eliza Herbert at
this period cannot be conceived. She was the only
bud from a parent stem of remarkable beauty; but,
alas! that stem was suddenly withered by consumption! Her father, also, fell a victim to the fierce
typhus fever only half a year after the death of his
wife. Little Eliza Herbert inherited, with her mother's beauty, her constitutional delicacy. Her figure
was so slight, that it almost suggested to the beholder
the idea of transparency; and there was a softness
and languor in her azure eyes, beaming through their
 ong silken lashes, which told of something too refined
for humanity. Her disposition fully comported with
her person and habits—arch, mild, and intelligent,
with a little dash of pensiveness. She loved the
shade of retirement. If she occasionally flitted for
a moment into the world, its glare and uproar seemed
almost to stun her gentle spirit. She was, almost
from infancy, devotedly fond of reading; and sought
with peculiar avidity books of sentiment. Her gifted
preceptress, one of the most amiable and refined of
women, soon won her entire confidence, and found
little difficulty in imparting to her apt pupil all the
stores of her own superior and extensive accomplishments. Not a day passed over that did not find Eliza
Herbert riveted more firmly in the hearts of all who
came near her, from her doting uncle down to the
most distant domestic. Every luxury that wealth
and power could procure was, of course, always at
her command; her own innate propriety and just
taste prompted her to prefer simplicity in all things.
Fla tery of all kinds she abhorred; and forsoo: the
house of a rich old English lady, who once told her
to her face she was a beautiful little angel! In
short, a more sweet, lovely, and amiable being than
Eliza Herbert never adorned the ranks of humanity.
The only fear which incessantly haunted those around
her, and kept Sir —— in a feverish flutter of apprehension every day of his life, was, that his niece

was, in his own words, "too good—too beautiful,
for this world;" and that unseen messengers from
above were already flitting around her, ready to
claim her suddenly for the skies. He has often described to me his feelings on this subject.   He
seemed conscious that he had no *right* to reckon on
the continuance of her life; he felt, whenever he
thought of her, an involuntary apprehension that
she would, at no distant period, suddenly fade from
his sight; he was afraid, he said, to let out the whole
of his heart's affections on her. Like the oriental
merchant, who shudders while freighting "one bark
—one little, fragile bark," with the dazzling stores
of his immense ALL, and committing it to the capri-
cious dominion of wind and waves,—so Sir ——
often declared, that at the period I am alluding to,
he experienced cruel misgivings, that if he embarked
the whole of his soul's loves on little Eliza Herbert,
they were fated to be shipwrecked. Yet he regarded
her every day with feelings which soon heightened
into absolute idolatry.

His fond anxieties soon suggested to him that so
delicate and fragile a being as his niece, supposing
for a moment the existence of any real grounds of
apprehension that her constitution bore an hereditary
taint, could not be thrown into a directer path for
her grave than in India; that any latent, lurking
tendency to consumption would be quickened and
developed with fatal rapidity in the burning atmosphere she was then breathing. His mind, once
thoroughly suffused with alarms of this sort, could
not ever afterward be dispossessed of them; and he
accordingly determined to relinquish his situation in
India the instant he should have realized, from one
quarter or another, sufficient to enable him to return
to England, and support an establishment suitable
to his station in society. About five years had
elapsed since his arrival in India, during which he
had contrived to save a large portion of his very

ample income when news reached him that a considerable fortune had fallen to him, from the sudden death of a remote relation. The intelligence made him comparatively a happy man. He instantly set on foot arrangements for returning to England, and procuring the immediate appointment of his successor.

Unknown to his niece, about a year after his arrival in India, Sir —— had confidentially consulted the most eminent physician on the spot. In obedience to the injunctions of the baronet, Dr. C—— was in the habit of dropping in frequently, as if accidentally, *to dinner*, for the purpose of marking Miss Herbert's demeanour, and ascertaining whether there was, so to speak, the very faintest adumbration of any consumptive tendency. But no—his quick and practised eye detected no morbid indications; and he reiteratedly gladdened the baronet's heart, by assuring him that, in any present evidence to the contrary, little Miss Herbert bade as fair for long and healthy life as any woman breathing, especially if she soon returned to the more salubrious climate of England. Though Dr. C—— had never spoken professionally to her, Eliza Herbert was too quick and shrewd an observer to continue unapprized of the object of his frequent visits to her uncle's house. She had not failed to notice his searching glances; and knew well that he watched almost every mouthful of food she eat, and scrutinized all her movements. He had once also ventured to feel her pulse, in a half-in-earnest, half-in-joke manner, and put one or two questions to the governess about Miss Herbert's general habits, which that good, easy, communicative creature unfortunately told her inquisitive little pupil. Now, there are few things more alarming and irritating to young people, even if consciously enjoying the most robust health, than suddenly to find that they have long been, and still are, the objects of anxious medical *surveillance*. They begin naturally to suspect that there must be very good reason for it, and especially in the case of nervous, irritable temperaments; their peace of mind is thenceforward destroyed by torturing apprehensions that they are the doomed victims of some insidious, incurable malady.   I have often and often known illustrations of this.   Sir —— also was aware of its ill consequences, and endeavoured to avert even the shadow of a suspicion from his niece's mind as to the real object of Dr. C——'s visits, by formally introducing him, from the first, as one of his own intimate friends He therefore flattered himself that his niece was profoundly ignorant of the existence of his anxieties concerning her health; and was not a little startled one morning by Miss Herbert's abruptly entering his study, and, pale with ill-disguised anxiety, inquiring if there was " any thing the matter with her."   Was she unconsciously *falling into a decline?* she asked, almost in so many words.   Her uncle was so confounded by the suddenness of the affair, that he lost his presence of mind, changed colour a little, and, with a consciously embarrassed air, assured her that it was " no such thing,"—" quite a mistake—a very ridiculous one,"—" a childish whim," &c. &c. &c He was so *very* earnest and energetic in his assurances that there was no earthly ground for apprehension, and, in short, concealed his alarm so clumsily, that his poor niece, though she left him with a kiss and a smile, and affected to be satisfied, retired to her own room, and from that melancholy moment resigned herself to her grave.   Of this she herself, three years subsequently, in England, assured me. She never afterward recovered that gentle buoyancy and elasticity of spirits which made her burst upon her few friends and acquaintance like a little lively sunbeam of cheerfulness and gayety.   She felt perpetually haunted by gloomy though vague suspicions that there was something *radically wrong* in her constitution; that it was from her birth sow-with the seeds of death; and that no earthly power could eradicate them. Though she resigned herse.f to the dominion of such harassing thoughts as these while alone, and even shed tears abundantly, she succeeded in banishing, to a great extent, her uncle's disquietude, by assuming even greater gayety of demeanour than before. The baronet took occasion to mention the little incident above related to Dr. C——; and was excessively agitated to see the physician assume a very serious air.

"This may be attended with more mischief than you are aware of, Sir ——," he replied. "I feel it my duty to tell you how miserably unfortunate for her it is that Miss Herbert has at last detected your restless uneasiness about her health, and the means you have taken to watch her constitution. Henceforward she may *appear* satisfied—but mark her if she can forget it. You will find her fall frequently into momentary fits of absence and thoughtfulness. She will brood over it," continued Dr. C——.

"Why, good God! doctor," replied the baronet, "what's the use of frightening one thus? Do you think my niece is the first girl who has known that her friends are anxious about her health? If she is really, as you tell her, free from disease—why, the devil!—can she *fancy* herself into a consumption?"

"No, no, Sir ——; but incessant alarm may accelerate the evil you dread, and predispose her to sink, her energies to droop, under the blow—however lightly it may at first fall—which has been so long impending. And besides, Sir ——, I did *not* say she was free from disease, but only that I had not discerned any present *symptoms* of disease."

"Oh, stuff, stuff, doctor! nonsense!" muttered the baronet, rising, and pacing the room with excessive agitation. "Can't the girl be *laughed* out of her fears?"

It may be easily believed that Sir —— spent every future moment of his stay in India in an agony of

apprehension. His fears exaggerated the slightest
indication of his niece's temporary indisposition into
a symptom of consumption; any thing like a cough
from her would send him to a pillow of thorns; and
her occasional refusal of food at meal-times was received with undisguised trepidation on the part of
her uncle. If he overtook her at a distance, walking
out with her governess, he would follow unperceived
and strain his eyesight with endeavouring to detec.
any thing like feebleness in her gait. These incessant and very natural anxieties about the only being
he loved in the world, enhanced by his efforts to
conceal them, sensibly impaired his own health and
spirits. He grew fretful and irritable in his demean
our towards every member of his establishment
and could not completely fix his thoughts for the
transaction of his important official business.

This may be thought an overstrained representa-
tion of Sir ——'s state of mind respecting his niece;
but by none except a young, thoughtless, or heartless
reader. Let the thousand—the million heart-wrung
parents who have mourned, and are now mourning,
over their consumptive offspring—let *them*, I say,
echo the truth of the sentiments I am expressing.
Let those whose bitter fate it is to see

"The bark, so richly freighted with their love,"

gradually sinking, shipwrecked before their very
eyes, say whether the pen or tongue of man can fur
nish adequate words to give expression to their anguished feelings!

———

Eighteen years of age, within a trifle, was Miss
Herbert when she again set foot on her native land,
and the eyes and heart of her idolizing uncle leaped
for joy to see her augmented health and loveliness,
which he fondly flattered himself might now be
destined to

'Grow w th her growth, and strengthen with her strength'

The voyage, though long and monotonous as usual, with its fresh breezy balminess, had given an impetus to her animated spirits; and as her slight figure stepped down the side of the gloomy colossal Indiaman which had brought her across the seas, her blue eye was bright as that of a seraph; her beauteous cheeks glowed with a soft and rich crimson, and there was a lightness, ease, and elasticity in her movements, as she tripped the short distance between the vessel and the carriage which was in waiting to convey them to town, that filled her doting uncle with feelings of almost phrensied joy.

"God Almighty bless thee, my darling! Bless thee—bless thee for ever, my pride! my jewel!—Long and happy be thy life in merry England!" sobbed the baronet, folding her almost convulsively in his arms as soon as they were seated in the carriage, and giving her the first kiss of welcome to her native shores. The second day after they were established at one of the hotels, while Miss Herbert and her governess were riding the round of fashionable shopping, Sir —— drove alone to the late Dr Baillie. In a long interview (they were personal friends) he communicated all his distressing apprehensions about his niece's state of health, imploring him to say whether he had any real cause of alarm whatever, immediate or prospective; and what course and plan of life he would recommend for the future. Dr. Baillie, after many and minute inquiries, contented himself with saying, that he saw no grounds for *present* apprehensions. "It certainly did *sometimes* happen, that a delicate daughter of a consumptive parent inherited her mother's tendencies to disease," he said. "And as for her future life and habits, there was not the slightest occasion for medicine of any kind; she must live almost entirely in the country, take plenty of fresh dry air and exercise—especially eschew late hours and company;" and he hinted, finally, the advantages, and almost a necessity, of an early matrimonial engagement.

It need hardly be said that Sir —— resolved most religiously to follow this advice to the letter

"I'll come and dine with you in Dover-street, at seven to-day," said Dr. Baillie, "and make my own observations."

"Thank you, doctor—but—but we dine out to-day," muttered the baronet, rather faintly, adding, inwardly, "no, no!—no more medical *espionage*—no, no!"

Sir —— purchased a very beautiful mansion, which then happened to be for sale, situated within ten or twelve miles of London; and thither he removed as soon as ever the preliminary arrangements could be completed.

The shrine and its divinity were worthy of each other. —— Hall was one of the most charming, picturesque residences in the county. It was a fine, antique, semi-Gothic structure, almost obscured from sight in the profound gloom of forest shade. The delicious velvet greensward, spread immediately in front of the house, seemed formed for the gentle foot steps of Miss Herbert. When you went there, if you looked carefully about, you might discover a little white tuft glistening on some part or other of the " smooth, soft-shaven lawn:" it was her pet lamb, cropping the crisp and rich herbage. Little thing! it would scarce submit to be fondled by any hand but that of its innocent indulgent mistress. She also might occasionally be seen there, wander-ing thoughtfully along, with a book in her hand—Tasso, probably, or Dante—and her loose light hair straying from beneath a gipsy bonnet, commingling in pleasant contact with a saffron-coloured riband. Her uncle would sit for an hour together, at a corner of his study-window, overlooking the lawn, and never remove his eyes from the figure of his fair niece.

Miss Herbert was now talked of every wheie in the neighbourhood as the pride of the place—the star of the county. She budded forth almost visibly and though her exquisite form was developing daily, till her matured womanly proportions seemed to have been cast in the mould of the Venus de Medici, though on a scale of more slenderness and delicacy, it was, nevertheless, outstripped by the precocious expanding of her intellect. The sympathies of her soul were attuned to the deepest and most refined sentiment. She was passionately fond of poetry, and never wandered without the sphere of what was first-rate. Dante and Milton were her constant companions by day and night; and it was a treat to hear the mellifluous cadences of·the former uttered by the soft and rich voice of Miss Herbert. She could not more satisfactorily evidence her profound appreciation of the true spirit of poetry than by her almost idolatrous admiration of the kindred genius of Handel and Mozart. She was scarcely ever known to play any other music than theirs; she would listen to none but the "mighty voices of those dim spirits." And then she was the most amiable and charitable creature that sure ever trod the earth! How many colds,—slight, to be sure, and evanescent,—had she caught, and how many rebukes from the alarmed fondness of her uncle had she suffered in conse quence, through her frequent visits, in all weathers, to the cottages of the poor and sick !—" You are describing an *ideal* being, and investing it with all the graces and virtues—one that never really existed," perhaps exclaims one of my readers. There are not a few now living who could answer for the truth of my poor and faint description with anguish and regret. Frequently, on seeing such instances of precocious developement of the powers of both mind and body, the curt and correct expression of Quintilian has occurred to my mind with painful force— " Quod observatum fere est, celerius occidere *festi-*

*natam maturn ttes :"** aptly rendered by the English proverb, "Soon ripe, soon rotten."

The latter part of Dr. Baillie's advice was anxiously kept in view by Sir ——; and soon after Miss Herbert had completed her twentieth year, he had the satisfaction of seeing her encourage the attentions of a Captain ——, the third son of a neighbouring nobleman. He was a remarkably fine and handsome young man, of a very superior spirit, and fully capable of appreciating the value of her whose hand he sought. Sir —— was delighted almost to ecstasy when he extracted from the trembling, blushing girl a confession that Captain ——'s company was any thing but disagreeable to her. The young military hero was, of course, soon recognised as her suitor; and a handsome couple, people said, they would make. Miss Herbert's health seemed more robust, and her spirits more buoyant than ever. How, indeed, could it be otherwise, when she was daily riding in an open carriage, or on horseback, over a fine, breezy, champaign country, by the side of the gay, handsome fascinating Captain ——?

The baronet was sitting one morning in his study, having the day before returned from a month's visit to some friends in Ireland, and engaged with some important letters from India, when Miss B——, his niece's governess, sent a message requesting to speak in private with him. When she entered, her embarrassed and somewhat flurried manner not a little surprised Sir ——.

"How is Eliza?—How is Eliza, Miss B——?" he inquired hastily, laying aside his reading-glasses. "Very well," she replied, "very;" and after a little fencing about the necessity of making allowance for the exaggeration of alarm and anxiety, she proceeded to inform him, that Miss Herbert had latterly passed

* De Inst. Orat. lib. iv   In proemio

~stless nights; that her sleep was not unfrequently broken by a cough—a sort of faint *churchyard* cough, she said, it seemed—which had not been noticed for some time, till it was accompanied by other symptoms—— "Gracious God! madam, how was this not told me before? Why—why did you not write to me in Ireland about it?" inquired Sir ——, with excessive trepidation. He could scarcely sit in his chair, and grew very pale; while Miss B——, herself equally agitated, went on to mention profuse night-sweats, a disinclination for food, exhaustion from the slightest exercise, a feverishness every evening, and a faint hectic flush—

"Oh, *plague-spot!*" groaned the baronet, almost choked, letting fall his reading-glasses. He tottered towards the bell, and the valet was directed to order the carriage for town immediately. " What—wha possible excuse can I devise for bringing Dr. Baillie here?" said he to the governess, as he was drawing on his gloves. " Well, well, I'll leave it to you; do what you can. For God's sake, madam, prepare her to see him somehow or another, for the doctor and I shall certainly be here together this evening. Oh! —say I'm called up to town on sudden business, and thought I might as well bring him on with me, as he is visiting a patient in the neighbourhood. Oh, any thing, madam, any thing!" He hardly knew what he was saying.

Dr. Baillie, however, could not come, being himself at Brighton an invalid, and the baronet was therefore pleased, though with ill-disguised chagrin, to summon me to supply his place. On my way down, he put me in possession of most of the facts above narrated. He implored me, in tenderness to his agitated feelings, to summon all the tact I had ever acquired, and alarm the object of my visit as little as possible. I was especially to guard against appearing to know too much; I was to beat about the bush—to extract her symptoms gradually, &c

&c. I never saw the fondest, the most doting father
or mother more agitated about an only child than
was Sir —— about his niece. He protested that he
could not survive her death; that she was the only
prop and pride of his declining years, and that he
must fall if he lost her; and made use of many similar expressions. It was in vain that I besought him
not to allow himself to be carried so much away
with his fears. He must let me see her, and have
an opportunity of judging whether there were any
real cause of alarm, I said; and he might rely on
my honour as a gentleman, that I would be frank
and candid with him to the very utmost—I would
tell him the worst. I reminded him of the possibility that the symptoms he mentioned might not really
exist; that they might have been seen by Miss B——
through the distorting and magnifying medium of
apprehension; and that, even if they did *really* exist
—why, that—that—they were not *always* the pre-
cursors of consumption, I stammered, against my
own convictions. It is impossible to describe the
emotions excited in the baronet by my simple uttering the word "consumption." He said it stabbed
him through the heart!

On arriving at —— Hall, the baronet and I instantly repaired to the drawing-room, where Miss
Herbert and her governess were sitting at tea. The
pensive sunlight of September shone through the
Gothic window near which they were sitting. Miss
Herbert was dressed in white, and looked really
dazzlingly beautiful; but the first transient glance
warned me that the worst might be apprehended. I
had that very morning been at the bedside of a dying
young lady, a martyr to that very disease, which
commenced by investing its victim with a tenfold
splendour of personal beauty, to be compensated for
by sudden and rapid decay! Miss Herbert's eyes
were lustrous as diamonds; and the complexion of
her cheeks, pure and fair as that of the lily, was sur-

mounted with an intense, circumscribed, crimson flush—alas, alas! the very "plague-spot" of hectic—of consumption. She saluted me silently, and her eyes glanced hurriedly from me to her uncle, and from him again to me. His disordered air defied disguise.

She was evidently apprized of my coming, as well as of the occasion of my visit. Indeed, there was a visible embarrassment about all four of us, which I felt I was expected to dissipate by introducing indifferent topics of conversation. This I attempted, but with little success. Miss Herbert's tea was before her, on a little ebony stand, untouched; and it was evidently a violent effort only that enabled her to continue in the room. She looked repeatedly at Miss B——, as though she wished to be gone. After about half an hour's time, I alluded complimentarily to what I had heard of her performance on the piano; she smiled coldly and rather contemptuously, as though she saw the part I was playing. Nothing daunted, however, I begged her to favour me with one of Haydn's sonatas; and she went immediatel to the piano, and played what I asked—I need hardly say, very exquisitely. Her uncle then withdrew, for the alleged purpose of answering a letter, as had been arranged between us; and I was then left alone with the two ladies. I need not fatigue the reader with a minute description of all that passed. I introduced the object of my visit as casually and gently as I could, and succeeded more easily than I had anticipated in quieting her alarms. The answers she gave to my questions amply corroborated the truth of the account given by Miss B—— to the baronet. Her feverish accelerated pulse, also, told of the hot blighting breathings of the destroying angel, who was already hovering close around his victim! I was compelled to smile with an assumed air of gayety and nonchalance, while listening to the poor girl's unconscious disclosures of various little

I.—M

matters, which amounted to infallible evidence that she was already beyond the reach of medicine. I bade her adieu, complimenting her on her charming looks, and expressing my delight at finding so little occasion for my professional services! She looked at me with a half-incredulous, half-confiding eye, and with much girlish simplicity and frankness put her hand into mine, thanking me for dispersing her fears, and begging me to do the same for her uncle. I afterward learned, that as soon as I left the room, she burst into a flood of tears, and sighed and sobbed all the rest of the evening.

With Sir —— I felt it my duty to be candid. Why should I conceal the worst from him, when I felt as certain as I was of my own existence that his beautiful niece was already beginning to wither away from before his eyes? Convinced that "hope deferred maketh sick the heart," I have always in such cases warned the patient's friends, long beforehand, of the inevitable fate awaiting the object of their anxious hopes and fears, in order that resignation might gradually steal thoroughly into their broken hearts.—To return. I was conducted to the baronet's study, where he was standing with his hat and gloves on, ready to accompany me as far as the high road, in order that I might wait the arrival of a London coach. I told him, in short, that I feared I had seen and heard too much to allow a doubt that his niece's present symptoms were those of the commencing stage of pulmonary consumption; and that though medicine and change of climate might possibly avert the evil day for a time, it was my melancholy duty to assure him that no earthly power could save her.

"Merciful God!" he gasped, loosing his arm from mine, and leaning against the park gate, at which we had arrived. I implored him to be calm. He continued speechless for some time, with his hands clasped.

"Oh, doctor, doctor!" he exclaimed, as if a gleam of hope had suddenly flashed across his mind, "we've forgot to tell you a most material thing, which perhaps will alter the whole case—oh, how could we have forgotten it!" he continued, growing heated with the thought; "my niece *eats* very heartily—nay, more heartily than any of us, and seems to relish her food more." Alas! I was obliged, as I have hundreds of times before been obliged, to dash the cup from his lips, by assuring him that an almost *ravenous* appetite was as invariably a forerunner of consumption as the pilot-fish of the shark!

"Oh, great God, what will become of me! What shall I do?" he exclaimed, almost frantic, and wringing his hands in despair. He had lost every vestige of self-control. "Then my sweet angel must DIE! Damning thought!. Oh, let me die too! I cannot, I will not survive her!—Doctor, doctor, you must give up your London practice, and come and live in my house—you must! By G—, I'll fling my whole fortune at your feet! Only save her, and you and yours shall wallow in wealth, if I go back to India to procure it!—Oh, whither—whither shall I go with my darling? To Italy—France?—My God! what shall I do when she is *gone* for ever!" he exclaimed, like one distracted. I entreated him to recollect himself, and endeavour to regain his self-possession before returning to the presence of his niece. He started. "Oh, mockery, doctor, mockery! How can I ever look on the dear girl again? She is no longer mine; she is in her grave—she is!"

Remonstrance and expostulation, I saw, were utterly useless, and worse, for they served only to irritate. The coach shortly afterward drew up; and, wringing my hands, Sir —— extorted a promise that I would see his niece the next day, and bring Dr. Baillie with me, if he should have returned to town. I was as good as my word, except that Dr. Baillie could not accompany me, being still at Brighton

My second interview with Miss Herbert was long,
and painfully interesting.   She and I were alone.
She wept bitterly, and recounted the incident before
mentioned which occurred in India, and occasioned
her first serious alarm.   She felt convinced, she told
me, that her case was hopeless; she saw, too, that
her uncle possessed a similar conviction, and sobbed
agonizingly when she alluded to his altered looks.
She had felt a presentiment, she said, for some
months past, which, however, she had never mentioned till then, that her days were numbered; and
attributed, too truly, her accelerated illness to the
noxious clime of India.   She described her sensations to be that of a constant void within, as if there
were a something wanting—an unnatural hollowness
—a dull, deep aching in the left side—a frequent inclination to relieve herself by spitting, which, when
she did, alas! alas! she observed more than once to
be streaked with blood.

"How long do you think I have to live, doctor?"
she inquired, faintly.

"Oh, my dear madam, do not, for heaven's sake,
ask such useless questions!   How can I possibly
presume to answer them, giving you credit for a
spark of common sense?"   She grew very pale, and
wiped her forehead.

"Is it likely that I shall have to endure much
pain?" she asked, with increasing trepidation.   I
could reply only, that I *hoped* not—that there was
no ground for *immediate* apprehension; and I faltered, that *possibly* a milder climate and the skill of
medicine might yet carry her through.   The poor
girl shook her head hopelessly, and trembled vio
lently from head to foot.

"Oh, poor uncle!—Poor, poor Edw——."   She
faltered, and fell fainting into my arms; for the latter
allusion to Captain —— had completely overcome
her.   Holding her senseless, sylphlike figure in my
arms, I hurried to the bell, and was immediately

joined by Sir ——, the governess. and one or two female attendants. I saw the baronet was beginning to behave like a madman, by the increasing boisterousness of his manner, and the occasional glare of wildness that shot from his eye. With the utmost difficulty I succeeded in forcing him from the room, and keeping him out till Miss Herbert had recovered.

"Oh, doctor, doctor!" be muttered hoarsely, after staggering to a seat, "this is worse than death. I pray God to take her and me, too, and put an end to our misery!"

I expostulated with him rather sternly, and represented to him the absurdity and impiousness of his wish.

"D—n—n!" he thundered, starting from his chair, and stamping furiously to and fro across the room. "What the —— do you mean by snivelling in that way, doctor? Can I see my darling dying—absolutely dying by inches—before my very eyes, and yet be cool and unconcerned? I did not expect such conduct from you, doctor;"—he burst into tears. "Oh! I'm going mad!—I'm going mad!" and he sunk again into his seat. From one or two efforts be made to gulp down again, as it were, the emotions which were swelling and dilating his whole frame, I seriously apprehended either that he would fall into a fit or go absolutely raving mad. Happily, however, I was mistaken. His fearful excitement gradually subsided. He was a man of remarkably strong and ardent feelings, which he had never been accustomed to control even in the moments of thei most violent manifestations; and on the present occasion, the maddening thought that the object cf his long, intense, and idolizing love and pride was about to be lost to him irretrievably—for ever—was sufficient to overturn his shaken intellects. I prevailed upon him to continue where he was till 1 returned from his niece for I was summoned to her chamber. I found her lying on the bed, only partially undressed. Her beautiful auburn hair hung disordered over her neck and shoulders, partially concealing her lovely marble-hued features. Her left hand covered her eyes, and her right clasped a little locket, suspended round her neck by a plain black riband, containing a little of Captain ——'s hair. Miss B——, her governess, her maid, and the housekeeper, with tears and sobs, were engaged in rendering various little services to their unfortunate young mistress; and my heart ached to think of the little—the nothing—*I* could do for her.

Two days afterward, Dr. Baillie, another physician, and myself, went down to see Miss Herbert; for a note from Miss B—— informed me that her ward had suffered severely from the agitation experienced at the last visit I had paid her, and was in a low nervous fever. The consumptive symptoms, also, were beginning to gleam through the haze of accidental indisposition with fearful distinctness. Dr. Baillie simply assured the baronet that my predictions were but too likely to be verified; and that the only chance of averting the worst form of consumption (a galloping one) would be an instant removal to Italy, that the fall of the year and the winter season might be spent in a more genial and fostering climate. We, at the same time, frankly assured Sir ——, who listened with a sullen, despairing apathy of manner, that the utmost he had to expect from a visit to Italy was the faintest chance of a temporary suspension of the fate which hovered over his niece. In a few weeks, accordingly, they were all settled at Naples.

But what have I to say, all this time, the reader is possibly asking, about the individual who was singled out by fate for the first and heaviest stroke inflicted by Miss Herbert's approaching dissolution? Where was the lover? Where was Captain ——? I have avoided allusions to him hitherto. because his distress and agitation transcended all my powers of description. He loved Miss Herbert with all the passionate romantic fervour of a first attachment; and the reader must ask his own heart what were the feelings by which that of Captain —— was lacerated.

I shall content myself with recording one little incident which occurred before the family of Sir —— left for Italy. I was retiring one night to rest, about twelve o'clock, when the startling summons of the night-bell brought me again down-stairs, accompanied by a servant. Thrice the bell rung with impatient violence before the door could possibly be opened, and I heard the steps of some vehicle let down hastily.

"Is Dr. —— at home?" inquired a groom, and being answered in the affirmative, in a second or two a gentleman leaped from the chariot standing at the door, and hurried into the room whither I had retired to await him. He was in a sort of half-military travelling dress. His face was pale, his eye sunk, his air disordered, and his voice thick and flurried. It was Captain ——, who had been absent on a shooting excursion in Scotland, and who had not received intelligence of the alarming symptoms disclosed by Miss Herbert till within four days of that which found him at my house, on the present occasion, come to ascertain from me the *reality* of the melancholy apprehensions so suddenly entertained by Sir —— and the other members of both families.

"Good God! is there no hope, doctor?" he inquired, faintly, after swallowing a glass of wine, which, seeing his exhaustion and agitation, I had sent for. I endeavoured to evade giving a direct answer—attempted to divert his thoughts towards the projected trip to the continent—dilated on the soothing, balmy climate she would have to breathe —it *had* done wonders for others, &c. &c.; and, in a word, exhausted the stock of inefficient subterfuges and palliatives to which all professional men are on such occasions compelled to resort. Captain —— listened to me silently, while his eye was fixed on me with a vacant unobserving stare. His utter wretchedness touched me to the soul; and yet what consolation had I to offer him? After several profound sighs, he exclaimed, in a flurried tone, " I see how it is. Her fate is fixed, and so is mine! Would to God—would to God I had never seen or known Miss Herbert!—*What* will become of us!" He rose to go. " Doctor, forgive me for troubling you so late, but really I can rest nowhere! I must go back to —— Hall." I shook hands with him, and in a few moments the chariot dashed off.

Really I can scarcely conceive of a more dreadful state of mind than that of Captain ——, or of any one whose "heart is in the right place," to use a homely but apt expression, when placed in such wretched circumstances as those above related. To see the death-warrant sealed of her a man's soul dotes on—who is the idolized object of his holiest, fondest, and possibly *first* affections!—yes, to see her bright and beautiful form suddenly snatched down into " utter darkness" by the cold, relentless grasp of our common foe—the " desire of our eyes taken away as with a stroke"—may well wither one! That man's soul which would not be palsied. prostrated by such a stroke as this is worthless. and worse—it is a foul libel on his kind. He cannot *love* a woman as she should and must be loved. Why am I so vehement in expressing my feelings on this subject? Because in the course of my professional intercourse my soul has been often sick- ened with listening to the expression of opposite sentiments. The poor and pitiful *philosophy*—that the word should ever have been so prostituted!— which is now sneaking in among us, fostered by foolish ears, and men with hollow hearts and barren brains. for the purpose of weeding out from the soul's garden its richest and choicest flowers, sympathy and sentiment—*this* philosophy may possibly prompt some reader to sneer over the agonies I have been attempting to describe; but, oh, reader, do you eschew it—trample on it—trample on it whenever, wherever you find it, for the reptile, though very little, is very venomous.

Captain ——'s regiment was ordered to Ireland; and as he found it impossible to accompany it, he sold out, and presently followed the heart-broken baronet and his niece to Italy. The delicious climate sufficed to kindle and foster for a while that deceitful *ignis fatuus*, hope, which always flits before in the gloomy horizon of consumptive patients, and leads them and their friends on—and on—and on— till it suddenly sinks quivering into their grave!— They staid at Naples till the month of July. Miss Herbert was sinking, and that with fearfully accelerated rapidity. Sir ——'s health was much impaired with incessant anxiety and watching; and Captain —— had been several times on the very borders of madness. His love for the dear being who could never be his increased ten thousand fold when he found it hopeless!—Is it not always so?

Aware that her days were numbered, Miss Herbert anxiously importuned her uncle to return to England. She wished, she said, to breathe her last in her native isle, among the green pastures and hills of ——shire, and to be buried with her father and mother. Sir —— listened to the utterance of these sentiments with a breaking heart. He could see no reason for refusing a compliance with her request; and accordingly the latter end of August beheld the unhappy family once more at —— Hall.

I once saw a very beautiful lily, of rather more than ordinary stateliness, whose stem had been snapped by the storm over-night; and on entering my garden in the morning, alas, alas! there lay the pride of all chaste flowers, pallid and prostrate on

the very bed where it had a short while before
bloomed so sweetly! This little circumstance was
forcibly recalled to my recollection on seeing Miss
Herbert fo the first time after her return from the
continent. It was in the spacious drawing-room at
—— Hall, where I had before seen her in the evening; and she was reclining on an ottoman, which
had been drawn towards the large fretted Gothic
window formerly mentioned. I stole towards it
with noiseless footsteps, for the hushing, cautioning
movements of those present warned me that Miss
Herbert was asleep. I stood and gazed in silence
for some moments on the lovely unfortunate, almost
afraid to disturb her even by breathing. She was
wasted almost to a shadow,—attenuated to nearly
ethereal delicacy and transparency. She was dressed
in a plain white muslin gown, and lying on an Indian
shawl, in which she had been enveloped for the purpose of being brought down from her bedchamber.
Her small foot and ankle were concealed beneath
white silk stockings and satin slippers, through
which it might be seen how they were shrunk from
the full dimensions of health. They seemed, indeed,
rather the exquisite chiselling of Canova, the repre-
sentation of recumbent beauty, than flesh and blood,
and scarcely capable of sustaining even the slight
pressure of Miss Herbert's wasted frame. The arms
and hands were enveloped in long white gloves,
which fitted very loosely; and her waist, encircled
by a broad violet-coloured riband, was rather that
of a young girl of twelve or thirteen than a full-
grown woman. But it was her countenance—her
symmetrical features, sunk, faded, and damp with
death-dews, and her auburn hair falling in rich, mat
'ed, careless clusters down each side of her alabaster
temples and neck—it was all this which suggested
the bitterest thoughts of blighted beauty, almost
breaking the heart of the beholder. Perfectly mo·
.enless and statuelike lay that fair creature, breath

ing so imperceptibly that a rose-leaf might have slept on her lips unfluttered. On an easy-chair, drawn towards the head of the ottoman, sat her uncle, Sir ——, holding a white cambric handkcr-chief in his hand, with which he from time to time wiped off the dews which started out incessantly on his niece's pallid forehead. It was affecting to see his hair changed to a dull iron-gray hue; whereas, before he had left for the continent, it was jet-black His sallow and worn features bore the traces of recent tears.

And where *now* is the lover? Where is Captain ——? again inquires the reader. He was then at Milan, raving beneath the tortures and delirium of a brain-fever, which flung him on his sick-bed only the day before Sir ——'s family set out for England. Miss Herbert had not been told of the circumstance till she arrived at home; and those who communi-cated the intelligence will never undertake such a duty again!

After some time, in which we around had main tained perfect silence, Miss Herbert gently opened her eyes; and seeing me sitting opposite her uncle, by her side, gave me her hand, and with a faint smile, whispered some words of welcome which I could not distinguish.

"Am I much altered, doctor, since you saw me last?" she presently inquired, in a more audible tone I said I regretted to see her so feeble and emaciated.

"And does not my poor uncle also look very ill?" inquired the poor girl, eying him with a look of sor-rowful fondness. She feebly extended her arms, as if for the purpose of putting them round his neck, and he seized and kissed them with such fervou. that she burst into tears. "Your kindness is killing me; oh, don't, don't!" she murmured. He was so overpowered with his emotions, that he abruptly rose and left the room. I then made many minute inquiries about the state of her health. I could hardly detect any pulsation at the wrist, though the blue veins and almost the arteries, 1 fancied, might be seen meandering beneath the transparent skin. * * * My feelings will not allow me, nor would my space, to describe every interview I had with her. She sunk very rapidly. She exhibited all those sudden deceitful rallyings which invariably agonize consumptive patients and their friends with fruitless hopes of recovery. Oh, how they are clung to! how hard to persuade their fond hearts to relinquish them! with what despairing obstinacy will they persist in "hoping against hope!" I recollect one evening, in particular, that her shattered energies were so un-accountably revived and collected—her eye grew so full and bright—her cheeks were suffused with so rich a vermilion—her voice soft and sweet as ever, and her spirits so exhilarated—that even *I* was stag-gered for a moment; and poor Sir —— got so ex-cited, that he said to me in a sort of ecstasy, as he accompanied me to my carriage, "Ah, doctor, *a phœnix*, doctor! a phœnix. She's rising from her ashes—ah! ha! She'll cheat you for once—darling!" and he raised his handkerchief to his eyes, for they were overflowing.

"Doctor, you're fond of music, I believe; you will not have any objection to listen to a little now, will you? I'm exactly in the mood for it, and it's almost the only enjoyment I have left, and Miss B—— plays enchantingly. Go, love, please, and play a mass from Mozart—the one we listened to last night," said Miss Herbert, on one occasion, about a week after the interview last mentioned. Miss B——, who was in tears, immediately rose, and took her seat at the piano. She played with exquisite taste and skill I held one of my sweet patient's hands in mine, as she lay on the sofa, with her face turned towards the window, through which the retiring sunlight was streaming in tender radiance on her wasted features, after tinting the amber-hued groves which were

visible through the window. I need not attempt to
characterize the melting music which Miss B——
was pouring from the piano. I have often thought
that there is a sort of *spiritual*, unearthly character
about some of the masses of Mozart, which draws
out the greatest sympathies of one's nature, striking
the deepest and most hidden chords of the human
heart. On the present occasion, the peculiar circumstances in which I was placed—the time—the
place—the dying angel whose hand was clasped in
mine—disposed me to a more intense appreciation
of Mozart's music than I had ever known before.
The soft, soothing, solemn, swelling cadences undulated one after another into my full heart, till they
forced the tears to gush from my eyes. I was utterly
overcome. Oh, that languishing, heart-breaking
music I can never forget! the form of Eliza Herbert
flits before me to this day when I hear it spoken of.
I will not listen to any one *play* it now; though I
have often wept since on hearing it from Miss B——,
to whom Miss Herbert bequeathed her piano.—To
return. My tears flowed fast; and I perceived also
the crystal drops oozing through the closed eyelids
of Miss Herbert. "Heart-breaking music, is it not,
doctor?" she murmured. I could make her no reply.
I felt at that moment as if I could have laid down
my life for her. After a long pause, Miss B——
continuing all the while playing, Miss Herbert sobbed,
"Oh, how I should like to be buried while the organ
is playing this music! And HE—HE was fond of it,
too!" she continued, with a long, shuddering sigh.
It was echoed, to my surprise, but in a profounder
tone, from that quarter of the room where the grand-
piano was placed. It could not have been from Miss
B——, I felt sure; and looking towards her, I beheld
the dim outline of Sir ——'s figure leaning against
the piano, with his face buried in his white handkerchief. He had stolen into the room unperceived—
for he had left it half an hour before, in a fit of sudden

agitation—and after continuing about five minutes, was compelled by his feelings again to retire. His sigh and the noise he made in withdrawing had been heard by Miss Herbert.

"Doctor—doctor," she stammered faintly, turning as white as ashes, "who—who is that? what was it?—Oh, dear—it can never be—no—no—it cannot"— and she suddenly fainted. She continued so long insensible that I began to fear it was all over. Gradually, however, she recovered, and was carried up to bed, which she did not leave again for a week.

———

I mentioned, I think, in a former part of this narrative, Miss Herbert's partiality for poetry, and that her readings were confined to that which was of the highest order. While sitting by her bedside, I have heard her utter often very beautiful thoughts, suggested by the bitterness of her own premature fate. All—all are treasured in my heart!

I have not attempted to describe her feelings with reference to Captain ——, simply because I cannot do them justice, without, perhaps, incurring the reader's suspicions that I am slipping into the character of the novelist. She did not know that Captain —— continued yet at death's door at Milan, for we felt bound to spare her feelings. We fabricated a story that he had been summoned into Egypt, to inquire after the fate of a brother who had travelled thither, and whose fate, we said, was doubtful. Poor girl! she believed us at last, and seemed rather inclined to accuse him of unkindness for allowing *any thing* to withdraw him from her side. She never, however, *said* any thing directly of this kind. It is hardly necessary to say that Captain —— never knew of the fiction. I have never, to this day, entirely forgiven myself for the part I took in it.

I found her one morning within a few days of her death wretchedly exhausted both in mind and body. She had passed, as usual, a restless night, unsoothed

..en by the laudanum, which had been administered to her in much larger quantities than her medical attendants had authorized. It had stupified, without at the same time composing and calming her. Poor —poor girl! almost the last remains of her beauty had disappeared. There was a fearful hollowness in her once lovely and blooming cheeks; and her eyes—those bright orbs which had a short while ago dazzled and delighted all they shone upon—were now sunk—quenched—and surrounded by dark halos! She lay with her head buried deep in the pillow, .ier hair folded back, matted with perspirations. Her hands—but I cannot attempt to describe her appearance any further. Sir —— sat by her bedside, as he had sat all through her illness, and was utterly worn out. I occupied the chair allotted to Miss B——, who had just retired to bed, having been up all night. After a long silence, Miss Herbert asked very faintly for some tea, which was presently brought her, and dropped into her mouth by . spoonfuls. Soon after she revived a little, and spoke to me, but in so low a whisper that I had great diffi culty in distinguishing her words. The exertion of utterance, also, was attended with so much evident pain, that I would rather she had continued silent.

"Laudanum—laudanum—laudanum, doctor! They don't give me enough of laudanum!" she muttered. We made her no reply. Presently she began murmuring at intervals somewhat in this strain : " Ah— among the pyramids—looking at them—sketching —ascending them, perhaps—oh! what if they should fall and crush him? Has he found his brother? .On his way—home—sea—ships—ship." Still we did not interrupt her, for her manner indicated only a dim, dreamy sort of half-consciousness. About an hour afterward (why did I linger there, it may be asked, when I could do nothing for her, and could ill spare the time? I know not—I *could* not leave) she again commenced, in a low, moaning, wander-

ing tone: "Uncle! what do you think? Chatterton
—poor, melancholy Chatterton, sat by my side all
night long—in that chair where Dr. —— is sitting
He died of a broken heart—or of my disease—didn't
he?—Wan—wan—sad—cold—ghostly—but so like
a poet!—Oh, how he talked—no one earthly like
him!—His voice was like the mysterious music ol
an Æolian harp—so solemn—soft—stealing!——
* * * He put his icy fingers on my bosom, and said
it must soon be as cold!—But he told me not to be
afraid—nor weep, because I was dying so young—
so early. He said I was a young little rose-tree,
and would have the longer to bloom and blossom
when he came for me." She smiled faintly and
sadly. "Oh, dear, dear!—I wish I had him here
again! But he looks very cold and ghostly—never
moves—nothing rustles—I never hear him come or
go—but I look, and there he is!—and I'm not at all
frightened, for he seems gentle—but I think he can't
be happy—happy—never smiles, never!—— * * *
Dying people see and hear more than others!"

This, I say, is the *substance* of what she uttered.
All she said was pervaded by a sad romance, which
showed that her soul was deeply imbued with poetry.

"Toll!—Toll!—Toll!—How solemn!—White
plumes!—White scarfs!—Hush—'*Earth to earth*'—
oh, dreadful!—It is crumbling on my breast! They
all go—they leave me all—poor, poor Eliza!—They
leave me all alone in the cold church.—*He'll* often
walk in the church by himself—his tears will fall on
the pavement—but *I* shall not hear him—nor see
him!—He will ne—ver see me!—Will the organ
play, I wonder?—It *may* wake me from sleep for a
while!" I listened to all this, and was fit for nothing
the rest of the day. Again—again I saw her, to let
fall tears over the withered petals—the blighted
blossoms of early beauty! It wrung my heart to
see her little more than a breathing corpse. Oh,
the gloom—anguish—desolation, diffused through

—— Hall! It could be *felt*, it *oppressed* you ol entering!

* * * On Saturday morning (the —— day ol November, 18—), I drove down early, having the preceding evening promised to be there as soon as possible the next day. It was a cold, scowling, bitter November morning, and my heart sunk within me as my chariot rattled rapidly along the hard highway towards —— Hall. But I was TOO LATE. The curtain had fallen, and hid poor Eliza Herbert from this world for ever! She had expired about half an hour before my arrival.

As I was returning to town, after attending the funeral of Miss Herbert, full of bitter and sorrowful thoughts, I met a travelling carriage and four thundering down the road. It contained poor Captain ——, his valet, and a young Italian medical attendant, all just returned from the continent. He looked white and wasted. The crape on my hat—my gloves—weepers—mourning suit, told all instantly. I was in a moment at his side, for he had swooned. As for the disconsolate baronet, little remains to be said. He disposed of —— Hall; and, sick of England—ill and irritable—he attempted to regain his Indian appointment, but unsuccessfully; so he betook himself to a solitary house belonging to the family in ——shire; and, in the touching language of one of old, "went on mourning to the end of his days."

The Spectral Dog—an Illusion.

· THE age of ghosts and hobgoblins is gone by, says worthy Dr. Hibbert; and so, after him, says almost everybody now-a-days. These mysterious visitants are henceforth to be resolved into mere optical delusion, acting on an excitable fancy and an irritable nervous temperament; and the report of a real *bona fide* ghost or apparition is utterly scouted *Possibly*

I.—N

this may *not* be going too far, even though it be in the teeth of some of the most stubborn facts that are on record. One or possibly two of this character I may perhaps present to the reader on a future occasion; but at present I shall content myself with relating a very curious and interesting case of acknowledged *optical delusion;* and I have no doubt that many of my medical readers can parallel it with similar occurrences within the sphere of their own observation.

Mr. D—— was a clergyman of the Church of England, educated at Oxford,—a scholar, " a ripe and good one,"—a man of remarkably acute and powerful understanding; but, according to his own account, destitute of even an atom of imagination. He was also an exemplary minister; preached twice willingly every Sunday; and performed all the othei duties of his office with zealous fidelity, and to the full satisfaction of his parishioners. If any man is less likely to be terrified with ghosts, or has less reason to be so, than another, surely it was such a character as Mr. D——.

He had been officiating on Sunday evening for an invalid friend, at the latter's church, a few miles' distance from London, and was walking homewards enjoying the tranquillity of the night, and enlivened by the cheerful beams of the full moon. When at about three miles' distance from town, he suddenly heard, or fancied he heard, immediately behind him, the sound of gasping and panting, as of a dog following at his heels, breathless with running. He looked round on both sides ; but, seeing no dog, thought he must have been deceived, and resumed his walk and meditations. The sound was presently repeated. Again he looked round, but with no better success than before. After a little pause, thinking there was something rather odd about it, it suddenly struck him, that what he had heard was nothing more than the noise of his own hard breathing, or casioned by the insensibly accelerated pace at which he was walking, intent upon some subject which then particularly occupied his thoughts. He had not walked more than ten paces further, when he again heard precisely similar sounds; but with a running accompaniment (if I may be allowed a pun) of the pit-pit-pattering of a dog's feet, following close behind his left side.

"God bless me!" exclaimed Mr. D—— aloud, stopping for the third time, and looking round in all directions, far and near; "why, really, that's *very* odd—very! Surely I could not have been mistaken again?" He continued standing still, wiped his forehead, replaced his hat on his head, and, with a *little* trepidation, resumed his walk, striking his stout black walking-stick on the ground with a certain energy and resoluteness which sufficed in reassuring his own flurried spirits. The next thirty or forty paces of his walk Mr. D—— passed over "*erectis auribus*," and hearing nothing similar to the sounds which had thrice attracted his attention, was relapsing into his meditative mood, when, in a few moments, the noise was repeated, apparently from his right-hand side; and he gave something like a start from the path-side into the road on feeling the calf of his leg brushed past, as he described it, by the shaggy coat of his invisible attendant. He looked suddenly down, and, to his very great alarm and astonishment, beheld the dim outline of a large Newfoundland dog—of a *blue* colour! He moved from the spot where he was standing—the phantom followed him; he rubbed his eyes with his hands, shook his head, and again looked; but there it still was, large as a young calf (to which he himself compared it), and had assumed a more distinct and definite form. The colour, however, continued the same—faint blue. He observed, too, its eyes—like dim-decaying firecoals, as it looked up composedly in his face. He poked about his walking-stick, and

moved it repeatedly through and through the form
of the phantom; but there it continued—indivisible
—impalpable—in short, as much a dog as ever, and
yet the stick traversing its form in every direction,
from the tail to the tip of the nose! Mr. D—— hurried on a few steps, and again looked;—there was
the dog! Now the reader should be informed that
Mr. D—— was a remarkably temperate man, and
had that evening contented himself with a solitary
glass of port by the bedside of his sick brother; so
that there was no room for supposing his perceptions
to have been disturbed with liquor.

"What *can* it be?" thought he, while his heart
knocked rather harder than usual against the bars
of its prison; " oh, it must be an *optical delusion*—
oh, 'tis clearly so! nothing in the world worse!
that's all. How odd!"—and he smiled, he thought,
very unconcernedly; but another glimpse of the
phantom standing by him in blue indistinctness instantly darkened his features with the hue of apprehension. If it really *was* an optical delusion, it was
the most fixed and pertinacious one he ever heard
of! The best part of valour is discretion, says
Shakspeare; and in all things; so, observing a stage
passing by at that moment, to put an end to the
matter, Mr. D——, with a little trepidation in his
tone, ordered it to stop: there was just room for *one*
inside; and in stepped Mr. D——, chuckling at the
cunning fashion after which he had succeeded in
jockeying his strange attendant. Not feeling inclined to talk with the fat woman who sat next him,
squeezing him most unmercifully against the side
of the coach, nor with the elderly grazier-looking
man fronting him, whose large, dirty, top-boots seriously incommoded him, he shut his eyes, that he
might pursue his thoughts undisturbed. After about
five minutes' riding, he suddenly opened his eyes
and the first thing that met them was the figure of

the blue dog, lying stretched in some unaccountable manner at his feet, half under the seat!

"I—I—hope THE DOG does not annoy you, sir?" inquired Mr. D——, a little flustered, of the man opposite, hoping to discern whether the dog chose to be visible to any one else.

"Sir!" exclaimed the person he addressed, staring from a kind of doze, and staring about in the bottom of the coach.

"Lord, sir!" echoed the woman beside him.

"A DOG, sir, did you say?" inquired several, in a breath.

"Oh—nothing—nothing, I assure you. 'Tis a little mistake," replied Mr. D——, with a faint smile; "I—I thought—in short, I find I've been *dreaming;* and I'm sure I beg pardon for disturbing you." Every one in the coach laughed except Mr. D——, whose eyes continued riveted on the dim blue outline of the dog lying motionless at his feet. He was now certain that he was suffering from an optical illusion of some sort or other, and endeavoured to prevent his thoughts from running into an alarmed channel, by striving to engage his faculties with the *philosophy* of the thing. He could make nothing out, however; and the Q.E.D. of his thinkings startled him not a little, when it came in the shape of the large blue dog, leaping at his heels out of the coach when he alighted. Arrived at home, he lost sight of the phantom during the time of supper and the family devotions. As soon as he had extinguished his bedroom candle and got into bed, he was nearly leaping out again on feeling a sensation as if a large dog had jumped on that part of the bed where his feet lay. He *felt* its pressure! He said he was inclined to rise, and make it a subject of special prayer to the Deity. Mrs. D—— asked him what was the matter with him? for he became very cold, and shivered a little. He easily quieted her with saying he felt a little chilled; and as soon

as she was fairly asleep, he got quietly out of bed,
and walked up and down the room. Wherever he
moved he beheld, by the moonlight through the window, the dim dusky outline of the dog, following
wherever he went! Mr. D—— opened the windows,
he did not exactly know why, and mounted the dressing-table for that purpose. On looking down before
he leaped on the floor, there was the dog waiting for
him, squatting composedly on his haunches! There
was no standing this any longer, thought Mr. D——,
delusion or no delusion ; so he ran to the bed, plunged
beneath the clothes, and, thoroughly frightened,
dropped at length asleep, his head under cover all
night! On waking in the morning, he thought it
must have been all a dream about the dog, for it had
totally disappeared with the daylight. When an
hour's glancing in all directions had convinced him
that the phantom was really no longer visible, he
told the whole to Mrs. D——, and made very merry
with her fears—for she would have it, it was " something supernatural," and, good lady, " Mr. D——
might depend upon it, the thing had its errand!"
Four times subsequently to this did Mr. D—— see
the spectral visitant—in nowise altered either in its
manner, form, or colour. It was always late in the
evenings when he observed it, and generally when
he was alone. He was a man extensively acquainted
with physiology; but felt utterly at a loss to what
derangement of what part of the animal economy to
refer it. So, indeed, was I—for he came to consult
me about it. He was with me once during the presence of the phantom. I examined his eyes with a
candle, to see whether the interrupted motions of
the irides indicated any sudden alteration of the
functions of the optic nerve; but the pupils con-
tracted and dilated with perfect regularity. On.
thing, however, was certain—his stomach had been
latterly a little out of order, and everybody knows
the intimate connexion between its functions and

the nervous system. But why he should see spectra
—why they should assume and retain the figure of
a dog, and of such an uncanine colour, too—and
why it should so pertinaciously attach itself to him,
and be seen precisely the same at the various intervals after which it made its appearance—and why
he should hear, or imagine he heard, it utter sounds,
—all these questions I am as unable to answer as
Mr. D—— was, or as the reader will be. He may
account for it in whatever way his ingenuity may
enable him. I have seen and known other cases of
spectra, not unlike the one above related ; and great
alarm and horror have they excited in the breasts
of persons blessed with less firmness and good sense
than Mr. D—— displayed.

The Forger.

A groom, in plain livery, left a card at my house
one afternoon during my absence, on which was the
name, " Mr. Gloucester, No. —, Regent-street ;"
and in pencil the words, " Will thank Dr. —— to
call this evening." As my red-book was lying on
the table at the time, I looked in it, from mere casual
curiosity, to see whether the name of " Gloucester"
appeared there ; but it did not. I concluded, therefore, that my new patient must be a recent comer.
About six o'clock that evening I drove to Regent-
street, sent in my card, and was presently ushered
by the man-servant into a spacious apartment, somewhat showily furnished. The mild, retiring sunlight
of a July evening was diffused over the room ; and
ample crimson window-curtains, half-drawn, miti
gated the glare of the gilded picture-frames which
hung in great numbers round the walls. There was
a large round table in the middle of the room covered
with papers, magazines, books, cards, &c. ; and, in
a word, the whole aspect of things indicated the residence of a person of some fashion and fortune. On

a side-table lay several pairs of boxing-gloves, foils, &c. &c. The object of my visit, Mr. Gloucester, was seated on an elegant ottoman, in a pensive posture, with his head leaning on his hand, which rested on the table. He was engaged with the newspaper when I was announced. He rose as I entered, politely handed me to a chair, and then resumed his seat on the ottoman. His countenance was rather pleasing—fresh-coloured, with regular features, and very light auburn hair, which was adjusted with a sort of careless fashionable negligence. I may perhaps be laughed at by some for noticing such an apparently insignificant circumstance; but the observant humour of my profession must sufficiently account for my detecting the fact, that his *hands* were not those of a *born and bred* gentleman—of one who, as the phrase is, "has never *done any thing*" in his life; they were coarse, large, and clumsy-looking. As for his demeanour, also, there was a constrained and over-anxious display of politeness—an assumption of fashionable ease and indifference that sat ill on him, like a court-dress fastened on a vulgar fellow. He spoke with a would-be jaunty, free-and-easy, small-swagger sort of air, and changed at times the tones of his voice to an offensive cringing softness, which, I dare say, he took to be monstrously insinuating. All these little circumstances put together prepossessed me with a sudden feeling of dislike to the man. These sort of people are a great nuisance to one, since there is no knowing exactly how to treat them. After some hurried expressions of civility, Mr. Gloucester informed me that he had sent for me on account of a deep depression of spirits to which he was latterly subject. He proceeded to detail many of the symptoms of a disordered nervous system. He was tormented with vague apprehensions of impending calamity; could not divest himself of an unaccountable trepidation of manner, which, by attracting observation seriously disconcerted him on many occasions; felt incessantly tempted to the commission of suicide; loathed society; disrelished his former scenes of amusement; had lost his appetite; passed restless nights, and was disturbed with appalling dreams. His pulse, tongue, countenance, &c. corroborated the above statement of his symptoms. I asked him whether any thing unpleasant had occurred in his family? Nothing of the kind. Disappointed in an *affaire du cœur?* Oh, no. Unsuccessful at play? By no means—he did not play. Well—had he *any* source of secret annoyance which could account for his present depression? He coloured, seemed embarrassed, and apparently hesitating whether or not he should communicate to me what weighed on his spirits. He, however, seemed determined to keep me in ignorance, and with some alteration of manner, said, suddenly, that it was only a constitutional nervousness—his family were all so—and he wished to know whether it was in the power of medicine to relieve him. I replied that I would certainly do all that lay in my power, but that he must not expect any sudden and miraculous effect from the medicines I might prescribe; that I saw clearly he had something on his mind which oppressed his spirits—that he ought to go into cheerful society—he sighed—seek change of air—that, he said, was, under circumstances, impossible. I rose to go. He gave me two guineas, and begged me to call the next evening. I left, not knowing what to make of him. To tell the plain truth, my suspicion was, that he was neither more nor less than a systematic London sharper—a gamester—a hanger-on about town—and that he had sent for me in consequence of some of those sudden alternations of fortune to which the lives of such men are subject. I was by no means anxious for a prolonged attendance on him.

About the same time next evening I paid him a second visit. He was stretched on the ottoman,

I.—C

enveloped in a gaudy dressing-gown, with his arms folded on his breast, and his right foot hanging ov he side of the ottoman, and dangling about as if in search of a stray slipper. I did not like this elaborately careless and conceited posture. A decanter or two, with some wine-glasses, stood on the table. He did not rise on my entering, but, with a languid air, begged me to be seated in a chair opposite him. "Good evening, doctor—good evening," said he, in a low and hurried tone; "I'm glad you are come, for if you had not, I'm sure I don't know what I should have done. I'm deusedly low to-night."

"Have you taken the medicines I prescribed, Mr. Gloucester?" I inquired, feeling his pulse, which fluttered irregularly, indicating a high degree of nervous excitement. He had taken most of the physic I had ordered, he said, but without perceiving any effect from it. "In fact, doctor," he continued, starting from his recumbent position to his feet, and walking rapidly three or four paces to and fro, "d—n me if I know what's come to me. I feel as if I could cut my throat." I insinuated some questions for the purpose of ascertaining whether there was any hereditary tendency to *insanity* in his family; but it would not do. He saw, he said "what I was *driving at*," but I was "on a wrong scent."

"Come, come, doctor, after all, there's nothing like *wine* for low spirits, is there? D—me, doctor, drink, drink. Only taste that claret;" and after pouring out a glass for me, which ran over the brim on the table (his hand was so unsteady), he instantly gulped down two glasses himself. There was a vulgar, offensive familiarity in his manner, from which I felt inclined to stand off; but I thought it better to conceal my feelings. I was removing my glove from my right hand, and putting my hat and stick on the table, when, seeing a thin slip of paper lying on the spot where I intended to place them (apparently a bill or promissory note). I was going to hand it over to Mr

Gloucester: but to my astonishment, he suddenly sprung towards me, snatched from me the paper with an air of ill-disguised alarm, and crumpled it up into his pocket, saying, hurriedly, " Ha, ha, doctor, d—me —this same little bit of paper—didn't see the *name*, eh ? 'Tis the bill of an extravagant young friend of mine, whom I've just come down a cool hundred or two for; and it wouldn't be the handsome thing to let his name appear—ha—you understand ?" he stammered, confusedly, directing to me as sudden and penetrating a glance as I ever encountered. I felt excessively uneasy, and inclined to take my depart ure instantly. My suspicions were now confirmed; I was sitting familiarly with a swindler—a gamblei —and the bill he was so anxious to conceal was evidently wrung from one of his ruined dupes. My demeanour was instantly frozen over with the most distant and frigid civility. I begged him to be reseated, and allow me to put a very few more questions to him, as I was in great haste. I was thus engaged, when a heavy knock was heard at the outer door. Though there was nothing particular in it, Mr. Gloucester started and turned pale. In a few moments I heard the sound of altercation; the door of the room in which we sat was presently opened, and two men entered. Recollecting suddenly a similar scene in my own early history, I felt faint. There was no mistaking the character or errand of the two fellows, who now walked up to where we were sitting: they were two sullen Newgate myrmidons and— gracious God! had a warrant to arrest Mr. Gloucester for FORGERY ! I rose from my chair, and staggered a few paces I knew not whither. I could scarce preserve myself from falling on the floor. Mr. Gloucester. as soon as he caught sight of the officers, fell back on the ottoman, suddenly pressed his hand to his heart, turned pale as death, and gasped, breathless with horror.

" Gentlemen what—what—do you want here ?"

" Isn't your name E—— T——?" asked the elder
of the two, coolly and unconcernedly.

" N—o, my name is Glou—ces—ter," stammered
the wretched young man, almost inaudibly.

" *Gloucester*, eh? Oh, d—me, none of that there
sort of blarney! Come, my kiddy, caged at last, eh!
We've been long after you, and now you must be off
with us directly. Here's your passport," said one
of the officers, pointing to the warrant. The young
man uttered a deep groan, and sunk senseless on the
sofa. One of the officers, I cannot conceive how,
was acquainted with my person; and taking off his
hat, said, in a respectful tone, " Doctor, you'll bring
him to his wits again, an't please you; we *must* have
him off directly." Though myself but a trifle removed from the state in which he lay stretched before
me, I did what I could to restore him, and succeeded
at length. I unbuttoned his shirt-collar, dashed in
his face some water brought by his man-servant, who
now stood looking on shivering with affright, and
endeavoured to calm his agitation by such soothing
expressions as I could command.

" Oh, doctor, doctor, what a horrid dream it was!
Are they gone?—are they?" he inquired, without
opening his eyes, and clasping my hand in his, which
was cold as that of a corpse.

" Come, come, none of these here tantrums; you
must *off* at once—that's the long and short of it," said
an officer, approaching, and taking from his coat-
pocket a pair of handcuffs; at sight of which and of
a large horse-pistol projecting from his breast-pocket,
my very soul sickened.

" Oh, doctor, doctor, save me! save me!" groaned
their prisoner, clasping my hands with convulsive
energy.

" Come, d—n your cowardly snivelling! Why
can't you behave like a man now, eh? Come—off
with this peacock's covering of yours—it was never
made for the like of *you*, I'm sure—and put on a plain

coat, and off to cage like a sensible bird," said one of the two, proceeding to remove the dressing-gown very roughly.

"Oh, my God!—oh, my God!—have mercy on me! Oh, strike me dead at once!" nearly shrieked their prisoner, falling on his knees on the floor, and glaring towards the ceiling with an almost maniac eye.

"I hope you'll not treat your prisoner with unnecessary severity," said I, seeing them disposed to be very unceremonious.

"No, not by no manner of means, if as how he behaves himself," replied one of the men, respectfully. Mr. Gloucester's dressing-gown was quickly removed, and his body-coat (himself perfectly passive the while) drawn on by his bewildered servant, assisted by one of the officers. It was nearly a new coat, cut in the very extreme of the latest fashion, and contrasted strangely with the disordered and affrighted air of its wearer. His servant placed his hat on his head, and endeavoured to draw on his gloves—showy, sky-coloured kid. He was standing with a stupified air, gazing vacantly at the officers, when he started suddenly to the window, manifestly with the intention of leaping out.

"Ha, ha! *that's* your game, my lad, is it!" coolly exclaimed one of the officers, as he snatched him back again with a vicelike grasp of the collar. "Now, since that's the sport you're for, why, you must be content to wear these little bracelets for the rest of your journey. D—me, it's your own seeking; for I didn't mean to have used them if as how you'd only behaved perfectly." And in an instant the young man's hands were locked together in the handcuffs. It was sickening to see the frantic efforts—as if he would have severed his hands from the wrists—he made to burst the handcuffs.

"Take me—to *hell*, if you choose!" he gasped, in a hoarse, hollow tone, sinking into a chair utterly exhausted, while one of the officers was busily engaged rummaging the drawers, desks, &c. in search of papers. When he had concluded his search, filled his pockets, and buttoned his coat, the two approached, and told him to rise and accompany them.

" Now, d—me, are you for a rough or a quiet passage, eh?" said one of them, seizing him not very gently by the collar. He received no answer. The wretched prisoner was more dead than alive.

" I hope you have a hackney-coach in waiting, and don't intend to drag the young man through the streets on foot?" I inquired.

" Why, true—true, doctor, it might be as well for us all; but who's to *stump up* for it?" replied one of the officers. I gave him five shillings, and the servant was instantly despatched for a hackney-coach. While they were waiting its arrival, conceiving I could not be of any use to Mr. Gloucester, and not choosing to be seen leaving the house with two police officers and a handcuffed prisoner, I took my departure, and drove home in such a state of agitation as I have never experienced before or since. The papers of the next morning explained all. The young man " living in Regent-street, in first-rate style," who had summoned me to visit him, had committed a series of forgeries for the last eighteen months to a great amount, and with so much secrecy and dexterity as to have till then escaped detection; and had for the last few months been enjoying the produce of his skilful villany in the style I witnessed, passing himself off in the circles where he associated under the assumed name of *Gloucester*. The immediate cause of his arrest was forging the acceptance of an eminent mercantile house to a bill of exchange for 45*l*. Poor fellow! it was short work with him afterward. He was arraigned at the next September sessions of the Old Bailey, the case clearly proved against him, he offered no defence, was found guilty, and sentenced to death. Shortly after this, while reading the papers one

Saturday morning at breakfast, my eye lit on the usual
gloomy annunciation of the Recorder's visit to Wind-
sor, and report to the King in council of the prison-
ers found guilty at the last Old Bailey sessions ; " all
of whom," the paragraph concluded, " his majesty
was graciously pleased to respite during his royal
pleasure, except E—— T——, on whom the law is
left to take its course next Tuesday morning."

Transient and any thing but agreeable as had been
my intimacy with this miserable young man, I could
not read this intelligence with indifference. He whom
I had so very lately seen surrounded with the life-
bought luxuries of a man of wealth and fashion, was
now shivering the few remaining hours of his life in
the condemned cells of Newgate! The next day
(Sunday) I entertained a party of friends at my house
to dinner; to which I was just sitting down, when
one of the servants put a note into my hand, of which
the following is a copy :—

" The chaplain of Newgate is earnestly requested
by E—— T—— (the young man sentenced to suffer
for forgery next Tuesday morning) to present his
humble respects to Dr. ——, and solicit the favour of
a visit from him in the course of to-morrow (Monday).
The unhappy convict, Mr. —— believes, has something on his mind which he is anxious to communicate to Dr. ——.   Newgate, September 28th, 182 —."

I felt it impossible, after perusing this note, to enjoy the company I had invited. What on earth could
the culprit have to say to me? what unreasonable
request might he put me to the pain of refusing?
ought I to see him at all? were questions which I
incessantly proposed to myself during the evening
but felt unable to answer. I resolved, however, at
last, to afford him the desired interview, and be at
the cell of Newgate in the course of the next evening
unless my professional engagements prevented me
About six o'clock, therefore, on Monday, after forti-
fying myself with a few extra glasses of wine (for

why should I hesitate to acknowledge that I apprehended much distress and agitation from witnessing so unusual a scene?) I drove to the Old Bailey, drew up opposite the governor's house, and was received by him very politely. He despatched a turnkey to lead me to the cell where my late patient, the *soi-disant* Mr. Gloucester, was immured, in chilling expectancy of his fate.

Surely horror has appropriated these gloomy regions for her peculiar dwelling-place! Who that has passed through them once can ever forget the long, narrow, lamp-lit passages,—the sepulchral silence, save where the ear is startled with the clangour of iron doors closing harshly before and behind,—the dimly-seen spectral figure of the prison patrol, gliding along with loaded blunderbuss,—and the chilling consciousness of being surrounded by so many fiends in human shape,—inhaling the foul atmosphere of all the concentrated crime and guilt of the metropolis! My heart leaped within me to listen even to my own echoing footfalls; and I felt several times inclined to return without fulfilling the purpose of my visit. My vacillation, however, was abruptly put an end to by my guide exclaiming "Here we are, sir." While he was unbarring the cell door, I begged him to continue at the outside of the door during the few moments of my interview with the convict.

"Holloa! young man there, here's Dr. —— come to see you!" said the turnkey, hoarsely, as he ushered me in. The cell was small and gloomy; and a little lamp lying on the table barely sufficed to show me the persons of the culprit and an elderly respectable-looking man, muffled in a drab great-coat, and sitting gazing in stupified silence on the prisoner. Great God, it was his FATHER! He did not seem conscious of my entrance; but his son rose, and feebly asked me how I was, muttered a few words of thanks, sunk again (apparently overpowered with his feelings) into his seat, and fixed his eyes on a page of the Bible which was lying open before him. A long silence ensued, for none of us seemed either able or inclined to talk. I contemplated the two with feelings of lively interest. How altered was the young culprit before me from the gay " Mr. Gloucester" whom I had visited in Regent-street! His face had now a ghastly, cadaverous hue; his hair was matted with perspiration over his sallow forehead; his eyes were sunk and bloodshot, and seemed incapable of distinguishing the print to which they were directed. He was dressed in a plain suit of mourning, and wore a simple black stock round his neck. How I shuddered when I thought of the rude hands which were soon to unloose it! Beside him, on the table, lay a white pocket handkerchief completely saturated either with tears or wiping the perspiration from his forehead, and a glass of water, with which he occasionally moistened his parched lips. I knew not whether he was more to be pitied than his wretched, heart-broken father. The latter seemed a worthy, respectable person (he was an industrious tradesman in the country), with a few thin gray hairs scattered over his otherwise bald head, and sat with his hands closed together, resting on his knees, gazing on his doomed son with a lack-lustre eye, which, together with his anguish-worn features, told eloquently of his sufferings!

" Well, doctor," exclaimed the young man, at length, closing the Bible, "I have now read that blessed chapter to the end; and I thank God I think I *feel* it. But now, let me thank you, doctor, for your good and kind attention to my request. I have something particular to say to you, but it must be in private," he continued, looking significantly at his father, as though he wished him to take the hint and withdraw for a few moments. Alas! the heart-broken parent understood him not, but continued with his eyes riveted, vacantly, as before.

" We *must* be left alone for a moment," said the

young man, rising, and stepping to the door. He
knocked, and when it was opened, whispered the
turnkey to remove his father gently, and let him wait
outside for an instant or two. The man entered for
that purpose, and the prisoner took hold tenderly of
his father's hand, and said, "Dear, dear father! you
must leave me for a moment while I speak in private
to this gentleman;" at the same time endeavouring
to raise him from the chair.

"Oh! yes—yes—what?—of course,". stammered
the old man, with a bewildered air, rising; and then,
as it were, with a sudden gush of full returning consciousness, flung his arms round his son, folded him
convulsively to his breast, and groaned—"Oh, my
son! my poor son!" Even the iron visage of the
turnkey seemed darkened with a transient emotion
at this heart-breaking scene. The next moment we
were left alone: but it was some time before the culprit recovered from the agitation occasioned by this
sudden ebullition of his father's feelings.

"Doctor," he gasped, at length, "we've but a few,
very few moments, and I have much to say. God
Almighty bless you," squeezing my hands convulsively, "for this kindness to a guilty, unworthy wretch
like me; and the business I wanted to see you about
is sad, but short. I have heard so much of your
goodness, doctor, that I'm sure you won't deny me
the only favour I shall ask."

"Whatever is reasonable and proper, if it lie in my
way, I shall certainly," said I, anxiously waiting to
see the nature of the communication he seemed to
have for me to execute.

"Thank you, doctor, thank you. It is only this—
in a word—guilty wretch that I am!—I have"—he
trembled violently—" seduced a lovely but poor girl
—God forgive me!—and—and—she is now—nearly
on the verge of her *confinement!*" He suddenly
covered his face with his handkerchief, and sobbed
bitterly for some moments. Presently he resumed—

" Alas! she knows me not by my real name; so that when she reads the account of—of—my execution in the papers of Wednesday, she won't know it is *her* Edward!   Nor does she know me by the name I bore in Regent-street.   She is not at all acquainted with my frightful situation, but she *must* be when all is over!   Now, dear, kind, good doctor," he continued, shaking from head to foot, and grasping my hand, " do, for the love of God, and the peace of my dying moments, promise me that you will see her; she lives at ——; visit her in her confinement, and gradually break the news of my death to her; and say my last prayers will be for her, and that my Maker may forgive me for her ruin!   You will find in this little bag a sum of 30*l.*—the last I have on earth—I beg you will take five guineas for your own fee, and give the rest to my precious—my ruined Mary!"   He fell down on his knees, and folded his arms round mine in a supplicating attitude.   My tears fell on him as he looked up at me.   " Oh, God be thanked for these blessed tears! they assure me you will do what I ask; may I believe you will?"

" Yes—yes—yes, young man," I replied, with a quivering lip; " it is a painful task, but I will do it— give her the money, and add ten pounds to the thirty should it be necessary."   " Oh, doctor, depend on it, God will bless you and yours for ever for this noble conduct!   And now, I have *one* thing more to ask— yes—one thing"—he seemed choked—" Doctor, your skill will enable you to inform me—I wish to know —is—the death I must die to-morrow"—he put his hand to his neck, and, shaking like an aspen leaf, sunk down again into the chair from which he had risen—" is—hanging—a painful—a tedious"— He could utter no more, nor could I answer him.

" Do not," I replied, after a pause, " do not put me to the torture of listening to questions like these. Pray to your merciful God; and rely on it, no one ever prayed sincerely in vain.   The thief on the cross"—I faltered; then feeling that if I continued in the cell a moment longer I should faint, I rose, and shook the young man's hands; he could not speak, but sobbed and gasped convulsively—and in a few moments I was driving home. As soon as I was seated in my carriage I could restrain my feelings no longer, but burst into a flood of tears. I prayed to God I might never be called to pass through such a bitter and afflicting scene again to the latest hour I breathed! I ought to have called on several patients that evening, but finding myself utterly unfit, I sent apologies, and went home. My sleep in the night was troubled; the distorted image of the convict I had been visiting flitted in horrible shapes round my bed all night long. An irresistible and most morbid restlessness and curiosity took possession of me to witness the end of this young man. The first time the idea presented itself it sickened me; I revolted from it. How my feelings changed I know not; but I rose at seven o'clock, and without hinting it to any one, put on the large top-coat of my servant, and directed my hurried steps towards the Old Bailey. I got into one of the houses immediately opposite the gloomy gallows, and took my station with several other visiters at the window. They were conversing on the subject of the execution, and unanimously execrated the sanguinary severity of the laws which could deprive a young man, such as they said E—— T—— was, of his life, for an offence of merely civil institution. Of course I did not speak. It was a wretched morning; a drizzling shower fell incessantly. The crowd was not great, but conducted themselves most indecorously. Even the female portion—by far the greater—occasionally vociferated joyously and boisterously, as they recognised their acquaintance among the crowd. At length St. Sepulchre's bell tolled the hour of eight—gloomy herald of many a sinner's entrance into eter nity!—and as the last chimes died away on the ear and were succeeded by the muffled tolling of the prison bell, which I could hear with agonizing distinctness, I caught a glimpse of the glistening gold-tipped wands of the two under-sheriffs, as they took their station under the shade at the foot of the gallows. In a few moments, the ordinary and another gray-haired gentleman made their appearance, and between them was the unfortunate criminal. He ascended the steps with considerable firmness. His arms were pinioned before and behind; and when he stood on the gallows, I could hear the exclamations of the crowd—"Lord, Lord, what a fine young man! —Poor fellow!" He was dressed in a suit of respectable mourning, and wore black kid gloves. His light hair had evidently been adjusted with some care, and fell in loose curls over each side of his temples. His countenance was much as I saw it on the preceding evening—fearfully pale; and his demeanour was much more composed than I had expected, from what I had witnessed of his agitation in the condemned cell. He bowed twice very low, and rather formally, to the crowd around; gave a sudden and ghastly glance at the beam over his head from which the rope was suspended, and then suffered the executioner to place him on the precise spot which he was to occupy, and prepare him for death. I was shocked at the air of sullen, brutal indifference with which the executioner loosed and removed his neckkerchief, which was white, and tied with neatness and precision—dropped the accursed noose over his head, and adjusted it round the bare neck—and could stand it no longer. I staggered from my place at the window to a distant part of the room, dropped into a chair, shut my eyes, closed my tingling ears with my fingers, and with a hurried aspiration for God's mercy towards the wretched young criminal, who within a very few yards of me was, perhaps, that instant surrendering his life into the hands which gave it, continued motionless for some minutes, till the noise

made by the persons at the window, in leaving, convinced me all was over! I rose and followed them
down stairs—worked my way through the crowd,
without daring to elevate my eyes, lest they should
encounter the suspended corpse—threw myself into
a coach, and hurried home. I did not recover the
agitation produced by this scene for several days
This was the end of a FORGER!

In conclusion, I may just inform the reader, that
I faithfully executed the commission with which he
had intrusted me; and a bitter, heart-rending business it was!

CHAPTER V.

"A MAN ABOUT TOWN."

I HATE humbug, and would eschew that cant and
fanaticism which are at present tainting extensive
portions of society, as sincerely as I venerate and
wish to cultivate a spirit of sober, manly, and rational
piety. It is not, therefore, to pander to the morbid
tastes of overweening saintliness, to encourage its
arrogant assumptions, sanction its hateful, selfish ex-
clusiveness, or advocate that spirit of sour, diseased,
puritanical seclusion from the innocent gayeties and
enjoyments of life, which has more deeply injured
the interests of religion than any of its professed
enemies; it is not, I repeat, with any such unworthy
objects as these that this melancholy narrative is
placed on record. But it is to show, if it ever meet
their eyes, your "men about town," as the *élite* of
the rakish fools and flutterers of the day are significantly termed, that some portions of the page of pro-
digacy are black—black with horror, and steeped ir

the tears, the blood of anguish and remorse wrung
from ruined thousands! that often the "iron is entering the very soul" of those who present to the
world's eye an exterior of glaring gayety and reck
lessness; that gilded guilt *must*, one day, be stripped
of its tinselry, and flung into the haze and gloom of
outer darkness. *These* are the only objects for which
this black passage is laid before the reader, in which
I have undertaken to describe pains and agonies
which these eyes witnessed, and that with all the true
frightfulness of reality. It has, indeed, cost me feelings of little less than torture to retrace the leading
features of the scenes with which the narrative con-
cludes.

"Hit him—pitch it into him! Go it boys—go it!
Right into your man, each of you, like good ones!
Top sawyers these! Hurra! Tap his claret-cask—
draw his cork! Go it—go it—beat him, big one! lick
him, little one! Hurra! Slash, smash—fib away—
right and left! Hollo! clear the way there! Ring'
ring!"

These and many similar exclamations may serve
to bring before the reader one of those ordinary
scenes in London—a street row; arising, too, out of
circumstances of equally frequent occurrence. A
gentleman (!) prowling about Piccadilly, towards
nightfall in the month of November, in quest of ad-
ventures of a certain description, had been offering
some impertinence to a female of respectable appearance, whom he had been following for some minutes. He was in the act of putting his arm round
her waist, or taking some similar liberty, when he
was suddenly seized by the collar from behind, and
jerked off the pavement so violently, that he fell
nearly at full length in the gutter. This feat was
performed by the woman's husband, who had that
moment rejoined her, having left her only a very short
time before, to leave a message at one of the coach-
offices, while she walked on, being in haste. Nc

man of ordinary spirit could endure such rough
handling tamely. The instant, therefore, that the
prostrate man had recovered his footing, he sprung
towards his assailant, and struck him furiously over
the face with his umbrella. For a moment the man
seemed disinclined to return the blow, owing to the
passionate dissuasions of his wife; but it was useless—his English blood began to boil under the idea
of submitting to a blow, and hurriedly exclaiming,
"Wait a moment, sir," he pushed his wife into the
shop adjoining, telling her to stay till he returned.
A small crowd stood round. "Now, by ——, sir, we
shall see which is the better man!" said he, again
making his appearance, and putting himself into a
boxing attitude. There was much disparity between
the destined combatants, in point both of skill and
size. The man last named was short in stature, but
of a square iron-build; and it needed only a glance
at his posture to see he was a scientific, perhaps a
thoroughbred, bruiser. His antagonist, on the contrary, was a tall, handsome, well-proportioned, gentlemanly man, apparently not more than twenty-eight
or thirty years old. Giving his umbrella into the
hands of a by-stander, and hurriedly drawing off his
gloves, he addressed himself to the encounter with
an unguarded impetuosity, which left him wholly at
the mercy of his cool and practised opponent.

The latter seemed evidently inclined to play a
while with his man, and contented himself with stopping several heavily-dealt blows, with so much quickness and precision that every one saw "the big one
had caught a Tartar" in the man he had provoked.
Watching his opportunity, like a tiger crouching
noiselessly in preparation for the fatal spring, the
short man delivered such a slaughtering left-handed
hit full in the face of his tall adversary, accompanied
by a tremendous "doubling-up" body-blow, as in
an instant brought him senseless to the ground. He
who now lay stunned and blood-smeared on the pave-

ment, surrounded by a rabble jeering the fallen "swell," and exulting at seeing the punishment he had received for his impertinence, the conqueror pithily told them, as he stood over his prostrate foe, was the honourable St. John Henry Effingstone, presumptive heir to a marquisate; and the victor, who walked coolly away as if nothing had happened, was Tom ——, the prize-fighter.

Such was the occasion of my first introduction to Mr. Effingstone; for I was driving by at the time this occurrence took place; and my coachman, seeing the crowd, slackened the pace of his horses, and I desired him to stop. Hearing some voices cry "Take him to a doctor," I let myself out, announced my profession, and seeing a man of very gentlemanly and superior appearance covered with blood and propped against the knee of one of the people round, I had him brought into my carriage, saying I would drive him to his residence close by, which his cards showed me was in —— street. Though much disfigured and in great pain, he had not received any injury likely to be attended with danger. He soon recovered; but an infinitely greater annoyance remained after all the other symptoms had disappeared —his left eye was sent into deep mourning, which threatened to last for some weeks; and could any thing be more vexatious to a gay man about town? for such was Mr. Effingstone—but no ordinary one. He did not belong to that crowded class of essenced fops, of silly coxcombs, hung in gold chains, and bespangled with a profusion of rings, brooches, pins, and quizzing-glasses, who are to be seen in fine weather glistening about town like fireflies in India. *He* was no walking advertisement of the superior articles of his tailor, mercer, and jeweller. No—Mr. Effingstone was really a *man about town*, and yet no puppy. He was worse—an abandoned profligate, a systematic debauchee, an irreclaimable reprobate. He stood pre-eminent amid the throng of men of

I.--P

fashion, a glaring form of guilt, such as Milton repre
sents Satan—

" In shape and gesture proudly eminent,"—

among his gloomy battalions of fallen spirits. He
had nothing in common with the set of men I have
been alluding to, but that he chose to drink deeper
from the same foul and maddening cup of dissipation. Their minor fooleries and "naughtinesses,"
as he termed them, he despised. Had he not neglected a legitimate exercise of his transcendent
talents, he might have become, with little effort, one
of the first men of his age. As for actual know
ledge, his powers of acquisition seemed unbounded.
Whatever he read he made his own ; good or bad, he
never forgot it. He was equally intimate with ancient and modern scholarship. His knowledge of
the varieties and distinctions between the ancient
sects of philosophers was more minutely accurate,
and more successfully brought to bear upon the
modern, tnan I am aware of having ever known in
another. Few, very few that ever I have been
acquainted with could make a more imposing and
effective display of the " dazzling fence of logic."
Fallacies, though never so subtle, so exquisitely
vraisemblant to the truth, and calculated to evade the
very ghost of Aristotle himself, me'ted away instantaneously before the first glance c. his eye. His
powers were acknowledged and feared by all who
knew him—as many a discomfited sciolist now living
can bear testimony. His acuteness of perception
was not less remarkable. He anticipated all you
meant to convey before you had uttered more than
a word or two. It was useless to kick or wince
under such treatment—to find your own words thrust
back agair down your own throat as useless, than
which few things are more provoking to men with
the slightest spice of petulance. A conviction of his

overwhelming power kept you passive beneath his grasp. He had, as it were, extracted and devoured the kernel, while you were attempting to decide on the best method of breaking the shell. His wit was radiant, and fed by a fancy both lively and powerful, it flashed and sparkled on all sides of you like lightning He had a strong bent towards satire and sarcasm, and that of the bitterest and fiercest kind. If you chanced unexpectedly to become its subject, you sneaked away consciously seared to your very centre. If, however, you really wished to acquire information from him, no one was readier to open the vast storehouses of his learning. You had but to start a topic requiring elucidation of any kind, and presently you saw, grouped around it, numerous, appropriate, and beautiful illustrations, from almost every region of knowledge. But then you could scarce fail to observe the spirit of pride and ostentation which pervaded the whole. If he failed any where—and who living is equally excellent in all things? it was in physics. Yes, here he *was* foiled. He lacked the patience, perseverance, and almost exclusive attention which the cold and haughty goddess presiding over them invariably exacts from her suitors. Still, however, he had that showy general intimacy with its outlines, and some of its leading features, which earned him greater applause than was doled out reluctantly and suspiciously to the profoundest masters of science.

Yet Mr. Effingstone, though such as I have described him, gained no distinctions at Oxford; and why? because he knew that all acknowledged his intellectual supremacy; that he had but to extend his foot and stand on the proudest pedestal of academical-eminence. This satisfied him. And another reason for his conduct once slipped out in the course of my intimacy with him :—his overweening, I may say, almost unparalleled pride could not brook the idea of the remotest chance of *failure*. The same

thing accounted for another manifestation of his peculiar character.   No one could conceive how, when,
or where he came by his wonderful knowledge.
He never *seemed* to be doing any thing; no one ever
saw him reading or writing, and yet he came into the
world *au fait* at almost every thing!   All this was
attributable to his pride, or, I should say more cor-
rectly, his vanity.   "*Results*, not processes, are for
the public eye," he was fond of saying.   In plain
English, he would shine before men, but would not
that they should know the pains and expense with
which his lamp was fed.   And this highly-gifted individual, as to intellect, it was, who chose to track
the waters of dissipation, to career among their sunk
rocks, shoals, and quicksands, even till he sunk and
perished in them!   By some strange omission in his
moral conformation, his soul seemed utterly destitute
of any sympathies for virtue ; and whenever I looked
at him, it was with feelings of concern, alarm, and
wonder, akin to those with which one might contemplate the frightful creature brought into being by
Frankenstein.   Mr. Effingstone seemed either wholly
incapable of appreciating moral excellence, or wilfully contemptuous of it.   While reflecting carefully
on his ἰδιοσυγκρισία, which several years' intimacy gave
me many opportunities of doing, and endeavouring
to account for his fixed inclination towards vice, and
that in its most revolting form and most frantic excesses, at a time when he was consciously possessed
of such capabilities of excellence of every description ; it has struck me that a little incident which
came to my knowledge casually afforded a clew to
the whole—a key to his character.   I one day
chanced to overhear a distinguished friend of his
father lamenting that a man "of Mr. St. John's
mighty powers" could prostitute them in the manner
he did; and the reply made by his father was, with a
sigh, that, "St. John was a *splendid* sinner, and he
knew it."   From that hour the key-stone was fixed

in the arch of his unalterable, irreclaimable depravity He felt a satanic satisfaction in the consciousness of being an object of regret and wonder among those who most enthusiastically acknowledged his intellectual supremacy. How infinitely less stimulating to his morbid sensibilities would be the placid approval of virtue—a commonplace acquiescence in the ordinary notions of virtue and religion! He wished rather to stand out from the multitude—to be severed from the herd. " Better to reign in hell than serve in heaven," he thought; and he was not long in sinking many fathoms lower into the abyss of atheism. In fact, he never pretended to the possession of religious principle; he had acquiesced in the reputed truths of Christianity like his neighbours; or at least, kept doubts to himself, till he fancied his reputation required him to join the crew of fools who blazon their unbelief. *This* was " *damned fine.*"

Conceive, now, such a man as I have truly, but perhaps imperfectly, described Mr. Effingstone—in the possession of 3000*l.* a year—perfectly his own master—with a fine person and most fascinating manners—capable of acquiring with ease every fashionable accomplishment—the idol, the dictator of all he met—and with a dazzling circle of friends and relatives:—conceive for a moment such a man as this *let loose upon the town !* Will it occasion wonder if the reader is told how soon nocturnal studies, and the ambition of retaining his intellectual character which prompted them, were supplanted by a blind, absorbing, reckless devotion—for he was incapable of any thing but *in extremes*—to the gaming-table, the turf, the cock-pit, the ring, the theatres, and daily and nightly attendance on those haunts of detestable debauchery which I cannot foul my pen with naming ?—that a two or three years' intimacy with such scenes as these had conduced, in the first instance, to shed a haze of indistinctness over the multifarious acquirements of his earlier and better days, and finally to blot out large portions with blank oblivion?—that his soul's sun shone in dim discoloured rays through the fogs—the vault-vapours of profligacy?—that prolonged desuetude was gradually, though unheededly, benumbing and paisying his intellectual faculties?—that a constant "feeding on garbage" had vitiated and depraved his whole system, both physical and mental?—and that, to conclude, there was a lamentable, an almost incredible, contrast between the glorious being, Mr. Effingstone, at twenty-one, and that poor faded creature —that prematurely superannuated debauchee, Mr Effingstone at twenty-seven?

I feel persuaded I shall not be accused of travelling out of the legitimate sphere of these " Passages," of forsaking the track of professional detail, in having thus attempted to give the reader some faint idea of the intellectual character of one of the most extraordinary young men that have ever flashed, meteor-like, across the sphere of my own observation. Not that in the ensuing pages it will be in my power to exhibit him such as he has been described, doing and uttering things worthy of his great powers. Alas, alas! he was " fallen, fallen, fallen" from that altitude long before it became my province to know him professionally. His decline and fall are alone what remain for me to describe. I am painting from the life, and those are living who know it: that I am describing the character and career of him who once lived,—who deliberately immolated himself before the shrine of debauchery; and they can, with a quaking heart, attest the truth of the few bitter and black passages of his remaining history which here follow.

The reader is acquainted with the circumstances attending my first professional acquaintance with Mr. Effingstone. Those of the second are in perfect keeping He had been prosecuting an enterprise of *seduction*, the interest of which was, in his eyes, enhanced a thousand fold, on discovering that the object of his illicit attentions was—married. The victim was, I understood, a very handsome, fashionable woman; and she fell—for Mr. Effingstone was irresistible! He was attending one of their assignations one night, which she was unexpectedly unable to keep; and he waited so long at the place of meeting, but slightly clad, in the cold and inclement weather, that when he returned home at an early hour in the morning, intensely chagrined, he felt inclined to be very ill. He could not rise to breakfast. He grew rapidly worse; and when I was summoned to his bedside, he exhibited all the symptoms of a very severe inflammation of the lungs. One or two concurrent causes of excitement and chagrin aggravated his illness. He had been very unfortunate in betting on the Derby, and was threatened with an arrest from his tailor whom he owed some hundreds of pounds which he could not possibly pay. Again—a wealthy remote member of the family, his godfather, having heard of his profligacy, altered his will, and left every farthing he had in the world, amounting to upwards of fifty or sixty thousand pounds, to a charitable institution, the whole of which had been originally destined to Mr. Effingstone. The only notice taken of him in the old gentleman's will was, "To St. John Henry Effingstone, my unworthy godson, I bequeath the sum of five pounds sterling, to purchase a Bible and prayer-book, believing the time may yet come when he will require them." These circumstances, I say, added to one or two other irritating concomitants, such as will sometimes succeed in stinging your *men about town* into something like reflection, brief and futile though it be, contributed to accelerate the inroads of his dangerous disorder. We were compelled to adopt such powerful antiphlogistic treatment as reduced him to within an inch of his life. Previous to, and in the course

of, this illness, he exhibited one or two characteristic
traits.

"Doctor, is delirium usually an attendant on this
disorder?" he inquired one morning. I told him it
was, very frequently.

"Ah! then I'd better become ἄγλωσσος, with one
of old, and bite out my tongue; for, d—n it! my life
won't bear ripping up! I shall say what will horrify
you all! Delirium blackens a poor fellow sadly
among his friends, doesn't it? Babbling devil—what
can silence it? If you should hear me beginning to
let out, suffocate me, doctor." * * *

"Any chance of my giving the GREAT CUT this
time, doctor, eh?" he inquired the same evening,
with great apparent nonchalance. Seeing my puzzled
air—for I did not exactly comprehend the low expression, "great cut"—he asked, quickly, "Doctor,
shall I die, d'ye think?" I told him I certainly apprehended great danger, for his symptoms began to
look very serious. "Then the ship must be cleared
for action. What is the best way of ensuring recovery, provided it is to be?" I told him that, among
other things, he must be kept very quiet—must not
have his mind excited by visiters.

"Nurse, please ring the bell for George," said he
suddenly interrupting me. The man in a few moments answered the summons. "George, d'ye value
your neck, eh?" The man bowed. "Then, harkee,
see you don't let in a living soul to see me, except
the medical people. Friends, relatives, mother, brothers, sisters—shut them all out—And, harkee, duns
especially. If —— should come and get inside
the door, kick him out again; and if —— comes,
and ——, and ——, tell them if they don't mind
what they are about, d—n them! I'll die, if it's only
to cheat them." The man bowed and retired. "And
—and—doctor, what else?"

"If you should appear approaching your end, M-

Effingstone, you would allow us, perhaps, to call in
a clergyman to assist you in your devo——"

"What—eh—a parson? Oh, —— it! no, no—out
of the question—*non ad rem*, I assure you," he replied,
hastily. "D'ye think I can't roll down to hell fast
enough without having my wheels oiled by *their*
hypocritical humbug? Don't name it again, doctor,
on any account, I beg."

* * * He grew rapidly worse, but ultimately
recovered. His injunctions were obeyed to the letter; for his man George idolized his master, and
turned a deaf ear to *all* applications for admission to
his master's chamber. It was well there was no one
of them present to listen to his ravings ; for the dis-
gorgings of his polluted soul were horrible. His
progress towards convalescence was by very slow
steps; for the energies of both mind and body had
been dreadfully shaken. His illness, however, had
worked little or no alteration in his moral sentiments
—or, if any thing, for the worse.

"It won't do at all, will it, doctor?" said Mr. Effingstone, when I was visiting him one morning at
the house of a titled relation in —— square, whither
ne had been removed to prepare for a jaunt to the
continent. "What do you allude to, Mr. Effingstone?
What won't do?" I asked, for I knew not to what he
alluded, as the question was the first break of a long
pause in our conversation, which had been quite of a
miscellaneous character. "*What* won't do? Why
the sort of life I have been leading about town these
two or three last years," he replied. "It has nearly
wound me up, has it not?"

"Indeed, Mr. Effingstone, I think so. You have had
a very, very narrow escape—have been within a hair's
breadth of your grave." "Ay," he exclaimed with
a sigh, rubbing his hand rapidly over his noble forehead, "'twas a complete toss up whether I should go
or stay! But come, come, the good ship has weath-
ered the storm bravely, though she *has* been battered

a little in her timbers!" said he, striking his breast,
" and she's fit for sea again already, with a little caulk-
ing, that is.   Heigho! what a d—d fool illness makes
a man! I've had some of the strangest, oddest
twingings—such gleams and visions! What d'ye
think, doctor, I've had dinging in my ears night and
day, like a d—d church-bell!   Why, a passage from
old Persius, and this is it (you know I was a *dab* at
Latin once, doctor), *rotundo ore,*

> ' Magne Pater divum! sævos punire tyrannos
> Haud aliâ ratione velis, quum dira libido
> Moverit ingenium, ferventi tincta veneno;
> —Virtutem videant—intabescantque relictâ !"[*]

'True and forcible enough, isn't it?"

  "Yes," I replied, and expressed my satisfaction at
his altered sentiments. "He might rely on it," I
ventured to assure him, "that the paths of virtue, of
religion"—— I was going too fast.

  "Pho, pho, doctor! No humbug, I beg—come,
come, no humbug—no nonsense of that sort! I
meant nothing of the kind, I can assure you! I'm a
better Bentley than you, I see! What d'ye think is
my reading of '*virtutem videant?*' Why—let them
get wives when they're worn out and want nursing—
ah, ha!—curse me! I'd go on raking—ay, d—n it, I
would, sour as you look about it! But I'm too
much the worse for wear at present—I must recruit
a little."

  "Mr. Effingstone, I'm really confounded at hearing
you talk in so light a strain! Forgive me, my dear
sir, but"——

  " Fiddle-de-dee, doctor! Of course I'll forgive
you, if you won't repeat the offence. 'Tis unpleasant—a nuisance—'*tis,* upon my soul! Well, however, what do you think is the upshot of the whole
—the practical point—the winding up of affairs—the

<hr>

[*] Pers. Sat. iii.

balancing of the books"—he delighted in accumula-
tions of this sort—" the shutting up of the volume,
eh? I'm going to get married! I'm at dead low-
watermark in money-matters—and, in short, I repeat it, I intend to marry—a gold bag! A good move,
isn't it? But to be candid, I can't take all the credit
of the thing to myself, either, having been a trifle
bored, bullied, *badgered* into it by the family. They
say the world cries shame on me! simpletons, why
listen to the world? I only laugh, ha, ha, ha' an)
cry, curse on the world—and so we are quits with
one another! By-the-way, the germ of that's to be
found in that worthy fellow Plautus!"

All this, uttered with Mr. Effingstone's characteristic emphasis and rapidity of tone and manner,
conveyed his real sentiments; and it was not long
before he carried them into effect. He spent two or
three months in the south of France; and not long
after his return to England, with restored health and
energies, he singled out from among the many, many
women who would have exulted in being an object
of the attentions of the accomplished, the celebrated
Mr. Effingstone, Lady E——— ———, the very flower
of English aristocratical beauty, daughter of a distinguished peer, and sole heiress to the immense
estates of an aged baronet in ———shire.

The unceasing, exclusive attentions exacted from
her suitor by this haughty young beauty operated
for a while as a salutary check upon Mr. Effingstone's reviving propensities to dissipation. So long
as there was the most distant possibility of his being
rejected, he was her willing slave at all hours, on all
occasions; yielding implicit obedience, and making
incessant sacrifices of his own personal conveniences.
As soon, however, as he had " run down the game,"
as he called it, and the young lady was so far com-
promised in the eyes of the world, as to render
retreat next to impossible, he began to slacken in his
attentions; not, however, so palpably and visibly as

to alarm either her ladyship or any of their mutual
relations or friends.   He compensated for the attentions he was obliged to pay her by day, by the most
extravagant nightly excesses.   The pursuits of
intellect, of literature and philosophy, were utterly
and apparently finally discarded—and for what? For
wallowing swinishly in the foulest sinks of depravity;
herding among the acknowledged outcasts, commingling intimately with the very scum and refuse
of society, and revelling amid the hellish orgies
celebrated nightly in haunts of nameless infamy.
Gambling, gluttony, drunkenness, harlotry, blas
phemy!   *   *

[I cannot bring myself to make public the shocking details with which the five following pages of
Dr ——'s Diary are occupied.   If printed, they wou.
appear to many absolutely incredible.   They ar
little else than a corroboration of what is advanced
in the sentences immediately preceding this inter-
jected paragraph.   What follows must be given only
in a fragmentary form—the cup of horror must be
poured out before the reader only κατὰ σταγόνα.*]

Mr. Effingstone one morning accompanied Lady
E—— and her mother to one of the fashionable
shops, for the purpose of aiding the former in her
choice of some beautiful Chinese toys to complete
the ornamental department of her boudoir.   After
having purchased some of the most splendid and
costly articles which had been exhibited, the ladies
drew on their gloves, and gave each an arm to Mr.
Effingstone, to lead them to the carriage.   Lady
E—— was in a flutter of unusually animated spirits,
and was complimenting Mr. Effingstone, in enthusi
astic terms, on the taste with which he had guided their
purchases; and they had left the shop-door, the foot
man was letting down the carriage-steps, when a very
young woman, elegantly dressed, who happened to be

* Also in Aphrodie

passing at that moment, seemingly in a state of deep dejection, suddenly started on seeing and recognising Mr. Effingstone, placed herself between them and the carriage, and lifting her clasped hands, exclaimed in piercing accents, " Oh, Henry, Henry, Henry! how cruelly you have deserted your poor ruined girl! What have I done to deserve it ?   I'm broken-hearted, and can rest nowhere! I've been walking up and down M —— street nearly three hours this morning to get a sight of you, but could not!   Oh, Henry! how differently you said you would behave before you brought me up from ——shire!"   All this was uttered with the impassioned vehemence and rapidity of highly-excited feelings, and uninterruptedly, for both Lady E —— and her mother seemed perfectly petrified, and stood pale and speechless. Mr. Effingstone, too, was for a moment thunder-struck; but an instant's reflection showed him the necessity of acting with decision one way or another. Though deadly pale, he did not disclose any other symptom of agitation ; and with an assumed air of astonishment and irrecognition, exclaimed, concernedly, " Poor creature! unfortunate thing! Some strange mistake this!"   " Oh, no, no, no, Henry! it's no mistake!   You know me well enough—I'm your own poor Hannah !"

" Pho, pho! nonsense, woman! *I* never saw you before."

" Never saw me ! never saw me!" almost shrieked the girl, " and is it come to this ?"

" Woman, don't be foolish—cease, or we must give you over to an officer as an impostor," said Mr. Effingstone, the perspiration bursting from every pore. " Come, come, your ladyships had better allow me to hand you into the carriage.   See, there's a crowd collecting."

" No, no, Mr. Effingstone," replied Lady E——'s mother, with excessive agitation: " this very singular, strange affair—if it *is* a mistake—had better be set right on the spot.   Here, young woman, can you tell me what is the name of this gentleman?" pointing to Mr. Effingstone.

"Effingstone, Effingstone, to be sure, ma'am," sobbed the girl, looking imploringly at him.   The instant she had uttered his name, the two ladies, dreadfully agitated, withdrew their arms from his, and, with the footman's assistance, stepped into their carriage and drove off rapidly, leaving Mr. Effingstone bowing, kissing his hand, and assuring them that he should "soon settle this absurd affair," and be at —— street before their ladyships.   They heard him not however; for the instant the carriage had set off Lady E—— fainted.

"Young woman, you are quite mistaken in me—I never saw you before.   Here is my card—come to me at eight to-night," he added, in an under-tone, so as to be heard by none but her he addressed.   She took the hint, appeared pacified, and each withdrew different ways—Mr. Effingstone almost suffocated with suppressed execrations.   He flung himself into a hackney-coach, and ordered it to —— street, intending to assure Lady E ——, with a smile, that he had instantly "put an end to the ridiculous affair." His knock, however, brought him a prompt "Not at home," though their carriage had but the instant before driven from the door.   He jumped again into the coach, almost gnashing his teeth with fury, drove home, and despatched his groom with a note and orders to wait an answer.   He soon brought it back, with the intelligence that Lord and Lady —— had given their porter orders to reject all letters or messages from Mr. Effingstone!   So there was an end of all hopes from *that* quarter.   This is the history of what was mysteriously hinted at in one of the papers of the day, as a "strange occurrence in high life which would probably break off a matrimonial affair long considered as settled."   But how did Mr. Effingstone receive his ruined dupe at the appointed

hour of eight? He answered her expected knock
himself.

"Now, look, —— !" said he, sternly, extending his
arm to her menacingly, "if ever you presume to
darken my doors again, by ——, I'll murder you! I
give you fair warning. You've ruined me—you have,
you accursed creature!"

"Oh, my God! What am I to do to live? What
is to become of me?" groaned the victim.

"Do? why go and be ——! And here's something
to help you on your way—there!" and he flung her a
check for 50l., and shut the door violently in her face.

Mr. Effingstone now plunged into profligacy with
a spirit of almost diabolical desperation. Divers
dark hints, stinging innuendoes, appeared in the papers, of his disgraceful notoriety in certain scenes
of an abominable description. But he laughed at
them. His family at length cast him off, and refused
to recognise him till he chose to alter his courses—
to "purge."

* * * * * *

Mr. Effingstone was boxing one morning with Be-
lasco—I think it was—at the latter's rooms; and was
preparing to plant a hit which the fighter had defied
him to do, when he suddenly dropped his guard,
turned pale, and in a moment or two fell fainting into
the arms of the astounded boxer. He had several
days previously suspected himself the subject of indisposition—how could it be otherwise, keeping such
hours and living such a life as he did—but not of so
serious a nature as to prevent him from going out as
usual. As soon as he had recovered and swallowed
a few drops of spirits and water, he drove home, intending to have sent immediately for Mr. ——, the
well-known surgeon; but on arriving at his rooms,
he found a travelling carriage-and-four waiting before
the door, for the purpose of conveying him instantly
to the bedside of his dying mother, in a distant part of
England, as she wished personally to communicate to

him something of importance before she died. This he learned from two of his relatives who were up-stairs giving directions to his servant to pack up his clothes and make other preparations for his journey, so that nothing might detain him from setting off the instant he arrived at his rooms. He was startled—alarmed—confounded at all this. Good God! he thought, what was to become of him? He was utterly unfit to undertake a journey, requiring instant medical attendance, which had already been too long deferred; for his dissipation had already made rapid inroads on his constitution. Yet what was to be done? His situation was such as could not be communicated to his brother and sister-in-law—for he did not choose to encounter their sarcastic reproaches. He had nothing for it but to get into the carriage with them, go down to ——shire, and when there devise some plausible pretext for returning instantly to town. That, however, he found impracticable. His mother would not trust him out of her sight one instant, night or day—but kept his hand close locked in hers; he was also surrounded by the congregated members of the family—and could literally scarce stir out of the house an instant. He dissembled his ill ness with tolerable success, till his aggravated agonies drove him almost beside himself. Without breathing a syllable to any one but his own man, whom he took with him, he suddenly left the house, and without even a change of clothes threw himself into the first London coach, and by two o'clock the next day was at his own rooms in M—— street, in a truly deplorable condition, and attended by Sir —— and myself. The consternation of his family in ——shire may be conceived. He trumped up some story about his being obliged to stand second in a duel—but his real state was soon discovered. Nine weeks of unmitigated agony were passed by Mr. Effingstone—the virulence of his disorder for a long time setting at defiance all that medicine could do. This illness also broke him

down sadly, and we recommended to him a second
sojourn in the south of France—for which he set
out the instant he could undertake the journey with
safety. Much of his peculiar character was developed in this illness; that haughty, reckless spirit of
defiance, that contemptuous disregard of the sacred
consolations of religion, that sullen indifference as
to the event which might await him, which his previous character would have warranted me in pre-
dicting.

* * * * * * * *

About seven months from the period last mentioned
(his return from the continent). I received one Sunday evening a note written in hurried characters
and a hasty glance at the seal, which bore Mr. Effingstone's crest, filled me with sudden vague apprehensions that some misfortune or other had befallen
him. This was the note :—

"Dear Doctor,—For God's sake come and see me
immediately, for I have this day arrived in London
from the continent, and am suffering the tortures of
the damned, both in mind and body. Come—come—
in God's name come instantly, or I shall go mad.
Not a word of my return *to any one* till I have seen
you. You will find me—in short my man will accompany you. Yours in agony, St. J. H. Effingstone
Sunday evening, November, 18—."

Tongue cannot utter the dismay with which this
note filled me. His unexpected return from abroad,
the obscure and distant part of the town (St. George's
in the East) where he had established himself, the
dreadful terms in which his note was couched, revived, amid a variety of vague conjectures, certain
fearful apprehensions for him which I had begun to
ontertain before he quitted England. I ordered out
my chariot instantly; his groom mounted the box
to guide the coachman, and we drove down rapidly.
A sudden recollection of the contents of several of
the letters he had sent me latterly from the continent

I.—Q

at my request served to corroborate my worst fears
I had given him over for lost, by the time my chariot
drew up opposite the house where he had so strangely
taken up his abode.   The street and neighbourhood,
though not clearly discernible through the fogs of a
November evening, contrasted strangely with the
aristocratical regions to which my patient had been
accustomed. —— row was narrow, and the houses
were small, yet clean and creditable-looking.   On
entering No. —, the landlady, a person of quiet respectable appearance, told me that *Mr. Hardy* (for
such it seems was the name he chose to go by in
these parts) had just retired to rest, as he felt fatigued
and poorly, and she was just going to make him some
gruel.   She spoke in a tone of flurried excitation,
and with an air of doubt, which were easily attributable to her astonishment at a man of Mr. Effingstone's appearance and attendance, with such superior travelling equipments, dropping into such a house
and neighbourhood as hers.   I repaired to his bedchamber immediately.   It was a small comfortably-
furnished room ; the fire was lit, and two candles
were burning on the drawers.   On the bed, the plain
chintz curtains of which were only half-drawn, lay
St. John Henry Effingstone.   I must pause a moment to describe his appearance, as it struck me at
first looking at him.   It may be thought rather far-
fetched, perhaps, but I could not help comparing him
in my own mind to a gem set in the midst of faded
tarnished embroidery : the coarse texture of the bed
furniture—the ordinary style of the room—its constrained dimensions, constrasted strikingly with the
indications of elegance and fashion afforded by the
scattered clothes, toilet, and travelling paraphernalia,
&c. of the person and manners of its present occupant, who lay on a bed all tossed and tumbled, with
only a few minutes' restlessness.   A dazzling dia-
mond ring sparkled on the little finger of his left
hand, and was the only ornament he ever wore

There was something also in the snowiness, simplicity, and fineness of his linen which alone might have evidenced the superior consideration of its wearer, even were that not sufficiently visible in the noble, commanding outline of the features, faded though they were, and shrinking beneath the inroads of illness and dissipation. His forehead was white and ample; his eye had lost none of its fire, though it gleamed with restless energy; in a word, there was that ease and loftiness in his bearing, that indescribable *manière d'être*, which are inseparable from high birth and breeding. So much for the appearance of things on my entrance.

"How are you, Mr. Effingstone—how are you, my dear sir?" said I, sitting down by the bedside.

"Doctor, the pains of hell have got hold upon me. I am undone," he replied, gloomily, in a broken voice, and extended to me a hand cold as marble.

"Is it as you suspected in your last letter to me from Rouen, Mr. Effingstone?" I inquired, after a pause. He shook his head, and covered his face with both his hands, but made me no answer. Thinking he was in tears, I said, in a soothing tone, "Come, come, my dear sir, don't be carried away; don't"——

"Faugh! Do you take me for a puling child or a woman, doctor? Don't suspect me again of such contemptible pusillanimity, low as I am fallen," he replied, with startling sternness, removing his hands from his face.

"I hope, after all, that matters are not so desperate as your fears would persuade you," said I, feeling his pulse.

"Doctor, don't delude me; all is over, I know it is. A horrible death is before me; but I shall meet it like a man. I have made my bed and must lie upon it."

"Come, come, Mr. Effingstone, don't be so gloomy, or hopeless; the exhausted powers of nature may yet be revived," said I, after having asked him many questions.

" Doctor ——, I'll soon end that strain of yours. 'Tis silly—pardon me—but it *is*. Reach me one of these candles, please." I did so. " Now I'll show you how to translate a passage of Persius.

> Tentemus fauces:—*tenero latet ulcus in ore*
> *Putre*, quod haud deceat plebeia raderebeta!'

Eh, you recollect it? Well, look! What say you to this; isn't it frightful?" he asked, bitterly raising the candle, that I might look into his mouth. It was, alas, as he said! In fact, his whole constitution had been long tainted, and exhibited symptoms of soon breaking up altogether! I feared, from the period of my attendance on him during the illness which drove him last to the continent, that it was beyond human power to dislodge the harpy that had fixed its cruel fangs deeply, inextricably in his vitals. Could it be wondered at, even by himself? Neglect, in the first instance, added to a persevering course of profligacy, had doomed him long, long before to premature and horrible decay! And though it can scarcely be credited, it is nevertheless the fact—even on the continent, in the character of a shattered invalid, the infatuated man resumed those dissolute courses which 'n England had already hurried him almost to death's door!

"My good God, Mr. Effingstone!" I inquired, almost paralyzed with amazement at hearing him describe recent scenes in which he had mingled, which would have made even satyrs skulk ashamed into the woods of old, " how *could* you have been so insane, so stark staring mad?"

" By instinct, doctor, by instinct! The *ncture* of the beast!" he replied, through his closed teeth, and with an unconscious clenching of his hands. Many inquiries into his past and present symptoms forewarned me that his case would probably be marked

by more appalling features than any that had ever
come under my care; and that there was not a ray of
hope that he would survive the long, lingering, and
maddening agonies which were " measured out to
him from the poisoned chalice" which he had "com-
mended to his own lips."

He shed no tears, and repeatedly strove, but in vain,
to repress sighs with which his breast heaved, nearly
to bursting, while I pointed out, in obedience to his
determination to know the worst, some portions of
the dreary prospect before him.

" Horrible! hideous!" he exclaimed, in a low, broken
tone, his flesh creeping from head to foot. " *How*
shall I endure it! Oh, Epictetus, how?" He relapsed into silence, with his eyes fixed on the ceiling
and his hands joined over his breast, and pointing upwards in a posture which I considered supplicatory.
I rejoiced to see it, and ventured to say, after much
hesitation, that I was delighted to see him at last
looking to the right quarter for support and consolation.

" Bah!" he exclaimed, impetuously, removing his
hands, and eying me with sternness almost approaching fury, " *why* will you persist in pestering your patients with twaddle of that sort?—*eandem semper ca-
nens cantilenam, ad nauseam usque*—as though you
carried a psalter in your pocket? When I want to
listen to any thing of that kind, why, I'll pay a parson! Haven't I a tide enough of horror to bear up
against already, without your bringing a sea of superstition upon me? No more of it—no more—'tis
foul." I felt roused myself, at last, to something
like correspondent emotions; for there was an insolence of assumption in his tone which I could not
brook.

" Mr. Effingstone," said I, calmly, " this silly swagger will not do. 'Tis unworthy of you—unscholarly
—ungentlemanly; you *force* me to say so. I beg I
may hear no more of it, or you and I must part. I

have never been accustomed to such treatment, and
I cannot now learn how to endure it from you.   From
what quarter can you expect support or fortitude,"
said I, in a milder tone, seeing him startled and surprised at the former part, " except the despised consolations of religion ?"

" Doctor, you are too superior to petty feelings not
to overlook a little occasional petulance in such a
wretched fellow as I am! You ask me whither I
look for support ?   I reply, to the energies of my own
mind—the tried, disciplined energies of my own mind,
doctor—a mind that never knew what fear was—that
no disastrous combinations of misfortune could ever
yet shake from its fortitude !   What but *this* is it that
enables me to shut my ears to the whisperings of
some pitying friend, who, knowing what hideous tortures await me, has stepped out of hell to come and
advise me to *suicide*—eh ?" he inquired, his eye glar
ing on me with a very unusual expression. " However, as religion, that is, your Christian religion, is a
subject on which you and I can never agree—an old
bone of contention between us—why, the less said
about it the better. It's useless to irritate a man
whose mind is made up. I shall *never* be a believer
—may I die first !" he concluded, with angry vehe
mence.

The remainder of the interview I spent in endea
vouring to persuade him to relinquish his present un-
suitable lodgings, and return to the sphere of his
friends and relations—but in vain. He was fixedly
determined to continue in that obscure hole, he said,
till there was about a week or so between him and
death and then he would return " and die in the bosom
of his family, as the phrase was." Alas! however, I
knew but too well, that in the event of his adhering
to that resolution, he was fated to expire in the bed
where he then lay ; for I foresaw but too truly that
the termination of his illness would be attended with
circumstances rendering removal utterly impos

sible. He made me pledge my word that I would not, without his express request or sanction, apprize any member of his family or any of his friends that he had returned to England. It was in vain that I expostulated, that I represented the responsibility imposed upon me; and reminded him that in the event of any thing serious and sudden befalling him, the censure of all his relatives would be levelled at me. He was immoveable. "Doctor, you know well I dare not see them, as well on my own account as theirs," said he, bitterly. He begged me to prescribe him a powerful anodyne draught; for that he could get no rest at nights; that an intense racking pain was gnawing all his bones from morning to evening, and from evening to morning: and what with this and other dreadful concomitants, he "was," he said, "suffering the tortures of the damned, and perhaps worse." I complied with his request, and ordered him also many other medicines and applications, and promised to see him soon in the morning. I was accordingly with him about twelve the next day. He was sitting up and in his dressing-gown before the fire, in great pain and suffering under the deepest dejection. He complained heavily of the intense and unremitting agony he had endured all night long, and thought that from some cause or other the laudanum draught I ordered had tended to make him only more acutely sensible of the pain. "It is a peculiar and horrible sensation, and I cannot give you an adequate idea of it," he said : "it is as though the marrow in my bones were transformed into something animated—into blind worms, writhing, biting, and stinging incessantly"—and he shuddered, as did I also, at the revolting comparison. He put me upon a minute exposition of the *rationale* of his disorder, and if ever I was at a loss for adequate expressions or illustrations, he supplied them with a readiness, an exquisite appositeness which, added to his astonishing acuteness in comprehending the mos

strictly technical details, filled me with admiration
for his great powers of mind, and poignant regret at
their miserable desecration.

"Well, I don't think you can give me any efficien
relief, doctor," said he, "and I am therefore bent on
trying a scheme of my own."

"And what, pray, may that be?" I inquired, curiously.

"I'll tell you my preparations. I've ordered nearly
a hundred weight of the strongest tobacco that's to
be bought, and thousands of pipes; and with these
I intend to smoke myself into stupidity, or rather insensibility, if possible, till I can't undertake to say
whether I live or not; and my good fellow George is
to be reading me Don Quixote the while." Oh, with
what a sorrowful air of forced gayety was all this
uttered!

One sudden burst of bitterness I well recollect.
I was saying, while putting on my gloves to go, that I
hoped to see him in better spirits the next time I called.

"Better spirits? Ha! ha! How the —— can I
be in better spirits—an exile from society—in such
a contemptible hovel as this—among a set of base-
born brutal savages?—faugh! faugh! It *does* need
something here—here," pressing his hand to his forehead, "to bear it—ay, it does!" I thought his tones
were tremulous, and that for the first time I had ever
known them so; and I could not help thinking the
tears came into his eyes; for he started suddenly
from me, and affected to be gazing at some passing
objects in the street. I saw he was beginning to sink
under a consciousness of the bitter degradation into
which he had sunk—the wretched prospect of his
"sun's going down in darkness!" I saw that the
strength of mind to which he clung so pertinaciously
for support was fast disappearing, like snow beneath
the sunbeam.　　*　　*　　*

[Then follow the details of his disease, which are
so shocking as to be unfit for any but professional

eyes. They represent all the energies of his nature as shaken beyond the possibility of restoration—his constitution wholly undermined: that the remedies resorted to had been almost more dreadful than the disease—and yet exhibited in vain! In the next twenty pages of the Diary, the shades of horror are represented as gradually closing and darkening around this wretched victim of debauchery; and the narrative is carried forward through three months. A few extracts only from this portion are fitting for the reader.]

Friday, January 5.—Mr. Effingstone continues in the same deplorable state described in my former entry. I found him engaged, as usual, deep in Petronius Arbiter! He still makes the same wretched show of reliance on the strength and firmness of his mental powers; but his worn and haggard features —the burning brilliance of his often half-phrensied eyes—the broken, hollow tones of his voice—his sudden starts of apprehension—belie every word he utters. He describes his bodily sufferings as frightful. Indeed, Mrs. —— has often told me that his groans both disturb and alarm the neighbours, even as far as over the way! The very watchman has several times been so much startled in passing at hearing his groans, that he has knocked at the door to inquire about them. Neither Sir —— nor I can think of any thing that seems likely to assuage his agonies. Even laudanum has failed us altogether, though it has been given in unprecedented quantities. I think I can say with truth and sincerity, that scarce the wealth of the Indies should tempt me to undertake the management of another such case. I am losing my appetite—loathe animal food—am haunted day and night by the piteous spectacle which I have to encounter daily in Mr. Effingstone. Oh, that Heaven would terminate his tortures—surely he has suffered enough! I am sure he would hail the prospect of death with ecstasy!

I.—R

Wednesday, 10.—Poor, infatuated, obstinate Effing
stone will not yet allow me to communicate with any
of his family or friends, though he knows they are
almost distracted at not hearing from him, fancying
him yet abroad. Colonel —— asked me the other
day, earnestly, when I last heard from Mr. Effing
stone? I wonder my conscious looks did not betray
me. I almost wish they had. Good God! in what
a painful predicament I am placed! What am I to
do? Shall I tell them all about him, and disregard
consequences? Oh, no, no; how can that be, when
my word and honour are solemnly pledged to the
contrary?

Saturday, 20.—Poor Effingstone has experienced
a signal instance of the ingratitude and heartlessness
of mere men of the world. He sent his man, some
time ago, with a confidential note to Captain ——,
formerly one of his most intimate acquaintances,
stating briefly the shocking circumstances in which
he was placed, and begging him to call and see him.
The captain sent back a *vivâ voce* (!) message, that
he should feel happy in calling on Mr. Effingstone in a
few days' time, and would then, but that he was busy
making up a match at billiards and balancing his betting book, &c. &c. &c. This day the fellow rode up
to the door, and *left a card for Mr. Effingstone, without
asking to see him!* Heartless, contemptible thing!
I drove up about a quarter of an hour after this gentleman had left. Poor Effingstone could not repress
tears while informing me of the above. "Would
you believe it, doctor," said he, "that Captain ——
was one of my most intimate companions, that he
has won many hundred pounds of my money, and
that I have stood his second in a duel?" "Oh, yes
I could believe it all, and much more!" "My poor
man George," he resumed, "is worth a million of
such puppies! Don't you think the good, faithful fel
low looks ill? He is at my bedside twenty times
a-night! Do try and do something for him! I've

left him a trifling annuity out of the wreck of my fortune, poor fellow!" and the rebellious tears again glistened in his eyes. His tortures are unmitigated.

Friday, 26.—Surely, surely I have never seen and seldom heard or read of such sufferings as the wretched Effingstone's. He strives to endure them with the fortitude and patience of a martyr, or rather is struggling to exhibit a spirit of sullen, stoical submission to his fate, such as is inculcated in Arrian's Discourses of Epictetus, which he reads almost all day. His anguish is so excruciating and uninterrupted, that I am astonished how he retains the use of his reason. All power of locomotion has disappeared long ago. The only parts of his body he can move now are his fingers, toes, and head—which latter he sometimes shakes about in a sudden ecstasy of pain, with such frightful violence as would, one should think, almost suffice to sever it from his shoulders! All sensation in the lower extremities has ceased for a fortnight! He describes the agonies about his stomach and bowels to be as though wolves were ravenously gnawing and mangling all within.

Oh, my God, if "men about town," in London or elsewhere, could but see the hideous spectacle Mr Effingstone presents, surely it would palsy them in the pursuit of ruin, and scare them into the paths of virtue!

Mrs. ——, his landlady, is so ill with attendance on him that she has gone to the house of a relative for a few weeks in a distant part of the town, having first engaged one of the poor neighbours to supply her place as Mr. Effingstone's nurse. The people opposite and on each side of the house are complaining again loudly of the strange nocturnal noises heard n Mr. Effingstone's room. They are his groanings!

Tuesday, 31.—Again I have visited that scene of loathsomeness and horror, Mr. Effingstone's chamber. The nurse and George told me he had been

raving deliriously all night long. I found him in-
credibly altered in countenance, so much so, that I
should hardly have recognised his features. He was
mumbling. with his eyes closed, when 1 entered the
room.

" Doctor," he exclaimed, in a tone of doubt and fear,
such as I had never known from him before, " you
have not heard me abuse the Bible lately, have you ?"

" Not *very* lately, Mr. Effingstone," I replied, pointedly.

" Good," said he, with his usual decision and energy
of manner. " There are awful things in that book.
aren't there, doctor ?"

"Many very awful things there are indeed."

" I thought so—I thought so. Pray"—his manner grew suddenly perturbed, and he paused for a
moment, as if to recollect himself; " Pray—pray"—
again he paused, but could not succeed in disguising
his trepidation—" do you happen to recollect whether
there are such words in the Bible as—as—' MANY
STRIPES ?' "

" Yes, there are; and they form part of a very
fearful passage," said I, quoting the verse as nearly
as I could. He listened silently. His features
swelled with suppressed emotion. There was horror
in his eye.

" Doctor, what a—a—remark—able—nay, hideous
dream I had last night! I thought a fiend came and
took me to a gloomy belfry, or some other such place
and muttered 'many stripes—many stripes,' in my
ear; and the huge bell almost tolled me into madness,
for all the damned danced round me to the sound of
it! ha, ha!" He added, with a faint laugh, after a
pause, " There's something cu—cur—cursedly *odd* in
the *coincidence*, isn't there? How it would have
frightened *some* wiseacres!" he continued, a forced
smile flitting over his haggard features, as if in
mockery. " But it is easily to be accounted for—the
intimate connexion—sympathy—between mind and

matter, reciprocally affecting each other—affecting each—ha, ha, ha! Doctor, it's no use keeping up this damned farce any longer; human nature won't bear it! D——n——n! I'm going down to HELL! I am!" said he, almost yelling out the words. I had never before witnessed such a fearful manifestation of his feelings. I almost started from the chair on which I was sitting.

" Why," he continued in nearly the same tone and manner, as if he had lost all self-control, "*what* is it that has maddened me all my life, and left me sober only at this ghastly hour—too late?" My agitation would not permit me to do more than whisper a few unconnected words of encouragement, almost inaudible to myself. In about ten minutes' time, neither of us having broken the silence of the interval, he said, in a calmer tone, " Doctor, be good enough to wipe my forehead, will you ?" I did so. " You know better, doctor, of course, than to attach any importance to the nonsensical rantings extorted by death-bed agonies, eh ? Don't dying people, at least those who die in great pain, almost always express themselves so ? How apt superstition is to rear its dismal flag over the prostrate energies of one's soul, when the body is racked by tortures like mine ? Oh, oh, oh, that maddening sensation about the centre of my stomach ! Doctor, go home and forget all the stuff you've heard me utter to-day—' Richard's himself again !' "

Thursday, 2*d February.*—On arriving this morning at —— row, I was shown into the back parlour, where sat the nurse, very sick and faint. She begged me to procure a substitute, for that she was nearly killed herself, and nothing should tempt her to continue in her present situation. Poor thing ! I did not wonder at it ! I told her I would send a nurse from one of the hospitals that evening, and then inquired what sort of a night Mr. Effingstone had passed. " Terrible," she said ; " groaning, shaking, and roaring all night long, ' many stripes,' 'many stripes,' 'oh, God of mercy!' and inquiring perpetually for you." I repaired to the fatal chamber immediately, though latterly my spirits began to fail me whenever I approached the door. I was going to take my usual seat in the arm-chair by the bedside.

"Don't sit there—don't sit there," groaned or rather gasped Mr. Effingstone, "for a hideous being sat in that chair all night long,"—every muscle in his face crept and shrunk with horror,—"muttering '*many stripes!*' Doctor, order that blighted chair to be taken away, broken up and burnt, every splinter of it! Let no human being ever sit in it again! And give instructions to the people about me never to desert me for a moment—or—or—carry me off!--they will! * * My phrensied fancy conjures up the ghastliest objects that can scare man into madness!" He paused.

"Great God, doctor! suppose, after all, what the Bible says should prove true!" he literally gnashed his teeth, and looked the truer image of despair than I have ever seen represented in pictures, on the stage, or in real life. "Why, Mr. Effingstone, if it *should*, it need not be to your sorrow, unless you choose to make it so," said I, in a soothing tone.

"Needn't it, needn't it?" with an abstracted air, "Needn't it? Oh, good!—hope.—There, there IT sat, all night long, there! I've no recollection of any distinct personality, and yet I thought it sometimes looked like—of course," he added, after a pause and a sigh of exhaustion, "of course these phantoms, or similar ones, must often have been described to you by dying people—eh?"

Friday, 3d.— * * * He was in a strangely altered mood to-day; for though his condition might be aptly described by the words "dead alive," his calm demeanour, his tranquillized features, and the mild expression of his eye, assured me he believed what he said when he told me that his disorder had "taken a turn,"—that the "crisis was past;" and he should *recover!* Alas, was it ever known that dead *mortified* flesh ever resumed its life and functions! To have saved himself from the spring of a hungry tiger, he could not have moved a foot or a finger, and that for the last week! Poor, poor Mr. Effingstone began to thank me for my attentions to him during his illness; said he " owed his life to my consummate skill;" he would " trumpet my fame to the Andes, if I succeeded in bringing him through."

" It has been a very horrible affair, doctor, hasn't it ?" said he.

" Very, very, Mr. Effingstone; and it is my duty to tell you there is yet much horror before you !"

" Ah! well, well! I see you don't want me to be too sanguine—too impatient; it's kindly meant— very! Doctor, when I leave here, I leave it an *altered man !* Come, does not that gratify you, eh ?"

I could not help a sigh. He *would* be an *altered man,* and that very shortly! He mistook the feelings which prompted the sigh. " Mind—not that I'm going to commence saint—far from it; but—but—I don't despair of being a Christian. I don't, upon my honour. The New Testament is a sublime—a—I believe—a true revelation of the Almighty. My heart is quite humbled ; yet—mark me—I don't mean exactly to say I'm a believer; not by any means but I can't help thinking that my inquiries might tend to make me so." I hinted that all these were indications of bettered feelings. I could say no more.

" I'm bent on leading a different life to what I have led before, at all events! Let me see—I'll tell you what I've been chalking out during the night. I shall go to Lord ——'s villa in ——, whither I've often been invited, and shall read Lardner and Paley and get them up thoroughly—I will, by ——!"

" Mr. Effingstone, pardon me"—

" Ah, I understand—'twas a mere slip of the tongue —what's bred in the bone, you know"—

"I was not alluding to the oath, Mr. Effingstone but—but it is my duty to warn you"—

"Ah—that I'm not going the right way to work, eh? Well, at all events, I'll consult a clergyman. The Bishop of —— is a distant connexion of our family, you know; I'll ask his advice! * * Oh, doctor, look at that rich, that blessed light of the sun! Oh, draw aside the window-curtain, let me feel it on me! What an image of the beneficence of the Deity! A smile flung from his face over the universe!" I drew aside the curtain. It was a cold, clear frosty day, and the sun shone into the room with cheerful lustre. Oh, how awfully distinct were the ravages which his wasted features had sustained! His soul seemed to expand beneath the genial influence of the sunbeams; and he again expressed his confident expectations of recovery.

"Mr. Effingstone, do not persist in cherishing false hopes! Once for all," said I, with all the deliberate solemnity I could throw into my manner, "I assure you, in the presence of God, that unless a miracle takes place, it is utterly impossible for you to recover, or even to last a week longer!" I thought it had killed him. His features whitened visibly as I concluded—his eye seemed to sink, and the eyelids fell. His lips presently moved, but uttered no sound. I thought he had received his death-stroke; and was immeasurably shocked at its having been from my hands, even though in the strict performance of my duty. Half an hour's time, however, saw him restored to nearly the same state in which he had been previously. I begged him to allow me to send a clergyman to him, as the best means of soothing and quieting his mind; but he shook his head despondingly. I pressed my point, and he said, deliberately, "*No.*" He muttered some such words as "The Deity has determined on my destruction, and is permitting his devils to mock me with hopes of this sort Let me go then to my own place!'" In this awful state

oi mind I was compelled to leave him. I sent a clergy
man to him in my chaise—the same whom I had
called to visit Mr. —— [alluding to the "Scholar's
Death-bed"]; but he refused to see him, saying, that
if he presumed to force himself into the room, he
would spit in his face, though he could not rise to
kick him out! The temper of his mind had changed
into something perfectly diabolical since my inter
view with him.

Saturday, 4th.—Really, my own health is suffering—my spirits are sinking through daily horrors I
have to encounter at Mr. Effingstone's apartment.
This morning I sat by his bedside full half an hour,
listening to him uttering nothing but groans that shook
my very soul within me. He did not know me when
I spoke to him, and took no notice of me whatever.
At length his groans were mingled with such expressions as these, indicating that his disturbed fancy had
wandered to former scenes.

"Oh! oh! Pitch it into him, Bob! Ten to two
on Cribb! Horrible! These dice are loaded, Wil
mington, by ——, I know they are ! *Seven's the main*
Ha! *done*, by ——! * * Hector, yes—(he was
alluding to a favourite race-horse)—won't 'bate a pound
of his price! Your Grace shall have him for six
hundred—Fore-legs, only look at them! There,
there, go it! away! away! neck and neck—In, in,
by ——! * * Hannah! what the ——'s become of
her—drown'd ? No, no, no,—What a fiend incarnate
that Bet —— is! * * Oh! horror, horror, horror!
Oh, that some one would knock me on the head, and
end me! * * Fire, fire ! Stripes, many stripes—
Stuff! You didn't fire fair. By ——, you fired before
your time—(alluding, I suppose, to a duel in which he
had been concerned)—d—n your cowardice!"

Such was the substance of what he uttered. It
was in vain that I tried to arrest the torrent of vile
recollections.   *   *   *

"Doctor, doctor, I shall die of fright !" he exclaimed,

an hour afterward; " what d'ye think happened to me last night? I was lying here with the fire burnt very low, and the candles out. George was asleep, poor fellow, and the woman gone out to get an hour's rest also. I was looking about, and suddenly saw the dim outline of a table, set, as it were, in the middle of the room. There were four chairs faintly visible, and three ghostly figures came through that door and sat in them one by one, leaving one vacant. They began a sort of horrid whispering, more like gasping—they were DEVILS, and talked about *my* damnation! The fourth chair was for me, they said, and all three turned and looked me in the face. Oh! hideous—shapeless—damned!" He uttered a shuddering groan.　　*　　*　　*

[Here follows an account of his interview with two brothers; the only members of the family—whom he had at last permitted to be informed of his frightful condition—who would come and see him.]　*　*　*
He did little else than rave and howl in a blasphemous manner all the while they were present. He seemed hardly to be aware of their being his brothers, and to forget the place where he was. He cursed me, then Sir ——, his man George, and charged us with compassing his death, concealing his case from his family, and execrated us for not allowing him to be removed to the west end of the town. In vain we assured him that his removal was utterly impossible—the time was past; I had offered it once. He gnashed his teeth and spit at us all! "What! die—die—DIE in this damned hole? I won't die here—I will go to —— street. Take me off! *Devils,* then, do *you* come and carry me there!—Come—out, out upon you! *　*　* You have killed me, all of you! You're twisting me!—You've put a hill of iron on me! I'm dead!—all my body is dead! [*　*　*] George, you wretch! why are you ladling fire upon me! Where do you get it? Out—out—out! I'm flooded with fire!—Scorched—scorched! *　* Now

—now for a dance of devils—Ha—I see! I see!—
There's ——, and ——, and ——, among them!—
What! all three of you dead—and damned before me?
W——! Where is your d—d loaded dice?—Filled with
fire, eh? * * * So you were the three devils I saw sitting at the table, eh? Well, I shall be last—but, d—e,
I'll be the chief of you!—I'll be king in hell! * * *
—What—what's that filthy owl sitting at the bottom
of the bed for, eh?—Kick it off—strike it!—Away—
out on thee, thou imp of hell!—I shall make thee sing
presently!—Let in the snakes—let them in—I love
them! I hear them writhing up stairs!" He began
to shake his head violently from side to side, his eyes
glaring like coals of fire, and his teeth gnashing. I
never could have imagined any thing half so frightful. What with the highly excited state of my feelings, and the horrible scents of death which were
diffused about the room, and to which not the strongest salts of ammonia, used incessantly, could render
me insensible, I was obliged to leave abruptly. I
knew the last act of the black tragedy was closing
that night! I left word with the nurse that so soon
as Mr. Effingstone should be released from his misery,
she should get into a hackney-coach and come to my
house. * * *

I lay tossing in bed all night long—my mind suffused with the horrors of the scene of which I have
endeavoured to give some faint idea above. Were I
to record half what I recollect of his hideous ravings
it would scare myself to read it!—I will not!
Let them and their memory perish! I fancied myself lying side by side with the thing bearing the
name of Effingstone—that I could not move away from
him—that his head, shaking from side to side as I have
mentioned above, was battering my cheeks and forehead; in short, I was almost beside myself! I was
in the act of uttering a fervent prayer to the Deity,
that even in the eleventh hour—the eleventh hour—
when a violent ringing of the night-bell made me

spring out of bed. It was as I suspected. The nurse
had come, and already all was over. My heart
seemed to grow suddenly cold and motionless. I
dressed myself and went down into the drawing-
room. On the sofa lay the woman : she had fainted.
On recovering her senses, I asked her if all was
over; she nodded with an affrighted expression!
A little wine and water restored her self-possession.
'When did it occur?" I asked. "Exactly as the
clock struck three," she replied. "George and I and
Mr. ——, the apothecary, whom we had sent for out
of the next street, were sitting and standing round
the bed. Mr. Hardy lay tossing his head about for
nearly an hour, saying all manner of horrible things.
A few minutes before three he gave a loud howl and
shouted, ' Here, you wretches—why do you put the
candles out—here—here—I'm dying!'

"'God's peace be with you, sir! The Lord have
mercy on you!'—we groaned, like people distracted.

"'Ha—ha—ha! D—n you! D—n you all! Dying?—D—n me! I won't die! I won't die! No—
no! D—n me—I won't—won't!—won't——' and
made a noise as if he was choked. We looked—yes,
he was gone!"

He was interred in an obscure dissenting burying-
ground in the immediate neighbourhood, under the
name of Hardy, for his family refused to recognise
him.

So lived and died a "man about town"—and so, alas!
will yet live and die many another MAN ABOUT TOWN

Death at the Toilet.

"'Tis no use talking to me, mother, I *will* go to
Mrs. P——'s party to-night, if I die for it—that's flat
You know as well as I do that Lieutenant N—— is
to be there, and he's going to leave town to-morrow
—so up I go to dress."

" Charlotte, why will you be so obstinate ? You

know how poorly you have been all the week, and
Dr. —— says late hours are the worst things in the
world for you."

" Pshaw, mother! nonsense, nonsense."

" Be persuaded for once, now, I beg! Oh dear
dear, what a night it is too—it pours with rain, and
blows a perfect hurricane! You'll be wet and catch
cold, rely on it. Come now, won't you stop and keep
me company to-night? That's a good girl!"

" Some other night will do as well for that, you
know; for now I'll go to Mrs. P——'s, if it rains cats
and dogs. So up—up—up I go!" singing jauntily

> " Oh she shall dance all dress'd in white,
>   So ladylike."

Such were very nearly the words, and such the
manner, in which Miss J—— expressed her determination to act in defiance of her mother's wishes
and entreaties. She was the only child of her wid-
owed mother, and had but a few weeks before completed her twenty-sixth year, with yet no other prospect before her than bleak single-blessedness. A
weaker, more frivolous and conceited creature never
breathed—the torment of her amiable parent, the
nuisance of her acquaintance. Though her mother's
circumstances were very straitened, sufficing barely
to enable them to maintain a footing in what is called
the middling genteel class of society, this young woman contrived by some means or other to gratify her
penchant for dress, and gadded about here, there, and
every where the most showily dressed person in the
neighbourhood. Though far from being even pretty
faced, or having any pretensions to a good figure, for
she both stooped and was skinny, she yet believed
herself handsome; and by a vulgar, flippant forward-
ness of demeanour, especially when in mixed company, extorted such attentions as persuaded her that
others thought so.

For one or two years she had been an occasional

patient of mine. The settled pallor, the tallowness of her complexion, conjointly with other symptoms, evidenced the existence of a liver complaint; and the last visits I had paid her were in consequence of frequent sensations of oppression and pain in the chest, which clearly indicated some organic disease of her heart. I saw enough to warrant me in warning her mother of the possibility of her daughter's sudden death from this cause, and the imminent peril to which she exposed herself by dancing, late hours, &c.; but Mrs. J——'s remonstrances, gentle and affectionate as they always were, were thrown away upon her headstrong daughter.

It was striking eight by the church clock when Miss J——, humming the words of the song above mentioned, lit her chamber-candle by her mother's and withdrew to her room to dress, soundly rating the servant-girl by the way for not having starched some article or other which she intended to have worn that evening. As her toilet was usually a long and laborious business, it did not occasion much surprise to her mother, who was sitting by the fire in their little parlour, reading some book of devotion, that the church chimes announced the first quarter past nine o'clock without her daughter's making her appearance. The noise she had made overhead in walking to and fro to her drawers, dressing-table, &c. had ceased about half an hour ago, and her mother supposed she was then engaged at her glass, adjusting her hair and preparing her complexion.

"Well, I wonder what can make Charlotte so very careful about her dress to-night!" exclaimed Mrs. J——, removing her eyes from the book and gazing thoughtfully at the fire; "Oh! it must be because young Lieutenant N—— is to be there. Well, I was young myself once, and it's very excusable in Charlotte—heigho!" She heard the wind howling so dismally without that she drew together the coals of her brisk fire, and was laying down the poker when the clock of —— church struck the second quarter after nine.

"Why, what in the world can Charlotte be doing all this while?" she again inquired. She listened—"I have not heard her moving for the last three quarters of an hour! I'll call the maid and ask." She rung the bell and the servant appeared.

· "Betty, Miss J—— is not gone yet, is she?"

"La, no, ma'am," replied the girl, "I took up the curling-irons only about a quarter of an hour ago, as she had put one of her curls out; and she said she should soon be ready. She's burst her new muslin dress behind, and that has put her into a way, ma'am.'

"Go up to her room then, Betty, and see if she wants any thing; and tell her it's half past nine o'clock," said Mrs. J——. The servant accordingly went up stairs and knocked at the bedroom-door once, twice, thrice, but received no answer. There was a dead silence, except when the wind shook the window. Could Miss J—— have fallen asleep? Oh, impossible! She knocked again, but unsuccessfully as before. She became a little flustered, and after a moment's pause opened the door and entered. There was Miss J—— sitting at the glass. "Why, la, ma'am," commenced Betty in a petulant tone, walking up to her, "here have I been knocking for these five minutes, and"—Betty staggered horror-struck to the bed, and uttering a loud shriek, alarmed Mrs. J——, who instantly tottered up stairs, almost palsied with fright. Miss J—— was dead!

I was there within a few minutes, for my house was not more than two streets distant. It was a stormy night in March: and the desolate aspect of things without—deserted streets—the dreary howling of the wind, and the incessant pattering of the rain, contributed to cast a gloom over my mind, when connected with the intelligence of the awful event that had summoned me out, which was deepened into horror by the spectacle I was doomed to witness

On reaching the house, I found Mrs. J—— in violent
hysterics, surrounded by several of her neighbours
who had been called in to her assistance. I repaired
instantly to the scene of death, and beheld what I
shall never forget. The room was occupied by a
white-curtained bed. There was but one window
and before it was a table, on which stood a looking
glass, hung with a little white drapery; and the vari
ous paraphernalia of the toilet lay scattered about—
pins, brooches, curling-papers, ribands, gloves, &c
An arm-chair was drawn to this table, and in it sat
Miss J——, stone dead. Her head rested upon her
right hand, her elbow supported by the table; while
her left hung down by her side, grasping a pair of
curling-irons. Each of her wrists was encircled by
a showy gilt bracelet. She was dressed in a white
muslin frock, with a little bordering of blonde. Her
face was turned towards the glass, which, by the light
of the expiring candle, reflected with frightful fidelity
the clammy fixed features, daubed over with rouge
and carmine—the fallen lower jaw, and the eyes di
rected full into the glass with a cold, dull stare that
was appalling. On examining the countenance more
narrowly, I thought I detected the traces of a smirk
of conceit and self-complacency, which not even the
palsying touch of death could wholly obliterate.
The hair of the corpse, all smooth and glossy, was
curled with elaborate precision, and the skinny, sallow
neck was encircled with a string of glistening pearls.
The ghastly visage of death thus leering through the
tinselry of fashion—the " vain show" of artificial joy
—was a horrible mockery of the fooleries of life!

Indeed it was a most humiliating and shocking
spectacle. Poor creature! struck dead in the very
act of sacrificing at the shrine of female vanity!
She must have been dead for some time, perhaps for
twenty minutes or half an hour, when I arrived, for
nearly all the animal heat had deserted the body,
which was rapidly stiffening. I attempted, but it

vain, to draw a little blood from the arm. Two or three women present proceeded to remove the corpse to the bed for the purpose of laying it out. What strange passiveness! No resistance offered to them while straightening the bent right arm, and binding the jaws together with a faded white riband which Miss J—— had destined for her waist that evening.

On examination of the body we found that death had been occasioned by disease of the heart. Her life might have been protracted, possibly for years, had she but taken my advice and that of her mother. I have seen many hundreds of corpses, as well in the calm composure of natural death as mangled and distorted by violence; but never have I seen so startling a satire upon human vanity, so repulsive, unsightly, and loathsome a spectacle, as a *corpse dressed for a ball!*

———

CHAPTER VI.

THE TURNED HEAD—THE WIFE.

The Turned Head.

HYPOCHONDRIASIS,* Janus-like, has two faces—a melancholy and a laughable one. The former, though oftener seen in actual life, does not present itself so frequently to the notice of the medical practitioner as the latter; though, in point of fact, one as imperatively calls for his interference as the other. It may be safely asserted, that a permanently morbid mood of mind invariably indicates a disordered state of some part or other of the physical

---

* Arising, as its name imports, from disease in the *hypo-chondres* (ύπό χόνδρος) i. e. the viscera lying under the cartilage of the *breast-bone* and false ribs, the *liver* *spleen*, &c.

I.—S

system ; and which of the two forms of hypochondria will manifest itself in a particular case, depends altogether upon the mental idiosyncrasy of the patient. Those of a dull, phlegmatic temperament, unstirred by intermixture and collision with the bustling activities of life, addicted to sombrous trains of reflection, and, by a kind of sympathy, always looking on the gloomy side of things, generally sink, at some period or other of their lives, into the " slough of despond"—as old Bunyan significantly terms it—from whence they are seldom altogether extricated. Religious enthusiasts constitute by far the largest portion of those afflicted with this species of hypochondria—instance the wretched Cowper; and such I have never known entirely disabused of these dreadful fantasies. Those, again, of a gay and lively fancy, ardent temperament, and droll, grotesque appetencies, exhibit the laughable aspect of hypochondriasis. In such you may expect conceits of the most astounding absurdity that could possibly take possession of the topsy-turvied intellects of a confirmed lunatic : and persisted in with a pertinacity—a dogged defiance of evidence to the contrary—which is itself as exquisitely ludicrous as distressing and provoking. There is generally preserved an amazing *consistency* in the delusion, in spite of the incipient rebuttals of sensation. In short, when once a crotchet of such a sort as that hereafter mentioned is fairly entertained in the fancy, the patient *will* not let it go ! It is cases of this kind which baffle the most adroit medical tactician. For my own part. I have had to deal with several during the course of my practice, which, if described coolly and faithfully on paper, would appear preposterously incredible to a non-professional reader. Such may possibly be the fate of the following. I have given it with a minuteness of detail, in several parts, which I think is warranted by the interesting nature of the case

by the rarity of such narratives,—and, above all, by
the peculiar character and talents of the well-known
individual who is the patient; and I am convinced
that no one would laugh more heartily over it than he
himself—had he not long lain quiet in his grave!

You could scarcely look on N—— without laughing. There was a sorry sort of humorous expression
in his odd and ugly features, which suggested to you
the idea that he was always struggling to repel some
joyous emotion or other with painful effort. There
was the rich light of intellect in his eye, which was
dark and full—you *felt* when its glance was settled
upon you;—and there it remained concentrated, at
the expense of all the other features;—in the clumsy
osseous ridge of eye-bone impending sullenly over
his eyes—the Pittlike nose, looking like a finger and
thumb-full of dough drawn out from the plastic mass,
with two ill-formed holes inserted in the bulbous
extremity—and his large liquorish, shapeless lips—
looked altogether any thing but refined or intellectual. He was a man of fortune—an obstinate bachelor—and was educated at Cambridge, where he
attained considerable distinction; and at the period
of his introduction to the reader was in his thirty-
eighth or fortieth year. If I were to mention his
name it would recall to the literary reader many
excellent and some admirable portions of literature
for the perusal of which he has to thank N——.
The prevailing complexion of his mind was sombrous—but played on occasionally by an arch-hu-
morous fancy, flinging its rays of fun and drollery
over the dark surface, like moonbeams on midnight
waters. I do believe he considered it sinful to
smile! There was a puckering up of the corner of
the mouth, and a forced corrugation of the eyebrows—the expression of which was set at naught
by the conviviality—the solemn drollery of the eyes
You saw Momus leering out of every glance of
them! He said many very witty things in conver-

sation, and had a knack of uttering the quaintest conceits with something like a whine of compunction in his tone, which ensured him roars of laughter. As for his own laugh—when he *did* laugh—there is no describing it—short, sudden, unexpected was it, like a flash of powder in the dark. Not a trace of real merriment lingered on his features an instant after the noise had ceased. You began to doubt whether he had laughed at all, and to look about to see where the explosion came from. Except on such rare occasions of forgetfulness on his part, his demeanour was very calm and quiet. He loved to get a man who would come and sit with him all the evening, smoking, and sipping wine in cloudy silence. He could not endure bustle or obstreperousness; and when he did unfortunately fall foul of a son of noise, as soon as he had had "a sample of his quality," he would abruptly rise and take his leave, saying, in a querulous tone. like that of a sick child, "I'll go!"—[probably these two words will at once recall him to the memory of more than one of my readers]—and he was as good as his word; for all his acquaintances—and I among the number—knew his eccentricities, and excused them.

Such was the man—at least as to the more prominent points of his character—whose chattering black servant presented himself hastily to my notice one morning, as I was standing on my door-steps, pondering the probabilities of wet or fine for the day He spoke in such a spluttering tone of trepidation that it was some time before I could conjecture what was the matter. At length I distinguished something like the words, " Oh, docta, docta, com-a, and see-a a massa! Com-a! Him so gashly—him so ill—ver dam bad—him say so—Oh, lorra-lorra-lorra! Com see-a a massa—him ver orrid!"

" Why, what on earth is the matter with you, you sable, eh?—Why can't you speak slower, and tell me plainly what's the matter?" said I, impatiently, fo-he seemed inclined to gabble on in that strain for some minutes longer. " *What's* the matter with your master, sirrah, eh?" I inquired, jerking his striped morning-jacket.

" Oh, docta! docta! Com-a—massa d—n bad! Him say so!—Him head turned! Him head turned"—

" Him *what*, sirrah?" said I, in amazement.

" Him *head turned*, docta—him head turned," replied the man, slapping his fingers against his forehead

" Oh, I see how it is, I see; ah, yes," I replied, pointing to my forehead in turn, wishing him to see that I understood him to say his master had been seized with a fit of insanity.

" Iss, iss, docta—him massa *head turned*—him head turned!—d—n bad!"

" Where is Mr. N——, Nambo, eh?"

" Him lying all 'long in his bed, massa—him d—n bad. But him 'tickler quiet—him head turned"—

" Why, Nambo, what makes *you* say your master's head's turned, eh? What d'ye mean?"

" Him massa self say so—him did—him head turned—d—n." I felt as much at a loss as ever; it was so odd for a gentleman to acknowledge to his negro-servant that his *head was turned*.

" Ah! he's gone *mad*, you mean, eh—is that it? Hem! *mad*—is it so?" said I, pointing, with a wink, to my forehead. "No, no, doctor—him head turned! —him *head*," replied Nambo; and raising both his hands to his head, he seemed trying to twist it round! I could make nothing of his gesticulations, so I dismissed him, telling him to take word that I should make his master's my first call. I may as well say, that I was on terms of friendly familiarity with Mr. N——, and puzzled myself all the way I went, with attempting to conjecture what *new* crotchet he had taken into his odd—and, latterly, I began to suspect, half-addled—head. He had never disclosed symptoms of what is generally understood by the word hypochondriasis; but I often thought

was not a likelier subject in the world for it. At
length I found myself knocking at my friend's door
fully prepared for some specimen of amusing ec
centricity—for the thought now crossed my mind
that he might be really ill. Nambo instantly an
swered my summons, and in a twinkling conducted
me to his master's bedroom. It was partially dark
ened, but there was light enough for me to discern
that there was nothing unusual in his appearance.
The bed was much tossed, to be sure, as if with the
restlessness of the recumbent, who lay on his back,
with his head turned on one side, and buried deep in
the pillow, and his arms folded together outside the
counterpane. His features certainly wore an air of
exhaustion and dejection, and his eye settled on me
with an alarmed expression from the moment that
he perceived my entrance.

"Oh, dear doctor!—Isn't this frightful!—Isn't it a
dreadful piece of business?"

"Frightful!—dreadful business?" I repeated, with
much surprise. "*What* is frightful? Are you ill—
have you had an accident, eh?"

"Ah—ah!—you may well ask that!" he replied;
adding, after a pause, "it took place this morning
about two hours ago!"

"You speak in parables, Mr. N——! Why, what
in the world is the matter with you?"

"About two hours ago—yes," he muttered, as if he
had not heard me. "Doctor, do tell me truly now,
for the curiosity of the thing, what did you think of
me on first entering the room?—Eh?—Feel inclined
to laugh, or be shocked—which?"

"Mr. N——, I really have no time for trifling, as I
am particularly busy to-day. Do, I beg, be a little
more explicit! Why have you sent for me?—
What is the matter with you?"

"Why, God bless me, doctor!" he replied, with
an air of angry surprise in his manner which I
never saw before. "I think, indeed, it's *you* who are

trifling! Have you lost your eyesight this morning? Do you pretend to say you do not see I have
undergone one of the most extraordinary alterations
in appearance that the body of man is capable of—
such as never was heard or read of before?"

"Once more, Mr. N——," I repeated, in a tone of
calm astonishment, "be so good as to be explicit.
What are you raving about?"

"Raving!—Egad, I think it's *you* who are raving,
doctor!" he answered; "or you must wish to insult
me! Do you pretend to tell me you do not see that
my head is turned?"—and he looked me in the face
steadily and sternly.

"Ha—ha—ha!—Upon my honour, N——, I've
been suspecting as much for this last five or ten
minutes! I don't think a patient ever described his
disease more accurately before!"

"Don't mock me, Doctor ——," replied N——,
sternly. "By ——, I can't bear it! It's enough for
me to endure the horrid sensations I do!"

"Mr. N——, what *do* you"——

"Why, d——n——n, Doctor ——! you'll drive me
mad!—Can't you see that the back of my head is in
front, and my face looking backwards? Horrible!" I
burst into loud laughter.

"Doctor ——, it's time for you and me to part-
high time," said he, turning his face away from me.
"I'll let you know that I'll stand your nonsense no
longer! I called you in to give me your advice, not
to sit grinning like a baboon by my bedside! Once
more,—finally: Doctor ——, are you disposed to be
serious and rational? If you are not, my man shall
show you to the door the moment you please." He
said this in such a sober, earnest tone of indignation,
that I saw he was fully prepared to carry his threat
into execution. I determined, therefore, to humour
him a little, shrewdly suspecting some temporary
suspension of his sanity—not exactly *madness*—but
at least some extraordinary hallucination. To adopt

an expression which I have several times heard him use—" I saw what o'clock it was, and set my watch to the time."

"Oh—well!—I see now how matters stand!—The fact is, I *did* observe the extraordinary posture of affairs you complain of—immediately I entered the room—but supposed you were joking with me, and twisting your head round in that odd way for the purpose of hoaxing me; so I resolved to wait and see which of us could play our parts in the farce longest!—Why, how's all this, Mr. N——? —Is it then *really* the case?—Are you—in—in earnest—in having your head turned?"—" *In earnest*, doctor!" replied Mr. N——, in amazement. "Why, do you suppose this happened by my own will and agency?—Absurd!"—"Oh, no, no—most assuredly not—it is a phenomenon—hem! hem!—a phenomenon—not unfrequently attending on the *nightmare*," I answered, with as good a grace as possible.

"Pho, pho, doctor!—Nonsense!—You must really think me a child, to try to mislead me with such stuff as that! I tell you again, I am in as sober possession of my senses as ever I was in my life; and, once more, I assure you, that in truth and reality my head is turned—literally so."

"Well, well!—So I see!—It is indeed, a very extraordinary case—a very unusual one; but I don't, by any means, despair of bringing all things round again!—Pray tell me how this singular and afflicting accident happened to you?"

"Certainly," said he, despondingly. "Last night, or rather this morning, I dreamed that I had got to the West Indies—to Barbadoes, an island where I have, as you know, a little estate left me by my uncle, C——; and that, a few moments after I had entered the plantation, for the purpose of seeing the slaves at work, there came a sudden hurricane, a more tremendous one than ever was known in those parts;

-trees—canes—huts—all were swept before it! Even the very ground on which we stood seemed whirled away beneath us! I turned my head a moment to look at the direction in which things were going, when, in the very act of turning, the blast suddenly caught my head, and—oh, my God! —blew it completely round on my shoulders, till my face looked quite—directly behind me—over my back! In vain did I almost wrench my head off my shoulders, in attempting to twist it round again; and what with horror, and—and—altogether—in short, I awoke—and found the frightful reality of my situation!—Oh, gracious Heaven!" continued Mr. N——, clasping his hands, and looking upwards, "what have I done to deserve such a horrible visitation as this?"

Humph! it is quite clear what is the matter *here*, thought I; so assuming an air of becoming professional gravity, I felt his pulse, begged him to let me see his tongue, made many inquiries about his general health, and then proceeded to subject all parts of his neck to a most rigorous examination; before, behind, on each side, over every natural elevation and depression, if such the usual varieties of surface may be termed, did my fingers pass; he all the while sighing, and cursing his evil stars, and wondering how it was that he had not been killed by the "dislocation!" This little farce over, I continued silent for some moments, scarcely able the while to control my inclination to burst into fits of laughter, as if pondering the possibility of being able to devise some means of cure.

' Ah,—thank God!—I have it—I have it"--

"What!—what—eh?—what is it?"

"I've thought of a remedy, which, if—if—if any thing in the world can bring it about, will set matters right again—will bring back your head to its former position."

"Oh, God be praised!—Dear—dear doctor!—if

you do but succeed, I shall consider a thousand pounds but the earnest of what I *will* do to evince my gratitude!" he exclaimed, squeezing my hand fervently "But I am not absolutely certain that we shall succeed," said I, cautiously. "We will, however, g've the medicine a twenty-four hours' trial; during all which time you must be in perfect repose, and consent to lie in utter darkness. Will you abide by my directions?"

"Oh, yes—yes—yes!—dear doctor!—What *is* the inestimable remedy? Tell me—tell me the name of my ransomer. I'll never divulge it—never!"

"That is not consistent with my plans at present, Mr N——," I replied, seriously; "but, if successful —of which I own I have *very* sanguine expectations —I pledge my honour to reveal the secret to you." "Well—but—at least you'll explain the nature of its operation—eh?" Is it internal—external—what?" The remedy, I told him, would be of both forms; the latter, however, the more immediate agent of his recovery; the former, preparatory—predisposing. I may tell the reader simply what my physic was to be: three *bread-pills* (the ordinary *placebo* in such cases) every hour; a strong laudanum draught in the evening; and a huge bread-and-water poultice for his neck, with which it was to be environed till the parts were sufficiently *mollified* to admit of the neck's being twisted back again into its former position; and when that was the case—why—to ensure its permanency, he was to wear a broad band of strengthening-plaster for a week!! This was the bright device, struck out by me—all at a heat; and explained to the poor victim with the utmost solemnity and deliberation of manner—all the wise winks and knowing nods, and hesitating "hems" and "has" of professional usage—sufficed to inspire him with some confidence as to the results. I confess I shared the most confident expectations of success. A sound night's rest, hourly pill-taking, and the clammy saturating sensation round about his neck, I fully believed, would bring him round :—and, in the full anticipation of seeing him disabused of the ridiculous notion he had taken into his head, I promised to see him the first thing in the morning, and took my departure. After quitting the house, I could not help laughing immoderately at the recollection of the scene I had just witnessed; and Mrs. M——, who happened to be passing on the other side of the street, and observed my involuntary risibility, took occasion to spread an ill-natured rumour, that I was in the habit of " making myself merry at the expense of my patients!"—I foresaw, that should this " crick in the neck" prove permanent, I stood a chance of listening to innumerable conceits of the most whimsical and paradoxical kind imaginable—for I knew N——'s natural turn to humour. It was inconceivable to me how such an extraordinary delusion could bear the blush of daylight, resist the evidence of his senses, and the unanimous simultaneous assurances of all who beheld him. Though it is little credit to me, and tells but small things for my self-control—I cannot help acknowledging, that at the bedside of my next patient, who was within two or three hours of her end, the surpassing absurdity of the " turned head" notions glared in such ludicrous extremes before me, that I was nearly bursting a blood-vessel with endeavours to suppress a perfect peal of laughter!

About eleven o'clock the next morning, I paid N—— a second visit. The door was opened as usual by his black servant, Nambo; by whose demeanour I saw that something or other extraordinary awaited me. His sable swollen features and dancing white eyeballs showed that he was nearly bursting with laughter. " He—he—he !" he chuckled, in a sort of *sotto voce*, " him massa head turned !—him back in front ! him waddle !—he—he—he !"—and he twitched his clothes—jerking his jacket, and pointing

to his breeches, in a way that I did not understand
On entering the room where N——, with one of his
favourite silent smoking friends (M——, the late
well-known counsel), were sitting at breakfast, I
encountered a spectacle which nearly made me
expire with laughter. It is almost useless to attempt describing it on paper—yet I will try. Two
gentlemen sat opposite each other at the breakfast-
table, by the fire: the one with his face to me was
Mr M.——; and N—— sat with his back towards the
door by which I entered. A glance at the former
sufficed to show me that he was sitting in tortures
of suppressed risibility. He was quite red in the
face—his features were swelled and puffy—and his
eyes fixed strainingly on the fire, as though in fear
of encountering the ludicrous figure of his friend.
They were averted from the fire, for a moment, to
welcome my entrance—and then redirected thither
with such a painful effort—such a comical air of
compulsory seriousness—as, added to the preposterous fashion after which poor N—— had chosen to
dress himself—completely overcame me. The thing
was irresistible; and my utterance of that peculiar
choking sound, which indicates the most strenuous
efforts to suppress one's risible emotions, was the
unwitting signal for each of us bursting into a long
and loud shout of laughter. It was in vain that I
bit my under lip almost till it brought blood, and that
my eyes strained till the sparks flashed from them,
in the vain attempt to cease laughing; in full before
me sat the exciting cause of it, in the shape of
N——, his head supported by the palm of his left
hand, with his elbow propped against the side of the
armchair. The knot of his neck-kerchief was tied,
with its customary formal precision, back at the nape
of his neck; his coat and waistcoat were buttoned
down his back;—and his trousers, moreover, to match
the novel fashion, buttoned behind, and, of course,
the hinder parts of them bulged out ridiculously in

front!—Only to look at the coat-collar fitting under
the chin, like a stiff military stock—the four tail
buttons of brass glistening conspicuously before, and
the front parts of the coat buttoned carefully over
his back—the compulsory handiwork of poor Nambo!

N——, perfectly astounded at our successive
shouts of laughter—for we found it impossible to
stop,—suddenly rose up in his chair, and, almost inarticulate with fury, demanded what we meant by
such extraordinary behaviour. This fury, however,
was all lost on *me;* I could only point, in an ecstasy
of laughter, almost bordering on phrensy, to his novel
mode of dress—as my apology. He stamped his
foot, uttered volleys of imprecations against us, and
then ringing his bell, ordered the servant to show us
both to the door. The most violent emotions, however, must in time expend their violence, though in
the presence of the same exciting cause; and so it
was with Mr. M—— and myself. On seeing how
seriously affronted N—— was, we both sat down,
and I entered into examination, my whole frame
aching with the prolonged convulsive fits of irre-
pressible laughter.

It would be in vain to attempt a recital of one of
the drollest conversations in which I ever bore part.
N——'s temper was thoroughly soured for some
time. He declared that my physic was all a humbug, and a piece of quackery; and the " d—d *pudding*
round his neck" the absurdest farce he ever heard
of; he had a great mind to make Nambo eat it, for
the pains he had taken in making it and fastening it
on—poor fellow!

Presently he lapsed into a melancholy, reflective
mood. He protested that the laws of locomotion
were utterly inexplicable to him—a practical para-
dox; that his volitions as to progressive and retro-
gressive motion neutralized each other; and the
necessary result was, a cursed circumgyratory motion—for all the world like that of a hen that had

lost one of its wings! That henceforward he shoulo be compelled to crawl, crablike, through life, all ways at once, and none in particular. He could not conceive, he said, which was the nearest way from one given point to another; in short, that all his sensations and perceptions were disordered and confounded. His situation, he said, was an admirable commentary on the words of St. Paul—"But I see another law in my members warring against the law of my mind." He could not conceive how the arteries and veins of the neck could carry and return the blood, after being so shockingly twisted—or "how the windpipe went in," affording a free course to the air through its distorted passage. In short, he said, he was a walking lie! Curious to ascertain the *consistency* of this anomalous state of feeling, I endeavoured once more to bring his delusion to the test of simple sensation by placing one hand c.i his nose and the other on his breast, and asking him which was which, and whether both did not lie in the same direction; he wished to know why I persisted in making myself merry at his expense. I repeated the question, still keeping my hands in the same position; but he suddenly pushed them off, and asked me, with indignation, if I was not ashamed to keep his head looking over his shoulder in that way—accompanying the words with a shake of the head, and a sigh of exhaustion, as if it had really been twisted round into the wrong direction. "Ah!" he exclaimed, after a pause, "if this unnatural state of affairs should prove permanent—hem!—I'll put an end to the chapter! He —he—he! He—he—he!" he continued, bursting suddenly into one of those short abrupt laughs, which I have before attempted to describe. "He— he—he! how d—d odd!" We both asked him, in surprise, what he meant, for his eyes were fixed on the fire in apparently a melancholy mood.

"He—he—he! exquisitely odd, by G—! He

he—he!" After repeated inquiries, he disclosed the occasion of his unusual cachinnations.

"I've just been thinking," said he, "suppose—He, he, he!—suppose it was to come to pass that I should be *hanged*—he, he, he! God forbid, by-the-way; but, suppose I should, how old Ketch would be puzzled! —my face looking one way, and my tied hands and arms pointing another! How the crowd would stare! He, he, he! **And** suppose," pursuing the train of thought, "**I were** to be publicly whipped— how I could superintend operations! And how the devil am I to ride on horseback, eh? with my face to the tail, or to the mane? In short, what is to become of me? I am, in effect, shut out from society!"

"You have only to *walk circumspectly*," said M——; "and as for *back*-biters—hem."

"That's odd—very—but impertinent," replied the hypochondriac, with a mingled expression of chagrin and humour.

"Come, come, N——, don't look so steadily on the dark side of things," said I.

"The *dark* side of things?" he inquired—"I think it is the *back*-side of things I am compelled to look at!"

"Look forward to better days," said I.

"*Look forward*, again! What nonsense!" he replied, interrupting me; "impossible! How can I *look forward?* My life will henceforth be spent in wretched *retrospectives!*" and he could not help smiling at the conceit. Having occasion during the conversation to use his pocket-handkerchief, he suddenly reached his hand behind as usual, and was a little confused to find that the usual position of his coat-pocket required that he should take it from before! This I should have conceived enough to put an end to his delusion, but I was mistaken.

"Ah! it will take some time to reconcile me to this new order of things—but practice—practice, you know!" It was amazing to me that his sensations, so contradictory to the absurd crotchet he had taken into his head, did not convince him of his error, especially when so frequently compelled to act in obedience to long-accustomed impulses. As, for instance, on my rising to go, he suddenly started from his chair, shook my hands, and accompanied me to the door, as if nothing had been the matter.

"Well now! what do you think of that?" said I, triumphantly.

"Ah—ah!" said he, after a puzzled pause, "but you little know the effort it cost me!"

*　*　*　*　*　*　*　*

He did not persevere long in the absurd way of putting on his clothes which I have just described; but even after he had discontinued it, he alleged his opinion to be, that the front of his clothes ought to be with his face! I might relate many similar fooleries springing from this notion of his turned head, but sufficient has been said already to give the reader a clear idea of the general character of such delusions. My subsequent interviews with him while under this unprecedented hallucination were similar to the two which I have attempted to describe. The fit lasted near a month. I happened luckily to recollect a device successfully resorted to by a sagacious old English physician, in the case of a royal hypochondriac abroad, who fancied that his nose had swelled into greater dimensions than those of his whole body besides; and forthwith resolved to adopt a similar method of cure with N——. *Electricity* was to be the wonder-working talisman! I lectured him out of all opposition, silenced his scruples, and got him to fix an evening for the exorcisation of the evil spirit—as it might well be called—which had taken possession of him. Let the reader fancy, then, N——'s sitting-room, about seven o'clock in the evening, illuminated with a cheerful fire, and four mould candles; the awful

electrifying machine duly disposed for action: Mr.
S—— of —— Hospital, Dr. ——, and myself, all
standing round it, adjusting the jars, chains, &c.; and
Nambo busily engaged in laying bare his master's
neck, N—— all the while eying our motions with
excessive trepidation. I had infinite difficulty in
getting his consent to one preliminary—the bandag-
ing of his eyes. I succeeded, however, at last, in
persuading him to undergo the operation blindfolded,
in assuring him that it was essential to success; for
that if he was allowed to see the application of the
conductor to the precise spot requisite, he might
start, and occasion its apposition to a wrong place!
The *real* reason will be seen presently; the great
manœuvre could not have been practised but on
such terms; for how could I give his head a sudden
twist round at the instant of his receiving the shock,
if he saw what I was about? I ought to have
mentioned that we also prevailed upon him to sit
with his arms pinioned, so that he was completely
at our mercy. None of us could refrain from an
occasional titter at the absurdity of the solemn
farce we were playing—fortunately, however, unheard by N——. At length, Nambo being turned
out, and the doors locked, lest seeing the trick he
might disclose it subsequently to his master, we
commenced operations. S—— worked the machine
—round, and round, and round, whizzing—sparkling
—crackling—till the jar was moderately charged:
it was then conveyed to N——'s neck, Dr. —— using
the conductor. N——, on receiving a tolerably
smart shock, started out of his chair, and I had not
time to give him the twist I had intended. After a
few moments, however, he protested that he felt
" something loosened" about his neck, and was easily
induced to submit to another shock considerably
stronger than the former. The instant the rod was
applied to his neck, I gave the head a sudden excruciating wrench towards the left shoulder, S——

I —T

striking him at the same moment a smart blow on the crown. Poor N——! "Thank God!" we all exclaimed, as if panting for breath.

"I—i—is it all over?" stammered N——, faintly—quite confounded with the effects of the threefold remedy we had adopted.

" Yes—thank God, we have at last brought your head round again, and your face looks forward now as heretofore!" said I.

" O, remove the bandage—remove it! Let my own eyesight behold it! Bring me a glass!"

"As soon as the proper bandages have been applied to your neck, Mr. N——."

" What, eh—a *second* pudding, eh?"

" No, merely a broad band of diachlum plaster, to prevent—hem—the contraction of the skin," said I. As soon as that was done, we removed the handkerchiefs from his eyes and arms.

"Oh, my God, how delightful!" he exclaimed, rising and walking up to the mirror over the mantelpiece. " Ecstasy! All really right again"—

"My dear N——, do not, I beg, do not work your neck about in that way, or the most serious disarrangement of the—the parts," said I—

"Oh, it's so, is it? Then I'd better get into bed at once, I think, and you'll call in the morning."

I did, and found him in bed. " Well, how does all go on this morning?" I inquired.

"Pretty well—middling," he replied, with some embarrassment of manner. " Do you know, doctor, I've been thinking about it all night long—and I strongly suspect"—His serious air alarmed me—I began to fear that he had discovered the trick. " I strongly suspect—hem—hem"—he continued.

" *What?*" I inquired, rather sheepishly.

" Why, that it was my *brains* only that were turned—and—that—that—most ridiculous piece of business—"

— 'Vhy, to be sure, Mr N——." * * * and he was

so ashamed about it, that he set off for the country immediately, and among the glens and mountains of Scotland endeavoured to forget that ever he dreamed that HIS HEAD WAS TURNED.

The Wife.

Monday Evening, 25*th July*, 18—.—Well! the poor martyr has at last been released from her sufferings, and her wasted remains now lie hid in the kindly gloom of the grave. Yes, sweet, abused, forgiving Mrs. T——! I this morning attended your funeral, and let fall a tear of unavailing regret! Shall I tell your sad story all in one word or two? The blow that broke your heart, was struck by YOUR HUSBAND!

Heaven grant me calmness in recording your wrongs! Let not the feelings of outraged humanity prompt me to " set down aught in malice ;" may I be dispassionately enough disposed to say but the *half*, nay, even the hundredth part only, of what I know, and my conscience will stand acquitted! Let not him who shall read these pages anticipate any thing of romance, of high-flown rodomontade, in what follows. It is all about a poor, ill-used, heart-broken WIFE: and such a one is, alas! too often met with in all classes of society to attract, in an ordinary case, any thing of public notice. The ensuing narration will not, however, be found an ordinary case. It is fraught with circumstances of such peculiar aggravation, and exhibits such a moving picture of the tenderness and unrepining fortitude of woman, that I am tempted to give it at some length. Its general accuracy may be relied upon, for I suc-ceeded in wringing it from the reluctant lips of the poor sufferer herself. I must, however, be allowed to give it in my own way; though at the risk of its being thereby divested of much of that sorrowful simplicity and energy—that touching *naïveté*, which characterized its utterance. I shall conclude with extracting some portions of my notes of visits made in a professional capacity.

Miss Jane C—— had as numerous a retinue of suitors as a pretty person, well-known sweetness of disposition, considerable accomplishments, and 10,000*l.* in the funds could not fail of procuring to the possessor of so many charms She was an orphan, and was left absolute mistress of her property on attaining her twenty-first year. All the members of her own family most strenuously backed the pretensions of the curate of the parish—a young man of ascertained respectability of character and family, with a snug stipend, and fair prospects of preferment. His person and manners were agreeable and engaging; and he could not conceal his inclination to fling them both at Miss C——'s feet. All who knew the parties said it would be an excellent match in all respects, and a happy couple they would make. Miss C—— herself could not look at the curate with indifference—at least if any inference might be drawn from an occasional flushing of her features at church, whenever the eyes of the clergyman happened to glance at her—which was much oftener than his duty required. In short, the motherly gossips of the place all looked upon it as a settled thing, and had pitched upon an admirable house for the future couple. They owned unanimously that " the girl *might* have gone further and fared worse," and so forth; which is a great deal for such people to say about such matters.

There happened, however, to be given a great ball by the lady of the ex-mayor, where Miss C—— was one of the stars of the evening; and at this party there chanced to be a young Londoner, who had just come down on a three-weeks' holyday. He was training for the law, in a solicitor's office, and was within six or seven months of the expiration of his articles. He was a personable sort of fellow to look at—a spice of a dandy—and had that kind of air about him which tells *of town*,—if not of the blandness, ease, and elegance of the West, still —*of town*,—which contrasted favourably with the comparative ungainliness of provincials. He was, in a word, a sort of small star; a triton among the minnows; and whatever he said or did *took instantly*. Apprized by some judicious relations of the united charms of Miss C——'s purse and person, he took care to pay her the most conspicuous attentions. Alas! the quiet claims of the curate were soon silenced by his bustling rival. This young spark chatted Miss C—— out of her calm senses. Wherever she went he followed; whatever she said or did he applauded. He put into requisition all his small acquirements—he sung a little, danced more, and talked an infinity. To be brief, he determined on carrying the fort with a *coup de main;* and he succeeded. The poor curate was forgotten for ever! Before the enterprising young lawyer left —— he was an accepted suitor of Miss C——'s. The coldness of all her friends and acquaintances signified nothing to her; her lover had, by some means or other, obtained so powerful a hold of her affections, that sneers, reproaches, remonstrances, threats on the part of all who had previously betrothed her to the curate, " passed by her as the idle wind, which she regarded not." She promised to become his wife as soon as his articles should have expired, and to live in London.

In due time, as matters approached a crisis, friends called in to talk over preliminaries. Mr. T—— proved to be comparatively penniless ; but what was that ? Miss C—— acted with very unusual generosity. She insisted on settling only half her fortune—and left the other half entirely at his disposal; receiving this intelligence from her own lips, the young man uttered the most frantic expressions of gratitude—promised her eternal love and faithfulness

—protested that he idolized her—and took her at her word. It was in vain that cautious relations stepped in to tender their remonstrances to Miss C——, on the imprudent extent to which she was placing her fortune beyond her own control. Opposition only consolidates the resolutions of a woman whose mind is once made up. The generous creature believed implicitly every word that her lover poured into her delighted ear; and was not startled into any thing like distrust, even when she found that her young husband had expended, at one fell swoop, nearly 3000*l.* of the 5000*l.* she had so imprudently placed at his disposal, in "establishing themselves in London," as he termed it. He commenced a rate of living which it required an income of at least 1000*l.* a-year to support; and when an uncle of his wife's took upon him to represent to Mr. T—— the ruinous extravagance—the profligate expenditure of his wife's funds—which all their mutual friends were lamenting and reprobating, he was treated with an insolence which for ever put an end to *his* inter-ference, and effectually prevented that of any other party.

All, however, might yet have gone right, had Mr. T—— paid but a moderate attention to business for his father had the command of an excellent town connexion, which soon put enough into his son's hands to keep two clerks in regular employment. His wife was soon shocked by hearing her husband make incessant complaints of the drudgery of the office, though he did not devote, on an average, more than two or three hours a-day to it. He was always proposing some new party, some delightful drive some enchanting excursion to her; and she dared not refuse, for he had already once disclosed symptoms of a most imperious temper whenever his will was interfered with. She began to grow very uneasy, as she saw him drawing check after check on the banker, without once replacing a

single sum! Good God, what was to become of
them? He complained of the tardy returns of busi
ness; and yet he left it altogether to the management of two hired clerks! He was beginning also
to grow irregular in his hours; reiteratedly kept
her waiting hours expecting his return to dinner in
vain; filled his table with frequent drafts from the
gayest and most dissipated of his professional acquaintance, whose uproar, night after night, alarmed
every one in the house, and disturbed the neighbours. Then he took to billiard-playing, and its
invariable concomitants—drinking and late hours;—
the theatres, frequented alone for the purpose—alas!
too notorious to escape even the chaste ears of his
unfortunate and insulted wife—of mingling with the
low wretches—the harpies—who frequent the slips
and saloons;—then "drinking-bouts" at taverns—
and midnight "larks"—in company with a set of
vulgar, ignorant young fellows, who always left him
to settle the reckoning. He sent one of the clerks
to his banker's, with a check for 10*l.* one morning;
which proved to be the exact amount by which he
had "overdrawn" his account—and worse—returned
without the usual accommodation afforded. He was
a little dismayed at finding such to be the state of
things, and went up stairs to his wife to tell her,
with a curse, of the "meanness"—the "d——d
stinginess" of Messrs ——.

"What! Is it *all* spent, George?" she inquired,
in a gentle and very faint tone of voice.

"Every rap—d—ee, Jane!" was the reply. She
turned pale and trembled, while her husband, putting
his hands in his pockets, walked suddenly to and fro
about the parlour. With trembling hesitation, Mrs.
T—— alluded to the near approach of her confinement, and asked, almost inaudible with agitation,
and the fear of offending him, whether he had made
any provision for the necessary expenses attending
it—had laid up *any thing*. He replied in the nega-

tive, in a very petulant tone.   She could not refrain from shedding tears.

"Your crying can't mend matters," said he, rudely walking to the window, and humming the words of some popular air.

"Dear, dear George, have you seen any thing in my conduct to displease you?" she inquired, wiping her eyes.

"Why do you ask me that, Mrs. T——!" said he, walking slowly towards her, and eying her very sternly.   She trembled, and had scarcely breath enough to answer, that she had feared such might have been the case, because he had become *rather* cool towards her of late.

"D'ye mean to say, ma'am, that I have used you ill, eh?   Because if you do, it's a d——"

"Oh, no, no, George, I did not mean any thing of the kind; but—but—kiss me, and say you have for-given me—do!" and she rose and stepped towards him with a forced smile.   He gave her his cheek with an air of sullen indifference, and said, "It's no use blubbering about misfortunes, and all that sort of thing.   The fact is, something must be done, or, d—ee! *I'm* done!   Look, here I am!   Bring your chair here, do!   What do you say to these?"   He pulled out of his pocket a crumpled mass of papers —bills which had been sent in during the week,— some of them of several months' standing : 70*l.* were due for wine and spirits; 90*l.* for articles of his dress; 35*l.* for the use of a horse and tilbury; 10*l.* for cigars and snuffs ; and, in short, the above are a sample of the items which swelled into the gross amount of nearly 300*l.*—all due—all from creditors who refused him longer credit, and all for articles which had ministered *nothing* to his poor wife's com-fort or necessities.   She burst into tears, as she looked over the bills scattered on the table, and flinging her arms round her husband's neck, implored him to pay more attention to business.

" I tell you I *do*," he replied, impatiently, suffering, not returning, her affectionate embrace.

" Well, dearest George! I don't mean to blame
you"——

" You had better not, indeed!" he replied, coldly ;
" but what's to be done, eh ?—That's what we ought
to be considering. Do you think—hem!—I am—
Could you, do you think—" He paused, and seemed
embarrassed.

" Could I *what*, dear George ?" she inquired,
squeezing his hands.

" D'ye think—D—ee!—no—I'll ask you some othei
day !" and he rose from his chair. What will be
imagined was his request ?—She learned some days
afterward, that it was for her to use her influence
with her aunt, an old widow lady, to lend him 500*l*. !
—To return, however.

He was standing opposite the fire, in moody con-
templation, when a rude puppy, dressed in the extreme of the fashion, with three different-coloured
waistcoats on, burst unceremoniously into the parlour, and disturbed the sorrowful *tête-à-tête* of T——
and his wife, by rushing up to the former, shaking
his hands, and exclaiming boisterously—" Ah !
T——, how d'ye do, d—ee ?—Bill Bunce's *chaffer*
has beat ——; he has, by —! I've won 15*l*. on it !
Oh, a thousand pardons, ma'am—I didn't see you ;
but there's been a great dog-fight, you see, and I
have been luckier than what Mr. T—— here has, for
I've won 15*l*. and he has lost 20*l*. !"

This precious puppy was one of T——'s bosom
friends !—Ay, incredible as it may seem, it was for
such worthless fellows, such despicable blockheads
as these, that Mr. T—— had squandered his generous wife's property, and forsaken her company !
On the present occasion,—a sample of what had occurred so often as to cause no surprise—nothing but
a gush of bitter tears after he was gone,—T——
eivilly bade her good morning, and departed arm-in-

I.—U

arm with his " friend," and did not return till past
two o'clock in the morning, almost dead-drunk.
Had he seen how the remainder of the day was spent
by his poor wife—in tears and terror—unsoothed by
the thought that her husband was absent on errands
of honourable employment—content with making a
scanty dinner of that at which the servant " turned
up her nose," as the phrase is—and sitting the rest of
the evening sewing and shedding tears by turns, till
the hour of midnight warned her to retire to a
sleepless bed: could he have felt the hurried beatings of the heart whenever her wakeful ear fancied
she heard the sound of his approaching footsteps on
the pavement beneath: could he have done this, he
might not, *possibly*, on waking in the morning, have
called her a ——, nor STRUCK HER on the mouth till
her under-lip was half cut through, for presuming to
rouse him before he had slept off the fumes of the
brandy, and all he had drunk over night—in order
that he might be in trim for a consultation appointed
for eleven o'clock. *He did do this;* and I was the
first person on earth to whom she reluctantly told
it—on her deathbed!

Though her delicate and interesting situation—
within a very few weeks of her accouchement—
might have kindled a spark of tenderness and pride
in the bosom of any husband who had not lost all
the feelings of honour and manliness, it sufficed, apparently, to inspire T—— with a determination to
treat her more unkindly and neglectfully than ever.
She scarcely ever saw him during the day; and
when he came home at night—more than once conducted by the watchman—he was almost invariably
stupified with liquor; and if ne had the power of
utterance, he seemed to take a demoniacal pleasure in
venting upon her the foulest expressions which he
could recollect being used by the riffraff of the
taverns where he spent his time. More than once
was she so horrified with what he said, that, at the

peril of her life, she insisted on leaving him, and sharing the bed of the servant! Her wretched looks might have broken a heart of stone; yet it affected not that of the wretch who called her his wife!

A few days after the occurrence above related, the maid-servant put a twopenny-post letter into her mistress's hands; and fortunate it was for Mrs. T—— that the girl happened to be in the room while she read it, awaiting orders for dinner. The note was in these words, written in a feigned, but still a lady's hand:—

"UNFORTUNATE MADAM!

"I feel it my duty to acquaint you that your husband, Mr. T——, is pursuing quite disgraceful courses all night and day, squandering away his money among sharpers and blacklegs, and that he is persuaded to back one of the boxers in a great fight that is to be; and above all, and what I blush to tell you,—but it is fitting Mrs. T—— should know it, in my opinion,—Mr. T—— is notoriously keeping a woman of infamous character, with whom he is constantly seen at the theatres and most other public places, and she passes as his *cousin*. Hoping that you will have prudence and spirit to act in this distressing business as becomes a lady and a wife, I am,

"Madam,
" With the truest respect and sympathy,
"A REAL FRIEND."

Mrs. T—— read this cruel letter in silence—motionless—and with a face that whitened sensibly as she proceeded; till, at the disgraceful fact mentioned in the concluding part, she dropped the paper from her hands—and the servant ran to her in time to prevent her falling from the chair, for she had swooned! It was long before she came to; and when that was the case, it was only that she might be carried to her bed—and she was confined that evening. The child was stillborn! All this came on the husband like a thunderstroke, and shocked him for a time into something like sobriety and compunction. The admirable qualities of his wife —her virtues and her meekness—shone before his startled eyes in angel hues. He forsook the scenes a constant frequenting of which had rendered him unworthy to live under the same roof with her, and betook himself to the regular pursuits of business with great earnestness. He soon found out what arduous up-hill work it was to bring again under his control affairs which had been so long and shamefully neglected. He felt several times disposed to throw it all over in disgust; for, alas! he had lost almost every vestige of the patience and accuracy of business-habits. He succeeded, with great difficulty, in appeasing the more clamorous of his creditors, and, in a word, he once more stood a chance of clearing his way before him. His poor wife, however, was brought several times to the very verge of the grave, and was destined for months to the monotonous hours of a bed of sickness. For nearly a month, she experienced the most affectionate attentions from her husband, that were consistent with a due attention to the business of his office. She felt revived and cheered by the prospect of his renewed attachment, and trusted in its permanency. But, alas! her husband was not made of such materials as warranted her expectations; he was little else than a compound of weakness, vanity, ignorance, and ill-temper; and for such a one the sober loveliness and attractiveness of domestic life had no charms. He had no sooner got his affairs a little into train, and succeeded in reviving the confidence of some of his principal clients, than he began to relax his efforts. One by one his old associates drew round him, and re-entangled him in the toils of dissipation. The first time that poor ill-fated Mrs. T—— came down into the parlour to dinner, after a three months' absence in her sick-chamber, she was doomed to dine alone—disappointed of the promised presence of her husband to welcome her—for the same low, contemptible coxcomb, formerly introduced to the reader as one of her husband's most intimate friends, had called in the course of the morning, and succeeded in enticing him away to a tavern-dinner with a " set of good ones," who were afterward to adjourn to one of the minor theatres. In vain was the little fillet of veal, ordered by her husband himself, placed on the table before his deserted wife ; she could not taste it, nor had strength enough to carve a piece for the nurse ! Mr. T—— had had the grace to send her a note of apology, alleging that his absence was occasioned by " an affair of business !" This cruel and perfidious conduct, however, met with its due punishment. One of his principal creditors—his tailor—happened to be swallowing a hasty dinner in a box adjoining the one in which T—— and his boisterous associates were dining, and accidentally cast eyes on his debtor T——. He saw and heard enough to fill him with fury ; for he heard his own name mentioned by the half-inebriated debtor, as one of the " *served-out snips*" whom he intended to " do"—an annunciation which was received by the gentlemanly young men who were dining with him, with cries of " Bravo, T——, do ! D—ee, I—and I—and I—have done it before this !"

The next morning he was arrested for a debt of 110*l* at the suit of the very " snip" whom he intended, in his own witty way, to " do," and carried off to a spunging-house in Chancery Lane. There he lay for two days without his wife's knowing any thing of the true state of things. He could get no one to stand bail for him, till one of his wife's insulted friends, and his own brother-in-law, came for-

ward reluctantly for that purpose, in order to calm
her dreadful agitation, which had flung her again on
a sick-bed. Her husband wrote her a most peniten-
tial letter from the spunging-house, imploring her
forgiveness of his misconduct, and promising amend-
ment. Again she believed him, and welcomed him
home with enthusiastic demonstrations of fondness.
He himself could not refrain from weeping; he
sobbed and cried like a child; for his feelings—what
with the most pungent sense of disgrace, and remorse, and conscious unworthiness of the sweet
creature, whose affections no misconduct of his
seemed capable of alienating—were quite overcome.
Three of his largest creditors commenced actions
against him, and nothing seemed capable of arresting
the ruin now impending over him. Where was he
to find the means of satisfying their claims? He
was in despair, and had sullenly and stupidly come
to a resolution to let things take their course, when,
as if Providence had determined to afford him one
chance more of retrieving his circumstances, the
sudden death of his father put him in possession
of 300*l.* in ready cash; and this sum, added to 200*l.*
advanced him by two of his wife's friends, who
could not resist her agonizing supplications, once
more set matters to rights.

* * * * * * * *

Passing over an interval of four years, spent with
disgrace to himself, and anguish to his wife, similar
to that described above, they must now be presented
to the reader occupying, alas! a lowered station of
society. They had been compelled to relinquish an
airy, respectable, and commodious residence, for a
small, bad house, in a worse neighbourhood. His
business had dwindled down to what was insufficient
to occupy the time of one solitary clerk, whom he
was scarcely able to pay regularly—and the more
respectable of his friends had deserted him in
disgust. The most rigorous—nay, almost starv'ng

—economy on the part of his wife barely sufficed to make both ends meet. She abridged herself of almost every domestic comfort, of all those little elegancies which a well-bred woman loves to keep about her, and did so without a murmur. The little income arising from the 5000*l*: her settlement-money, might surely of itself, with only ordinary prudence on his part, have enabled them to maintain their ground with something like respectability, especially if he had attended to what remained of his business. But, alas! alas! T——'s temper had by this time been thoroughly and permanently soured. He hated his good wife—his business—his family—himself—every thing except liquor and low company! His features bore testimony to the sort of life he led—swelled, bloated, and his eyes languid and bloodshot. Mrs. T—— saw less of him than ever; for not far from his house there was a small tavern, frequented by not the most respectable sort of people; and there was T—— to be found, evening after evening, smoking and drinking himself into a state of stupid insensibility, till he would return home redolent of the insufferable stench and fumes of tobacco-smoke and brandy-and-water! In the daytime he was often to be found for hours together at an adjoining billiard-room, where he sometimes lost sums of money, which his poor wife was obliged to make up for by parting, one by one, with her little trinkets and jewelry! What could have infatuated him to pursue such a line of conduct? it may be asked. Why, as if of set purpose, to ruin the peace of mind of one of the fondest and most amiable wives that ever man was blessed with? A vulgar but forcible expression may explain all,—it was "the nature of the beast." He had no intellectual pleasures—no taste for the quiet enjoyments of home; and had, above all, in his wife, too sweet, confiding, and unresisting a creature! Had she proved a ter-magant, the aspect of things might have been very different; *she* might have *bullied* him into something like a sense of propriety. But here, however, he had it all his own way—a poor creature, who allowed him to break her heart without remonstrance or reproach; for the first she *dared* not—the second she could not! It would have melted a heart of stone to see her! She was wasted to a skeleton, and in such a weak, declining state of health, that she could scarcely stir out of doors. Her appetite was almost entirely gone; her spirits all fled long ago! Now, shall I tell the reader *one* immediate cause of such physical exhaustion? I will, and truly. Mr. T—— had still a tolerable share of business, but he could scarcely be brought to give more than two hours' attendance in his office a-day, and sometimes not even that. He therefore imprudently left almost every thing to the management of his clerk, a worthy young man, but wholly incompetent to such a charge. He had extorted from even his idle and unworthy master frequent acknowledgments of his obligations for the punctuality with which he transacted all that was intrusted to him, and, in particular, for the neatness, accuracy, and celerity with which he copied drafts of pleadings, leases, agreements, &c. His master often hiccoughed to him his astonishment at the rapidity with which he "turned them out of hand." Little did the unworthy fellow imagine that in saying all this, he was uttering, not his clerk's, but his WIFE's praises! For *she* it was, poor creature! who, having taken the pains to learn a lawyer's hand, engrossing, &c. from the clerk, actually sat up almost regularly till two or three o'clock in the morning, plodding, occasionally through papers and parchments—making long and laborious abstracts—engrossing settlements, indentures, &c. and copying pleadings, till her wearied eyes and her little hands could no longer perform their office! I could at this moment lay my hands on a certain legal instrument of tiresome prolixity, which was engrossed, every word, by Mrs. T——! *This* was the way in which his wife spent the hours of midnight, to enable him to squander away his time and money in the unworthy, the infamous manner above related!

Was it wonderful that her health and spirits were wholly borne down by the pressure of so many accumulated ills! Had not her husband's eye been dulled, and his perceptions deadened, by the perpetual stupors of intoxication, he might have discerned the hectic flush—the coming fever—the blood-spitting, which foretel—consumption! But that was too much to be expected. As for the evenings—that part of his day was invariably spent at his favourite tavern, sotting hour after hour among its lowest frequenters; and as for her night-cough and blood-spitting, he was lulled by liquor into too profound a repose to be roused by the sounds which were, in effect, his martyred wife's death-knell! If, during the daytime, he was, in a manner, forced to notice her languor—her drooping spirits—the only notice, the only sympathy it called forth on his part, was a cold and careless inquiry, why she did not call in a medical man! I shall conclude this portion of my narrative with barely reciting four instances of that conduct on the part of Mrs. T——'s husband. which at last succeeded in breaking her heart; and which, with many other similar vices, were communicated to me with tears of tortured sensibility.

I. Half-drunk, half-sober, he one evening introduced to her, at tea, a familiar "friend," whose questionable appearance might, at first sight, have justified his wife's refusal to receive her. Her conversation soon disclosed her real character; and the insulted wife abruptly retired from the room that was polluted by the presence of the infamous creature, whom he avowed to be *his mistress!* He sprung after her to the door, for the purpose of dragging her back; but her sudden paleness, and the faint tones in which she whispered—"Don't stop me—

don't—or I shall die!" so shocked him, that he allowed her to retire, and immediately dismissed the wretch, whom he could have brought thither for no other purpose than to insult his wife! Poor creature! did a portion of her midnight earnings go towards the support of the wretch who was kept by her husband? Was not such a consideration sufficient to stab her to the heart?

II. Having occasion, late one evening, to rummage among her husband's office-papers, in search of something which was to be engrossed that night, her eye happened to light on a document, with a pencil superscription—"*Copy, case for counsel, concerning Mrs. T——'s marriage-settlement.*" A very excusable curiosity prompted her to peruse what proved to be a series of queries submitted to counsel, on the following points, among others: What present powers he had under her marriage-settlement?—whether her own interest in it could be legally made over to another, with her consent, during her lifetime, and if so, how?—whether or not he could part with the reversion, provided she did not exercise her power of willing it away elsewhere?—From all this, was it possible for her not to see how heartlessly he was calculating on the best method of obtaining possession of the remnant of her fortune?

" Oh, cruel—cruel—cruel George! So impatient! —Could you not wait a month or two? I'm sure I shall not keep you out of it long! I always intended to leave it you, and I won't let this alter my mind, though it is cruel of you!" sobbed Mrs. T——, till her heart seemed breaking. At that moment she heard her husband's loud obstreperous knock at the door, and hastily crumpling up the paper into the drawer of the desk from which she had taken it, she put out the candle, and leaving her midnight labours, flew up stairs to bed—to a wretched and sleepless one!

III. Mrs. T——'s child, which was about three

years and a half old, was suddenly seized with convulsive fits, as she was one evening undressing it for bed. Fit after fit followed in such rapid succession that the medical man who was summoned in prepared her to expect the worst. The distraction of her feelings may be easier conceived than described, as she held on her knee the little creature on whose life were centred all the proud and fond feelings of a mother's love, deepened into exclusive intensity—for it seemed the only object on earth to return her love;—as she held it, I say, but with great difficulty, for its tiny limbs were struggling and plunging about in a dreadful manner. And then the frightful rolling of the eyes! They were endeavouring to pour a tea-spoonful of Dalby's carminative, or some such medicine, through the closed teeth, when the room-door was suddenly thrown open, and in reeled Mr. T——, more than half-seas over with liquor, and in a merrier mood than usual, for he had been successful at billiards! He had entered unobserved through the street-door, which had been left ajar by the distracted servant-girl, and hearing a bustle in the room, he had entered for the purpose of seeing what was the matter.

"Wh—wh—what is the matter, good fo—olks, eh?" he stammered, reeling towards where Mrs. T—— was sitting, almost fainting with terror at seeing the frightful contortions of her infant's countenance. She saw him not, for her eyes were fixed in agony on the features of her suffering babe.

"What the—the—the d—l is the matter with all of you here, eh?" he inquired, chucking the servant-girl under the chin, who, much agitated, and shedding tears, had approached to beg he would leave the room. He tried to kiss her, and in the presence of the medical man—who sternly rebuked him for his monstrous conduct.

"D—n you, sir—who the d—l are *you?*" he said putting his arms a-kimbo: "I will know what's th matter !"   He came near—he saw all !--the leaden hand, quivering features, the limbs now rigid, and struggling violently, the starting eyeballs.

" Why, for God's sake, what's the matter, eh ?" he stammered, almost inaudibly, while the colour fled from his face, and the perspiration started upon his forehead.   He strove to steady himself, but that was impossible.   He had drunk too deeply.

" What are you doing to the child—what—what ?" he again inquired, in a feeble and faltering voice, interrupted by a hiccough.   No notice whatever was taken of him by ——, who did not seem to see or hear him.—" Jane, tell me," addressing his wife, " has the child had"—hiccough—" an—an—ac—ci—dent ?"   The infant that moment gave a sudden and final plunge ; and Mrs. T——'s faint shriek and the servant-girl's wringing of the hands announced that all was over!   The little thing lay dead in the arms of its mother.

" Sir, your child is dead," said the apothecary, somewhat sternly, shaking Mr. T—— by the arm—for he stood gazing on the scene with a sullen, vacant stare, scarcely able to steady himself.

" Wh—wh—at ! *D—e—a—d!*" he muttered.

" Oh, George, my darling is—is dead!" groaned the afflicted mother, for the first time looking at and addressing her husband.   The word seemed to sober him in an instant.

" What !—Dead !   And I DRUNK !"

The medical man who stood by told me he could never forget the scenes of that evening!   When Mrs. T—— discovered, by his manner, his disgraceful condition, she was so utterly overcome with her feelings of mingled grief, shame, and horror, that she fell into violent hysterics, which lasted almost all night long.   As for T——, he seemed palsied all the next day.   He sat alone during the whole of the next morning. in the room where the dead infant lay gazing upon it with emotions which may be imagined, but not described!

IV. Almost the only piece of ornamental furniture, ner last remaining means of amusement and consolation, was her piano. She played with great taste and feeling, and many a time contrived to make sweet sounds pour an oblivious charm over her sorrows and sufferings, by wandering over the airs which she had loved in happier days. Thus was she engaged one afternoon with one of Dr. Arne's exquisite compositions, the air beginning, "Blow, blow, thou bitter wind." She made several attempts to accompany the music with her voice—for she had a very sweet one, and *could* sing—but, whenever she attempted, the words seemed to choke her. There was a sorrowful appropriateness in them, a touching echo of her own feelings, which dissolved her very spirit within her. Her only child had died, as the reader was informed, about six months before, and her husband had resumed his ill courses, becoming more and more stern and sullen in his demeanour—more unreasonable in his requirements. The words of the air, as may be easily conceived, were painfully appropriate to her situation, and she could not help shedding tears. At that moment her husband entered the room, with his hat on, and stood for some moments before the fire in silence.

"Mrs. T——!" said he, as soon as she had concluded the last stanza.

"Well, George?" said she, in a mild tone.

"I—I must *sell that piano*, ma'am—I must!" said he.

"What!" exclaimed his wife, in a low whisper, turning round on the music-stool, and looking him in the face with an air of sorrowful surprise. "Oh, you cannot be in earnest, George!"

"'Pon my life, ma'am, but I am—I can't afford you superfluities while we can hardly afford the means of keeping body and soul together."

"George—dear George—do forgive me, but I   I—
I *cannot* part with my poor piano!" said she.

"Why not, ma'am, when *I* say you MUST?"

"Oh, because it was the gift of my poor mother!"
she replied, bursting into tears.

"Can't help that, ma'am—not I.   It must go.   I
hate to hear its cursed noise in the house—it makes
me melancholy—it does, ma'am—you're always
playing such gloomy music," replied her husband, in
a severe and less decisive tone.

"Well, well! if that's all, I'll play any thing you
like—only tell me, dear George! what shall I play
for you, now?" said she, rising from the music-stool
and approaching him.

"Play a farewell to the piano; for it *must* go, and
it shall!"

"Dear, kind George! let me keep it a little longer,"
said she, looking him beseechingly in the face—" a
little—a *little* longer"—

"Well, ma'am, sit down and play away till I come
in again, any thing you like."

He left the room; and in less than half an hour—
oh, hardness of heart unheard of!—returned with a
stranger, who proved to be a furniture broker, come
to value the instrument!   That evening it was sold
to him for 15*l.*; and it was carried away the first
thing in the morning, before his wife came down
stairs!   What will be supposed the cause of this
cruelty?   It was to furnish Mr. T—— with money
to pay a bill of the infamous creature more than
once alluded to, and who had obtained a complete
ascendency over him!

It was a long-continued course of such treatment
as this that called *me* upon the scene, in a professional capacity merely at first; till the mournful
countenance of my patient inspired me with feelings
of concern and friendly sympathy, which eventually
led to an entire confidence.   She came to me in the
unostentatious character of a morning patient, in a

hackney-coach, with an elderly female friend. She
looked quite the lady, though her dress was of but
an ordinary quality, yet exquisitely neat and clean,
and she had still a very interesting and somewhat
pretty face, though long-continued sorrow had made
sad havoc with her features! These visits, at intervals of a week, she paid me, and compelled me to
take my fee of one guinea, on each occasion—though
I would have given *two* to be enabled to decline it
without hurting her delicacy. Though her general
health had suffered severely, still I thought that
matters had not gone quite so far as to destroy all
hopes of recovery, with due attention ;—though her
cheeks disclosed, almost every evening, the death-
rose, the grave-flowers of hectic, and night-sweats
and a faint cough were painfully regular in their
recurrence, still I saw nothing, for a long time, to
warrant me in warning her of serious danger. I insisted on her allowing me to visit her at her own house,
and she at last permitted me, on condition that I
would receive at least half-a-guinea—poor creature!
—for every visit. That, however, I soon dropped ;
and I saw her almost every day gratuitously, whenever any temporary aggravations of her symptoms
required my attendance. The first time I saw her
husband I could not help taking a prejudice against
him, though she had never breathed a syllable to me
of his ill conduct. He was apparently about forty
years old, though his real age was not more than two
or three-and-thirty. His manners and habits had
left a sufficiently strong impress upon him to enable
a casual beholder to form a shrewd conjecture as to
his character. His features, once rather handsome
than otherwise, were now reddened and swollen with
long-continued excess; and there was altogether an
air of truculence—of vulgar assurance and stupid sul-
lenness about him which prepossessed me strongly
against him. When, long afterward, Mrs. T——
gave me that description of his appearance and

manners under which he is first placed before the reader of this narrative, I could not help frequently interrupting her with expressions of incredulity, and reminding her of his present ill-favoured looks : but as she went on with her sad story my skepticism vanished.   Personal deterioration was no incredible attendant on moral declension!

March 28th, 18——.—There can be no longer any doubt as to the nature of Mrs. T——'s symptoms. She is the destined victim of consumption. The oftener I go to her house the stronger are my suspicions that she is an unhappy woman, and that her husband ill-uses her. I have many times tried to hint my suspicions to her, but she will declare nothing. She *will* not understand me. Her settled despondency, however, accompanied with an undue current of feverish nervous trepidation, which she cannot satisfactorily explain, convinces me something or other is wrong. I see very little of her husband, for he is scarcely ever in her company when I call. Though his business is that of an attorney, and his house and office are one, I see scarcely any indications of business stirring. I am afraid they are in sinking circumstances. I am *sure* that she, at least, was born and bred for a higher station than she now occupies. Her manners have that simplicity, ease, and elegance which tell of a higher rank in society. I often detect her alone in tears, over a low fire. In a word, I am sure she is wretched, and that her husband is the cause of it. That he keeps late hours I *know*—for she happened to let slip as much one day to me, when I was making inquiries about the time of her retiring to sleep. I feel a great interest in her; for whenever I see her, her appearance reminds me of "Patience on a monument, smiling at Grief,"—

> "Sorrow deck'd
> In the poor faded garb of tarnish'd joy
> Ill fitting to her wasted form."

April 5th.—To-day I found them both together—sitting one on each side of the fireplace, he smok-ing—in the parlour,—and she, with a little flower-ing-work in her lap. I thought he seemed somewhat embarrassed at my entrance; which probably had put an end to some scene of unpleasantness, for her face was suffused with crimson. *It* soon retired, however, and left the wanness to which I had been accustomed in her.

" So my wife's ill, sir, it seems," said Mr. T——, putting his pipe on the hob, and addressing me.

" I'm sorry to say she *is*, Mr. T——," I replied, "and that she is worse to-day than she has been for some time."

Mrs. T—— let fall tears.

" Sorry to hear you say so, doctor; I've just been telling her it's all owing to her own *obstinacy* in not calling entirely on ——."

" I think you might have used a milder word, sir," said I, with involuntary sternness, at the same time directing my attention exclusively to his wife, as if for the purpose of hinting the propriety of his re-tiring.

" What's the matter with her, sir?" he inquired, in a more respectful tone than he had hitherto as-sumed.

" General debility, sir, and occasional pain," said I, coldly.

" What's it owing to ?"

I looked suddenly at Mrs. T——; our eyes met—and hers had an expression of apprehension. I determined, however, to give a hint that I suspected all was not right, and replied—" I fear she does not take suitable nourishment—keeps irregular hours—and has something or other in her mind which harasses her." The latter words I accompanied with a steady look in his face. He seemed a little flushed.

' You're mistaken, sir," said he, with a *brusque* air
I.—X

"she may eat what she likes—that I can afford—may go to bed at what hour she likes—and it's all ner own fault that she will sit moping over the fire night after night, and week after week—waiting for my return—till two or three o'clock in the morning"—

"*That* is, of itself, sufficient to account for her illness," said I, pointedly. He began to lose his temper, for he saw the shameful acknowledgment he had unwittingly made.

"Pray, Mrs. T——," he inquired, looking angrily at his wife, who sat pale and trembling by his side, —"*Have* you any thing on your mind—eh?—if so—why—speak out—no sneaking!"

"No!" she stammered; "and I never said I had—I assure you. Did I ever give you even the mos' distant hint of the kind, doctor?" she continued, appealing to me.

"By no means, madam,—not in the slightest, on any occasion," I replied; "it was only a conjecture—a suspicion of my own." I thought he looked as if he would have made some instant reply, for his eye glared furiously on me. He bit his lips, however, and continued silent. His conscience "pricked him." I began to feel uneasy about the future quiet of Mrs. T——, lest any observations of mine should have excited her husband's suspicions that she made disclosures to me of family matters.

"What would you advise for her, sir?" he asked, coldly.

"Removal, for a few weeks, to the seaside, a liberal diet, and lively society."

"Very well, sir," said he, after a puzzled pause; "very good, sir—very; it shall be attended to.—Perhaps you want to be alone—eh?—So I'll leave you!" and directing a peculiar look towards his wife, as if warning her against something or other, he left the room. She burst into tears directly he was gone.

"My dear madam, forgive me for saying that I suspect your husband's behaviour towards you is somewhat harsh, and, perhaps, *unkind*," said I, in as soothing a tone as I could command, and pressing her hand kindly in mine.

"Oh no, doctor,—no!" she replied, adding in an altered manner, indicating displeasure, "what makes you think so, sir?"

"Why, madam, simply because I cannot shut my eyes or my ears to what passes even while I am here—as, for instance—only just now, madam—just now."

She sighed, and made me no reply. I told her I was in earnest in recommending the course I had mentioned to her husband.

"Oh dear, doctor, no, no,—we could not afford it," said she, with a sigh. At that moment her husband returned,—and resumed his former seat in sullen silence. I soon after took my departure.

April 7th.—Does not the following make one blush for one's species?—I give it merely as I received it from the lips of Mrs. T——. Inestimable woman! why are you fated to endure such pangs?—

About twelve o'clock at noon, hearing her husband come in, and thinking from his looks, of which she caught a casual and hasty glance through the window, that he was fatigued, and stood in need of some refreshment, she poured out a glass of port wine, almost the last in a solitary bottle which she had purchased, under my directions, for medicinal purposes, and, with a biscuit, brought it herself down stairs—though the effort so exhausted her feeble frame, that she was obliged to sit down for several moments on the last stair to recover her breath. At last she ventured to knock at the door of the little back-office where he was sitting, holding the little waiter with the glass of wine and the biscuit in her left hand.

"Who's there?" inquired the gruff voice of T——

"It's only I, my dear. May I come in, please?" replied the gentle voice of his wife.

"What brings *you* here, eh?—What the d—l do you want with me, now?" said he, surlily.

"I've brought you something, my dear," she replied, and ventured to open the door. T—— was sitting before some papers or parchments, alone, and his countenance showed that he was in a worse humour than usual. So soon as he saw her errand, he suddenly rose from his chair, and exclaiming, in an angry tone—"What the —— brings you here in this way, plaguing me while engaged at business, you ——! Eh, woman?" Oh, my God! In a sudden fit of fury he struck the waiter, wine, biscuit and all, out of her trembling hands to the floor, rudely pushed her out of the room, and slammed the door violently in her face. He did not reopen it, though he could not but have heard her fall upon the floor, the shock was so sudden and violent.

There, stretched across the mat, at the bottom of the staircase, lay that suffering creature, unable to rise, till her stifled sobbings brought the servant-girl to her assistance.

"I can't help saying it's most abominable usage of you, ma'am; it is—and I don't care if master hears me say so neither," said the girl, herself crying; "for I'm sure he isn't worthy of the very shoes you wear—he isn't." She was endeavouring to lift her mistress, when Mrs. T—— suddenly burst into a loud unnatural laugh, and went off into violent hysterics. Mr. T——, hearing the noise of talking and laughing, sprung to the door, threw it open, and shouted to them to be "off with their noise—disturbing business!"—but the piteous spectacle of his prostrate wife stopped him—and, almost petrified with horror, he knelt down for the purpose of assisting her all he could.   *   *   *

About an hour after this occurrence I happened to call—and found her lying in bed, alone—her husband

having left her on business. When the servant told
me—and her mistress reluctant.y corroborated what
she said—the circumstances above related, I felt such
indignation swelling my whole frame, that had he
been within reach, I could not have resisted caning
the scoundrel within an inch of his unworthy life!
The recollection of this occurrence tortures me even
now, and I can ha.dly believe that such brutality as
T——'s could have been shown by man!

Mrs. T—— kept her room from that hour, and never
left it till she was carried out for burial!—But this
is anticipating.

April 8th, 9th, 10th, 11th.—I see clearly that poor
Mrs. T—— will never rise from her bed again. She
has drained the bitter cup of grief to the dregs!—
She is one of the meekest sufferers I ever had for a
patient. She says little to me, or to any one : and
shows a regard—a love for her unworthy husband.
which, I think, can be called by no other name than
absolute infatuation. I have never yet heard her
breathe a hint to his disadvantage. He is not much
with her; and from what little I have seen, I feel
convinced that his eyes are opening to a sense of the
flagrant iniquity of his past conduct. And what are
.he effects produced by his feelings of shame and
remorse? He endeavours to forget all in the continual
stupor induced by liquor!

April 12th.—Mrs. T—— delirious. Raved while
I was there about her child—convulsions—said something about " cruel of Mr. T—— to be drunk while
his child lay dying,"—and said many other things
which shocked me unutterably, and convinced me
that her primary disorder was,—a broken heart. I
am sure she must have endured a series of brutal
usage from her husband!

—— *13th.*—The whole house upside down—in disorder and confusion from the top to the bottom—for
there is an *execution* in it, and the officers and an appraiser are making an inventory of the furniture :—

poor—poor—poor Mrs. T—— lying all the while on her death-bed !—The servant told me afterward, that her mistress, hearing strange steps and voices, called what was the matter; and on receiving word of the real state of matters, lifted up her hands, burst into an agony of weeping, and prayed that the Almighty would be pleased to remove her from such a scene of wretchedness. T—— himself, I learned, was sitting cowering over the kitchen fire, crying like a child !—Brute ! coward ! fool !—Such was the state of things at the time of my arrival. I was incon-ceivably shocked, and hurried to Mrs. T——'s room, with unusual haste and trepidation. I found her in tears—sobbing, and exclaiming, " Why won't they let us rest a little ?—why strip the house before I am gone ?—can they not wait a little ?—where, where is Mr. T——?"

I could not for several minutes speak myself, for tears. At length I succeeded in allaying her ex-citement and agitation. At her request, I sent for the appraiser into her room. He came—and seemed a respectable and feeling man.

" Were you bent upon stripping the house, sir, while this lady is lying in her present dangerous state ?"

" Indeed, sir, indeed, sir," replied the man, with considerable emotion—" I'm sorry for it—very—but it is my duty—duty—ordered—" he continued, com-posedly ; " if I had my own way, sir"—

" But at least you need not approach this cham-ber, sir," said I, rather sternly. He stammered something like the words, " obliged—sorry—court of law," &c. &c. Mrs. T—— again burst into an agony of tears.

" Retire, sir, for the present," said I, in an authori-tative tone, " and we will send for you soon." I then entered into a conversation with my poor persecuted patient, and she told me of the 5000l. settled to her separate use, and which she intended, under a power in the deed of settlement, to will to her husband. I spontaneously promised to stand security for the satisfaction of the execution, provided the creditors would defer proceedings for three months. She blessed me for it!—This, however, I afterward learned would be illegal, at least so I was told; and I therefore wrote a check on my banker for the amount awarded by the court, and thus put an end to distress from that quarter.

At Mrs. T——'s request, I returned to her bedside that evening. I found a table, with writing materials placed before a chair, in which she begged me to be seated. She then dictated to me her will—in which, after deducting the sum I had advanced in satisfaction of the execution, and leaving me, in addition, sufficient to purchase a plain mourning-ring, she bequeathed the whole absolutely and unreservedly to her husband; and added, my hand shaking while I wrote it down. " hoping that he will use it prudently, and not entirely forget me when I am gone. And if he should—if he should—" her utterance was choked— "and if he should—*marry again*—" again she paused.

"Dear, dear madam! compose yourself! Take time! This dreadful agitation will accelerate the event we are all dreading!" said I.

"No—don't fear. I beg you will go on! If he should marry again, may he use her—use her—No, no, no!—strike all the last clause out! Give me the pen!" I did as she directed me—struck out from the words, " and if he should," &c., and put the pen into her hand. With trembling fingers she traced the letters of her name; I witnessed it, and she said, "Now, is all right?"—"Yes, madam," I replied. She then burst into a flood of tears, exclaiming, "Oh, George! George! this will show you that, however tired you may have grown of *me*, I have loved you to the end—I have—I have!" She burst into louder weeping.

"Oh, it's hard, it's hard to part with him, though

he *might*—he *might* have used me—No !" she paused
I suffered her excited feelings to grow calm ; and
after some time spent in endeavouring to soothe her,
I took my departure from witnessing one of the most
heart-breaking scenes I have ever encountered. Her
husband could not be prevailed on to enter her room
that day; but all night long, I was told, he sat
outside the door, on one of the steps of the stairs,
and more than once startled her with his sighs.

April 14*th to May* 6*th.*—Sinking rapidly. I shall
be astonished if she survive a week. She is comparatively in a happy frame of mind, and has availed
herself of the consolations of religion to some
purpose. On this day (May 6th) I succeeded in extracting from her the facts which compose the former
part of this narrative. Her gentle, palliating way
of telling it divested the conduct of her husband of
almost all blameworthiness ! She would not allow
me to make a harsh or condemnatory comment all
the way through ! She blamed herself as she went
on ; accused herself of want of firmness ; said she
was afraid Mr. T—— had been disappointed in her
disposition ; said that if he HAD done any thing
wrong, it was owing to the bad companions who had
enticed him from the path of duty into that of dis
sipation ; that he had not exactly *neglected* her, or
wilfully ill-used her ; but—but—she could say nothing
to extenuate his guilt, and I begged her not ! I left
her in tears myself.

O woman ! woman ! woman ! " We had been
brutes without you," and the mean and miserable
T—— was a brute *with* you !

May 8*th.*—Mrs. T—— wasted to a shadow : all
the horrors of consumption ! Her husband, though
apparently broken-hearted, cannot, though probably
no one will believe it—he *cannot* refrain from frequenting the public-house ! He pretends that his
spirits are so low, so oppressed, that he requires the
use of stimulating liquors ! Mrs. T—— made me

promise this morning that I would see her coffin closed ; and a small locket, containing a portion of her child's and husband's hair, placed next her heart. I nodded acquiescence, for my tongue refused me words !

10*th.*—I was summoned this evening to witness the exit from our world of one of the sweetest, loveliest spirits, that it was, and is, unworthy of! I was not sent for under the apprehension that her end was at hand, but on account of some painful symptoms which had manifested themselves since my visit in the morning. It was about nine o'clock when I arrived, and found her in a flow of spirits, very unexpected and unusual in her situation. Her eye was bright, and she could talk with a clearness and rapidity of utterance to which she had long been a stranger. She told me that she had been awakened from sleep by hearing the sound of sweet singing— which, I need hardly say, was wholly imaginary. She was in a very happy frame of mind; but evi dently in a state of dangerous excitement. Her sottish husband was sitting opposite the fire, his face entirely hid in his hands: and he maintained a stupid silence, undisturbed even by my entrance. Mrs. T—— thanked me, in almost enthusiastic terms, for my attention to her throughout her illness, and regretted that I would not allow her to testify her sense of it by leaving me a trifling legacy.

" George—George !" she exclaimed, with sudden and startling energy—an inspiration of tone which brought him in an instant, with an affrighted air, to the foot of the bed.

" George, I've a message from heaven for you! Listen—God will never bless you, unless you alter your courses !" The man shrunk and trembled under the scorching, burning, overpowering glance of her eye. " Come, dearest, come—Doctor —— will let you sit beside me for a few moments !" I removed, and made way for him. She clasped his hand in hers.

"Well, George, we must part!" said she, closing her eyes, and breathing fast. The husband sobbed like a child, with his face buried in his handkerchief. —"Do you forgive me?" he murmured, half-choked with emotion.

"Yes, God knows I do, from my heart! I forgive all the little you have ever grieved me about!"

"Oh, Jane—Jane—Jane!" groaned the man, suddenly stooping over the bed, and kissing her lips in an apparent ecstasy. He fell down on his knees, and cried bitterly.

"Rise, George, rise," said his wife, faintly. He obeyed her, and she again clasped his hand in hers.

"George are you there—are you?" she inquired, in a voice fainter and fainter.

"Here I am, love!—oh, look on me!—look on me!" he sobbed, gazing steadily on her features. "Say once more that you forgive me! Let me hear your dear, blessed voice once again—or—or"—

"I do! Kiss me—kiss me," she murmured, almost inaudibly; and her unworthy husband kissed away the last expiring breath of one of the loveliest and most injured women whose hearts have been broken by a husband's brutality!

12th.—This evening I looked in at the house where my late patient lay dead, for the purpose of fulfilling my promise, and seeing her locket placed near her heart, and the coffin closed. I then went into the parlour, where sat the bereaved husband, in company with his clerk, who had, ever since his engagement, showed a deep regard and respect for Mrs. T——. After I had sat some moments in their company,—

"I've something on my mind, Mr. T——," said the young man with emotion, "which I shall not be happy till I've told you."

"What is it?" inquired his master, languidly.

"Do you recollect how often you used to praise

my draft-copying, and wondered now I got through so much work ?"

"Why, yes, d—n you, yes!" replied his master, angrily; "what have you brought *that* up for now eh ?"

" To tell you, sir, that I did not deserve your praises"—

" Well—well—no more," interrupted his master, impatiently.

" But *I* must, and *will* tell you that it was all done by poor Mrs. T—— ,who learned engrossing, and sat up whole nights together writing, that you might not lose your business, till she was nearly blinded, poor dear lady ! and she would not even let me tell you ! And I shall make free to tell you," continued the young man, rising, and bursting into tears,—" I shall make free to tell you, that you have behaved shame-fully—brutally to her, and have broken her poor heart—you have—and God will remember you for it!"—And he left the room, and never again en-tered the house, the scene of his beloved mistress's martyrdom.

Mr. T—— listened to all this without uttering a word—his eyes dilated—and he presently burst into a fit of loud and lamentable weeping, which lasted long after I left; and that evening he attempted to commit *suicide*, unable, like one before him, to en-dure the heavy smitings of a guilty conscience.

CHAPTER VII.

THE SPECTRE-SMITTEN.

Few topics of medical literature have occasioned more wide and contradictory speculation than that of insanity, with reference as well to its predisposing and immediate causes as its best method of treatment;—since experience is the only substratum of real knowledge, the easiest and surest way of arriving at those general principles which may regulate both our pathological and therapeutical researches,—especially concerning the subtle, almost inscrutable disorder, *mania*—is, when one does meet with some striking, well-marked case, to watch it closely throughout, and be particularly anxious to seize on all those smaller features, those more transient evanescent indications which are truer characteristics of the complaint than perhaps any other. With this object did I pay close attention to the very singular and affecting case detailed in the following narrative. I have not given the *whole* of my observations—far from it; those only are recorded which seemed to me to have some claims to the consideration of both medical and general readers. The apparent eccentricity of the title will be found accounted for in the course of the narrative.

Mr. M——, as one of a very large party, had been enjoying the splendid hospitality of Lady ——, and did not leave till a late, or rather early, hour in the morning. Pretty women, music, and champaign, had almost turned his head ; and it was rather fortunate for him that a hackney-coach stand was within a stone's throw of the house he was leaving. Muffling his cloak closely around him, he contrived to move towards it in a tolerably direct line, and a few moments' time beheld him driving, at the usual snail's pace of those rickety vehicles, to Lincoln's-Inn; for Mr. M—— was a law student. In spite of the transient exhilaration produced by the scenes he had just quitted, and the excitement consequent on the prominent share he took in an animated discussion, in the presence of about thirty of the most elegant women that could well be brought together, he found himself becoming the subject of a most unaccountable depression of spirits. Even while at Lady ——'s, he had latterly perceived himself talking often for mere talking's sake—the chain of his thoughts perpetually broken—and an impatience and irritability of manner towards those whom he addressed, which he readily resolved into the reaction following high excitement. M——, I ought before, perhaps, to have mentioned, was a man of great talent, chiefly, however, imaginative, and had that evening been particularly brilliant on his favourite topic—*diablerie* and mysticism ; towards which he generally contrived to incline every conversation in which he bore a part. He had been dilating, in particular, on the power which Mr. Maturin had of exciting the most fearful and horrific ideas in the minds of his readers, instancing one of his romances, the title of which I have forgotten. Long before he had reached home, the fumes of wine had evaporated, and the influence of excitement subsided; and with reference to intoxication, he was as sober and calm as ever he was in his life. *Why*, he knew not, but his heart seemed to grow heavier and heavier, and his thoughts gloomier, every step by which he neared Lincoln's-Inn. It struck three o'clock as he entered the sombrous portals of the ancient inn of court. The perfect silence—the moonlight shining sadly on the dusky buildings—the cold quivering stars—all these, together, combined to enhance his nervousness. He described it to me as though things seemed to wear a strange, spectral, supernatural aspect. Not a watchman of the inn was heard crying the hour—not a porter moving—no living being but himself visible in the large square he was crossing. As he neared his staircase, he felt his heart fluttering; in short, he felt under some strange, unaccountable influence, which, had he reflected a little, he would have discovered to arise merely from an excitable nervous temperament, operating on an imagination peculiarly attuned to sympathize with terror. His chambers lay on the third floor of the staircase; and on reaching it, he found his door-lamp glimmering with its last expiring ray. He opened his door, and after groping some time in the dark of his sitting-room, found his chamber candlestick. In attempting to light it, he put out the lamp. He went down stairs, but found that the lamp of every landing had shared the fate of his own; so he returned, rather irritated, thinking to amerce the porter of his customary Christmas-box for his niggard supply of oil. After some time spent in the search, he discovered his tinder-box, and proceeded to strike a light. This was not the work of a moment. And where is the bachelor to whom it is? The potent spark, however, dropped at last into the very centre of the soft tinder. M—— blew—it caught—spread—the match quickly kindled, and he lighted his candle. He took it in his hand, and was making for bed, when his eyes caught a glimpse of an object which brought him senseless to the floor. The furniture of his room was disposed as when he had left it; for his laundress had neglected to come and put things in order; the table with a few books on it, drawn towards the fireplace, and by its side the ample-cushioned easy-chair. The first object visible, with sudden distinctness, was a figure sitting in the arm-chair. It was that of a gentleman, dressed in dark-coloured clothes, his hands, white as alabaster, closed together over his lap, and the face looking away; but it turned slowly towards

M- -, revealing to him a countenance of a ghastly hue—the features glowing like steel heated to a white heat, and the two eyes turned full towards him, and blazing—absolutely blazing—he described it—with a most horrible lustre. The appalling spectre, while M——'s eyes were riveted upon it, though glazing fast with fright, slowly rose from its seat, stretched out both its arms, and seemed approaching him, when he fell down senseless on the floor, as if smitten with apoplexy. He recollected nothing more, till he found himself, about the middle of the next day, in bed, his laundress, myself, an apothecary, and several others, standing round him. His situation was not discovered till more than an hour after he had fallen, as nearly as could be subsequently ascertained, nor would it then, but for a truly fortunate accident. He had neglected to close either of his outer-doors (I believe it is usual for chambers in tne inns of court to have double outer-doors), and a woman, who happened to be leaving the adjoining set, about five o'clock, on seeing Mr. M——'s doors both open at such an untimely hour, was induced, by feelings of curiosity and alarm, to return to the rooms she had left for a light, with which she entered his chambers, after having repeatedly called his name without receiving any answer. What will it be supposed had been her occupation at such an early hour in the adjoining chambers? Laying out the corpse of their occupant, a Mr. T——, who had expired about eight o'clock the preceding evening!

Mr. M—— had known him, though not very intimately: and there were some painful circumstances attending his death, which, even though on no other grounds than mere sympathy, M—— had laid much to heart. In addition to this, he had been observed by his friends as being latterly the subject of very high excitement, owing to the successful prosecution of an affair of great interest and importance. We all recounted for his present situation, by referring it to some apoplectic seizure; for we were of course ignorant of the real occasion, fright, which I did not learn till long afterward. The laundress told me that she found Mr. M——, to her great terror, stretched motionless along the floor, in his cloak and full dress, and with a candlestick lying beside him. She at first supposed him drunk; but on finding all her efforts to rouse him unsuccessful, and seeing his fixed features and rigid frame, she hastily summoned to her assistance a fellow-laundress, whom she had left in charge of the corpse next door, undressed him, and laid him on the bed. A neighbouring medical man was then called in, who pronounced it to be a case of epilepsy; and he was sufficiently warranted by the appearance of a little froth about the lips—prolonged stupor, resembling sleep—and frequent convulsions of the most violent kind. The remedies resorted to produced no alleviation of the symptoms; and matters continued to wear such a threatening and alarming aspect, that I was summoned in by his brother, and was at his bedside by two o'clock. His countenance was dark and highly intellectual: its lineaments were naturally full of power and energy; but now overclouded with an expression of trouble and horror. He was seized with a dreadful fit soon after I had entered the room. Oh, it is a piteous and shocking spectacle to see the human frame subject to such demoniacal twitchings and contortions, which are so sudden—so irresistible, as to give the idea of some vague, terrible exciting cause, which cannot be discovered: as though the sufferer lay passive in the grasp of some messenger of darkness *" sent to buffet him."**

* The popular etymology of the word *epilepsy*, sanctioned by several reputable class-books of the profession, which are now lying before me —i. e. "ἐπιλΕΙψις," is totally erroneous, and more—nonsensical. For the information of *general* readers, I may state, that its true derivation is from λαμβάνω, through its Ionic obsolete form λήβω: whence ἐπί-λΗψις —a "seizing," a "holding fast." Therefore we speak of an ATTACK of epilepsy. This etymology is highly descriptive of the disease in question, for the sudden prostration, rigidity, contortions, &c. of the patient, strongly

M—— was a very powerful man; and during the fits it was next to impossible for all present, united to control his movements. The foam at his mouth suggested to his terrified brother the harrowing suspicion that the case was one of hydrophobia. None of my remonstrances or assurances to the contrary sufficed to quiet him, and his distress added to the confusion of the scene. After prescribing to the best of my ability, I left, considering the case to be one of simple epilepsy. During the rest of the day and night, the fits abated both in violence and frequency; but he was left in a state of the utmost exhaustion, from which, however, he seemed to be rapidly recovering, during the space of the four succeeding days; when I was suddenly summoned to his bedside, which I had left only two hours before, with the intelligence that he had disclosed symptoms of more alarming illness than ever. I hurried to his chambers, and found that the danger had not been magnified. One of his friends met me on the staircase, and told me that about half an hour before, while he and Mr. C—— M——, the patient's brother, were sitting beside him, he suddenly turned to the latter, and inquired, in a tone full of apprehension and terror—"Is Mr. T—— dead?"

"Oh dear, yes—he died several days ago"—was the reply.

"Then it was he"—he gasped—"it was he whom I

suggest the idea that he has been *taken* or *seized* ($\epsilon\pi\iota\lambda\eta\phi\vartheta\epsilon\iota\varsigma$) by, as it were, some external invisible agent.—It is worthy of notice, by-the-way, that $\epsilon\pi\iota\lambda\eta\pi\tau\iota\kappa\delta\varsigma$ is used by ecclesiastical writers to denote a person *possessed by a demon*. 'Ε$\pi\iota\lambda\epsilon\iota\psi\iota\varsigma$, signifies simply "failure, deficiency." I shall conclude this note with a practical illustration of the necessity which calls it forth—the correction of a prevalent error. A flippant student, who, I was given to understand, plumed himself much among his companions on his Greek, was suddenly asked by one of his examiners for a definition of *epilepsy*, grounded on its etymology. I forget the definition, which was given with infinite self-sufficiency of tone and manner; but the fine trick of scholarship with which it was finished off I well recollect:—"From $\epsilon\pi\iota\lambda\epsilon\iota\psi\iota\varsigma$ — $\epsilon\pi\iota\lambda\epsilon\iota\pi\omega$—I fail, am wanting); therefore, sir, epilepsy is *a failure of animal functions!*"—The same sage definition is regularly given by a well-known metropolitan lecturer'

I.—Y

saw, and he is surely—*damned!*——Yes, merciful Maker!—he is!—he is!"—he continued, elevating his voice to a perfect roar—"and the flames have reduced his face to ashes!—Horror! horror! horror!"—He then shut his eyes, and relapsed into silence for about ten minutes: when he exclaimed—" Hark you, there—secure me! tie me! make me fast, or I shall ourst upon you and destroy you all—for I'm going mad—I feel it!"—He ceased, and commenced breathing fast and heavily—his chest heaving as though under the pressure of enormous weight; and his swelling, quivering features, evidencing the dreadful uproar within. Presently he began to grind his teeth, and his expanded eyes glared about in all directions, as though following the motions of some frightful object, and muttering fiercely through his closed teeth— " O save me from him—save me—save me!"—It was a fearful thing to see him lying in such a state—grinding his teeth as though he would crush them to powder—his livid lips crested with foam—his features swollen—writhing—blackening; and, which gave his face a peculiarly horrible and fiendish expression, his eyes distorted or inverted upwards, so that nothing but the glaring whites of them could be seen—his whole frame rigid—and his hands clenched, as though they would never open again!—It is a dreadful tax on one's nerves to have to encounter such objects, familiar though medical men are with such and similar spectacles; and in the present instance, every one round the bedside of the unfortunate patient stood trembling with pale and momentarily-averted faces. The ghastly, fixed, up-turning of the eyes in epileptic patients fills me with horror whenever I recall their image to my mind!

The return of these epileptic fits, in such violence, and after such an interval, alarmed me with apprehensions, lest, as is not unfrequently the case, apoplexy should supervene, or even ultimate insanity

was rather singular that M—— was never known

to have had an epileptic fit previous to the present
seizure, and he was then in his twenty-fifth year. I
was conjecturing what sudden fright or blow, or' accident of any kind, or congestion of the vessels of
the brain from frequent inebriation, could have
brought on the present fit—when my patient, whose
features had gradually sunk again into their natural
disposition, gave a sigh of exhaustion—the perspiration burst forth, and he murmured—some time before
we could distinctly catch the words—" Oh—spectre-
smitten ! — spectre-smitten !" — which expression I
have adopted as the title of this paper—" I shall never
recover again !"—Though sufficiently surprised and
perplexed about the import of the words, we took
no notice of them ; but endeavoured to divert his
thoughts from the fantasy, if such there were, which
seemed to possess them, by inquiring into the nature
of his symptoms. He disregarded us, however ; feebly grasped my hand in his clammy fingers, and
looking at me languidly, muttered—" What—Oh,
what brought the *fiend* into *my* chambers ?"—and I
felt his whole frame shiver—" Poor T——! Horrid
fate !"—On hearing him mention T——'s name, we
all looked simultaneously at one another, but without speaking ; for a suspicion crossed our minds,
that his highly-wrought feelings, acting on a strong
imagination, always tainted with superstitious ter-
rors, had conjured up some hideous object, which had
scared him nearly to madness—probably some fancied apparition of his deceased neighbour. He began
again to utter long deep-drawn groans, that gradually
gave place to the heavy stertorous breathing which,
with other symptoms—his pulse, for instance, beating about 115 a-minute—confirmed me in the opinion
that he was suffering from a very severe congestion
of the vessels of the brain. I directed copious vene-
section—his head to be shaven, and covered perpetually with cloths soaked in evaporating lotions—and
blisters behind his ears, and at the nape of the neck

—and appropriate internal medicines. I then left him, apprehending the worst consequences: for I had once before a similar case under my care—one in which a young lady was, which I strongly suspected to be the case with M——, absolutely frightened to death, and went through nearly the same round of symptoms as were beginning to make their appearance in my present patient: a sudden epileptic seizure, terminating in outrageous madness, which destroyed both the physical and intellectual energies, and the young lady expired. I may possibly hereafter prepare for publication some of my notes of *her* case, which had some very remarkable features.

The next morning, about eleven, saw me again at Mr. M——'s chambers, where I found three or four members of his family—two of them his married sisters—seated round his sitting-room fire, in melancholy silence. Mr. ——, the apothecary, had just left, but was expected to return every moment, to meet me in consultation. My patient lay alone in his bed-room asleep, and apparently better than he had been since his first seizure. He had had only one slight fit during the night; and though he had been a little delirious in the earlier part of the evening, he had been on the whole so calm and quiet, that his friends' apprehensions of insanity were beginning to subside; so he was left, as I said, *alone*, for the nurse, just before my arrival, had left her seat by his bedside for a few moments, thinking him " in a comfortable and easy nap," and was engaged, in a low whisper, conversing with the members of M——'s family who were in the sitting-room. Hearing such a report of my patient, I sat down quietly among his relations, determining not to disturb him, at least till the arrival of the apothecary. Thus were we engaged, questioning the nurse in an undertone, when a loud laugh from the bed-room suddenly silenced our whisperings, and turned us all pale. We started to our feet, with blank amazement in each countenance, scarcely crediting the evidence of our senses. Could it be M——! It *must*; there was none else in the room. What, then, was he laughing about?

While we were standing silently gazing on one another with much agitation, the laugh was repeated, but longer and louder than before, accompanied with the sound of footsteps, now crossing the room—then, as of one jumping! The ladies turned paler than before, and seemed scarcely able to stand. They sunk again into their chairs, gasping with terror. "Go in, nurse, and see what's the matter," said I, standing by the side of the younger of the ladies, whom I expected every instant to fall into my arms in a swoon.

"Doctor!—go in?—I—I—I dare not!" stammered the nurse, pale as ashes, and trembling violently.

"Do you come *here*, then, and attend to Mrs.——," said I, "and I will go in." The nurse staggered to my place, in a state not far removed from that of the lady whom she was called to attend; for a third laugh,—long, loud, uproarious,—had burst from the room while I was speaking. After cautioning the ladies and the nurse to observe profound silence, and not to attempt following me till I sent for them, I stepped noiselessly to the bed-room door, and opened it slowly and softly, not to alarm him. All was silent within; but the first object that presented itself when I saw fairly into the room, can never be effaced from my mind to the day of my death. Mr. M—— had got out of bed, pulled off his shirt, and stepped to the dressing-table, where he stood stark-naked before the glass, with a razor in his right hand, with which he had just finished shaving off his eyebrows; and he was eying himself steadfastly in the glass, holding the razor elevated above his head. On seeing the door open and my face peering at him, he turned full towards me—(the grotesque aspect of his countenance denuded of so prominent a feature as the eyebrows, and his head completely shaved, and the wildfire of madness flashing from his staring eyes, exciting the most frightful ideas)—brandishing the razor over his head with an air of triumph, and shouting nearly at the top of his voice—"Ah, ha, ha! —What do you think of this?"

Merciful Powers! May I never be placed again in such perilous circumstances, nor have my mind overwhelmed with such a gush of horror as burst over it at that moment! What was I to do? Obeying a sudden impulse I had entered the room, shutting the door after me; and should any one in the sitting-room suddenly attempt to open it again, or make a noise or disturbance of any kind, by giving vent to their emotions, what was to become of the madman or ourselves? He might, in an instant, almost sever his head from his shoulders, or burst upon me or his sisters, and do us some deadly mischief! I felt conscious that the lives of all of us depended on my conduct; and I do devoutly thank God for the measure of tolerable self-possession which was vouchsafed me at that dreadful moment. I continued standing like a statue—motionless—silent—endeavouring to fix my eye on him, that I might gain the command of *his; that* successful, I had some hopes of being able to deal with him. He, in turn, now stood speechless—and I thought he was quailing— that I had over-mastered him—when I was suddenly fit to faint with despair—for at that awful instant I heard the door-handle tried—the door pushed gently open—and the nurse, I supposed—or one of the ladies —peeping through it. The maniac also heard it— the spell was broken—and, in a phrensy, he leaped several times successively in the air, brandishing the razor over his head as before.

While he was in the midst of these feats, I turned my head hurriedly to the person who had so shamefully disobeyed my orders, and thereby jeopardied my life—whispered in low, affrighted accents—"A the peril of your lives—of mine—shut the door, away —away, hush! or we are all murdered!" I was obeyed—the intruder withdrew, and I heard a sound as if she had fallen to the floor—probably in a swoon. Fortunately the madman was so occupied with his antics, that he did not observe what had passed at the door. It was the nurse who made the attempt to discover what was going on, I afterward learned— but unsuccessfully, for she had seen nothing. My injunctions were obeyed to the letter, for they maintained a profound silence, unbroken but by a faint sighing sound, which I should not have heard, but that my ears were painfully sensitive to the slightest noise. But to return to myself and my fearful chamber companion.

"Mighty talisman!" he exclaimed, holding the razor before him, and gazing earnestly at it, "how utterly unworthy—how infamous the common use men put thee to!" Still he continued standing, with his eyes fixed intently upon the deadly weapon—1 all the while uttering not a sound, nor moving a muscle, but waiting for our eyes to meet once more.

"Ha—Doctor ——!—How easily I keep you at bay, though little my weapon—*thus*"—he exclaimed gayly, at the same time assuming one of the postures of the broadsword exercise—but I observed that he *cautiously avoided meeting my eyes again.* I crossed my arms submissively on my breast, and continued in perfect silence, endeavouring, but in vain, to catch a glance of his eye. I did not wish to excite any emotion in him, except such as might have a tendency to calm, pacify, disarm him. Seeing me stand thus, and manifesting no disposition to meddle with him, he raised his left hand to his face, and rubbed his fingers rapidly over the site of his shaved eyebrows. He seemed, I thought, inclined to go over them a second time, when a knock was heard at the outer chamber-door, which I instantly recognised as that of Mr —— the apothecary. The madman also heard it, turned suddenly pale, and moved away from the glass opposite which he had been stooping. "Oh —oh!" he groaned, while his features assumed an air of the blankest affright, every muscle quivering, and every limb trembling from head to foot. "Is that— is—is that T—— come for ME?" He let fall the razor on the floor, and clasping his hands in an agony of apprehension, he retreated, crouching and cowering down, towards the more distant part of the room, where he continued peering round the bedpost, his eyes straining as though they would start from their sockets, and fixed steadfastly upon the door. I heard him rustling the bed-curtain, and shaking it; but very gently, as if wishing to cover and conceal himself within its folds.

Oh, humanity!—Was *that* poor being—that silly slavering idiot—was *that* the once gay, gifted, brilliant M——?

To return. My attention was wholly occupied with one object, the razor on the floor. How I thanked God for the gleam of hope that all might yet be right—that I might succeed in obtaining possession of the deadly weapon, and putting it beyond his reach! But how was I to do all this? I stole gradually towards the spot where the razor lay, without removing once my eye from his, nor he his from the dreaded door, intending, as soon as I should have come pretty near it, to make a sudden snatch at the horrid implement of destruction. I did—I succeeded—I got it into my possession, scarcely crediting my senses. I had hardly grasped my prize, when the door opened, and Mr. —— the apothecary entered, sufficiently startled and bewildered, as it may be supposed, with the strange aspect of things.

"Ha—ha—ha! It's *you*, is it—it's you—you anatomy! You plaster! How dare you mock me in this horrid way, eh?" shouted the maniac, and springing like a lion from his lair, he made for the spot where the confounded apothecary stood. stupified with ter

ror. I verily believe he would have been destroyed,
torn to pieces, or cruelly maltreated in some way or
other, had I not started and thrown myself between
him and the unwitting object of his vengeance, exclaiming at the same time, as a *dernier resort*, a sudden and strong appeal to his fears—" Remember!—
T——! T——! T——!" •

"I do—I—do!" stammered the maniac, stepping
back, perfectly aghast. He seemed utterly petrified,
and sunk shivering down again into his former position at the corner of the bed, moaning—" Oh me!
wretched me! Away—away—away!" I then stepped
to Mr. ——, who had not moved an inch, directed
him to retire instantly, conduct all the females out
of the chambers, and return immediately with two
or three of the inn-porters, or any other able-bodied
men he could procure on the spur of the moment;
and I concluded by slipping the razor unobservedly,
as I thought, into his hands, and bidding him remove
it to a place of safety. He obeyed, and I found myself once more alone with the madman.

"M——! dear Mr. M——! I've got something to
say to you—I have, indeed; it's very—very particular." I commenced, approaching him slowly, and
speaking in the softest tones conceivable.

" But you've forgotten THIS, you fool, you!—you
have!" he replied, fiercely, approaching the dressing-
table, and suddenly seizing *another razor*—the fellow
of the one I had got hold of with such pains and
peril—and which, alas, alas! had never once caught
my eye! I gave myself up for lost, fully expecting
that I should be murdered, when I saw the blood-
thirsty spirit with which he clutched it, brandished it
over his head, and with a smile of fiendish derision,
shook it full before me! I trembled, however, the
next moment, for himself, for he drew it rapidly to
and fro before his throat, as though he would give
the fatal gash, but did not touch the skin. He
gnashed his teeth with a kind of savage satisfaction

I.—Z

at the dreadful power with which he was consciously
armed.

"Oh, Mr. M——! think of your poor mother and
sisters!" I exclaimed, in a sorrowful tone, my voice
faltering with uncontrollable agitation. He shook
the razor again before me with an air of defiance,
and really "grinned horribly a ghastly smile."

"Now suppose I choose to finish your perfidy, you
wretch! and do what you dread, eh?" said he, holding the razor as if he was going to cut his throat.

"Why, wouldn't it be nobler to forgive and forget,
Mr. M——?" I replied, with tolerable firmness, and
folding my arms on my breast, anxious to appear
quite at ease.

"'Too—too—too, doctor! Too—too—too!—Ha, by-
the-way!—What do you say to a *razor hornpipe*—
eh?—Ha, ha, ha—a novelty, at least!" He began
forthwith to dance a few steps, leaping frantically
high, and uttering at intervals a sudden, shrill, disso-
nant cry, resembling that used by those who dance
the Highland "fling," or some other species of Scottish dance. I affected to admire his dancing, even
to ecstasy—clapping my hands, and shouting, "Bravo,
bravo!—Encore!" He seemed inclined to go over
it again, but was too much exhausted, and sat down
panting on the window-seat, which was close behind
him.

"You'll catch cold, Mr. M——, sitting in that
draught of air naked, and perspiring as you are.
Will you put on your clothes?" said I, approaching
him.

"No!" he replied, sternly, and extending the razor
threateningly. I fell back, of course—not knowing
what to do, nor choosing to risk either his destruction or my own by attempting any active interference; for what was to be done with a madman who
had an open razor in his hand? Mr. ——, the apo-
hecary, seemed to have been gone an age; and I
found even my *temper* beginning to fail me—for I

was tired with his tricks, deadly dangerous as they were. My attention, however, was soon riveted again on the motions of the maniac. "Yes—yes, decidedly so—I'm too hot to do it now—I am!" said he, wiping the perspiration from his forehead, and eying the razor intently. "I must get calm and cool—and then—*then* for the sacrifice! Ah, ha, the sacrifice!—An offering—expiation—even as Abraham—ha, ha, ha!—But, by-the-way, how did Abraham do it—that is, how did he intend to have done it?—Ah, I must ask my familiar!"

"A *sacrifice*, Mr. M——?—Why, what do you mean?" I inquired, attempting a laugh—I say, *attempting*—for my blood trickled chillily through my veins, and my heart seemed frozen.

"What do I mean, eh? Wretch! Dolt!—What do I mean?—Why, a peace-offering to my Maker for a badly-spent life, to be sure!—One would think you had never *heard* of such a thing as religion—you sow!"

"I deny that the sacrifice would be accepted, and for two reasons," I replied, suddenly recollecting that he plumed himself on his casuistry, and hoping to engage him on some new crotchet, which might keep him in play till Mr. —— returned with assistance—but I was mistaken!

"Well, well, Doctor ——! Let *that* be, now—I can't resolve doubts now—no, no," he replied, solemnly,—"'tis a time for action—for action—for action," he continued, gradually elevating his voice, using vehement gesticulations, and rising from his seat.

"Yes, yes," said I, warmly; "but though you've followed closely enough the advice of the Talmudist, in shaving off your eyebrows, as a preparatory"——

"Aha! aha!—What! have *you* seen the Talmud! —Have you, really?—Well," he added, after a doubtful pause, "in what do you think I've failed, eh?"

[I need hardly say, that I myself scarcely knew

what led me to utter the nonsense in question; but
I have several times found, in cases of insanity, that
suddenly and readily *supplying a motive for the patient's conduct*—referring it to a *cause*, of some sort
or other, with steadfast intrepidity—even be the said
cause never so preposterously absurd—has been
attended with the happiest effects, in arresting the
patient's attention—chiming in with his eccentric fancies, and *piquing* his disturbed faculties into *acquiescence* in what he sees coolly taken for granted, as
quite true—a thing of course—mere matter-of-fact—
by the person he is addressing. I have several times
recommended this little device to them who have
been intrusted with the care of the insane, and have
been assured of its success.]

"You are very near the mark, I own; but it strikes
me that you have shaved them off too equally—too
uniformly. You ought to have left some little
ridges—furrows—hem, hem!—to—to—terminate, or
resemble the—the—the *striped stick* which Jacob held
up before the ewes!"

"Oh—ay—ay! Exactly—true!—Strange over-
sight!" he replied, as if struck with the truth of the
remark, and yet puzzled by vain attempts to corroborate it by his own recollections—"I—I recollect
it now—but it isn't too late yet—is it?"

"I think not," I replied, with apparent hesitation,
hardly crediting the success of my strange stratagem. "To be sure, it will require very great delicacy; but as you've not shaved them off *very* closely,
I think I can manage it," I continued, doubtfully.

"Oh, oh, oh!" growled the maniac, while his eyes
flashed fire at me. "There's one sitting by me tha
tells me you are dealing falsely with me—oh, you
villain! oh, you wretch!" At that moment the door
opened gently behind me, and the voice of Mr. ——,
the apothecary, whispered, in a low hurried tone,
"Doctor, I've got three of the inn-porters here, in
the sitting-room." Though the whisper was almost

inaudible even to me, when uttered close to my ear to my utter amazement, M—— had heard every syl- lable of it, and understood it too, as if some official minion of the Devil himself had quickened his ears, or conveyed the intelligence to hi.n.

"Ah—ha—ha !—Ha, ha, ha !—Fools ! Knaves ! Harpies !—and what are you and your three hired desperadoes, to *me ?*—Thus—thus do I outwit you, fools—thus!" and springing from his seat, he sud- denly drew up the lower part of the window-frame, and looked through it—then at the razor—and again at me, with one of the most awful glances—full of dark diabolical meaning, the momentary suggestion of the*great tempter, that I ever encountered in my life.

"Which!—which!—which!" he muttered fiercely through his closed teeth, while his right foot rested on the window-seat, ready for him to spring out, and his eye travelled, as before, rapidly from the razor to the window.   Can any thing be conceived more pal- sying to the beholders ! ' Why did not you and your strong reinforcement spring at once upon him, and overpower him ?' possibly some one is asking.— Aha ! and he armed with a *naked razor ?* His head might have been severed from his shoulders, before we could have over-mastered him—or we might our- selves—at least one of us—have been murdered in the attempt. We knew not *what* to do! M—— sud- denly withdrew his head from the window, through which he had been gazing, with a shuddering, horror- stricken motion, and groaned—"No! no! no!—I won't—can't—for there's T—— standing just be- neath, his face all blazing, and waiting with out- spread arms to catch me," standing at the same time shading his eyes with his left hand—when I whis- pered,—"Now, now! go up to him—secure him—all three spring on him at once, and disarm him!" They obeyed me, and were in the act of rushing into the room. when M—— suddenly planted himself in a posture of defiance, elevated the razor to his throat, and almost *howled*—" One step—one step nearer—and I —I—I—so !" motioning as though he would draw it from one ear to the other. We all fell back, horror-struck, and in silence. What could we do ? If we moved towards him, or made use of any threatening gesture, we should see the floor in an instant deluged with his blood. I once more crossed my arms on my breast, with an air of mute submission.

"Ha—ha !" he exclaimed, after a pause, evidently pleased with such a demonstration of his power, " obedient, however !—come—that's one merit ! But still, what a set of cowards—bullies—cowards you must all be !—What !—all four of you afraid of *one* man ?" In the course of his frantic gesticulations he had drawn the razor so close to his neck that its edge had slightly grazed the skin under his left ear, and a little blood trickled from it over his shoulders and breast.

" Blood !—*blood?*—What a strange feeling! How coldly it fell on my breast !—How did I do it?—Shall —I—go—on, as I have made a beginning ?" he exclaimed, drawling the words at great length. He shuddered, and—to my unutterable joy and astonishment—deliberately closed the razor, replaced it in its case, put both in the drawer; and having done all this, before we ventured to approach him, he fell at his full length on the floor, and began to yell in a manner that was perfectly frightful; but in a few moments he burst into tears, and cried and sobbed like a child. We took him up in our arms, he groaning—" Oh, shorn of my strength !—shorn! shorn ! like Samson !—Why part with my weapon ?—The Philis-tines be upon me !"—and laid him down on the bed, where, after a few moments, he fell asleep. When he woke again, a strait-waistcoat put all his tremendous strugglings at defiance—though his strength seemed increased in a tenfold degree—and prevented his attempting either his own life or that of any one near him. When he found all his writhings and heavings utterly useless, he gnashed his teeth, the foam issued from his mouth, and he shouted, "I'll be even with you, you incarnate devils!—I will!—I'll suffocate myself!" and he held his breath till he grew black in the face, when he gave over the attempt. It was found necessary to have him strapped down to the bed; and his howlings were so shocking and loud, that we began to think of removing him, even in that dreadful condition, to a madhouse. I ordered his head to be shaved again, and kept perpetually covered with cloths soaked in evaporating lotions—blisters to be applied behind each ear, and at the nape of the neck—leeches to the temples, and the appropriate internal medicines in such cases—and left him, begging I might be sent for instantly in the event of his getting worse.* Oh, I shall never forget this harrowing scene!—my feelings were wound up almost to bursting; nor did they receive their proper tone for many a week. I cannot conceive that the people whom the New Testament speaks of as being "possessed of devils," could have been more dreadful in appearance, or more outrageous in their actions, than was Mr. M——; nor can I help suggesting the thought, that, possibly, they were in reality nothing more than maniacs of the worst kind. And is not a man transformed into a devil when his reason is utterly overturned?

On seeing M—— the next morning, I found he had passed a terrible night—that the constraint of the strait-waistcoat filled him incessantly with a fury that was absolutely diabolical. His tongue was dreadfully lacerated; and the whites of his eyes, with perpetual straining, were discoloured with a

---

* I ought to have mentioned, a little way back, that in obedience to my hurried injunctions, the ladies suffered themselves, almost fainting with fright, to be conducted silently into the adjoining chambers; and it was well they did. Suppose they had uttered any sudden shriek or attempted to interfere, or made a disturbance of any kind, what would have become of us all!

reddish hue, like ferrets' eyes. He was truly a piteous spectacle! One's heart ached to look at him, and think, for a moment, of the fearful contrast he formed to the gay Mr. M—— he was only a few days before,—the delight of refined society, and the idol of all his friends! He lay in a most precarious state for a fortnight; and though the fits of outrageous madness had ceased, or become much mitigated, and interrupted, not unfrequently, with "lucid intervals" —as the phrase is,—I began to be apprehensive of his sinking eventually into that hopeless, deplorable condition, idiotcy. During one of his intervals of sanity —when the savage fiend relaxed, for a moment, the hold he had taken of the victim's faculties—M—— said something according with a fact which it was impossible for him to have any knowledge of by the senses, which was to me singular and inexplicable. It was about nine o'clock in the morning of the third day after that on which the scene above described took place, that M——, who was lying in a state of the utmost lassitude and exhaustion, scarcely able to open his eyes, turned his head slowly towards Mr. ——, the apothecary, who was sitting by his bedside, and whispered to him—" They are preparing to bury that wretched fellow next door—hush! hush!—one of the coffin-trestles has fallen—hush !" Mr. ——, and the nurse, who had heard him, both strained their ears to listen, but could hear not even "a mouse stirring"—"there's somebody come in—a lady, kissing his lips before he's screwed down—oh, I hope she won't be scorched—that's all ?" He then turned away his head, with no appearance of emotion, and presently fell asleep. Through mere curiosity, Mr. —— looked at his watch; and from subsequent inquiry ascertained that—sure enough— about the time when his patient had spoken, they *were* about burying his neighbour; that one of the trestles *did* slip a little aside, and the coffin, in consequence, was near falling; and finally, marvellous to tell, that a lady, one of the deceased's relatives, I believe, did come and kiss the corpse, and cry bitterly over it! Neither Mr. —— nor the nurse heard any noise whatever during the time of the burial preparations next door, for the people had been earnestly requested to be as quiet about them as possible, and really made no disturbance whatever. By what strange means he had acquired his information —whether or not he was indebted for it to the exquisite delicacy, the morbid sensitiveness of the organs of hearing, I cannot conjecture; especially am I at a loss to account for the latter part of what he uttered, about the lady's kissing the corpse. On another occasion, during one of his most placid moods, but *not* in any lucid interval, he insisted on my taking pen, ink, and paper, and turning amanuensis. To quiet him I acquiesced, and wrote what he dictated; and the manuscript now lies before me, and is, *verbatim et literatim*, as follows:—

"I, T—— M——, saw,—what saw I? A solemn silver grove—there were *innumerable spirits* sleeping among the branches—(and it is this, though unobserved of naturalists, that makes the aspen-tree's leaves to quiver so much—it is this, I say, namely, the rustling movements of the spirits)—and in the midst of this grove was a beautiful site for a statue, and one there assuredly was—but *what* a statue! Transparent, of stupendous size, through which (the sky was cloudy and troubled) a ship was seen sinking at sea, and the crew at cards; but the *good spirit* of the HIM saved them; for he showed them the key of the universe, and a shoal of sharks, with murderous eyes, were disappointed of a meal. Lo, man, behold—another part of this statue—what a one!—has a FISSURE in it—it opens—widens into a parlour, in darkness; and shall be disclosed the *horror of horrors*, for, lo, some one sitting—sitting—easy-chair—fiery-face—fiend—fiend—oh, God! oh, God! save me," cried he. He ceased speaking, with a shudder—nor did he resume the dictation, for he seemed in a moment to have forgotten that he had dictated at all. I preserved the paper; and gibberish though it is, I consider it both curious and highly characteristic throughout. Judging from the latter part of it, where he speaks of a "*dark parlour with some fiery-faced fiend sitting in an armchair;*" and coupling this with various similar expressions and allusions which he made during his ravings, I felt convinced that his fancy was occupied with some one individual image of horror, which had scared him into madness, and now clung to his disordered faculties like a fiend. He often talked about " spectres," " spectral"—and uttered incessantly the words, " spectre-smitten." The nurse once asked him what he meant by these words; he started—grew disturbed—his eye glanced with affright—and he shook his head, exclaiming, " horror!" A few days afterward he hired an amanuensis, who, of course, was duly apprized of the sort of person he had to deal with; and after a painfully ludicrous scene—he attempting to beat down the man's terms from a guinea and a half a week to *half a crown*—he engaged him for *three guineas*, he said, and insisted on his taking up his station at the side of the bed, in order that he might take down every word that was uttered. M—— told him he was going to dictate a *romance!* It would have required, in truth, the " pen of a ready writer" to keep pace with poor M——'s utterance ; for he raved on at a prodigious rate, in a strain, it need hardly be said, of unconnected absurdities. Really it was inconceivable nonsense, rhapsodical rantings in the Maturin style, full of vaults, sepulchres, spectres, devils, magic—with here and there a thought of real poetry. It was piteous to peruse it! His amanuensis found it impossible to keep up with him, and therefore profited by a hint from one of us, and, instead of writing, merely moved his pen rapidly over the paper, scrawling all sorts of

ragged lines and figures, to resemble writing! M——
never asked him to read it over, nor requested to see
it himself; but, after about fifty pages were done,
dictated a titlepage—pitched on publishers—settled
the price and the number of volumes—*four!*—and
then exclaimed—" Well!—thank God—*that's* off my
mind at last!" He never mentioned it afterward;
and his brother committed the *whole* to the flames
about a week after.

M—— had not, however, yet done with his amanuensis—but put his services in requisition in quite another capacity—that of reader. Milton was the book
he selected—and actually they went through very
nearly nine books of it,—M—— perpetually interrupting him with comments, sometimes saying sur-
passingly absurd, and occasionally very fine, forcible
things. All this formed a truly touching illustration
of that beautiful often-quoted sentiment of Horace—

> "Quo semel est imbuta recens, servabit odorem
>   Testa diu."
> *Epist. Lib. I. Ep.* 2. 69, 70.

As there was no prospect of his speedily recovering the use of his reasoning faculties, he was removed to a private asylum, where I attended him
regularly for more than six months. He was re
duced to a state of drivelling idiotcy; complete
fatuity! Lamentable! heart-rending! Oh, how deplorable to see a man of superior intellect—one whose
services are really wanted in society—the prey of
madness!

Dr. Johnson was well known to express a peculiar
horror of insanity. " Oh, God! afflict my body with
what tortures thou willest; but *spare my reason.*"
Where is he that does not join him in uttering such
a prayer?

It would be beside my purpose here to enter into
abstract speculations or purely professional details

concerning insanity; but one or two brief and simple remarks, the fruits of much experience and consideration, may perhaps be pardoned me. It is still a *vexata questio* in our profession, whether persons of strong or weak minds—whether the ignorant or the highly cultivated, are most frequently the subjects of insanity. If we are disposed to listen to a generally shrewd and intelligent writer [Dr. Munro, in his *Philosophy of Human Nature"*], we are to understand, that "children and people of weak minds are *never* subject to madness; for," adds the doctor, "how can he despair who cannot think?" Though the logic here is somewhat loose and leaky, I am disposed to agree with the doctor in the main; and I ground my acquiescence, first, on the truth of Locke's distinction, laid down in his great work (book ii. c. ii. § 12 and 13), where he mentions the difference "between idiots and madmen," and thus states the sum of his observations:

"In short, herein seems to lie the difference between idiots and madmen, that madmen put wrong ideas together, and do make wrong propositions, but argue and reason *right* from them; but idiots make very few or no propositions, and reason scarce at all."

Secondly, On the corroboration afforded to it by my own experience. I have generally found that those persons who are most *distinguished* for their powers of thought and reasoning when of sound mind, continue to exercise that power, but incorrectly, and be distinguished by their exercise of that power when of unsound mind,—their understanding retaining, even after such a shock and revolution of its faculties, the bent and bias impressed upon it beforehand; and I have found, further, that it has been chiefly those of such character—*i. e.* thinkers—that have fallen into madness; and that it is the perpetual straining and taxing of their strong intellects,

...t the expense of their bodies, that has brought them into such a calamity. Suppose, therefore, we say, in short, that *madness* is the fate of strong minds, or at least of minds many degrees removed from weak; and *idiotcy* of weak, imbecile minds. This supposition, however, involves a sorry sort of compliment to the fair sex; for it is notorious that the annual majority of those received into lunatic asylums are *females!* I have found imaginative, fanciful people the most liable to attacks of insanity; and have had under my care four such instances, or at least very nearly resembling the one I am now relating, in which insanity has ensued from sudden *fright*. And it is easily accounted for. The imagination—the predominant faculty—is immediately appealed to—and, eminently lively and tenacious of impressions, exerts its superior and more practised powers at the expense of the judgment or reason, which it tramples upon and crushes. There is then nothing left in the mind that may make head against this unnatural dominancy; and the result is generally not unlike that in the present instance. As for my general system of treatment, it may all be comprised in a word or two—acquiescence ; submission ; suggestion ; soothing.* Had I pursued a different plan with M——, what might have been the disastrous issue !

To return, however. The reader may possibly recollect seeing something like the following expression, occurring in " The Broken Heart :"† " A candle flickering and expiring in its socket, which suddenly shoots up into an instantaneous brilliance, and then is utterly extinguished." I have referred to it, merely because it affords a very apt illustration—apter far than any that now suggests itself to me, of what sometimes takes place in madness. The roaring flame of insanity sinks suddenly into the sullen.

* See the case " *Int iguing and Madness* p. 91.
† Page 121

smoul lering embers of complete fatuity, and remams
so for months; when, like that of the candle just
alluded to, it will instantaneously gather up and con-
centrate its expiring energies into one terrific blaze·
—one final paroxysm of outrageous mania—and lo !
it has consumed itself utterly—burnt itself out--and
the patient is unexpectedly restored to reason. The
experience of my medical readers, if it have lain at
all in the track of insanity, must have presented such
cases to their notice not unfrequently. However
metaphysical ingenuity may set us speculating about
the " why and wherefore" of it—the *fact* is undenia-
ble. It was thus with Mr. M——. He had sunk into
the deplorable condition of a simple, harmless, melancholy idiot, and was released from formal constraint:
but suddenly, one morning, while at breakfast, he
sprung upon the person who always attended him·-
and had not the man been very muscular, and practised in such matters, he must have been soon overpowered, and perhaps murdered. A long and deadly
wrestle took place between them. Thrice they threw
each other—and the keeper saw that the madman
several times cast a longing eye towards a knife
which lay on the breakfast-table, and endeavoured to
swing his antagonist so as to get himself within its
reach. Both were getting exhausted with the prolonged struggle—and the keeper, really afraid for his
life, determined to settle matters as soon as possible.
The instant, therefore, that he could get his right arm
disengaged, he hit poor Mr. M—— a cruel blow on the
side of the head, which felled him, and he lay senseless on the floor, the blood pouring fast from his ears
nose, and mouth. He was again confined in a strait·
waistcoat, and conveyed to bed—when, what with
exhaustion, and the effect of the medicines which
had been administered, he fell into profound sleep,
which continued all day, and, with little intermission,
through the night. When he awoke in the morning,
lo ! he was " in his right mind !" His calmed, tran-

quillized features, and the sobered expression of his eyes, showed that the sun of reason had really once more dawned upon his long-benighted faculties. ·Ay—he was

——" himself again !"

I heard of the good news before I saw him, and on hastening to his room, I found it was indeed so—his altered appearance at first sight amply corroborated it!   How different the mild, sad smile now beaming on his pallid faded features, from the vacant stare—the unmeaning laugh of idiotcy—or the fiendish glare of madness!—the contrast was strong as that between the soft, stealing, expansive twilight, and the burning blaze of noonday. He spoke in a very feeble, almost inarticulate voice, complained of dreadful exhaustion, and whispered something indistinctly about " waking from a long and dreary dream ;" and said that he felt, as it were, only half awake—or alive. All was new—strange—startling! Fearful of taxing too much his new-born powers, I feigned an excuse, and took my leave, recommended him cooling and quieting medicines, and perfect seclusion from visiters.   How exhilarated I felt my own spirits all that day!

He gradually, very gradually, but surely, recovered. One of the earliest indications of his reviving interest in life—

" And all its busy, thronging scenes,"

was an abrupt inquiry whether Trinity term had commenced—and whether or not he was now eligible to be called to the bar. He was utterly unconscious that *three* terms had flitted over him, while he lay in the gloomy wilderness of insanity ; and when I satisfied him of this fact, he alluded with a sigh to the beautiful thought of one of our old dramatists, who, illustrating the unconscious lapse of years over " Endymion"—makes one tell him—

" Lo, the twig against which thou lean dst when thou didst fall asleep is now become a tree when thou awakest "'

It was not till several days after his restoration to reason that I ventured to enter into any thing like detailed conversation with him, or to make particular allusions to his late illness; and on this occasion it was that he related to me his rencounter with the fearful object which had overturned his reason—adding, with intense feeling, that not ten thousand a-year should induce him to live in the same chambers any more.

During the course of his progress towards complete recovery, memory shot its strengthening rays further and further back into the inspissated gloom in which the long interval of insanity had shrouded his mind; but it was too dense—too "palpable an obscure"—to be ever completely and thoroughly illuminated. The rays of recollection, however, settled distinctly on some of the more prominent points; and I was several times astonished by his sudden reference to things which he had said and done, during the "depth of his disorder." He asked me once, for instance, whether he had not made an attempt on his life, and with a razor, and how it was that he did not succeed. He had no recollection, however, of his long and deadly struggle with his keeper—at least he never made the slightest allusion to it,—nor of course did any one else.

"I don't much mind talking these horrid things over with you, doctor—for you know all the *ins and outs* of the whole affair; but if any of my friends or relatives presume to torture me with any allusions or inquiries of this sort—I'll fight them! they'll drive me mad again!" The reader may suppose the hint was not disregarded. All recovered maniacs have a dread—an absolute horror—of any reference being made to their madness, or any thing they have said or done during the course of it: and is it not easily accounted for?

" Did the horrible spectre which occasioned your illness, in the first instance, ever present itself to you afterward!" I once inquired. He paused and turned pale. Presently he replied, with considerable agitation—" Yes, yes—it scarcely ever left me. It has not always preserved its spectral consistency, but has entered into the most astounding—the most preposterous combinations conceivable, with other objects and scenes—all of them, however, more or less of a distressing or fearful character—many of them terrific!" I begged him, if it were not unpleasant to him, to give me a specimen of them.

" It is certainly far from gratifying to trace scenes of such shame and horror—but I will comply as far as I am able," said he, rather gloomily. " Once I saw him," meaning the spectre, " leading on an army of huge speckled and crested serpents against me ; and when they came upon me—for I had no power to run away—I suddenly found myself in the midst of a pool of stagnant water, absolutely alive with slimy shapeless reptiles ; and while endeavouring to make my way out, *he* rose to the surface, his face hissing in the water, and blazing bright as ever! Again, I thought I saw him in single combat, by the gates of Eden, with Satan—and the air thronged and heated with swart faces looking on !" This was unquestionably some dim confused recollection of the Milton-readings, in the earlier part of his illness. " Again, I thought I was in the act of opening my snuff-box, when *he* issued from it, diminutive at first 'n size—but swelling soon into gigantic proportions, and his fiery features diffusing a light and heat around, that absolutely scorched and blasted! At another time I thought I was gazing upwards on a sultry summer sky—and in the midst of a luminous fissure in it, made by the lightning—I distinguished *his* accursed figure, with his glowing features wearing an expression of horror, and his limbs outstretched, as if he had been hurled down from some height or other, and was falling through the sky towards *me*. He came—he came—flung himself into

I.—A A

my recoiling arms—and clung to me—burning, scorching, withering my soul within me! I thought further, that I was all the while the subject of strange, paradoxical, contradictory feelings towards him ;— that I at one and the same time loved and loathed— feared and despised him !" He mentioned several other instances of the confusions in his "chamber of imagery." I told him of his sudden exclamation concerning Mr. T——'s burial, and its singular corroboration ; but he either did not, or affected not to recollect any thing about it. He told me he had a full and distinct recollection of being for a long time possessed with the notion of making himself a "sacrifice" of some sort or other, and that he was seduced or goaded on to do so by the spectre, in the most dazzling temptations—and under the most appalling threats—one of which latter was, that God would plunge him into hell for ever, if he did not offer up himself;—that if he did so, he should be a sublime spectacle to the universe," &c. &c. &c.

"Do you recollect of dictating a novel or a romance ?" He started as if struck with some sudden recollection. "No—but I'll tell you what I recollect well—that the spectre and I were set to copy all the tales and romances that ever had been written, in a large, bold, round hand, and then translate them into Greek or Latin verse !" He smiled, nay, even laughed at the thought, almost the first time of his giving way to such emotions since his recovery. He added, that as to the latter, the idea of the utter hopelessness of ever getting through such a stupendous undertaking never once presented itself to him, and that he should have gone on with it, but that he lost his inkstand !!

"Had you ever a clear and distinct idea that you had lost the right use of reason ?"

"Why, about that, to tell the truth, I've been puzzling myself a good deal, and yet I cannot say any thing decisive. I *do* fancy that at times I had short, transient glimpses into the real state of things, but they were so evanescent. I am conscious of feeling at these times incessant fury arising from a sense of personal constraint, and I longed once to strangle some one who was giving me medicine."

But one of the most singular of all is yet to come. He still persisted *then*, after his complete recovery as we supposed, in avowing his belief that we had hired a huge boa serpent from Exeter 'Change, to come and keep constant watch over him, to constrain his movements when he threatened to become violent; that it lay constantly coiled up under his bed for that purpose; that he could now and then feel the motions—the writhing undulating motions of its coils—hear it utter a sort of *sigh*, and see it often elevate its head over the bed, and play with its soft, slippery, delicate forked tongue over his face, to soothe him to sleep. When poor M——, with a serious, sober, earnest air, assured me he STILL believed all this, my hopes of his complete and final restoration to sanity were dashed at once! How such an absurd—in short I have no terms in which I may adequately characterize it—how, I say, such an idea could possibly be persisted in I was bewildered in attempting to conceive. I frequently strove to reason him out of it, but in vain. To no purpose did I burlesque and caricature the notion almost beyond all bounds; it was useless to remind him of the blank impossibility of it; he regarded me with such a face as I should exhibit to a fluent personage, quite in earnest in demonstrating to me that the moon was made of green cheese.

I have once before heard of a patient who, after recovering from an attack of insanity, retained one solitary crotchet—one little stain or speck of lunacy—about which, and which alone, he was mad to the end of his life. I supposed such to be the case with M——. It was possible—barely so, I thought—that he might entertain his preposterous notion about the boa, and yet be sound in the general texture of his mind.   I prayed God it might; I " hoped against hope."   The last evening I ever spent with him was occupied with my endeavouring, once for all, to dis-abuse him of the idea in question; and in the course of our conversation he disclosed one or two other little symptoms—specks of lunacy—which made me leave him filled with disheartening doubts as to the probability of a permanent recovery.

*   *   *   *   *   *   *   *

My worst fears were awfully realized.   In about five years from the period above alluded to, M——, who had got married, and had enjoyed excellent general health, was spending the summer with his family at Brussels—and one night destroyed him-self—alas, alas! *destroyed* himself in a manner too horrible to mention!

CHAPTER VIII.

The Martyr-Philosopher.

It has been my lot to witness many dreadful death-beds.   I am not overstating the truth, when I assert that nearly eight out of every ten that have come under my personal observation—of course excluding *children*—have more or less partaken of this char-acter.   I know only one way of accounting for it, and some may accuse me of cant for adverting to it —men will not LIVE as if they were to die.   They are content to let that event come upon them " like a thief in the night."*   They grapple with their final

* One of my patients, whom a long course of profligacy had brought to a painful and premature death-bed, once quoted this striking and scriptural expression when within less than an hour of his end, and with a thrill of horror.

foe, not merely unprepared, but absolutely inca-
pacitated for the struggle, and then wonder and wail
at their being overcome and "trodden under foot."
I have, in some of the foregoing chapters, attempted
to sketch three or four dreary scenes of this description, my pencil trembling in my hand the while; and
could I but command colours dark enough, it is yet
in my power to portray others far more appalling
than any that have gone before—cases of those who
have left life "clad in horror's hideous robe"—
whose sun has gone down in darkness—if I may be
pardoned for quoting the fearful language of a very
unfashionable book!

Now, however, for a while at least, let the storm
pass away; the accumulated clouds of guilt, despair,
madness, disperse; and the lightning of the fiercer
passions cease to shed its disastrous glare over our
minds. Let us rejoice beneath the serened heavens;
let us seek sunnier spots—by turning to the more
peaceful pages of humanity. Let me attempt to lay
before the reader a short account of one whose exit
was eminently calm, tranquil, and dignified; who did
not skulk into his grave with shame and fear, but laid
down life with honour: leaving behind him the influence
of his greatness and goodness, like the evening sun—
who smiles sadly on the sweet scenes he is quitting, and
a holy lustre glows long on the features of nature—

> "Quiet as a nun
> "Breathless with adoration."*

Even were I disposed, I could not gratify the
reader with any thing like a fair sketch of the early
days of Mr. E——. I have often lamented, that,
knowing as I did the simplicity and frankness of his
disposition, I did not once avail myself of several
opportunities which fell in my way of becoming
acquainted with the leading particulars of his life.

* Wordsworth, I believe.

Now, however, as is generally the case, I can but deplore my negligence, when remedying it is impossible.   All that I have it now in my power to record is some particulars of his latter days.   Interesting I know they will be considered: may they prove instructive.   I hope the few records I have here preserved will show how a mind long disciplined by philosophy, and strengthened by religious principle, may triumph over the assault of evils and misfortunes combined against its *expiring* energies.   It is fitting, I say, the world should hear how nobly E——— surmounted such a sudden influx of disasters as have seldom before burst overwhelmingly upon a deathbed.

And should this chapter of my Diary chance to be seen by any of his relatives and early friends, I hope the reception it shall meet with from the public may stimulate them to give the world some fuller particulars of Mr. E——'s valuable, if not very varied life. More than seven years have elapsed since his death; and as yet, the only intimation the public has had of the event, has been in the dreary corner of the public prints allotted to "*Deaths,*"—and a brief enumeration in one of the quarterly journals of some of his leading contributions to science.   The world at large, however, scarce know that he ever lived—or at least, *how* he lived or died; but how often is such the fate of modest merit!

My first acquaintance with Mr. E——— commenced accidentally, not long before his death, at one of the evening meetings of a learned society of which we were both members.   The first glimpse I caught of him interested me much, and inspired me with a kind of reverence for him.   He came into the room within a few minutes of the chair's being taken, and walked quietly and slowly, with a kind of stooping gait, to one of the benches near the fireplace, where he sat down without taking off his great-coat, and crossing his gloved hands on the knob of a high walking-

stick, he rested his chin on them, and in that attitude
continued throughout the evening.   He removed his
hat when the chairman made his appearance; and I
never saw a finer head in my life.   The crown was
quite bald, but the base was fringed round, as it were,
with a little soft, glossy, silver-hued hair, which in
the distance looked like a faint halo.   His forehead
was of noble proportions; and, in short, there was
an expression of serene intelligence in his features,
blended with meekness and dignity, which quite
enchanted me.

"Pray, who is that gentleman?" I inquired of my
friend Dr. D——, who was sitting beside me.   "Do
you mean that elderly thin man sitting near the fireplace with a great-coat on?"—"The same."—"Oh, it
is Mr. E——, one of the very ablest men in the room,
though he talks the least," whispered my friend;
"and a man who comes the nearest to my *beau ideal*
of a philosopher of any man I ever knew or heard
of in the present day!"

"Why, he does not seem very well known here,"
said I, observing that he neither spoke to nor was
spoken to by any of the members present.   "Ah,
poor Mr. E—— is breaking up, I'm afraid, and that
very fast," replied my friend, with a sigh.   "He
comes but seldom to our evening meetings, and is
not ambitious of making many acquaintances."   I
intimated an eager desire to be introduced to him.
"Oh, nothing easier," replied my friend, "for I
know him more familiarly than any one present, and
he is, besides, simple as a child in his manners, even
to eccentricity, and the most amiable man in the
world.   I'll introduce you when the meeting's over."
While we were thus whispering together, the subject
of our conversation suddenly rose from his seat, and
with some trepidation of manner addressed a few
words to the chair, in correction of some assertions
which he interrupted a member in advancing.   It
was something, if I recollect right, about the atomic

theory, and was received with marked deference by the president, and general " Hear! hears!" from the members. He then resumed his seat, in which he was presently followed by the speaker whom he had evidently discomfited; his eyes glistened, and his cheeks were flushed with the effort he had made, and he did not rise again till the conclusion of the sitting. We then made our way to him, and my friend introduced me. He received me politely and frankly. He complained, in a weak voice, that the walk thither had quite exhausted him, that his health was failing him, &c.

" Why, Mr. E——, you *look* very well," said my friend.

" Ah, perhaps I do, but you know how little faith is to be put in the hale looks of an old and weak man. Age generally puts a good face on bad matters, even to the last," he added, with a smile and a shake of the head.

" A sad night!" he exclaimed, on hearing the wind howling drearily without, for we were standing by a window at the north-east corner of the large building; and a March wind swept cruelly by, telling bitter things to the old and feeble who had to face it. " Allow me to recommend that you wrap up your neck and breast well," said I.

" I intend it, indeed," he replied, as he was folding up a large silk handkerchief. " One must guard one's candle with one's hand, or death will blow it out in a moment. That's the sort of treatment we old people get from him; no ceremony—he waits for one at a bleak corner, and puffs out one's expiring light with a breath, and then hastens on to the more vigorous torch of youth."

" Have you a coach?" inquired Dr. D——.

" A coach! I shall *walk* it in less than twenty minutes," said Mr. E——, buttoning his coat up to the chin.

" Allow me to offer you both a seat in mine," said

1; "it is at the door, and I am driving towards your neighbourhood." He and Dr. D—— accepted the offer, and in a few minutes' time we entered, and drove off. We soon set down the latter, who lived close by; and then my new philosophical friend and I were left together. Our conversation turned, for a while, on the evening's discussion at the society: and in a very few words, remarkably well chosen, he pointed out what he considered to have been errors committed by Sir —— and Dr. ——, the principal speakers. I was not more charmed by the lucidness of his views than by the unaffected diffidence with which they were expressed.

"Well," said he, after a little pause in our conversation, "your carriage motion is mighty pleasant; it reduces one into a feeling of indolence! These delicious soft-yielding cushioned backs and seats, they would make a man loath to use his legs again' Yet I never kept a carriage in my life, though I have often wanted one, and could easily have afforded it once." I asked him why? He replied, "It was not because he feared childish accusations of ostentation, nor yet in order to save money, but because he thought it becoming to a rational being to be content with the natural means God has given him, both as to matter of necessity and pleasure. It was an insult," he said, "to nature, while she was in full vigour, and had exhibited little or no deficiency in her functions, to hurry to *art*. For my own part," said he, "I have always found a quiet but exquisite satisfaction in continuing independent of *her* assistance, though at the cost of some occasional inconvenience: it gives you a consciousness of relying incessantly on Him who made you and sustains you in being. Do you recollect the solemn saying of Johnson to Garrick, on seeing the immense levies the latter had made on the resources of ostentatious, ornamental art? 'Davie, Davie, these are the things that make a death-bed terrible!'" I said something about

Diogenes. "Ah," he replied, quickly, "the other extreme! He accused nature of superfluity, redun-
dancy. A proper subordination of externals to her
use is part of her province; else why is she placed
among so many materials, and with such facilities
of using them? My principle, if such it may be
called, is, that art may *minister* to nature, but not
pamper and *surfeit* her with superfluities.

"You would laugh, perhaps, to come to my house,
and see the extent to which I have carried my principles into practice. I,—yes, I,—whose life has
been devoted, among other things, to the discovery
of mechanical contrivances! You, accustomed, perhaps, to the elegant redundancies of these times, may
consider my house and furniture absurdly plain and
naked—a tree stripped of its leaves, when the birds
are left to lodge on the bare branches! But I want
little, and do not 'want that little long.' But stop,
here is my house! Come—a laugh, you know, is
good before bed—will you have it now? Come, see
a curiosity—a Diogenes, but no cynic!" Had the
reader seen the modesty, the cheerfulness, the calmness of manner with which Mr. E——, from time to
time, joined in the conversation, of which the above
is the substance, and been aware of the weight due
to his sentiments, or those of one who had actually
LIVED UP to them all his life, and earned a very high
character in the philosophical world—if he be aware
how often old age and pedantry, grounded on a small
reputation, are blended in repulsive union, he might
not consider the trouble I have taken thrown away
in recording this my first conversation with Mr.
E——. He was, indeed, an instance of "philosophy
teaching by example;" a sort of character to be
sought out for in life, as one at whose feet we may
safely sit down and learn. I could not accept of
Mr. E——'s invitation that evening, as I had a patient to see a little farther on; but I promised him
an early call. All my way home my mind was filled

with the image of E——, and partook of the tranquillity and pensiveness of its guest.

I scarce know how it was, but with all my admiration of Mr. E——, I suffered the month of May to
approach its close before I again encountered him
It was partly owing to a sudden increase of business,
created by a raging scarlet fever, and partly occasioned by illness in my own family. I often thought
and talked, however, of the philosopher, for that was
the name he went by with Dr. D—— and myself.
Mr. E—— had invited us both to take "an old-fashioned friendly cup of tea" with him; and accordingly,
about six o'clock, we found ourselves driving down
to his house. On our way, Dr. D—— told me that
our friend had been a widower nearly five years;
and that the loss, somewhat sudden, of his amiable
and accomplished wife had worked a great change
in him, by divesting him of nearly all interest in life
or its concerns. He pursued even his philosophical
occupations with languor, more from a kind of habit
than inclination. Still he retained the same even-
ness and cheerfulness which had distinguished him
 hrough life. But the blow had been struck which
severed him from the world's joys and engagements.
He might be compared to a great tree torn up by the
root, and laid prostrate by a storm, yet which dies
not all at once. The sap is not instantaneously
dried up; but for weeks, or even months, you may
see the smaller branches still shooting unconsciously
into short-lived existence, all fresh and tender from
the womb of their dead mother; and a rich green
mantle of leaves long concealing from view the poor
fallen trunk beneath. Such was the pensive turn
my thoughts had taken by the time we had reached
Mr. E——'s door. It was a fine summer evening—
the hour of calm excitement. The old-fashioned win-
dow-panes of the house we had stopped at shone like
small specks of fire in the steady slanting rays of the
retiring sun. It was the first house of a very respect

able antique-looking row, in the suburbs of London, which had been built in the days of Henry the Eighth. Three stately poplars stood sentries before the gateway.

" Well, here we are at last at *Plato's Porch*, as I've christened it," said Dr. D——, knocking at the door. On entering the parlour, a large old-fashioned room, furnished with the utmost simplicity consistent with comfort, we found Mr. E—— sitting near the window, reading. He was in a brown dressing-gown and study cap. He rose and welcomed us cheerfully. " I have been looking into La Place," said he, in the first pause which ensued, " and a little before your arrival, had flattered myself that I had detected some erroneous calculations; and only look at the quantity of evidence that was necessary to convince that I was a simpleton by the side of La Place !" pointing to two or three sheets of paper crammed with small algebraical characters in pencil—a fearful array of symbols —" $\sqrt{\qquad} = 3\,a^2,\ \square\ \frac{y^2}{z^2} + 9 - n = 9;\ n \times \log. e$"— and sines, co-sines, series, &c. &c. without end. I had the curiosity to take up the volume in question, while he was speaking to Dr. D——, and noticed on the fly leaf the autograph of the Marquis La Place who had sent his work to Mr. E——. Tea was presently brought in; and as soon as the plain old-fashioned china, &c. &c. had been laid on the table by the man-servant, himself a knowing old fellow as I ever saw in my life, Miss E——, the philosopher's niece, made her appearance, an elegant, unaffected girl, with the same style of features as her uncle.

" I can give a shrewd guess at your thoughts, Dr. ——," said Mr. E——, smiling, as he caught my eye following the movements of the man-servant till he left the room. " You fancy my keeping a man-servant to wait at table does not tally very well with what I said the 'ast time I had the pleasure of seeing you."

"Oh dear, I'm sure you're mistaken, Mr. E——! I was struck with the singularity of his countenance and manners—those of a stanch old family servant."

"Ah, Joseph is a vast favourite with my uncle," said Miss E——, "I can assure you, and fancies himself nearly as great a man as his master."

"Why, as far as the *pratique* of the laboratory is concerned, I doubt if his superior is to be found in London. He knows *it*, and all my ways as well as he knows the palm of his own hand! He has the neatest way in the world of making hydrogen gas, and, what is more, found it out himself," said Mr. E——, explaining the process; "and then he is a miracle of cleanliness and care! He has not cost me ten shillings in breakage since I knew him. He moves among my brittle wares like a cat on a glass wall."

"And then he writes and reads for my uncle—does all the minor work of the laboratory—goes on errands—waits at table—in short, he's quite invaluable," said Miss E——.

"Quite a *factotum*, I protest," exclaimed Dr D——.

"You'd lose your *better half*, then, if he were to die. I suppose?" said I, quickly.

"No! *that* can happen but *once*," replied Mr. E——, with a sigh, alluding to the death of his wife. Conversation flagged for a moment. "You've forgotten," at length said E——, breaking the melancholy pause, "the very chief of poor Joseph's accomplishments—what an admirable, unwearied *nurse* he is to me." At that moment Joseph entered the room with a note in his hand, which he gave to Mr. E——. I guessed where it came from; for happening a few moments before to cast my eye to the window, I saw a footman walking up to the door; and there was no mistaking the gorgeous scarlet liveries of the Duke of ——. E——, after glancing over the letter, begged us to excuse him for a minute or two, as the man was waiting for an answer.

"*You*, of course, knew what my uncle alluded to," said Miss E——, addressing Dr. D—— in a low tone, as soon as E—— had closed the door after him, "when he spoke of Joseph's being a *nurse;* don't you?" Dr. D—— nodded. "My poor uncle," she continued, addressing me, "has been for nearly *twenty-five* years afflicted with a dreadful disease in the spine; and during all that time has suffered a perfect martyrdom from it. He could not stand *straight* up, if it were to save his life; and he is obliged to sleep in a bed of a very curious description, the joint contrivance of himself and Joseph. He takes half an ounce of laudanum every night at bedtime, without which the pains, which are always most excruciating at nighttime, would not suffer him to get a moment's sleep. Oh, how often have I seen him rolling about on this carpet and hearth-rug— yes, even in the presence of visiters—in a perfect ecstasy of agony, and uttering the most heartbreaking groans."

"And I can add," said Dr. D——, "that he is the most perfect Job, the most angelic sufferer I ever saw."

"Indeed, indeed he is," rejoined Miss E——, with emotion. "I can say with perfect truth that I never once heard him murmur or complain at his hard fate. When I have been expressing my sympathies, during the extremity of his anguish, he has gasped, ' Well, well, it *might* have been worse.' " Miss E—— suddenly raised her handkerchief t) her eyes, for they were overflowing.

"Do you see that beautiful little picture hanging over the mantelpiece?" she inquired, after a pause, which neither Dr. D—— nor I seemed inclined to interrupt; pointing to an exquisite oil-painting of the crucifixion. "I have seen my poor uncle lying down on the floor, while in the most violent paroxysms of pain, and with his eyes fixed intently on that picture, exclaim, '*Thine* were greater; thine were greater!' And then he has presently clasped his hands upwards, a smile has beamed upon his pallid, quivering features, and he has told me the pain was abated."

"I was once present during one of these painfully interesting scenes," said Dr. D——, "and have seen such a heavenly radiance on his countenance as could not have been occasioned by the mere sudden cessation of the anguish he had been suffering."

"Does not this strange disorder abate with his increasing years?" I inquired.

"Alas, no!" replied Miss E——; "but is, if possible, more frequent and severe in its seizures. Indeed, we all think it is wearing him out fast. But for the unwearied services of that faithful creature Joseph, who sleeps in the same room with him, my uncle must have died long ago."

"How did this terrible disorder attack Mr. E——, and when?" I inquired. I was informed that he himself originated the complaint with an injury he sustained when a very young man. He was riding one day on horseback; and his horse suddenly reared backward, and Mr. E——'s back came in violent contact with a plank projecting from behind a cart loaded with timber. He was, besides, however, subject to a constitutional feebleness in the spine, derived from his father and grandfather. He had consulted almost every surgeon of eminence in England, and a few on the Continent; and spent a little fortune among them,—but all had been in vain!

"Really, you will be quite surprised, Dr. ——," said Miss E——, "to know, that though such a martyr to pain, and now in his sixty-fourth year, my uncle is more active in his habits and regular in his hours than I ever knew any one. He rises almost invariably at four o'clock in summer, and at six in

winter; and this, though so helpless, that without
Joseph's assistance he could not dress himself—."
"Ah, by-the-way,"—interrupted Dr. D——, "that is
another peculiarity in Mr. E——'s case; he is subject
to a sort of nightly paralysis of the upper extremities,
from which he does not completely recover till he
has been up for some two or three hours." How
little had I thought of the under-current of agony,
flowing incessantly beneath the calm surface of his
cheerful and dignified demeanour! Oh, philosophy
—Oh, Christian philosophy!—I had failed to detect
any marks of suffering in his features, though I had
now had two interviews with him—so completely,
even hitherto, had "his unconquerable mind con-
quered the clay,"—as one of our old writers expresses
it. If I had admired and respected him heretofore,
on the ground of Dr. D——'s opinion, how did I now
feel disposed to adore him! I looked on him as an
instance of long-tried heroism and fortitude, almost
unparalleled in the history of man. Such thoughts
were passing through my mind when Mr. E——
re-entered the room. What I had heard during his
absence made me now look on him with tenfold
interest. I wondered that I had overlooked his
stoop, and the permanent print of pain on his pallid
cheek. I gazed at him, in short, with feelings of
sympathy and reverence, akin to those called forth
by a picture of one of the ancient martyrs.

"I'm sorry to have been deprived of your company so long," said he; "but I have had to answer
an invitation, and several questions besides, from—
I dare say you know whom?" addressing Dr. D——.

"I can guess, on the principle *ex ungue*—the gaudy
livery 'vaunts of royalty'—eh? Is it —— ?"

"Yes. He has invited me to dine with Lord ——,
Sir ——, and several other members of the ——
Society, at ——, this day week, but I have declined.
At my time of life I can't stand late hours and excite-
ment. Besides, one must learn betimes to *wean*

from the world, or he suddenly snatched from it screaming like a child," said Mr. E——, with an impressive air.

" I believe you are particularly intimate with ——· at least I have heard so. Are you?" inquired Dr. D——.

" No. I might possibly have been so, for —— has shown great consideration towards me; but I can assure you, I am the sought rather than the seeker, and have been all my life."

" It is often fatal to philosophical independence to approach too frequently and too nearly the magic circle of the court," said I.

" True. Science is, and should be, aspiring. So is the eagle; but the royal bird never approaches so near the sun as to be drowned in its blaze. —— has been nothing since he became a courtier." * * *

" What do you think of ——'s pretensions to science generally, and his motives for seeking so anxiously the intimacy of the learned?" inquired Dr. D——.

" Why, ——," replied E——, with some hesitation; " 'tis a wonderful thing for him to know even a fiftieth part of what he does. He is popularly acquainted with the outlines of most of the leading sciences. He went through a regular course of readings with my friend ——; but he has not the *time* necessary to ensure a successful prosecution of science. It is, however, infinitely advantageous to science and literature to have the willing and active patronage of royalty. I never knew him exhibit one trait of overbearing dogmatism; and that is saying much for one whom all flatter always. It *has* struck me, however, that he has rather too anxious an eye towards securing the character and applause of a MECÆNAS."

" Pray, Mr. E——, do you recollect mentioning to me an incident which occurred at a large dinner-party given by——, when you were present, when

I.—B b

Dr. —— made use of these words to — — : ‘ *Does no
your* —— *think it possible for a man to pelt another
with potatoes, to provoke him to fling peaches in ret
for want of other missiles ?*’—and the furious answ
was —— ——.”

“ We will drop that subject, if you please,” said
E——, coldly, at the same time colouring, and giving
my friend a peculiar monitory look.

“ I know well, personally, that —— has done very
many noble things in his day—most of them, comparatively, in secret; and one munificent action he
has performed lately towards a man of scientific
eminence, who has been as unfortunate as he is deserving, which will probably never come to the public
ear, unless —— and —— die suddenly,” said Mr.
E——.   He had scarcely uttered these words, when
he turned suddenly pale, laid down his teacup with
a quivering hand, and slipped slowly from his chair
to the floor, where he lay at his full length, rolling to
and fro, with his hands pressed upon the lower part
of his spine—and all the while uttering deep sighs
and groans.   The big drops of perspiration rolling
from his forehead down his cheeks, evidenced the
dreadful agony he was enduring.   Dr. D—— and I
both knelt down on one knee by his side, proffering
our assistance—but he entreated us to leave him to
himself for a few moments, and he should soon be
better.

“ Emma !” he gasped, calling his niece—who, sobbing bitterly, was at his side in a moment, “ kiss
me—that’s a dear girl—and go up to bed—but, on
your way, send Joseph here directly.”   She retired,
and in a few moments Joseph entered hastily, with a
broad leathern band, which he drew round his master’s waist and buckled tightly.   He then pressed
with both his hands for some time upon the immediate seat of the pain.   Our situation was both em
barrassing and distressing—both of us medical men,
and yet compelled to stand by mere passive spec

ators of agonies we could neither alleviate nor remove.

"Do you absolutely *despair* of discovering what the precise nature of this complaint is ?" I inquired in an under-tone.

"Yes—in common with every one else that has tried to discover it, but in vain. That it is an affection of the spinal chord is clear; but what is the immediate exciting cause of these tremendous paroxysms I cannot conjecture," replied Dr. D——.

"What have been the principal remedies resorted to ?"

"Oh, every thing—almost every thing that the wit of man could devise : local and general bleedings to a dreadful extent; irritations and counter-irritations without end; electricity—galvanism—all the resources of medicine and surgery have been ransacked to no purpose.—Look at him!" whispered Dr. D——, "look—look ;—do you see how his whole body is drawn together in a heap, while his limbs are quivering as though they would fall from him ?—See —see—how they are now struck out, and plunging about, his hands clutching convulsively at the carpet —scarce a trace of humanity in his distorted features—as if this great and good man were the sport of a demon !"

"Oh ! gracious God ! Can we do *nothing* to help him ?" I inquired, suddenly approaching him, almost stifled with my emotions. Mr. E—— did not seem conscious of our approach; but lay rather quieter, groaning—" Oh—oh—oh—that it would please God to dismiss me from my sufferings !"

"My dear, dear Mr. E——," exclaimed Dr. D——, excessively agitated, "can we do nothing for you ? Can't we be of *any* service to you ?"

"Oh, none—none—none !" he groaned, in tones expressive of utter hopelessness. For more than a quarter of an hour did this victim of disease continue writhing on the floor, and we standing by,

"physicians of no value !" The violence of the paroxysm abated at length, and again we stooped, for
the purpose of raising him and carrying him to the
sofa—but he motioned us off, exclaiming so faintly
as to be almost inaudible—" No—no, thank you—I
must not be moved for this hour—and when I am, it
must be to bed."—" Then we will bid you good
evening, and pray to God you may be better in the
morning."—" Yes—yes.—Better—better : good--
good-by," he muttered, indistinctly.

" Master's falling asleep, gentlemen, as he always
does after these fits," said Joseph, who had his arm
round his suffering master's neck. We, of course,
left immediately, and met Miss E—— in the passage,
muffled in her shawl, and sobbing as if she would
break her heart.

Dr. D—— told me as we were walking home, that
about two years ago, E—— made a week's stay with
him ; and that, on one occasion, he endured agonies
of such horrible intensity, as nothing could abate, or
in any measure alleviate, but two doses of laudanum
of nearly six drachms each, within half an hour of
each other ; and that even then he did not sleep for
more than two hours. "When he awoke," continued my friend, "he was lying on the sofa in a
state of dreadful exhaustion, the perspiration running from him like water. I asked him if he did not
sometimes yield to such thoughts as were suggested
to Job by his impetuous friends—to 'curse God and
die,'—to repine at the long and lingering tortures he
had endured nearly all his life, for no apparent crime
of his own ?" " No, no," he replied, calmly ; " I've
suffered too long an apprenticeship to pain for that !
I own I was at first a little disobedient—a little
restive—but now I am learning resignation ! Would
not useless fretting serve to enhance—to aggravate
my pains !"

" Well !" I exclaimed, " it puzzles my theology -
if any thing could make me skeptical." E—— saw

the train of my thoughts, and interrupted me, laying his white wasted hand on mine—"I always strive to bear in mind that I am in the hands of a God as good as great, and that I am not to doubt his goodness because I cannot exactly see *how* he brings it about. Doubtless there are *reasons* for my suffering what I do, which, though at present incomprehensible to me would appear abundantly satisfactory could I be made acquainted with them. Oh, Dr. D——, *what* would become of me," said E——, solemnly, " were I, instead of the rich consolations of religion, to have nothing to rely on but the disheartening speculations of infidelity?—if in *this* world only I have hope," he continued, looking steadfastly upwards ," I am, of all men, most miserable '"—" 's not it dangerous to know such a man, lest one should feel inclined to fall down and worship him ?" inquired my friend. Indeed I thought so. Surely E—— was a *miracle* of patience and fortitude ! and how he had contrived to make his splendid advancements in science, while subject to such almost unheard-of tortures, both as to duration and intensity—had devoted himself so successfully to the prosecution of studies requiring habits of long, patient, profound abstraction—was to me inconceivable.

How few of us are aware of what is suffered by those with whom we are most intimate! How few know the heavy counterbalancings of popularity and eminence; the exquisite agonies, whether physical or intellectual, inflicted by one irremoveable " thorn in the flesh!" Oh! the miseries of that eminence whose chief prerogative too often is—

> "Above the vulgar herd *to rot in state!*"

How little had I thought, while gazing at the —— rooms, on this admirable man, first fascinated with the *placidity* of his noble features, that I looked at one who had equal claims to the character of a MAR

TYR and a philosopher! How my own petty griev-
ances dwindled away in comparison of those endured
by E——! How contemptible the pusillanimity I had
often exhibited!

And do you, reader, who, if a man, are, perhaps,
in the habit of cursing and blaspheming while smarting under the toothache, or any of those minor "ills
that flesh is heir to," think, at such times, of poor
meek, suffering E——, and be silent!

I could not dismiss from my mind the painful image
of E—— writhing on the floor, as I have above described, but lay the greater part of the night reflecting on the probable nature of his unusual disorder.
Was it any thing of a spasmodic nature? Would not
such attacks have worn him out long ago? Was it
one of the remoter effects of partial paralysis? Was a
preternatural pressure on the spinal chord, occasioned
by fracture of one of the vertebræ, or enlargement of
the intervertebral ligaments?—Or was it owing to a
thickness of the medulla-spinalis itself?

Fifty similar conjectures passed through my mind,
excited as well by the singularity of the disease, as
by sympathy for the sufferer. Before I fell asleep, I
resolved to call on him during the next day, and
inquire carefully into the nature of his symptoms,
in the forlorn hope of hitting on some means of miti-
gating his sufferings.

By twelve o'clock at noon I was set down again
at his door. A maid-servant answered my summons, and told me that Mr. E—— and Joseph were
busily engaged in the "*labbory!*" She took in my
card to him, and returned with her master's compliments, and he would thank me to step in. I followed
the girl to the laboratory. On opening the door, I
saw E—— and his trusty work-fellow, Joseph, busily
engaged fusing some species of metal. The former
was dressed as on the preceding evening, with the
addition of a long black apron,—looked heated and
flushed with exercise; and, with his stooping gait,

was holding some small implement over the furnace, while Joseph, on his knees, was puffing away at the fire with a small pair of bellows.—To anticipate for a moment: how little did E—— or I imagine that this was very nearly the *last time* of his ever again entering the scene of his long and useful scientific labours!

I was utterly astonished to see one whose sufferings over night had been so dreadful, quietly pursuing his avocations in the morning as though nothing had happened to him!

"Excuse my shaking hands with you for the present, doctor," said E——, looking at me through a huge pair of tortoise-shell spectacles, "for both hands are engaged, you see.   My friend Dr. —— has just sent me a piece of platina, and you see I'm already playing pranks with it!   Really, I'm as eager to spoil a plaything to see what my rattle's made of as any philosophical child in the kingdom!   Here I am analyzing—dissolving—transmuting—and so on :—but I've really an important end in view here—trying a new combination of metal, and Dr. —— is anxious to know if the result of my process corresponds with *his*—now, now, Joseph," said E——, breaking off suddenly, "it is ready ; bring the—" At this critical instant, by some unlucky accident, poor Joseph suddenly overthrew the whole apparatus—and the compounds, ashes, fragments, &c. were spilled on the floor!   Really, I quite lost my own temper with thinking of the vexatious disappointment it would be to E——.   Not so, however, with him.

"Oh, dear—dear, dear me!   Well, here's an end of our day's work before we thought of it!   How did you do it, Joseph, eh ?" said E——, with an air of chagrin, but with perfect mildness of tone.   What a ludicrous contrast between the philosopher and his assistant!   The latter, an obese little fellow, with a droll cast of one eye—was quite red in the face, and wringing his hands, exclaimed—"Oh Lord—oh Lord —Oh Lord! what *could* I have been doing, master?"

—"Why, that's surely *your* concern more than mine," replied E——, smiling at me. "Come, come, it can't be helped—you've done yourself more harm than me, by giving Dr. —— such a specimen of your awkwardness as *I* have not seen for many a month. See and set things to rights as soon as possible," said E——, calmly, and putting away his spectacles.

"Well, Dr. ——, what do you think of my little workshop?" he continued, addressing me, who still stood with my hat and gloves on, surprised and delighted to see that his temper had stood this trial, and that such a provoking *contre-temps* had really not at all ruffled him. From the position in which he stood, the light fell strongly on his face, and I saw his features more distinctly than heretofore. I noticed that sure index of a thinking countenance—three strong perpendicular marks or folds between the eyebrows, at right angles with the deep wrinkles that furrowed his forehead, and then the " untroubled lustre" of his cold, clear, full, blue eyes, rich and serene as that

> ——" through whose clear medium the great sun
> Loveth to shoot his beams, all brightening, all
> Turning to gold."

Reader, when you see a face of this stamp, so marked, and with such eyes and forehead, rest assured you are looking at a gifted, if not an extraordinary man. The lower features were somewhat shrunk and sallow—as well they might, if only from a thousand hours of agony, setting aside the constant wearing of his "ever-waking mind;" yet a smile of cheerfulness—call it rather resignation—irradiated his pale countenance, like twilight on a sepulchre. He showed me round his laboratory, which was kept in most exemplary cleanliness and order; and then, opening a door, we entered the "sanctum sanctorum"—his study. It had not more, I should think, than five or six hundred books; but all of them—in

plain, substantial bindings—had manifestly seen good
service.   Immediately beneath the window stood
several portions of a splendid astronomical apparatus—a very large telescope, in exquisite order—a
recently invented instrument for calculating the par-
allaxes of the fixed stars—a chronometer of his own
construction, &c.   " Do you see this piece of furniture ?" he inquired, directing my attention to a sort
of sideless sofa, or broad inclined plane, stuffed, the
extremity turned up, to rest the feet against—and
being at an angle of about forty-five degrees with
the floor.   " Ah ! could that thing speak, it might tell
a tale of my tortures, such as no living being may !
For, when I feel my daily paroxysms coming on me,
if I am any where near my study, I lay my wearied
limbs here, and continue till I find relief !"   This put
conversation into the very train I wished.   I begged
him to favour me with a description of his disease ;
and he sat down and complied.   I recollect him comparing the pain to that which might follow the incessant stinging of a wasp at the spinal marrow—
sudden, lacerating, accompanied by quivering sensations throughout the whole nervous system—followed by a strange sense of numbness.   He said that
at other times it was as though some one was in the
act of drilling a hole through his backbone, and
piercing the marrow !   Sometimes, during the moments of his most ecstatic agonies, he felt as though
his backbone was rent asunder all the way up.   The
pain was, on the whole, local—confined to the first of
the lumbar vertebræ ; but occasionally fluctuating
between them and the dorsal.   When he had finished
the dreary details of his disease, I was obliged to
acknowledge, with a sigh, that nothing suggested
itself to me as a remedy, but what I understood from
Dr. D—— had been tried over and over, and over
again.—" You are right," he replied, sorrowfully.
" Dreadful as are my sufferings, the bare thought of
undergoing more medical or surgical treatment
makes me shudder.   My back is already frightfully

I.—C c.

disfigured with the searings of caustic, seaton-marks,
cupping, and blistering;—and I hope God will give
me patience to wait till their perpetual knockings, as
it were, shall have at length battered down this frail
structure."

"Mr. E——, you rival some of the old martyrs!"
said I, as we rose to leave the study.

"In point of bodily suffering, I may; but their
holiness! those who are put into the keenest parts—
the very heart of the 'fiery furnace'—will come out
most refined at last!"

"Well, you may be earning a glorious reward
hereafter for your constancy—"

"Or I may be merely smarting for the sins of my
forefathers!" exclaimed E——, mournfully.

Monday, July, 18—. Having been called to a
patient in the neighbourhood of E——, I took that
opportunity of calling upon him on my return. It
was about nine o'clock in the evening; and I found
the philosopher sitting pensively in the parlour
alone; for his niece, I learned, had retired early,
owing to indisposition. A peculiar semicircular
lamp, of his own contrivance, stood on the table,
which was strewed with books, pamphlets, and
papers. He received me with his usual gentle
affability.

"I don't know how it is, but I feel in a singular mood
of mind to-night," said he; "I ought to say rather
many moods: sometimes so suddenly and strongly
excited, as to lose the control over my emotions—at
others, sinking into the depths of despondency. I've
been trying for these two hours to glance over this
new view of the Neptunian theory," pointing to an
open book on the table, "which —— has sent me, to
review for him in the ——; but 'tis useless; I cannot
command my thoughts." I felt his pulse: it was
one of the most irregular I had ever known. "I
know what you suspect," said he, observing my eyes
fixed with a puzzled air on my watch, and my

finger at his wrist, for several minutes; "some o·
ganic mischief at the heart. Several of your frater-
nity have latterly comforted me with assurances to
that effect." I assured him I did not apprehend any
thing of the kind, but merely that his circulation
was a little disturbed by recent excitement.

"True—true," he replied, "I *am* a little flustered,
as the phrase is—"

"Oh—here's the secret, I suppose?" said I, reaching to a periodical publication of the month, lying
on the table, and in which I had a few days ago read
a somewhat virulent attack on him. "You're very
rudely handled here, I think?" said I.

"What, do you think *that* has discomposed me?"
he inquired, with a smile. "No, no—I'm past feeling
these things long ago! Abuse—mere personality·
now excites in me no emotion of any kind!"

"Why, Mr. E——, surely you are not indifferent
to the opinion of the public, which may be misled
by such things as these, if suffered to go unan-
swered?"

"I am not afraid of that. If I've done any thing
good in my time, as I have honestly tried to do, sensible people won't believe me an impostor, at any
man's bidding. Those who *would* be so influenced
are hardly worth undeceiving."*

* * "There's a good deal of acuteness in the paper,
and in one particular, the reviewer has fairly caught
me tripping. He may *laugh* at me as much as he
pleases; but why go about to put himself in a passion? The subject did not require it. But if he is
in a passion, should I not be foolish to be in one too?
—Passion serves only to put out truth; and no one
would indulge it that had truth only in view. * *

* "This gentleman's speculations have long served to amuse children
and old people : now that he has become old himself, he also may hope
for amusement from them."—"This mountain has so long brought forth
mice, that, now it has become enfeebled and worn out, it may amuse
itself with looking after its progeny."—"Chimeras of a diseased brain."
—"Quackery."—*Review*. [Neither the Edinburgh nor Quarterly.] *Mr
E—— knew wh. was the writer this article.*

The real occasion of my nervousness," he continued, "is far different from what you have supposed—a little incident which occurred only this evening, and I will tell it you.

"My niece, feeling poorly with a cold, retired to bed as soon as she had done tea; and after sitting here about a quarter of an hour, I took one of the candles, and walked to the laboratory, to see whether all was right—as is my custom every evening. On opening the door, to my very great amazement, I saw a stranger in it, a gentleman in dark-coloured clothes, holding a dim taper in one hand, and engaged in going round the room, apparently putting all my instruments in order. I stood at the door almost petrified, watching his movements, without thinking of interrupting them, for a sudden feeling of something like awe crept over me. He made no noise whatever, and did not seem aware that any one was looking at him—or if he was, he did not seem disposed to notice the interruption. I saw him as clearly, and what he was doing, as 1 now see you playing with your gloves! He was engaged leisurely putting away all my loose implements,—shutting boxes, cases, and cupboards, with the accuracy of one who was perfectly well acquainted with his work. Having thus disposed of all the instruments and apparatus which had been used to-day—and we have had very many more than usual out—he opened the inner-door leading to the study, and entered—I following in mute astonishment. He went to work the same way in the study; shutting up several volumes that lay open on the table, and carefully replacing them in their proper places on the shelves.

"Having cleared away these, he approached the astronomical apparatus near the window, put the cap on the object-end of the telescope, pushed in the joints, all noiselessly, closed up in its case my new chronometer, and then returned to the table where my desk lay, took up the inkstand, poured out the ink into the fireplace, flung all the pens under the grate, and then shut the desk, locked it, and laid the key on the top of it. When he had done all this he walked towards the wall, and turned slowly towards me, looked me full in the face, and shook his head mournfully. The taper he held in his hand slowly expired—and the spectre, if such it were, disappeared. The strangest part of the story is yet to follow. The pale, fixed features seemed perfectly *familiar* to me—they were those which I had often gazed at, in a portrait of Mr. Boyle, prefixed to my quarto copy of his 'Treatise of Atmospheric Air.' As soon as I had a little recovered my self-possession, I took down the work in question, and examined the portrait. I was right! I cannot account for my not having spoken to the figure, or gone close up to it. I think I could have done either, as far as *courage* went. My prevailing idea was, that a single word would have dissolved the charm, and my curiosity prompted me to see it out. I returned to the parlour and rung the bell for Joseph.

" ' Joseph,' said I, ' have you set things to rights in the laboratory and study to-night ?"—' Yes, master,' he replied, with surprise in his manner; ' I finished it before tea-time, and set things in *particular* good order—I gave both the rooms a right good cleaning out—I'm sure there's not even a pin in its wrong place.'

" ' What made you fling the pens and ink in the fireplace and under the grate ?'

' Because I thought they were of no use—the pens worn to stumps, and the ink thick and clotted—too much *gum* in it.' He was evidently astonished at being asked such questions—and was going to explain further, when I said, simply, ' that will do,' and he retired. Now, what am I to think of all this! If it were a mere ocular spectrum, clothed with its functions from my own excited fancy, there was yet a unity of purpose in its doings that is extraordinary!

Something very much like '*shutting up the shop*'—eh?" inquired E——, with a melancholy smile.

"'Tis touching—very! I never heard a more singular incident," I replied, abstractedly, without removing my eyes from the fire; for *my* reading of the occurrence was a sudden and strong conviction, that, ghost or no ghost, E—— had toiled his *last* in the behalf of science—that he would never again have occasion to use his philosophical machinery! This melancholy presentiment invested E——, and all he said or did, with tenfold interest in my eyes. " Don't suppose, doctor, that I am weak enough to be seriously disturbed by the occurrence I have just been mentioning. Whether or not it really portends my approaching death I know not. Though I am not presumptuous enough to suppose myself so important as to warrant any special interference of Providence on my behalf—yet I cannot help thinking I am to look on this as a warning—a solemn premonition—that I may ' set my house in order, and die.'"

Our conversation during the remainder of our interview turned on the topic suggested by the affecting incident just related. I listened to all he uttered, as to the words of a doomed—a dying man! All E—— advanced on this difficult and interesting subject was marked not less by sound philosophy than unfeigned piety. He ended with avowing his belief, that the omnipotent Being who formed both the body and the soul, and willed them to exist unitedly, could surely, nevertheless, if he saw good, cause the one to exist separately from the other; either by endowing it with *new properties* for that special purpose, or by enabling it to exercise, in its disembodied state, those powers which continued *latent* in it during its connexion with the body. Did it follow—he asked—that neither body nor soul possessed any *other qualities* than those which were necessary to enable them to exist together? Why should the soul be incapable of a substantially distinct personal existence? Where the *impossibility* of its being made visible to organs of sense? Has the Almighty no means of bringing this to pass? Are there no latent properties in the organs of vision—no subtle *sympathies* with immaterial substances—which are yet un-discovered—and even undiscoverable? Surely this *may* be the case—though *how*, it would be impossible to conjecture. He saw no bad philosophy, he said, in this; and he who decided the question in the negative before he had brought forward some evidence of its moral or physical *impossibility* was guilty of most presumptuous dogmatism.

This is the substance of his opinions; but, alas! I lack the chaste, nervous, philosophical eloquence in which they were clothed. A distinguished living character said of E——, that he was the most fascinating talker on abstruse subjects he ever heard. I could have staid all night listening to him. In fact, I fear I *did* trespass on his politeness even to inconvenience. I staid and partook of his supper—simple, frugal fare—consisting of roasted potatoes, and two tumblers of new milk. I left about eleven: my mind occupied but with one wish, all the way home, —that I had known E—— intimately for as many *years* as hours!

Two days afterward, the following hurried note was put into my hands, from my friend Dr. D——: "My dear ——, I am sure you will be as much affected as I was, at hearing that our inestimable friend Mr. E——, had a sudden stroke of the palsy this afternoon about two o'clock, from which I very much fear he may never recover; for this, added to his advanced age, and the dreadful chronic complaint under which he labours, is surely sufficient to shatter the small remains of his strength. I need hardly say, that all is in confusion at ——. I am going down there to-night, and shall be happy to drive you down also, if you will be at my *house* by seven. Yours," &c. &c. I was grieved and agitated, but in

nowise surprised at this intelligence. What passe
the last time I saw him prepared me for something
of this kind !

On arriving in the evening we were shown into
the parlour, where sat Miss E—— in a paroxysm of
hysterical weeping, which had forced her a few moments before to leave her uncle's sick-room.   It was
some time before we could calm her agitated spirits,
or get her to give us any thing like a connected account of her uncle's sudden illness.   " Oh, these will
tell you all !" said she, sobbing, and taking two letters from her bosom, one of which bore a black seal;
" It is these cruel letters that have broken his heart !
Both came by the same post this morning !" She
withdrew, promising to send for us when all was
ready, and we hastily opened the two letters she had
left.   What will the reader suppose were the two
heavy strokes dealt at once upon the head of Mr.
E—— by an inscrutable Providence ?   The letter I
opened, conveyed the intelligence of the sudden
death, in childbed, of Mrs. ——, his only daughter,
to whom he had been most passionately attached.
The letter Dr. D—— held in his hand disclosed an
instance of almost unparalleled perfidy and ingratitude.   I shall here state what I learned afterward—
that many years ago, Mr. E—— had taken a poor lad
from one of the parish schools, pleased with his
quickness and obedience, and had apprenticed him
to a respectable tradesman.   He served his articles
honourably, and Mr. E—— nobly advanced him
funds to establish himself in business.   He pros-
pered beyond every one's expectations : and the
good, generous, confiding E—— was so delighted
with his conduct, and persuaded of his principles,
that he gradually advanced him large sums of money
to increase an extensive connexion ; and, at last, invested his *all*, amounting to little short of £15,000,
in this man's concern, for which he received 5 per
cent.   Sudden success, however, turned this young

man's head; and Mr. E—— had long been uneasy at hearing current rumours about his protegé's unsteadiness and extravagance. He had several times spoken to him about them; but was easily persuaded that the reports in question were as groundless as malignant. And as the last half-year's interest was paid punctually, accompanied with a hint that if doubts were entertained of his probity, the man was ready to refund a great part of the *principal*, Mr. E——'s confidence revived. Now, the letter in question was from this person; and stated that, though "circum stances" had compelled him to withdraw from his creditors for the present—in other words, to abscond— he had no doubt that if Mr. E—— would wait a little, he should in time be able to pay him a "fair dividend!" —"Good God! why E—— is *ruined!*" exclaimed Dr. D - - -, turning pale, and dropping the letter, after having read it to me.

"Yes, ruined!—all the hard savings of many years' labour and economy *gone* at a stroke!"

"Why, was *all* his small fortune embarked in this man's concern?"

"All, except a few hundreds lying loose at his banker's!—What is to become of poor Miss E——?"

"Cannot this infamous scoundrel be brought to justice?" I inquired.

"If he were, he may prove, perhaps, not worth powder and shot,—the viper!'

Similar emotions kept us both silent for several moments.

"This will put his philosophy to a dreadful trial," said I. "How do you think he will bear it, should he recover from the present seizure so far as to be made sensible of the extent of his misfortunes?"

"Oh, nobly, nobly! I'll pledge my existence to it! He'll bear it like a Christian, as well as a philosopher! I've seen him in trouble before this."

"Is Miss E —— entirely dependent on her uncle; and has he made no provision for her?"

"Alas! he had appropriated to her 5000*l* of the 15,000*l*. in this man's hands, as a marriage-portion—I know it, for I am one of his executors. The circumstance of leaving her thus destitute will, I know, prey cruelly on his mind." Shortly afterward we were summoned into the chamber of the venerable sufferer. His niece sat at the bedside, near his head, holding one of his cold motionless hands in hers. Mr. E——'s face, deadly pale, and damp with perspiration, had suffered a shocking distortion of the features—the left eye and the mouth being drawn downwards to the left side. He gazed at us vacantly, evidently without recognising us, as we took our stations, one at the foot, the other at the side of the bed. What a melancholy contrast between the present expression of his eyes, and that of acuteness and brilliance which eminently characterized them in health! They reminded me of Milton's sun, looking

> "Through the horizontal misty air,
> Shorn of its beams."

The distorted lips were moving about incessantly, as if with abortive efforts to speak, though he could utter nothing but an inarticulate murmuring sound, which he had continued almost from the moment of his being struck. Was it not a piteous—a heart-rending spectacle? Was *this* the philosopher?

After making due inquiries, and ascertaining the extent of the injury to his nervous system, we withdrew to consult on the treatment to be adopted. In accounting for the seizure, I considered that the uncommon quantities of laudanum he had so long been in the habit of receiving into his system alone sufficiently accounted for his present seizure. Then, again, the disease in his spine—the consequent exhaustion of his energies—the sedentary, thoughtful life he led—all these were at least predisposing causes. The sudden shock he had received in the

morning merely *accelerated* what had long been advancing on him. We both anticipated a speedily
fatal issue, and resolved to take the earliest oppor-
unity of acquainting him with his approaching end

[He lies in nearly the same state during Thursday
and Friday.]

Saturday.—We are both astonished and delighted
to find that E——'s daily paroxysms have deserted
him, at least he has exhibited no symptoms of their
appearance up to this day. On entering the room,
we found to our inexpressible satisfaction that his
disorder had taken a very unusual and happy course
—having been worked out of the system by *fever.*
This, as my medical readers will be aware, is a very
rare occurrence.—[Three or four pages of the Diary
are occupied with technical details, of no interest
whatever to the general reader.]—His features were
soon restored to their natural position; and, in short,
every appearance of palsy left him.

Sunday evening.—Mr. E—— going on well, and
his mental energies and speech perfectly restored. I
called on him alone. Almost his first words to me
were—"Well, doctor, good Mr. Boyle was right, you
see!" I replied that it yet remained to be proved.

"God sent me a noble messenger to summon me
hence, did he not? One whose character has always
been my model, as far as I could imitate his great
and good qualities."

"You attach too much weight, Mr. E——, to that
creature of imagination"—

"What! do you really doubt that I am on my
death-bed? I assuredly shall not recover. The
pains in my back have left me, that my end may be
easy. Ay, ay, the 'silver cord is loosed.'" I inquired about the sudden cessation of his chronic
complaint. He said, it had totally disappeared;
leaving behind it only a sensation of numbness. "In
this instance of His mercy towards an unworthy
worm of the earth, I devoutly thank my Father—my

God!" he exclaimed, looking reverentially upward.
—"Oh, how could I in patience have possessed my
soul, if to the pains of dying had been superadded
those which had imbittered life!—My constant
prayer to God has been, that, if it be His will, my life
may run out clear to the last drop; and though the
stream has been a little troubled," alluding to the intelligence which had occasioned his illness, " I may
yet have my prayer answered—Oh, sweet darling
Anne! why should I grieve for *you?* Where I am
going, I humbly believe you are! Root and branch
—both gathered home!" He shed tears abundantly,
but spoke of the dreadful bereavement in terms of
perfect resignation. * * * " You are no doubt
acquainted," he continued, " with the other afflicting
news, which, I own, has cut me to the quick! My
confidence has been betrayed,—my sweet niece's
prospects utterly blighted,—and I made a beggar of
in my old age. This ungrateful man has squandered
away infamously the careful savings of more than
thirty years—every penny of which has been earned
with the sweat of my brow. I do not so much care
for it myself, as I have still enough left to preserve
me from want during the few remaining days I have
left me; but my poor, dear Emma! My heart aches
to think of it!"

"I hope you may yet recover *some* portion of your
property, Mr. E——; the man speaks in his letter
of paying you a fair dividend."

"No, no; when once a man has deliberately acted
n such an unprincipled manner as he has, it is foolish to expect restitution. Loss of character and the
confidence of his benefactor makes him desperate.
I find, that, should I linger on earth longer than a
few weeks, I cannot now afford to pay the rent of this
house—I must remove from it—I cannot die in the
house in which my poor wife breathed her last—this
very room!" His tears burst forth again, and mine
started to my eyes. " A friend is now looking out

lodg.ngs for me in the neighbourhood; to which 1 shall remove the instant my health will permit. It goes to my heart, to think of the bustling auctioneer disposing of all my apparatus,"—tears again gushed from his eyes—"the companions of many years"—

"Dear, dear sir!—Your friends will ransack heaven and earth before your fears shall be verified," said I, with emotion.

"They—you—are very good; but you would be unsuccessful!—You must think me very weak to let these things overcome me in this way—one can't help feeling them!—A man may writhe under the amputating knife, and yet acknowledge the necessity of its use! My spirit wants disciplining."

"Allow me to say, Mr. E——, that I think you bear your misfortunes with admirable fortitude—true philosophic"—

"Oh doctor! doctor!" he exclaimed, interrupting me, with solemn emphasis, "believe a dying man, to whom all this world's fancied realities have sunk into shadows—*nothing* can make a death-bed easy, but RELIGION—a humble, hearty faith in Him whose Son redeemed mankind! Philosophy—science—is a nothing—a mockery—a delusion—if it be only of this world!—I believe from the bottom of my heart, and have long done so, that the essence—the very crown and glory of true philosophy, is to surrender up the soul entirely to God's teaching, and practically receive and appreciate the consolations of the gospel of Jesus Christ!" Oh, the fervency with which he expressed himself—his shrunk clasped hands pointed upwards, and his features beaming with devotion! I told him it did my heart good to hear such opinions avowed by a man of his distinguished attainments.

"Don't—don't—don't talk in that strain, doctor!" said he, turning to me with a reproving air. "Could a living man but know how compliments fall upon a dying man's ear! * * * I am going shortly into the presence of Him who is wisdom itself; and shall I go pluming myself on my infinitely less than glowworm glimmer, in the presence of that pure effulgence?   Doctor, I've felt, latterly, that I would give worlds to forget the pitiful acquirements which I have purchased by a life's labour, if my soul might meet a smile of approbation when it first flits into the presence of its Maker—its Judge!" Strange language! thought I, for the scientific E——, confessedly a master-mind among men.—Would that the shoal of sciolists, now babbling abroad their infidel crudities, could have had one moment's interview with this dying philosopher! Pert fools, who are hardly released from their leading-strings—the very go-cart, as it were, of elemental science—before they strut about and forthwith proceed to pluck their Maker by the beard—and this, as an evidence of their "independence," and being released from the "trammels of superstition!"

Oh, Lord and Maker of the universe!—that thou shouldst be so "long-suffering" towards these insolent insects of an hour!

To return. I left E—— in a glowing mood of mind, disposed to envy him his death-bed, even with all the ills which attended it! Before leaving the house, I stepped into the parlour to speak a few words to Miss E——. The sudden illness of her uncle had found its way into the papers; and I was delighted to find it had brought a profusion of cards every morning, many of them bearing the most distinguished names in rank and science. It showed that E——'s worth was properly appreciated. I counted the cards of five noblemen, and very many members of the Royal and other learned societies.

———

Wednesday, 15th August.—Well, poor E—— was yesterday removed from his house in —— Row, where he had resided upwards of twenty-five years —which he had fitted up, working often with his own hands, at much trouble and expense—having built the laboratory-room since he had the house—he was removed, I say, from his house, to lodgings in the neighbourhood. He has three rooms on the first floor, small, indeed, and in humble style—but perfectly clean, neat, and comfortable. Was not this itself sufficient to have broken many a haughty spirit! His extensive philosophical apparatus, furniture, &c. &c., had *all been sold*, at less than a *twentieth* part of the sum they had originally cost him! No tidings as yet have been received of the villain who has ruined his generous patron! E—— has ceased, however, to talk of it; but I see that Miss E—— feels it acutely. Poor girl, well she may! Her uncle was carried in a sedan to his new residence, and fainted on the way, but has continued in tolerable spirits since his arrival. His conduct is the admiration of all that see or hear of him! The first words he uttered as he was sitting before the fire in an easy chair, after recovering a little from the exhaustion occasioned by his being carried up stairs, were to Dr. D——, who had accompanied him. "Well!"—he whispered, faintly, with his eyes shut—"What a gradation!—Reached the *half-way-house* between —— Row and the 'house appointed for all living!'"

"You have much to bear, sir!" said Dr. D——. "And more to be thankful for!" replied E——. "If there were such a thing as a Protestant *calendar*,' said Dr. D—— to me, enthusiastically, while recounting what is told above, "and I could canonize, E—— should stand first on the list, and be my patron saint!" When I saw E——, he was lying in bed in a very low and weak state, evidently declining rapidly. Still he looked as placid as his fallen features would let him.

"Doctor," said he, soon after I had sat down "how very good it is of you to come so far out of your regular route to see me!"

" Don't name it," said I, " proud and happy"—

" But excuse me, I wish to tell you that when I am gone you will find I knew how to be grateful, as far as my means would warrant."

" Mr. E——! my dear sir!" said I, as firmly as my emotions could let me, " if you don't promise this day to erase every mention of my name or services from your will, I leave you, and solemnly declare I will never intrude upon you again! Mr. E——, you distress me—you do, beyond measure!"

" Well—well—well—I'll obey you—but may God bless you! God bless you!" he replied, turning his head away, while the tears trickled down.   Indeed! —as if a thousand guineas could have purchased the emotions with which I felt his poor damp fingers feebly compressing my hand!

*   *   *   *   *   *   *   *

" Doctor!" he exclaimed, after I had been sitting with him some time, conversing on various subjects connected with his illness and worldly circumstances, " don't you think God can speak to the soul as well in a night as in a day-dream? Shall I presume to say he has done so in my case!" I asked him what he was alluding to.

" Don't you recollect my telling you of an optical, or spectral illusion, which occurred to me at —— Row? A man shutting up the shop—you know?" I told him I did.

" Well—last night I *dreamed*—I am satisfied it was a dream—that I saw Mr. Boyle again ; but how different!   Instead of gloomy clothing, his appearance was wondrously radiant—and his features were not, as before, solemn, sad, and fixed. but wore an air of joy and exultation ; and instead of a miserable expiring taper, he held aloft a light like the kindling lustre of a star!   What think you of that, doctor? Surely, if both these are the delusions of a morbid fancy, *if* they are, what a light they fling over the dark valley' I am entering !"

I hinted my dissent from the skeptical sneers of the day, which would resolve all that was uttered on death-beds into delirious rant—confused disordered faculties—superstition.

"I think you are right," said he. "Who knows what new light may stream upon the soul, as the wall between time and eternity is breaking down? Who has come back from the grave to tell us that the soul's energies decay with the body, or that the body's decay destroys or interrupts the exercise of the soul's powers, and that all a dying man utters is mere gibberish? The *Christian* philosopher would be loath to do so, when he recollects that God chose *the hour of death* to reveal futurity to the patriarchs and others of old! Do you think a superintending Providence would allow the most solemn and instructive period of our life, the close—scenes where men's hearts and eyes are open, if ever, to receive admonition and encouragement—to be mere exhibitions of absurdity and weakness? Is that the way God treats his servants?"

Friday afternoon.—In a more melancholy mood than usual, on account of the evident distress of his niece about her altered prospects. He told me, however, that he felt the confidence of his soul in nowise shaken. "I am," said he, "like one lying far on the shores of Eternity, thrown there by the waters of the world, and whom a high and strong wave reaches once more and overflows. One may be pardoned a sudden chilliness and heart-fluttering.—After all," he continued, "only consider what an easy end mine is, comparatively with that of many others! How very—very thankful should I be for such an easy exit as mine seems likely to be! God be thanked that I have to endure no such agonies of horror and remorse as ——!" (alluding to Mr. ——, whom I was then attending, and whose case I had mentioned on a former occasion to Mr. E——; the one described in a former part of this Diary, under the

I.—D d

title, "*A Man about Town*")—"that I am writhing
under no accident—that I have not to struggle with
utter destitution!—Why am I not left to perish in a
prison? To suffer on a scaffold? To be plucked
suddenly into the presence of my Maker in battle,*
' with all my sins upon my head?' Suppose I were
grovelling in the hopeless darkness of skepticism or
infidelity? Suppose I were still to endure the agonies arising from disease in my spine?—Oh God!"
exclaimed Mr. E——, " give me a more humble and
grateful heart!"

Monday, 19*th September*.—Mr. E—— is still alive,
to the equal astonishment of Dr. D—— and myself.
The secret must lie, I think, in his tranquil frame of
mind.   He is as happy as the day is long!   Oh, that
my latter days may be like his! I was listening
with feelings of delight unutterable to E——'s description of the state of his mind—the perfect peace
ne felt towards all mankind, and his humble and
strong hopes of happiness hereafter—when the landlady of the house knocked at the door, and on entering, told Mr. E—— that a person was down-stairs
very anxious to see him.—"Who is it?" inquired
E——. She did not know. " Has he ever been
here before?"—" No; but she thought she had
several times seen him about the neighbourhood."—
" What sort of a person is he?" inquired E——, with
a surprised air.—" Oh, he is a tall, pale man, in a
brown   great-coat."   E—— requested her to go
down and ask his name. She returned, and said,
" Mr. H——, sir." E——, on hearing her utter the
word, suddenly raised himself in bed; the little
colour he had fled from his cheeks: he lifted up his
hands and exclaimed, " What can the unhappy man
want with me?" He paused thoughtfully for a few
moments. " You're of course aware who this is?"
he inquired of me in a whisper. I nodded. " Show

* This was at the time of the Peninsular campaigns.

&c. up stairs," said he, and the woman withdrew. " For your own sake I beg you to be calm ; don't allow your feelings"— I was interrupted by the door opening, and just such a person as Mrs.—— had described entered, with a slow, hesitating step, into the room. He held his hat squeezed in both his hands, and he stood for a few moments motionless, just within the door, with his eyes fixed on the floor. In that posture he continued till Mrs. —— had retired, shutting the door after her, when he turned suddenly towards the easy-chair by the fire, in which Mr. E—— was sitting, much agitated—approached, and falling down on his knees, he covered his eyes with his hands, through which the tears presently fell like rain ; and after many choking sobs and sighs, faltered, " Oh, Mr. E—— !"

" What do you want with ME, Mr. H——?" inquired Mr. E——, in a low tone, but very calmly.

" Oh, kind, good, abused sir ! I have behaved like a villain to you"—

" Mr. H——, I beg you will not distress me ; consider I am in a very poor and weak state."

" Don't for God's sake speak so coldly, sir ! I am heartbroken to think how shamefully I have used you !"

" Well, then, strive to amend."—

" Oh, dear, good Mr. E——! can you forgive me ?" Mr. E—— did not answer. I saw he *could* not. The tears were nearly overflowing. The man seized his hand, and pressed it to his lips with fervency.

" Rise, Mr. H——, rise ! I *do* forgive you, and I hope that God will ! Seek his forgiveness, which will avail you more than *mine!*"

" Oh, sir !" exclaimed the man again, covering his eyes with his hands,—" how very—VERY ill you look —how pale and thin. It's *I* that have done it all—I, the d——dest"—

" Hush, hush, sir !" exclaimed Mr. E——, with

more sternness than I had ever seen him exhibit, "do not curse in a dying man's room."

"Dying—dying—*dying*, sir?" exclaimed the man, hoarsely, staring horror-struck at Mr. E——, and retiring a step from him.

"Yes, James," replied E——, mildly, calling him for the first time by his Christian name, "I am assuredly dying—but not through *you*, or any thing you have done. Come, come, don't distress yourself unnecessarily," he continued, in the kindest tones; for he saw the man continued deadly pale, speechless, and clasping his hands convulsively over his breast—"Consider, James, my daughter, Mrs. ——."

"Oh, no, no, sir—no! It's *I* that have done it all; my ingratitude has broken your heart—I know it has! —What will become of me?"—the man resumed, still staring vacantly at Mr. E——.

"James, I must not be agitated in this way—it agitates me—you must leave the room unless you can become calm. What is done *is* done; and if you really repent of it"—

"Oh, I do, sir; and could almost weep tears of blood for it! But indeed, sir, it has been as much my misfortune as my fault."

"Was it your *misfortune* or your fault that you kept that infamous woman on whom you have squandered so much of your property—of *mine* rather?" inquired Mr. E——, with a mild expostulating air. The man suddenly blushed scarlet, and continued silent.

"It is right I should tell you that it is *your* misconduct which has turned me out, in my old age from the house which has sheltered me all my life, and driven me to die in this poor place! You have beggared my niece, and robbed me of all the hard earnings of my life—wrung from the sweat of my brow, as you well know, James. James, how could your heart let you do all this?" The man made him no answer. "I am not *angry* with you—that is past

—but I am grieved—disappointed—shocked to find my confidence in you has been so much abused."

"Oh, sir, I don't know what it was that infatuated me; but—never trust a living man again, sir—never," replied the man, vehemently.

"It is not likely I shall, James—I shall not have the opportunity," said Mr. E——, calmly. The man's eye continued fixed on Mr. E——, his lip quivered in spite of his violent compression, and the fluctuating colour in his cheeks showed the agitation he was suffering.

"Do you forgive me, sir, for what I have done?" he asked, almost inaudibly.

"Yes—if you promise to amend—yes! Here is my hand—I *do* forgive you, as I hope for my own forgiveness hereafter!" said Mr. E——, reaching out his hand. "And if your repentance is sincere, should it ever be in your power, remember whom you have most heavily wronged, not *me*, but—but—Miss E——, my poor niece. If you should ever be able to make her any reparation—" the tears stood in Mr. E——'s eyes, and his emotions prevented his completing the sentence. "Really you *must* leave me, James—you must—I am too weak to bear this scene any longer," said E——, faintly, looking deadly pale.

"You had better withdraw, sir, and call some other time," said I. He rose, looking almost bewildered; thrust his hand into his breast-pocket, and taking out a small packet laid it hurriedly on Mr. E——'s lap—snatched his hand to his lips, and murmuring, "Farewell, farewell, best of men!"—withdrew. I watched him through the window; and saw that as soon as he had left the house, he set off, running almost at the top of his speed. When I returned to look at Mr. E——, he had fainted. He had opened the packet, and a letter lay open in his lap, with a great many bank notes. The letter ran as follows: "Injured and revered sir,—When you read this epistle, the miserable writer will have fled from his country and

be on his way to America.   He has abused the confidence of one of the greatest and best of men, but
hopes the enclosed sum will show he repented what
he had done! If it is ever in his power he will do
more. J—— H——." The packet contained bank
notes to the amount of 3000*l.* When E—— had
recovered from his swoon, 1 had him conveyed to
bed, where he lay in a state of great exhaustion. He
scarce spoke a syllable during the time I continued
with him.

Tuesday.—Mr. E—— still suffers from the effects
of yesterday's excitement.   It has, I am confident,
hurried him far on his journey to the grave.   He told
me he had been turning over the affair in his mind,
and considered that it would be wrong in him to retain the 3000*l.*, as it would be illegal, and a fraud on
H——'s other creditors: and this upright man had
actually sent in the morning for the solicitor to the
bankrupt's assignees, and put the whole into his
hands, telling him of the circumstances under which
he had received it, and asking him whether he should
not be wrong in keeping it.   The lawyer told him
that he might perhaps be legally, but not morally
wrong—as the law certainly forbade such payments,
and yet he was by very far the largest creditor.
"Let me act right, then, in the sight of God and
man!   Take the money, and let me come in with the
rest of the creditors."   Mr. —— withdrew.   He must
have seen but seldom such an instance of noble con-
scientiousness!   I remonstrated with Mr. E——.
"No, no, doctor," he replied, "I have endeavoured
strictly to do my duty during life—I will not begin
roguery on my death-bed!"—"Possibly you may
not receive a penny in the pound, Mr. E——," said I.
   "But I shall have the comfort of quitting life with
a clear conscience!"

*   *   *   *   *   *   *   *

Monday.—[A week afterward.]—The "weary
wheels of life" will soon "stand still!"   All is calm

and serene with E—— as a summer evening's sun-
set! He is at peace with all the world, and with
his God. It is like entering the porch of heaven,
and listening to an angel, to visit and converse with
E——. This morning he received the reward of his
noble conduct in the matter of H——'s bankruptcy.
The assignees have wound up the affairs, and found
them not near so desperate as had been apprehended.
The business was still to be carried on in H——'s
name; and the solicitor who had been sent for by
E—— to receive the 3000*l.* in behalf of the assignees,
called this morning with a check for 3500*l.*, and a
highly complimentary letter from the assignees.
They informed him that there was every prospect of
the concern's yet discharging the heavy amount of his
claim, and that they would see to its being paid to
whomsoever he might appoint. H—— had set sail
for America, the very day he had called on E——,
and had left word that he should never return. E——
altered his will this evening, in the presence of myself and Dr. D——. He left about 4000*l.* to his
niece, "and whatever sums might be from time to time
paid in from H——'s business; five guineas for a
yearly prize to the writer of the best summary of the
progress of philosophy every year, in one of the
Scotch colleges; and ten pounds to be delivered
every Christmas to ten poor men, as long as they
lived, and who had already received the gratuity for
several years; and to J—— H——, his full and
hearty forgiveness, and prayers to God that he may
return to a course of virtue and true piety, before it
is too late." * * * "How is it," said he, addressing Dr. D—— and me, "that you have neither of you
said any thing to me about examining my body after
my decease?" Dr. D—— replied, that he had often
thought of asking his permission, but had kept delay-
ing from day to day. "Why?" inquired E——, with
a smile of surprise; "do you fancy I have any silly
fears or prejudices on the subject? That I am anxious

about the shell when the kernel is gone! I can assure you that it would rather give me pleasure than otherwise, to think that by an examination of my body the cause of medical science might be advanced, and so minister a little to my species. I must, however, say you NAY; for I promised my poor wife that I would forbid it. *She* had prejudices, and I have a right to respect them."

Wednesday.—He looked much reduced this evening. I had hurried to his lodgings, to communicate what I considered would be the gratifying intelligence, that the highest prize of a foreign learned society had just been awarded him for his work on ———, together with a fellowship. My heated and hurried manner somewhat discomposed him; and before I had communicated my news, he asked, with some agitation, "What!—Some new misfortune?" —When I had told him my errand,—"Oh, bubble! bubble! bubble!" he exclaimed, shaking his head with a melancholy smile, "would I not give thousands of these for a poor man's blessing? Are these, *these* the trifles men toil through a life for?—Oh, if it had pleased God to give me a single glimpse of what I now see, thirty years ago, how true an estimate I should have formed of the littleness—the vanity of human applause! How much happier would my end have been! How much nearer should I have come to the character of a true philosopher—an impartial, independent, sincere teacher of the truth, for its own sake!"—"But honours of this kind are of admirable service to science, Mr. E———," said I, "as supplying strong incentives and stimulants to a pursuit of philosophy."

"Yes; but does it not argue a defect in the constitution of men's minds to require them? What is the use of stimulants in medicine, doctor?—Don't they presuppose a morbid sluggishness in the parts they are applied to? Do you ever stimulate a *healthy* organ?—So is it with the little honours and distinc-

tions we are speaking of.   Directly a man becomes
anxious about obtaining them, his mind has lost its
healthy tone—its sympathies with truth—with real
philosophy."

"Would you, then, discourage striving for them?
Would you banish honours and prizes from the scientific world?"

"Assuredly—altogether—did we but exist in a better state of society than we do. * * What is the
proper spirit in which, as matters at present stand,
a philosopher should accept of honours?—Merely as
evidences, testimonials, to the multitude of those
who are *otherwise* incapable of appreciating his merits,
and would set him down as a dreamer—a visionary
—but that they saw the estimation in which he was
held by those who are likely to canvass his claims
strictly.   They *compel* the deference, if not respect of the δι πολλοι.   A philosopher ought to receive
them, therefore, as it were, in *self-defence*—a shut-
mouth to babbling, envious gainsayers.   Were all the
world philosophers, in the *true* sense of the word,
not merely would honours be unnecessary, but an
insult—a reproach.   Directly a philosopher is conscious that the love of fame—the ambition to secure
such distinctions, is gradually insinuating—inter-
weaving itself with the very texture of his mind;
that considerations of that kind are becoming *necessary in any degree* to prompt him to undertake or
prosecute scientific pursuits, he may write Icha-
bod on the door of his soul's temple—for the glory
is departed.   His motives are spurious; his fires
false!   To the exact extent of the necessity for such
motives is, as it were, the pure ore of his soul adul-
terated.   Minerva's jealous eyes can detect the
slightest vacillation or inconsistency in her votaries,
and discover her rival even before the votary himself
is sensible of her existence; and withdraws from
her faithless admirer in cold disdain perhaps never to
return   Do you think that Archimedes, Plato, or Sir

Isaac Newton would have cared a straw for even
royal honours ? The true test, believe me—the almost
infallible criterion of a man's having attained to true
greatness of mind—to the true philosophic temper,
is his utter indifference to all sorts of honours and
distinctions.   Why ?—What seeks he—or proposes,
to seek—but TRUTH ?   Is he to stop in the race, to
look after Atalanta's apples ?   He should *endure* honours, not go out of his way to seek them.   If one
apple hitches in his vest, he may carry it with him,
not stop to dislodge it.   Scientific distinctions are
absolutely necessary in the present state of society,
because it is defective.   A mere ambitious struggle
for college honours through rivalry has induced
many a man to enter so far upon philosophical studies
as that their charms, unfolding in proportion to his
progress, have been *of themselves* at last sufficient to
prevail upon him to go onwards—to love science for
herself alone.   Honours make a man open his eyes,
who would else have gone to his grave with them
shut: and when once he has seen the divinity of
truth, he laughs at obstacles, and follows it through
evil and good report—if his soul be properly con-
stituted—if it have in it any of the nobler sympathies
of our nature.—That is my *homily on honours*," said
he, with a smile, " I have not wilfully preached and
practised different things, I assure you," he continued,
with a modest air, " but through life have striven to
act upon these principles.   Still, I never saw so
clearly as at this moment how small my success has
been—to what an extent I have been influenced by
incorrect motives—as far as an over-valuing of the
world's honours may be so considered.   Now I see
through no such magnifying medium; the mists and
vapours are dispersing; and I begin to see that these
objects are in themselves little, even to nothingness.
—The general retrospect of my life is far from satisfactory," continued E——, with a sigh—" and fills
me with real sorrow !"—" Why ?"—I inquired, with

surprise. "Why, for this one reason—because I have in a measure sacrificed my *religion* to philosophy! Oh—will my Maker thus be put off with the mere lees—the refuse—of my time and energies? For *one hour* in the day that I have devoted to him, have I not given twelve or fourteen to my own pursuits? What shall I say of this shortly—in a few hours—perhaps moments—when I stand suddenly in the presence of GOD—when I see Him face to face! Oh, doctor!—my heart sinks and sickens at the thought!—shall I not be *speechless*, as one of old?"

I told him I thought he was unnecessarily severe with himself—that he "wrote bitter things against himself."

"I thought so once, nay, all my life, myself—doctor"—said he, solemnly—"but mark my words, as a dying man—you will think as I do now when you come to be in my circumstances!"

The above, feebly conveyed perhaps to the reader, may be considered THE LAST WORDS OF A PHILOSOPHER. They made an impression on my mind which has never been effaced; and I trust never will. The reader need not suspect him of "prosing." The above were uttered with no pompous, swelling, pedantic swagger of manner, but with the simplest, most modest air, and in the most silvery tones of voice I ever listened to. He often paused from faintness: and at the conclusion his voice grew almost inaudible, and he wiped the thick-standing dews from his forehead. He begged me, in a low whisper, to kneel down and read him one of the church-prayers —the one appointed for those in prospect of death: I took down the prayer-book and complied, though my emotions would not suffer me to speak in more than an often-interrupted whisper. He lay perfectly silent throughout, with his clasped hands pointing upwards; and when I had concluded, he responded, feebly, but fervently, "Amen—Amen!"—and the tears gushed down his cheeks. My heart was melted within me. The silk cap had slipped from his head, and his long, loose, silvery hair streamed over his bed-dress: his appearance was that of a dying prophet of old! But I find I am going on at too great length for the reader's patience, and must pause. For my own part I could linger over the remembrances of these solemn scenes for ever: but I shall hasten on to the "last scene of all." It did not take place till near a fortnight after the interview above narrated. His manner during that time evinced no tumultuous ecstasies of soul; none of the boisterous extravagance of enthusiasm. His departure was like that of the sun, sinking gradually and finally, lower—lower—lower—no sudden upflashings —no quivering—no flickering unsteadiness about his fading rays!

Tuesday, 13th October.—Miss E—— sent word that her uncle appeared dying, and had expressed a wish to see both Dr. D—— and me. I therefore despatched a note to Dr. D——, requesting him to meet me at a certain place, and then hurried through my list of calls, so as to have finished by three o'clock. By four we were both in the room of the dying philosopher. Miss E—— sat by his bedside, her eyes swollen with weeping, and was in the act of kissing her uncle's cheek when we entered. Mr. F——, an exemplary clergyman, who had been one of E——'s earliest and dearest friends, sat at the foot of the bed with a copy of Jeremy Taylor's " Holy Living and Dying," from which he was reading in a low tone, at the request of E——. The appearance of the latter was very interesting. At his own instance, he had not long before been shaved, washed, and had a change of linen ; and the bed was also but recently made, and was not at all tumbled or disordered. The mournful tolling of the church-bell for a funeral was also heard at intervals, and added to the solemnity of the scene. I have seldom felt in such a state

of excitement as I was on first entering the room.
He shook hands with each of us, or rather we shook
his hands, for he could hardly lift them from the bed
" Well—thank you for coming to bid me farewell '"
said he, with a smile ; adding, pleasantly, " Will you
allow Mr. F—— to proceed with what he is reading ?" Of course we nodded, and sat in silence listening.   I watched E——'s features; they were
much wasted—but exhibited no traces of pain. His
eye, though rather sunk in the socket, was full of the
calmness and confidence of unwavering hope, and
often directed upwards with a devout expression. A
most heavenly serenity was diffused over his countenance.   His lips occasionally moved, as if in the utterance of prayer.   When Mr. F—— had closed the
book, the first words uttered by E—— were, " Oh
the infinite goodness of God !"

" Do you feel that your ' anchor is within the veil ?"
inquired F——.

" Oh !—yes—yes !—My vessel is steadily moored
—the tide of life goes fast away—I am forgetting
that I ever sailed on its sea !" replied E——, closing
his eyes.

" The star of faith shines clearest in the night of
expiring nature !" exclaimed F——.

" The sun—the sun of faith, say rather," replied
E——, in a tone of fervent exultation ; " it turns my
night into day—it warms my soul—it rekindles my
energies !—Sun—sun of righteousness !"—he exclaimed, faintly.   Miss E—— kissed him repeatedly,
with deep emotion. " Emma, my love !" he whispered, " hope thou in God ! See how he will support thee in death !"—She burst into tears.—" Will
you promise me, love, to read the little Bible I gave
you, when I am gone—especially the *New Testament?*
—Do—do, love."

" I will—I—," replied Miss E——, almost choked
with her emotions. She could say no more.

" Dr. ——," he addressed me, " I feel more to-

wards you than I can express; your services—services—" he grew very pale and faint.   I rose and
poured out a glass of wine, and put it to his lips.
He drank a few teaspoonfuls, and it revived him.

"Well!" he exclaimed, in a stronger voice than I
had before heard him speak.   "I thank God I leave
in perfect peace with all mankind!   There is but
one thing that grieves me—the general neglect of
religion among men of science."   Dr. D—— said, it
must afford him great consolation to reflect on the
steadfast regard for religion which *he* himself had
always evidenced.   "No, no—I have gone nearly
as far astray as any of them; but God's rod has
brought me back again.   I thank God devoutly that
he ever afflicted me as I have been afflicted through
life—He knows I do!" * * * Some one mentioned
the prevalence of materialism.   He lamented it bitterly; but assured us that several of the most eminent men of the age—naming them—believed firmly
in the immateriality and immortality of the human
soul.

"Do *you* feel firmly convinced of it—on natural
and philosophical grounds?" inquired Dr. D——.

"I do; and have, ever since I instituted an inquiry
on the subject.   *I* think the *difficulty* is to believe the
reverse—when it is owned on all hands, that nothing
in nature's changes suggests the idea of annihilation.
I own that doubts have very often crossed my mind
on the subject—but could never see the reason of
them!"

"But *your* confidence does not rest on the barren
grounds of reason," said I; "you believe Him who
brought 'life and immortality' into the world."

"Yes—'Thanks be to God, who giveth us the victory through our Lord Jesus Christ!'"

"Do you *never* feel a pang of regret at leaving life?"
I inquired.

"No, no, no!" he replied, with emphasis; "life and
I are grown unfit for each other!   My sympathies—

my hopes—my joys, are too large for it! Why should
I, just got into the haven, think of risking shipwreck
again?"

*   *   *   *   *   *   *   *

He lay still for nearly twenty minutes without
speaking. His breathing was evidently accomplished
with great difficulty; and when his eyes occasionally
fixed on any of us, we perceived that their expression was altered. He did not seem to see what he
looked at. I noticed his fingers also slowly twitch
ing or scratching the bedclothes. Still the expression of his features was calm and tranquil as ever.
He was murmuring something in Miss E——'s ear;
and she whispered to us, that he said, "Don't go—*I
shall want you at six.*" Within about a quarter of
six o'clock, he inquired where Emma was, and Dr.
D——, and Mr. F——, and myself. We severally
answeied, that we sat around him.

"I have not *seen* you for the last twenty minutes.
Shake hands with me!" We did. "Emma, my
sweet love! put your arm round my neck—I am cold,
cold." Her tears fell fast on his face. "Don't cry,
·—love—don't—I am quite happy!—God—God—
bless you, love!"

His lower jaw began to droop a little.

Mr. F——, moved almost to tears, rose from his
chair, and noiselessly kneeled down beside him.

"Have faith in our Lord Jesus Christ!" he exclaimed, looking steadfastly into his face.

"I do!" he answered distinctly, while a faint smile
stole over his drooping features.

"Let us pray!" whispered Mr. F——; and we all
knelt down in silence. I was never so overpowered
in my life. I thought I should have been choked
with suppressing my emotions. "O Lord, our heavenly Father!" commenced Mr. F——, in a low
tone, "receive thou the spirit of this our dying brother—" E—— slowly elevated his left hand, and
kept it pointing upwards for a few moments, when it

suddenly dropped, and a long deep respiration announced that this great and good man had breathed his last!

No one in the room spoke or stirred for several minutes; and I almost thought I could hear the beatings of our hearts. He died within a few moments of six o'clock. Yes—there lay the sad effigy of our deceased " guide, philosopher, and friend ;"—and yet, why call it sad? I could detect no trace of sadness in his features—he had left in peace and joy ; he had lived well, and died as he had lived. I can now appreciate the force of that prayer of one of old—" Let ME die the death of the righteous, and let MY last end be like his !"

There was some talk among his friends of erecting a tablet to his memory in Westminster Abbey; but it has been dropped. We soon lose the recollection of departed excellence, if it require any thing like active exertion.

END OF VOL. I.